# The Cook's Temptation

# The Cook's Temptation

Joyce Wayne

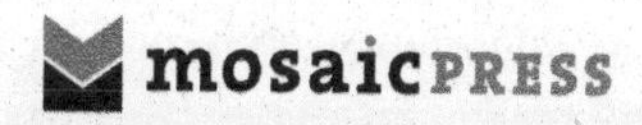

LIBRARY AND ARCHIVES CANADA CATALOGUING IN PUBLICATION

WAYNE, JOYCE, 1951-, AUTHOR
*THE COOK'S TEMPTATION* / JOYCE WAYNE.

ISSUED IN PRINT AND ELECTRONIC FORMATS.
ISBN 978-1-77161-045-2 (PBK.).--ISBN 978-1-77161-046-9 (HTML).--ISBN 978-1-77161-047-6 (PDF)

I. TITLE.

PS8645.A92C66 2013 C813'.6 C2013-906450-8
C2013-906451-6



Published by Mosaic Press, Oakville, Ontario, Canada, 2013.
Distributed in the United States by Bookmasters (www.bookmasters.com).
Distributed in the U.K. by Gazelle Book Services (www.gazellebookservices.co.uk).

MOSAIC PRESS, Publishers

Published in December 2013 in Canada.
Published in March 2014 in the United States.
Cover design and book layout by Eric Normann
Cover photograph: Digital image courtesy of the Getty's Open Content Program.
More at: www.getty.edu/about/opencontent.html#sthash.GfnDNtp8.dpuf

Printed and Bound in Canada.
ISBN Paperback 978-1-77161-045-2
ePub 978-1-77161-046-9
ePDF 978-1-77161-047-6

MOSAIC PRESS
1252 Speers Road, Units 1 & 2
Oakville, Ontario L6L 5N9
phone: (905) 825-2130
info@mosaic-press.com

www.mosaic-press.com

"No one is such a liar as the indignant man."
Friedrich Nietzsche, *Beyond Good and Evil*

"Is there anything in nature that makes such hard hearts?"
*King Lear*

To Hannah

# Book One

DEVIL'S STONE INN
SHEBBEAR, COUNTY DEVON
1881

# - I -

THE FIRST TIME I set eyes on Frederick Wendice, he was hovering in the corner of the dining room of the Devil's Stone Inn, trying to stay out of Maman's way. It was four years ago, in 1877, and he isn't likely to remember me since I was still a girl then, with slim hips and a flat chest. As usual, I was well concealed by Maman's long, protective shadow.

Today Wendice graces the door of the Devil's Stone Inn on the anniversary of the turning of the ancient devil's stone, the huge slab of rock perched in the centre of the village of Shebbear. It's April 5, and the yearly ritual of turning the stone by the Vicar of St. Michael's means that the square across from our inn is overflowing with revellers from the County Devon and far beyond. No one can actually calculate how the mysterious boulder, weighing more than one ton, dropped into the middle of Shebbear, but our visitors steadfastly hold to the belief that the stone dropped from Satan's pocket as he descended from heaven to hell. Although she doesn't say as much I understand that Maman believes we are living in her very own version of hell, and why shouldn't she?

On this day, the odd, the inordinately curious, the superstitious and the pious congregate in the village square. Maman always claims that the strangest people in all of Christendom assemble in the northern heart of County Devon on the anniversary of the falling of the stone from heaven to earth, and I must agree with her. As I count the unseemly numbers of those hobbling on crutches, those brandishing white canes, those maimed or disfigured from disease, pestilence or gross misfortune, I can only imagine what hidden infirmities are obscured beneath their bodily ailments. Many of those who are drawn to the village square of Shebbear for this bizarre event, more pagan than Christian in appearance, brandish a look of shame and I can only imagine the perversions of the mind that compel these revellers to travel from near and far to Shebbear. Everyone in the square surely carries the burden of their own secret, the curse of the body or the soul that confounds and wreaks havoc with their daily existence. Each one of them is ashamed to be among us. I can see it in their faces, but they cannot resist, they cannot stop themselves from witnessing the turning of the Devil's stone.

As for Frederick Wendice, I'm not certain if he joins us on this occasion by accident or design. On the surface a blancmange, but beneath? His hands are continuously moving, the thumb and forefingers squeezed together nervously as he waits to be admitted to the inn. As he inhales a long breath, his eyes role upward. I suspect a turbulent nature restrained by his station. He is, after all, the wealthiest man in the West Country. Yet I'd wager he is not entirely unlike the others assembled in the square or the privileged few anticipating the celebratory dinner at Maman's legendary table after the turning is done. Beneath the comportment of a gentleman, there is something amiss with Mr. Wendice's heart.

Maman, who rules our kitchen with an iron fist, is herding her guests to their seats inside the inn. Local toffs can regularly be observed darkening the doorway of our white stucco inn, with its thatch roof and smoking chimney spewing spice-tinged flavours into the clear white, English air, but on this night the collection of the high and mighty of industry and the church are most apparent. Maman remains outwardly calm. This evening, as always, she is in control, claiming it's the only way, if we wish to turn the fine profit needed to purchase the fabric to decorate our cottage or the books she imports from London and Paris to educate me, her only daughter. Maman and I are like two peas in a pod: we adore luxurious things that cost a fortune and we both love reading books until our eyes fall out of our heads. When Maman was young she was as lovely as I am now, she always reminds me, cautioning that beauty is fleeting and that I must make the most of my good looks before they abandon me.

Naturally, I recognize Frederick Wendice right off, as soon as he lumbers onto the stoop of Devil's Stone Inn. As he crosses the doorstep onto the flagged surface of the dining hall, I am able to examine him more closely: the nervous hand movements, watery blue eyes roaming in their sockets. Everyone in the West Country speaks with respect, afflicted by a hint of trepidation when gossipping about Wendice. Everyone from the sheep farmer near Tiverton to the quarryman at Tintagel depend on his wealth and beneficence. He is the source of wages for labour and the dispenser of alms for charity. The economy of our little corner of England runs on his diligence as an industrialist.

I cannot recall anyone speaking lovingly about this man. Only that he is a "confirmed bachelor," never having found a wife who would suit his purposes, whatever they may be. Bowing slightly before Maman, he asks politely for a place at her table. He is on his own, with only his valet and coachmen for company and they, of course, eat with the servants in the shed behind the inn.

What he actually thinks of our establishment, I have no idea. If he looks down his nose at us, the Tilleys of Shebbear, I cannot smell it on him, at least not yet. The Devil's Stone, with its ancient stone floor and three open fireplaces, is not the fanciest inn in County Devon, but I would wager my last penny that the food we serve is the finest in all of England. It's French, just like Maman, and she spares not a shilling when fixing her nightly concoctions that never fail to impress our good West Country customers.

In anticipation of the commerce surrounding tonight's celebration, the white washed walls of the inn are sparkling clean. The huge black beams supporting the ceiling of the dining room are adorned with sprigs of rosemary, sage and tarragon, Maman's favourite spices. And there they are: Maman's salivating customers, unbuttoning their waistcoats before tucking into her hors d'oeuvres of mushroom stuffed artichokes and devilled eggs, sweating with anticipation as the first heavenly bite touches their greedy tongues.

In this respect, Wendice is no different from the other locals, although he is unduly cautious not to allow a droplet of food to fall from his lips. Before the soup is served he tucks his napkin under his chin. It is a green pea and asparagus cream, followed by steamed mussels and veal gently stewed in freshly pickled tomatoes. Next comes the lamb garnished with garlic-simmered fava beans. Conversation in the room comes to a dead halt as the men, healthy or sick, whole or disfigured, wealthy or skirting bankruptcy, devour their meals.

Four years ago, upon his earlier visit to the inn, Mr. Wendice was wary of Maman, who was ordering the scullery maids about and swinging a huge wooden spoon at the customers who wouldn't remain exactly where she put them. On festive nights, when the inn is full with Devon farmers, travelling merchants and clergymen, she prefers using the long trestle dinner table. The customers sit in two long rows, the high and the low, saints and sinners, relishing their first exquisite bite of Maman's cooking. It's fair to say that no one, not even Frederick Wendice, can resist Maman's gastronomic delights forever.

"It's all hogwash," Maman says tonight, in her best English, to Mr. Wendice when he speculates why the Stone across from the inn is turned by the good reverend each year on this exact date. Tonight Maman's eyes shine and I can imagine how enchanting she once was. My Pa never notices how his wife's beauty has faded. Nor does he notice what is left of it: the elegant turn of her swan-like neck and the fine way she holds her head high when she addresses Mr. Wendice.

"Not even you, Madeleine Tilley, can calculate how this mysterious boulder dropped into the middle of Shebbear on this very date," Pa roars from behind the bar and across the room to where Mr. Wendice is certain to hear him. I loathe it when my father interrupts Maman. My five brothers, who are pouring brown beer down their throats, stop drinking for a moment, to nod their heads in agreement. Four of my brothers resemble Pa. Four of these creatures are enormous muscled men with lifeless ginger hair, thick lips and small beady eyes. Only my eldest brother, Albert, looks like Maman: frail, with bird-like bones, coal black hair and a fine chiselled nose. If I care for anyone in our family, other than Maman, it is Albert, for he is the most thoughtful of the Tilley men.

As usual, Maman pays Pa no mind, but eagerly resumes her conversation with Mr. Wendice, who she is apprising as a possible suitor for me. I can tell by the sharp glint in her eye as she speaks with him. Four of my brothers, louts that they are, continue with their drinking. Albert, with his expression of pure mischief, pinches a waiting maid's bottom as she clears crockery from the long table for the next course of tonight's feast. Then he winks at me, showing that he, too, knows that Maman is scheming on my behalf.

"Rubbish," Maman says firmly. "Of course, some say the Stone fell from Satan's pocket on April 5th, as he descended from heaven to hell, but educated people such as we don't believe in such foolishness, do we Mr. Wendice?"

"I might," Frederick admits sheepishly, without looking up from his plate piled high with Maman's culinary creations.

Pa, never one to back down from an argument, interjects: "The only way to keep Old Nick from causing mayhem is to turn the Stone every year. Only once in four hundred years, has it not been turned on April 5th, and that was the night my daughter, Cordelia, was born. That's when the old vicar took deathly ill and the midwife was too occupied with Madeleine, here, to save our poor reverend before he perished." Pa points his finger directly at Maman and shakes it hard. "The apple doesn't fall far from the tree," he shouts, moving his hand in my direction.

Yes, it's my birthday. Pa has neglected to extend his good wishes, acting as if the anniversary of my birth is an insult to him. But Maman and I celebrated on our own before the revellers descended and the madness began. We prefer to keep to ourselves.

As Maman and Pa carry on in their usual manner, Mr. Wendice appears to be more interested in dessert than the superstition surrounding the Stone. I, for one, recognize the sly look of gluttony on his round face. He can't wait to get his mouth around Maman's apple crepes. She serves them with sour cream and freshly ground cinnamon. Recklessly, he inquires if Devon cream could be spooned on top.

"Of course, Mr. Wendice, anything else, a slice of our ripened cheese?" Maman certainly is putting her best foot forward tonight. She thinks of everything. "More Turkish coffee? A cheroot from the Orient?"

"I don't mind if I do," Wendice says, leaning back in his seat to make a smidgen of room between his stomach and the table. He is spooning crepes and cream into his mouth at a great rate, managing to get not one morsel on the napkin now tucked into his trousers. Presently, he asks for another helping.

Maman has that effect on people. Making them beg for more no matter how proud they are.

"Anything that tastes this divine," the curate sitting opposite Mr. Wendice suddenly remarks, "must be touched by Satan's hand." Then he smacks his thin lips as he dips his tablespoon into a bowl of Maman's brandied fruit trifle.

Maman ignores men of the cloth. She is afraid of them. This Catholic priest, who is on his way to the Americas, terrifies her. For good reason. Her family was expelled from Spain during the Inquisition, along with the other 500,000 Jews who fled because they refused to convert to Catholicism. After the Rosenblums were settled and secure in France for 300 years, the Roman church in Angers blamed them for poisoning the well water at the Oblate monastery. The family, purveyors of fine food and wine, was ruined. Maman's hands tremble when she serves the priest.

Tonight she is trying to focus on winning Mr. Wendice's attention. "May I inquire how your mother and father are faring?" she asks him.

"Mater is in perfect health," he says, gazing up to the heavens in thanks. But poor Pater passed on to his reward last winter."

"What a blow it must be to your family!" Maman sounds stricken with grief, although she, like everyone residing in Devon, is aware of the elder Wendice's death. "Now the weight of the entire Wendice establishment falls on your shoulders, am I not correct?"

"Indeed. The copper works at Morwellham Quay and the many slate quarries at Tintagel."

"Broad shoulders, I might add," Maman says, coyly. "Would you be wanting a room for the night, then, Mr. Wendice?"

There is only one room left unoccupied in the inn and she doesn't want the Roman priest to snatch it up before our mining potentate and potential suitor. Now that I'm nineteen and have grown smart in the way of the world, I often notice that certain customers take rooms at the inn rather than returning to their good wives after they've been fed by Maman. The prettiest maidens, hired by Maman to lend a hand in the scullery, can be seen giggling at the men's low humour. At times, if the spring rain is sweet or the sun lingers heavy in the western sky, I watch as a girl settles in on a traveller's lap while he unbuttons her loose-fitting shirt to slyly nuzzle the milkmaid's bosom. Maman plays down this side of the business, worried that the Quality will steer clear if it's public knowledge, but if I were running the Devil's Stone Inn, I wouldn't be ashamed of the services we offer.

It is as he is paying for his room that I catch Frederick Wendice staring at me. For a moment, I believe that he recognizes me from when I was a girl, but how could that be, concealed as I was by Maman? Now, I am standing beside the registry desk, offering to carry his case to his room. My red hair, like a halo around my head, falls in curls down my sturdy, straight back. He looks directly into my hazel eyes and I surmise that he is taking note of the freckles on my fair skin. The bodice of my frock is tight and he peers down at my nipples pointing sharply through the thin muslin. Although he attempts to conceal it, I can discern the lasciviousness of his gaze.

"I wouldn't dream of it, Miss Tilley. I'll arrange for my valet to carry the case to the room," he says, unable to take his eyes from me. Again he squeezes his pudgy fingers together pressing so strongly I can observe the white bloodless skin of his thumbs poking out from his starched shirt.

"Now there's a gentleman for you," Maman whispers in my ear. "The exact opposite of your Pa." She gives me the look that tells me to swing my broad hips and lick my full lips.

"Do you remember me, Mr. Wendice?" I inquire. "I remember you."

## – 2 –

This morning from the window of our thatch cottage, across the tiny square from the inn, I watch Mr. Wendice's face turn beet red with exertion as he lifts himself into his stately carriage. When the door of the carriage swings open, I catch a brief glimpse of the green leather seats and polished brass fittings inside the coach.

Before pulling out from the inn, Maman runs toward the carriage to wish him a safe trip. She's packed a wicker hamper for Wendice, filled it with her finest smoked trout, leek and potato soup, chicken croquettes and a half of her apple torte, neatly wrapped in blue linen. He does not demur when she hands him the basket of goodies. She is bowing and scraping like the lowliest of servant girls. It pains me to see her this way. To see her trying so hard.

"You should have come down to wish him off," she says to me later in the day when I'm scrubbing the stone floor of the inn's dining parlour. The water in the bucket beside me is brown with the filth and scraps of last evening's festivities.

Why Maman believes she can bully me into this romance, I have no idea. I must find a way to distract her, put her off Mr. Wendice's scent. "It's best that I don't appear too eager," I reply smartly.

She grins when she adds that she just might have knocked some sense into me after all. I notice when she smiles that her teeth are yellow and splintered. Her gums bleed whenever she eats.

If truth be told there is nothing I would like better than to please my dear Maman, but I'm not remotely convinced that Mr. Wendice is the beau for me. A polite person would describe him as a broadly built man. In reality, he is one of those men who as early as adolescence acquire a protruding belly rounding over his buckling trousers and plush hips that would look saucy on a girl. He looks like an amorphous jellyfish bobbing up and down on the placid sea.

Although I can't imagine Mr. Wendice touching me with his pudgy hands, Maman is trying to convince me that he is a gentleman above reproach. "Do you wish to spend your days, like me, on your hands and knees, scrubbing the floors of this lowly establishment, taking more guff from your father and brothers than an ocean could swallow? Is that what you want, my fine missy?"

Maman's words get me thinking about how my days would be spent if I did manage to snag the great Mr. Wendice, lord of all he surveys.

"He's Christian," I blurt out. Whenever Maman dreams of a union between Mr. Wendice and me, I quickly realize that I must put as many barriers in her face as I'm able to construct. Maman is a master at forcing me to do things her way. In this case, the stakes are too high for me to acquiesce.

"Don't I know it?" Maman replies wearily as she wipes down the long trestle table that is streaked with grease from Friday night's feast. "But what can we do, daughter? There are a handful of Jews in this County and they're old and poor. That won't do for you, my girl. If you marry Mr. Wendice, you must keep up our traditions, privately, as I do, as you've observed me doing since you were a babe in arms. "

Last night, just before sundown, Maman and I did manage to sneak back to the cottage to say the Hebrew blessing over the candles and wish each other a "good *Shabbas*". The prayers are our secret, an imaginary place where we enter a private world, one that is highly exotic and more complex than the Tilleys could possibly appreciate. Our devotions are a well-guarded secret. They distinguish us from the others, and bind us firmly together.

It is no secret, however, that Maman and Pa do not get on, he being the earthy English publican sort and she being the spoiled child of once wealthy French provisioners. I guess that makes me who I am today, neither fish nor fowl, neither Quality nor servant, but somewhere in-between where no one understands you.

When Maman tells the story of why she married Pa and came to live with him at the Devil's Stone Inn, it sounds as if he kidnapped her. But then stories are misleading that way, with one person seeing it one way and the other disputing it with all her heart. In the end, it's up to the listener to decide what is true and what is not. Pa claims that he rescued his bride from a fate worse than death by bringing her to England. It is one of the many things upon which they will never agree.

"Mr. Wendice is much older than I and you have told me repeatedly to marry a man my own age or I'll be nursing him on his death bed," I declare boldly, advancing my case against marriage to Wendice. Pa is ten years older than Maman.

"True enough, *Cherie*, but Wendice is so wealthy, it matters not a *sou*. Cooks and maids and stable boys will be yours. You'll be a rich widow before you know it."

"I don't want to hire a cook. And I certainly don't intend to be a young widow."

"Why might that be?" Maman is becoming exasperated with me.

"I wish to rule the kitchen one day, to follow in your footsteps, and cook for all the County. I fancy it, making their mouths' water. Right here at the Devil's Stone Inn."

I roll out another sopping wet rag on the stained floor.

"Haven't I taught you anything? Can't you see me, old before my time, withered and worn? Is that what you aspire to?" Maman wrings the greasy rag she used on the table into the wash bucket before she places her wrinkled hand on the small of her back. Her fingers are cracked with raw, red streaks from the lye in the wash water. She shrewdly observes the expression on my face. It is untrue that I do not see her clearly, but the bargain she presents is not worth the cost to my happiness, I fear.

"An idiot, I have spawned another idiot child. First your brothers and now you. I suppose you imagine you'll be madly in love with your husband."

I answer by asserting that I never spoke a word about love.

## – 3 –

It is an entire week since Mr. Wendice spent the night at the inn, but we've received not a word from him—and I can't say that I'm chagrined. I ought to have received a letter by now, adorned by the Wendice crest, asking my permission to visit on an afternoon in April and thereby offering me the opportunity to turn down his proposal.

The more Maman natters on about him, the more uninviting a prospect he becomes, not that I condemn her hopes and dreams for my future. I suspect she would do anything to deliver me from the hell she considers the Devil's Stone Inn to be. Why shouldn't she? She was born into wealth, the only daughter of well-educated and refined French Jews. To her, cooking at the inn is lower in station than the maid-of-all-work at her home in Angers.

Possibly Wendice sees through us in ways my own people cannot, he being a man of sophistication and experience and they being ignorant country bumpkins. How could they understand me, having never ventured past the confines of the West Country? Nor have I, of course. Not physically, but with my mind I've travelled to all the best capital cities: Paris, London, Rome and Moscow. When I was an innocent, Maman made certain to show me the world by entreating me to read her books. I've been to Italy with Mr. Shakespeare, France with Monsieur Flaubert, London with Mr. Thackeray and Russia with Count Tolstoy. By reading, I've looked into the many faces of human nature, and memorized the big, important words famous authors employ. Rather than saying someone is two-faced and sneaky, a famous author will say someone is d-u-p-l-i-c-i-t-o-u-s and c-o-n-n-i-v-i-n-g. It sounds so much superior. So much more intriguing!

I understand that Maman has thrown herself too wholeheartedly into introducing me to the finer things in life—books, painting, music and fashion—to watch me waste my talents with the Tilley men and their ilk. Her ambition for me knows no bounds. But to my mind, there must be a superior way to launch me into society than by marrying me off to Mr. Wendice. If only his sly look of lasciviousness was not so obvious to me.

Even as her intentions for me grow more pressing, Maman looks increasingly frail and more worn with each passing day. When I take her hand in my own, it feels like a collection of dry sticks in a sack of cheesecloth. Her olive skin is turning a faded yellow and I fear she is becoming ill. A rumour is circulating in the village that typhoid is spreading throughout the West Country and that a dozen folk have already fallen under its ghastly spell.

Maman could not have picked a worse time to get sick: today is pig-splitting day! At the Devil's Stone Inn, after fattening the pig each winter, Pa is always eager to splice the beast wide open for Easter Sunday's feast.

As soon as I wake, I can hear Pa hollering to his sons, still fast asleep in the second-floor attic rooms of the family cottage.

"Lads, today's the day!" From my perch in the upstairs dormer window, I can see Pa wrapping the oilskin apron around his ample gut. He is carrying his blood encrusted Wellies in one hand and the freshly sharpened butcher's blade in the other. There is a bounce to his step as he walks to the stone shed where the beast will be strung up. "Lads, get out here and give us a hand," he shouts. Pa doesn't speak very often, but when he does he yells.

The stone shed where Pa hides his knives and pipes and tobacco and who knows what else is twenty feet from the inn, but it is his private domain. Maman and I are not allowed to enter the shed because we are "Nosey Parkers," he claims and I doubt that I will ever see the inside of it. The shed and the inn skirt the River Torridge. Today, the river is high and the salmon are spawning. The forest below is a lush, verdant green, showing off our ancient little village of Shebbear at its best.

Downstairs, I watch Pa from the front door of the inn. First, he slices open the pig's throat. Next, the animal is hoisted up feet first on the meat hook with its pumping heart draining blood into the wooden bucket beneath it. By the time the blood overruns the rim and begins soaking the earth below the poor beast, Pa is passing around the Scrumpy, not just to the brothers, who are drowning in it, but to the customers, the ones lucky enough to participate in the spring pig splitting at the Devil's Stone Inn. Most of the onlookers are hardworking Devon farmers, but a handful are local toffs thoroughly enjoying this bloody-thirsty spectacle.

"Tilley, my man," shouts a young toff intoxicated by the cider and the bloodletting. "Next thing you know, we'll be stripping off our clothing like savages and dancing under the full moon!"

Pa is so pleased by the revelry, he circles around the dead pig, humming and shaking the butcher's knife at the crowd.

I look back into the kitchen to where Maman is chopping carrots and potatoes for tonight's dinner. Naturally being raised in the Jewish faith, Maman will not brook any bacon in her kitchen, although each and every Easter Pa insists on roasting the pig sizzling on the spit beside the stone shed. I dread the day. The rift between Maman and Pa is most apparent on this day, more so than any other in the year.

Today Pa decides to carry the wooden pail overflowing with blood into the kitchen. He chooses not to acknowledge my presence as I stare resentfully at him.

"Woman, make us some blood pudding. There's a good lass," he bellows at Maman.

Without hesitation, she kicks the pail of blood onto the flagstone where it will surely leave a permanent brown stain.

"Now Madeleine," Pa says. "Are you going to pitch a fit right here in the kitchen of my inn or are you going to do as you're told?"

By now I'm cowering beside the cast iron stove, trying to stay out of reach. In another second, Maman will begin throwing her cooking utensils at Pa. Her skin is looking a more sickly yellow by the moment as she hollers at Pa: "How many times have I told you I won't have pork in my kitchen?"

But Pa is adamant and tries another tack. "Just this once, darlin', make us some blood pudding, the way me own dear mum would make. There's more where this lot comes from." Pa points to the pig strung upside down in the yard. His words stoke the fire of her simmering indignation and so she launches into her rant.

"Haven't you hurt me enough, Thomas Tilley?" she asks. "You tricked *mon pere* into giving me to you. As if I were a discarded china bowl in a rummage sale." She makes rummage sound exotic, pronouncing it in the French way.

When the Roman Church accused the Rosenblums of poisoning the water at the monastery's well, the town of Angers turned its back and locked their doors to the family. Purveyors of fine food and wine could be found elsewhere. The Rosenblum's larders, where raw cheese ripened and pickled meat turned spicy, festered with mould; the underground cellars housing a famous collection of hundreds of bottles of white and red wines remained locked and unattended. Even the great farm, skirting the town of Angers, where Papa Rosenblum kept a herd of more than fifty white cattle, fertile and maintained manicured acres of fresh vegetables, herbs and flowers, and orchards of succulent fruits and berries, were left to degenerate. No one would purchase the family's products now that they were labeled Christian killers. No matter how many times Maman tells the story of her family's demise, the pain in her face never lessens.

Pa, who is drunk with cider and the slaughter, suddenly turns sober. "No, that's not true. Your blessed Papa begged me to take you off his hands. He offered me his prize herd of white cattle if I would marry you and bring you to England."

"He was trying to save me, in the face of ruin. He panicked. The Church left us with nothing, not one *sou* by the time they were done with us. Papa truly believed that I could lead a superior life in England; it was commonly perceived that the wicked superstitions about Jews do not exist here. How wrong he was! The English fear the Jews; insinuate that we have mysterious powers. They are obsessed with how we make our money. How was Papa to know that he was selling me into bondage, in a country plagued by superstition and prejudice?"

"You were part of the bargain. You came with the cattle, as plain as that," Pa says brusquely.

For once, Maman accepts his explanation. She nods and closes her eyes. She is flustered and exhausted and her ankles are swelling. "I've born you eleven children, six alive and five dead. I work like a slave every day at the Devil's Stone Inn. All I ask of you is that you keep pork out of my kitchen."

As Pa collects his bucket, I observe him sneering at her sudden show of weakness. Usually, Maman fights back, flinging horrible names at him in French and in English. Today she is subdued, shaky on her feet, and Pa does not know how to react. They have been locked in this vindictive ritual for too long for either of them to emerge as the winner.

Once Pa leaves the inn, Maman puts her hand feebly to her forehead and collapses to the floor.

## – 4 –

As I feared, Maman has fallen prey to typhoid fever. She is resting in the inn where I can care for her. Since there isn't a doctor in Shebbear, Albert is riding to Black Torrington to fetch the physician and bring him to us. In the meantime, my youngest brother, Georgie, has also fallen ill. I've put him in the guest room next to Maman. The inn is becoming an infirmary.

Last night after midnight, a strange woman checked into the Devil's Stone Inn. Her name is Polly Turney or that's how she signed the guestbook. Although she plays the part of a lady—she is tall, with a tiny waist and thick black ringlets cascading from her fine feathered hat—her cheek is bruised and the skin surrounding her left eye is yellow and blue. Someone has assaulted her, or my name isn't Cordelia Tilley.

Before dawn, she enters Maman's sickroom unbidden. I am resting on the spindle rocker, trying to catch a few winks before the day's chores begin. Mrs. Turney claims to be a nurse en route to a gathering of women engaged in helping the less fortunate of our sex. She has come to the right place. I am curious how a congregation of lady do-gooders will approach this Mrs. Turney of the blackened eye. Will they embrace her as one of their own or regard her as one of those who requires assistance? Will they wonder if she has come to join them or to feast off them?

Mrs. Turney is nonplussed by illness, she announces nonchalantly. Many times she has tended to the sick overcome with this disease and she has suffered from it herself, she informs me. Maman's illness does not deter her from staying at the inn. I admire her fearlessness and her stalwart belief that typhoid never infects the same body twice. Since no one can recall a time when the filthy disease invaded Shebbear, it's impossible to know if she is right. She offers to lend a hand with Maman and Georgie, which is more than I can say for the rest of the family hovering outside the sick rooms. Pa is riding to Heatherleigh to buy ammunition for a guest's shooting party. He ignores Maman when she needs him most. I inform Mrs. Turney that I will call for her if I require assistance. She looks at me quizzically, as if to say, you have no idea what you are up against. I return her gaze with my glare. I'm not certain I wish Mrs. Turney at my side. She leans up against me with a familiarity that I disdain.

"When I was girl," Maman murmurs under the influence of her soaring fever, "the yyyyoung fellows ... *gentilshommes* who courted me ... suave and wwwwell-mannered. They wore tailored topcoats; they straightened their silk cravats before they dared approach our house." She is slurring her words. "Even Thomas asked Papa's permission to enter the parlour."

"Yes, Maman." I've heard all her stories before.

"Our parlour in Angers was covered in gold-flecked brocade wallpaper, with a mahogany panelled library, bound with leather first editions."

"Yes, Maman." I am holding cold compresses to her head and the back of her neck. She is burning with fever.

"Only the finest Persian carpets covered the floor. Behind the velvet divan was a gorgeous tapestry depicting the Holy Land ..."

"Yes, Maman everything was perfect."

"*Ma fille,* I must have my copy of Baudelaire. I must have it next to me."

It is too far to run to our cottage to fetch the book of poems, so I place a worn copy of the King James Bible in Maman's hands. How will she know the difference now that the fever is overwhelming her?

In our cottage Maman's library is magnificent, the best in the north of Devon, I expect, more entertaining, more original than the gentry's prized ancient collections, whose tomes, Maman claims, are so predictable they are not worth reading. Maman's library is our special domain, a world apart from the drudgery of the inn. In Maman's collection are the latest novels from France: Balzac, Dumas, Flaubert, of course, George Sand, and Zola. Before Maman fell ill we were reading Zola's

*Therese Raquin* aloud to each other while surrounded by her French books. The collection is bound in burnished Spanish leather adorned with gilt lettering. Maman ships the books to a seasoned Jewish bookbinder on the Charing Cross Road in London, who she trusts to spare not one detail with her most prized possessions. It is my fondest wish to visit all the literary bookshops in London. Perhaps some day I shall. While there I might meet a dignified gentleman, a poet of some repute and substantial means who will immediately recognize my worth. He will respect my person and hesitate before approaching me. On our first meeting he shall hand me his embossed card and ask permission to call on me of an afternoon at my London address.

Suddenly Maman sits up straight. "Cordelia, your father ..."

"He's a brute of the lowest order, I know."

"I mmmust tell you ..." but she no longer has the strength to remain sitting. She collapses and her sweat-soaked hair streaks across the pillow. "He is not who you think he is ..."

"Shush, Maman," I am attempting to quiet her. "Rest now. There will be plenty of time to dissect Pa when you are recovered."

Before long Maman is falling in and out of consciousness. What if I contract typhoid fever? Who will care for me? I stick my head out of the sick room to call for Griselda, Albert's wife. She is the Irish tinker's daughter, who wafted into Shebbear during the potato famine. Maman considers Griselda an entirely unsuitable match for her firstborn son.

Griselda dares not cross me when I ask for her help, but I can only imagine how grudgingly she agrees to lend a hand. She is a large woman, with a broad muscular back and shoulders the size of a stevedore's. Her dark brown hair is loosely tied in a bun. Her face reminds me of a rodent's: pointed and hungry. As I rush to Georgie's room, carrying another bowl of cooling water, I overhear her babbling away to Maman, who is too ill to respond. "You know what the villagers call you: the Jewish dragon, because you are all vinegar and bad blood. If they had an ounce of courage, they would say it directly to your face, but they don't."

I can hear Maman moaning from the next room as Griselda goes on with her stream of pent-up resentment: "Always acting like you're too good for me and my kin, you and your snooty daughter. When you're dead and gone, I'll rule the kitchen and the first thing I'll do is get rid of the fancy fixings you push on the customers. It's simple country fare I'll be serving at the Devil's Stone Inn, not foie gras and petit fours."

---

If Maman had any strength left in her at all, she would smack Griselda hard, across the face, as I've seen her do many times before. But as I turn back into her sickroom, I see her lying limply on the bed, holding the Bible in her hand and crying out to the Jewish God I hardly know or can comprehend.

"Get out!" I order Griselda. "She'll be dead fast enough, you ugly, unforgiving cow." I am screaming now, holding Maman in my arms and trying to douse her fever. Without her, where will I stand in this family of ne'er do wells, braggarts and Irish tinkers? Griselda shoots me a dirty look before leaving the room.

"Who will protect me, who will teach me?" I beg Maman to fight the fever.

I plead with her to sip a spoonful of clear broth, but she can no longer swallow or speak. Her tongue is so thickened with white protrusions I cannot imagine how she can breathe. I am terrified that without her encouragement, her huge, overweening ambition for me, I shall never rise above an existence that Maman has spent all of our time together convincing me is too narrow, too tedious, too banal to settle for. I imagine the walls of the inn closing in on me.

"Maman, you have been right all along!" I cry. Surely, I owe it to myself to escape from the inn and take my place in English society, as she has tutored me to do since I was a child. I must not waste my days here, slaving in the kitchen, until I have no strength to fight even the mildest of illnesses, let alone the typhoid fever. In the end, what has Maman's life come to? I dare not think.

## – 5 –

Maman is fast giving in to this foulest of diseases. She has no fight left in her. The fever is taking her quickly.

I can hardly keep my eyes open. Between caring for her and Georgie, I am exhausted and sure to come down with the fever myself. Maman would not want that for me. She would wish for me to survive.

Albert returns with the doctor who drinks a tankard of ale before he examines Maman and Georgie.

"Your mother will live or die," he says glumly.

"Is that so? " I inquire, taken by the brilliance of his prognosis.

"I'm afraid it is out of my hands and in God's hands now. Same goes for your brother."

"There must be something you can do," I plead, while wishing to kick the drunken fool in the backside. But the doctor says Maman's fever has reached 104 degrees.

"If she makes it through the night, which I doubt, she will live," the physician states.

Pa is giving the inn a wide berth. He is sleeping on the cot in the stone shed, beside the pigpen. The butchered pig is wrapped in burlap. Flies are buzzing around its head. There will be no Easter Sunday feast tonight. A sign is posted outside the inn: "Typhoid House," it reads.

The only guest brave enough to remain at the inn is Mrs. Turney. Throughout this ordeal, she remains calm, dressed in a white frock dappled with swirls of green and brown. Her eyes reflect the verdant green of the budding leaves on the bushes caressing the windows of the inn. She belongs in the orchard with Maman's apple trees. The other guests, including Pa's shooting party, have packed their bags and left, praying they have escaped this plague.

Mrs. Turney comes round to the sick room when she notices that I have fallen asleep sitting outside Maman's door. She wakes me gently with a touch of her kid-leather gloved hand and I can smell the sweet scent of lavender. She helps me to stand, leads me into the kitchen to pour me a glass of brandy.

"Will you allow me to help you, Miss Tilley?" she asks directly. "Drink up, now," she says, taking my hand in her own gloved one. "Gloves protect us from spreading the disease. If we remove them, that is, before we leave the sick room. Would you wish to borrow a pair of mine?" she offers sweetly.

I decline. "If the fever is going to befall me a pair of gloves won't change its course," I retort.

"Not so, Miss Tilley," she says. "I happen to know quite a bit about the causes of contagion."

We approach Maman together, she in her gloved hands and me with my alabaster skin exposed. What if she is correct, and gloves could protect me? Mrs. Turney could be a woman worth befriending. I must admit that I am drawn to her in inexplicable ways completely unknown to me. At this moment, I yearn to reach out my hand and touch her cheek, however silly the action. Yet, I remain hard as a stone. She is interfering with my intention to nurse Maman on my own, drawing away my attention on what might be done to comfort Maman.

Maman has soiled the bedclothes and I do not have the stomach to clean her. Mrs. Turney takes over. Within a half hour, my poor Maman is almost comfortable, fresh linen covers the bed and Mrs. Turney is holding up Maman's head, trying to spoon a droplet of water into her mouth. To me she orders, "Tend to your brother."

I do as I am told, but Georgie's delirium is even more pronounced than Maman's. He is sweating profusely, so much so that his shirt is soaking with sweat. Green bile is dripping from his chin. He is raging on about the inn's water well being poisoned by Jews. Little red spots are breaking out over his chest and abdomen.

"The filthy disease, I'm dying of the filthy disease," he rants. "The Jews' disease."

I would prefer to leave him to die alone. There is nothing to be done for Georgie.

Outside in the cooling spring air, I notice Pa sitting under the willow tree near his shed. There is an uncanny resemblance between him and the ancient tree: gnarled, stolid and blissfully impervious to the surroundings.

As I approach him, he says: "Your Maman will go to hell because she has never accepted Jesus Christ as her saviour. She'll burn for eternity, that one." Pa says this matter-of-factly, without a hint of regret in his voice.

At that very moment, I begin to retch and father, who is fearful of catching the typhoid, leaves me crouching on the ground at his feet. He calls out lamely for help and it is only Mrs. Turney and brother Albert who come to my aid. My head is swimming as they place me in the third sickroom. Albert sits at the foot of my bed reading to me from *Madame Bovary*, my favourite novel. Mistakenly, he believes it will calm me, but stories written by authors of passion and intellect aren't meant as salve; they are meant to invigorate the soul while turning our minds to singular adventures. I ask Albert to bring me my composition book so I can write down my thoughts about the illness. Although I am frightened, miraculously, it occurs to me that I am not terribly ill, not to the same degree as Maman or Georgie. When Albert forces a spoonful of broth between my burning lips, I'm able to keep it down. I ask for more and he smiles, almost amused. Pa remains outside the inn, tending to his pigs, although his wife and two of his children are suffering from the filthy disease.

## - 6 -

Georgie is dead. I can't say that I'm sorry. The little blighter was always a stone lodged in my ear, but I suppose I'll miss his constant nattering and tagging after Maman and me when we were too busy to pay him any mind.

Polly Turney, who tends to me when Albert sleeps, reports that Maman is exceedingly ill. She will not live through the night. Polly tries to console me, but I wish to be left in peace. I have much to consider.

Maman's fever has not gone down and although she fooled the drunken doctor and lasted for two long days in this desperate condition, I believe she will die tonight, as Polly predicts. Polly knows more about this disease than the useless physician. I admire her strength and her knowledge.

I will survive. Already I am recovering. My fever is going down. Polly says I have the mildest case of typhoid she has ever witnessed. She also informs me that Frederick Wendice has sent a letter to me through the post. Although he doesn't offer to visit, he does offer the services of his physician, Mr. Ealing, "a medical man of impeccable repute," from the village of Holsworthy. If I recall correctly, Wendice's great house is in that very town, a dreary place that is home to the country's largest slaughterhouse. It would be just like Frederick Wendice to choose to live there, amid the stalls of helpless animals, waiting to die, rather than at that great pile, his ancestral home, the Abbey at Hartland Point. What an odd duck he is! Pretending that he is one with the people of Devon when in actual fact, brother Albert informs me that he sells more tin and copper to every corner of the world than anyone in England. Most strangely, Wendice adds that I must not be alarmed by the cost of the physician; that he would be honoured to cover the expense, as a friend of the family and as an admirer.

Polly reads the note aloud to me, in a stagey voice, with a tone that is not unlike Frederick's.

"How do you know what he sounds like?" I inquire and she replies that most toffs sound exactly the same.

I snatch the note from her hand. "You're right about that."

Maman is dying. Time is short. If I knew what to do, I would give her a Jewish burial, no matter who discovered our religion, but I am entirely ignorant of the custom. If only there were friends or relations to ask, but members of the Rosenblum family have spread across the continent of Europe, some to Salonika in the Balkans, others to darkest ends of Europe, to Budapest and Warsaw, remote places too uncivilized to consider and when I do attempt to imagine my relations in Eastern Europe what I see is a large family huddled on a dirt floor near a ceramic stove. They are eating red cabbage borscht from bowls. Thinking about my far-flung family sends shivers down my spine and makes my fever rise. My body is desperately cold and then unbearably hot. I feel light headed again when I should be clear of mind.

Instead of worrying about my lost relations, I must concentrate on my own future and get on with it now that Maman will not be here to protect me. I must not allow Griselda to preside over the inn's kitchen. I must force myself out of this bed and back into the kitchen the moment I am able to stand straight. I must assert my control or I am done for at the Devil's Stone Inn. Yet when I attempt to rise, my body will not co-operate and I fall back against the pillow. Perhaps I should invite Mr. Wendice to the first Friday night dinner, which I'll be preparing without Maman. It is important to seat the right people around my table if I am to establish my supremacy in reigning over the kitchen at the Devil's Stone Inn.

Perhaps this one time, I shall allow myself to sleep, fading into dreams until the fever subsides.

When I wake, my face is cool although my body is limp. I force myself from the bed, heaving my weight from the bed and onto my legs. My nightdress is stained with sweat so I tie a dressing gown tightly about me. In bare feet, I make my way to Maman's room, scratching along the wooden boards like an invalid. I must be with her at the end. With day turning into night, I alone must sit with Maman as she dies. I observe her face closely. In the last light of the evening, it is wrinkled like that of an ancient, old woman's and her death rattles drowns out the sound of my sobbing. Just a few years ago, she was exquisite, but now her beauty has deserted her entirely. Not a trace remains. Not a hint of her former radiance, not the shimmer of her black hair, or the glow of her exotic olive complexion. Certainly not the red blush of her sensual lips turned to a pout as she paused between reading passages of her precious novels. Instead she leaves this world with nothing but regrets. A girlhood of promise, her adulthood wasted: that is what she would scream if she could, raging at the Jewish God who has forsaken her.

I keep telling myself that I must survive without Maman, but for the moment it is not survival that concerns me. My head is churning with visions of isolation. Since the fever struck me I've become the prisoner of my dreams. I see myself as a leather-skinned hag, soured by the salt air, isolated, deserted, living inside a stone cave facing the sea. It is abandonment that frightens me. Much too late, I realize that Maman was my only true friend. She cared for me, fiercely, as no one ever will again. I am completely alone.

## – 7 –

Maman's sad little funeral was yesterday. Georgie's the day before yesterday. From the front window of the inn, I watched the tiny procession of mourners follow Maman's coffin to the furthest reaches of the graveyard. For Georgie's, the square was overflowing with mourners. Not so, for Maman. Her plain coffin was resting inside an ornate wood and glass box pulled by one black mare. The windows of the glass box were decorated with swiggles of black and gilt paint and the horse wore a ridiculous headdress with one black feather sticking straight into the air. Albert must have been the one to have gone to this expense for the funeral. He is the only Tilley who would bother. No one shed a tear. Griselda and the other sisters-in-law sang a pathetic hymn about Jesus that Maman would detest. Pa walked with a slight sprint in his step and I could tell that he was relieved that Maman was dead. He believed his troubles were over forever. He did nothing to conceal his happiness.

Most of the villagers avoided the wake since our house remained quarantined with the broad red mark of the plague painted on our front door. True to form, Pa insisted that the service be held at St. Michael's and on a Saturday, Maman's Sabbath, and the day that Jewish law forbids funerals. Although there is a synagogue in Exeter, Pa insisted that Maman be given a Christian burial. I was not allowed to attend since I am not completely recovered and everyone, except Polly, was concerned that I would spread the fever far and wide.

---

"I shouldn't think you are contagious now that the worst of your fever has passed," Polly says to me as I walk between the inn's vestibule and the empty scullery. There are no guests and Polly encourages me to exercise my limbs regularly to regain my strength. "You are no longer dangerous to others. Your father is wrong," she states reassuringly.

"He usually is." I am still curious about how this woman knows so much about disease and contagion, why she came alone and bearing signs of an assault.

"As soon as you are well, I'll be returning to Plymouth. My affairs are in shambles and I must attempt to put them in order."

How intriguing are her comments! "Are you living with your husband, Mrs. Turney?" I inquire. "You never mention him." There is no longer any sign of a black eye.

"No need to pretend you didn't see my eye," she says with a wry smile. "That was the last time he will strike me. I've left him."

"Did you call the peelers on him?"

"What good would it have done? No, I threatened to kill him myself," she says while darting her pink tongue from her mouth, "and he knows I meant it. He's a seaman and by next Sunday he's off to America with the Royal Navy. The blow to my face was his parting gift."

"How will you survive, on your own, that is?" I ask, in a quandary about how a woman on her own might make her way in the grand port city of Plymouth.

"My lodging house. I've never needed him. I am a nurse and I keep women who are … indisposed, so to speak … who require my protection and attention."

"Like Florence Nightingale?"

"Different from Florence Nightingale. My lodgers are my charges."

"Do you ask them for room and board while they are recuperating?"

"In a manner of speaking, yes. Have you heard of the Contagious Disease Act?"

"Of course." I don't wish to appear the country mouse entirely, but I only dimly recall Maman mentioning it.

"Then, you do know about the dreadful Act? The peelers in Plymouth are doing their best to strictly enforce it, although my friends and I are fighting to have it repealed by Parliament. With all the sailors and the dollymops cavorting on the street, and going at it day and night, they've grown accustomed to throwing the poor girls in the

Royal Albert Hospital, diseased or healthy. The surgeons depend on the business, examining the dollymops for the clap."

I pretend to be utterly shocked rather than what I am: curious.

"Excuse me for speaking so bluntly," she says upon witnessing my discomfort, but her words provoke a profound awakening in me. This woman comes from a world beyond my experience, one recognized only by my reading of Maman's novels. I'm tempted to ask her more about the seamy side of Plymouth. In fact, I'd wager that Mrs. Polly Turney is operating a brothel rather than a lodging house for respectable women. Well, why not? She must conduct herself the best way she knows how, particularly if her man is a lout who beats her.

"It is my way of helping the girls. Providing them with safe and sanitary rooms where the police have no excuse to intrude."

No wonder Polly was so adept at caring for Maman. She's seen much worse than the sick rooms in our little inn. Appearances can be frightfully deceiving. When she first arrived—except for her black eye –she looked quite respectable. But she is nothing of the sort. When she invites me to leave the inn and travel to Plymouth with her, as her companion, I'm not entirely certain what she means by "companion."

Imagine that, I could say farewell to the inn, Pa, the Tilley brothers and their gormless wives, in one fell swoop. Leave the dullards to run the kitchen of the Devil's Stone without me. Just let them try!

## – 8 –

If Polly weren't quite so friendly, I might consider her offer. But there is something suspicious about the way she sidles up to me when I am standing at the window. Once she even swung her arms around my shoulders and kissed me on the neck. Her kiss felt lovely, I must admit. I remain intrigued about what she means by suggesting that I would be her companion.

If Maman were alive, to hear me speak about love between two women, she'd probably give me a good jab to the head, but I don't see how it is worse than the love between a man and a woman. Last summer, two spinsters shared a room at our inn. They appeared to be perfectly normal, two middle-aged women embarking on a holiday to walk the Cornish coast. Normal. Until I carried up their morning tea and discovered them locked in a heated embrace. I might have knocked, but I didn't. Although country life can be exceedingly dull, there are little dramas you are not intended to witness when you run an inn, but you do. I make it a habit to take a peek. At the time, I wondered how their union could be worse that what occurred between Maman and Pa, eleven pregnancies and not one of them bargained for, or so she claimed?

Today, Frederick sends another missive to me by post. Maman certainly left an impression on Mr. Wendice. He writes in his letter, "I am hoping the disease has not left you changed." How he knows that I am almost completely recovered, I'll never know. Who might have relayed this choice bit of information to him?

He is asking if he may call on me after I am fully recovered. He is sorry he has not visited, but he claims he was in Tintagel at the great stone pits of Penpithy. A section of rock collapsed into the sea carrying three men to their deaths, he reports, and his presence was needed to quell the skittish quarrymen. "Work must continue, no matter how severe the conditions," he writes to me. "It is my duty as a Christian and a Reformer to keep the men occupied in the pits or they will get up to no good, they will fall into the ways of the Devil." He also inquires in the postscript, rather indiscreetly I might add, if I have any scars from the fever or if my red hair has fallen out of my head.

Now that Maman is buried in a Christian graveyard, against her final wishes, I have no one to help me decide if I should allow Mr. Wendice to court me. He is a gentleman of means and stature even if his stomach protrudes over his trousers. It's gauche not to attempt to cover it up. I've always expected to belong to a dapper man, not particularly handsome in a classic way, but engaging in the way of Coleridge, let's say. In the representations of Samuel Coleridge's visage, at which I've spent many rapturous hours gazing, I perceive a man of character and courage, however boyish.

Of course, Maman would encourage me, no, force me to entertain Mr. Wendice. But now that she is gone, I feel as if I am a beached fish floundering on dry land. There is no one to rail against. Before she took ill, I'd fully intended to oppose her scheme to wed Wendice. After all, as long as she ruled the inn, I was safe from the whims of my Pa or the brothers, louts that they are. Now, even Polly is about to depart for Plymouth and I'll have no one at all on my side. In a pinch, Albert will defend his wife Griselda, the Tinker's daughter, against me. Mr. Wendice, unattractive as he is, is beginning to look slightly more appealing than I could possibly have imagined.

## – 9 –

Soon the May flowers will burst into full bloom, the purple delphiniums and pink phlox that Maman cared for, pruning and weeding and taking cuttings to her Jewish friends in the village of Holsworthy. I met these people years ago, but I've long forgotten their names or what they looked like. I'm certain that they don't fraternize with Wendice since they are Jewish and from another stratum of society.

Polly has stayed at the inn longer than expected. She encircles me like a lioness inspecting her prey. Unlike my sister-in-law Griselda, she appreciates my fine cooking. Tonight I concoct a dish of sweetbreads simmered in creamed onions and fennel. As I trim the membranes from the sweetbreads and slide them in the pan for searing, the aroma fills the kitchen and I feel myself for the first time in days.

"I could use an accomplished chef in my kitchen," she remarks. "You'd have free rein with me."

"In all things?" I inquire demurely.

Polly's smile is most beguiling. "Perhaps not in all things. You might find yourself enjoying my company more than you're able to concede at this moment."

What a thought! I haven't yet given up on winning the war at the Devil's Stone Inn. Perhaps more Tilleys will drop dead of typhoid before the month ends. Mr. Wendice is arriving tomorrow. If I'm lucky Polly and Wendice will meet.

## – 10 –

Just as Polly is climbing into the dray, with Albert driving her to the rail station in Holsworthy to catch the train to Plymouth, Frederick arrives by coach. He is dressed in a fine topcoat with a red silk vest and matching cravat. He has come to court me; I can see it by the set of his simpering yet greedy expression. He is wondering if I can cook like my

Maman. His stomach, thrust forward, stretches his vest to the point where the bejewelled buttons are about to pop.

Before Polly departs, she calls us both to her. "Mr. Wendice, have we not met before? In Plymouth?"

Frederick turns as crimson as his vest. "I think not, I rarely visit Plymouth and then solely for business purposes."

"I distinctly recall seeing you ... in my parlour." Polly winks at me.

"No," he insists wiping his brow with his handkerchief. "Impossible. I swear I have never set eyes on you before." Frederick turns to walk toward the inn, cutting Polly sharply while muttering a recitation from a poem. "On the touch of this bosom, there worketh a spell."

How odd! I daresay it is from "Christabel", one of Maman's and my favourite rhymes. How many times we have read it aloud in the safety of her library! Out in the open air, it sounds surprisingly ominous. But, then, everything is altered since Maman succumbed to the sickness. My maidenhood is ending before I am prepared to let it go.

"Before you embark on this new course in life, I suggest you consider it carefully," Polly states in haste to me. I admire her fearlessness; she cares not if Wendice hears her warning.

Turning to brother Albert, who has taken his place at the reins of the dray, she continues, "Your sister's suitor is not exactly as he appears. Mind her welfare. It is your duty as the eldest now that your mother is dead." With this, she hands me her calling card, inviting me to visit her whenever I fancy.

***

Mr. Wendice courts me most strangely. Although I question him severely about Polly, about why he cut her when she was only attempting to rekindle their friendship, he avoids answering me. He insists he has never set eyes on Mrs. Turney before, but he and I both know that he is dissembling. It surprises me that Frederick would go to such lengths to deny his knowledge of Polly Turney since no one is more revered in North Devon than Frederick Wendice. What could he possibly be concealing?

Shortly after Frederick arrives, he launches into a recitation of poetry. More lines from "Christabel." Pa and the brothers are overjoyed to be making great fun of him. Even Albert, who hankers after the finer things in life, remarks, "A quick pinch of your rounded bottom would do the trick rather than all this gibberish about love and romance."

"Myself, I prefer whispering lewd propositions in a maid's ear," adds Pa. His wife still warm in the ground and I bet he's already thinking of taking on a new woman, one considerably younger than himself, I suspect. She would become my stepmother.

There were times, when I was younger and more innocent than I am now, that I wished for Maman to give Pa a chance, to embrace him. Every little girl wants her mother and father to love each other. But as I observe the new widower, Thomas Tilley, how he sheds not one tear for his wife and how his spirits have lifted since her death, I wonder how I might have been so naïve. Maman was always right. I must remember that as I try to craft my life without her. Before she died from the filthy disease, Maman tried to convince me that Frederick Wendice was my only way to a better life, a proper life. I might have assured her that I would, at least, consider her petitions, but I did not.

Yet I am hesitant. What if there are things between a man and a woman that Maman has failed to tell me about? Feelings of passion absent from her life and, so far, from mine. I have no idea about what ingredients make for a happy marriage. Could it be as simple as following a recipe, combining the right number of eggs with flour and watching the mixture rise like the soufflés in Maman's kitchen? Looking back, I suspect Maman and I spent altogether too much time investigating the foibles of restless women, grasping at myriad ways to escape their marriages.

As for the opposite sex, I know next to nothing, except for what I learned in novels. Of course, there are my brothers, who will not give me the time of day, other than Albert, who watches over me like a father. As for Pa, anyone with eyes in her head can see it: he carries a grudge against me for a reason inexplicable to me. It cannot simply be that I was born on the day of the turning of the Devil's Stone. Or can it? Pa is a harsh man. There are no soft edges to him. No forgiveness.

In contrast with Pa, there is a gentle, contemplative quality about Frederick that I must admit to finding attractive. Maman was right. With her worldly experience, she saw Wendice more clearly than I. Perhaps it's worth considering him. What do I know of a kind but steady hand on my shoulder in times of need? It has always been Maman and me against the men in the family. I know more about what I don't want, than what I do.

Wendice makes absolutely no demands on my person; he hasn't tried to kiss me yet, even when we walk down to the River Torridge, hand-in-hand. At the river, he confesses he was dreadfully upset when he learned that I'd come down with the fever.

"It was so strange, Cordelia," he admits shyly. "If I may call you Cordelia?"

I nod in agreement and squeeze his hand. He brings my hand close to his lips while examining it—almost as if he has never held a woman's hand before, but refrains from actually touching my skin with his mouth.

"Are you absolutely certain, that you are cured of the filthy disease?" Frederick inquires.

"Would I be wandering about in the woods with the likes of you, Mr. Wendice, if I were sick?"

Even with Frederick's fear of contagion, I can sense that he is entirely taken with me. Why he remains so reserved, I cannot imagine. Surely, he can discern that I am no longer ill.

"What was it like for you, struck down by the disease? Were you disfigured? Was your face swollen or your body marked?" he asks, his voice ringing with curiosity.

Why this man wishes to know how I looked when I was sick, I cannot begin to comprehend.

"Was your friend, Mrs. Turney ill? Illness breeds in the darkest corners of Plymouth," he adds salaciously, sidling up close to me, careful not to touch me. "Dirt and disease radiate from Plymouth."

"Mrs. Turney suffered from the disease years ago. Now she is perfectly healthy."

"That's what she told you," he says, a sly look crossing his face. "I wouldn't be naïve about your friend."

I inquire of Mr. Wendice why he believes me to be naïve, but his gaze is fixed on my body. On my breasts, to be exact. He lifts his hand to touch my face, but immediately pulls back in fear, as if I might contaminate him.

What I wish to know is why not just give it a try? Touch me! Kiss me square on the lips and confess his undying love and devotion? He can see for himself I'm fully recovered and that my complexion has returned to its usual pink. Perhaps Quality are different than plain country folk.

"I could not sleep or eat or concentrate after seeing you that day at the inn and when I discovered that you were ill, I became indisposed myself. My mood turned black as I considered your illness. What would I do if you ... if you succumbed? Mater tried to drag me from my bed, but I wouldn't budge."

"Does your mother live with you?" I inquire.

"No, she prefers the old Abbey at Hartland, where she was raised. "It is I who decided to live in town at the manor house and mingle with the common folk. One day I shall make a run at Parliament, for the Reformers, of course."

"Of course."

If I felt the same way as Frederick obviously does about me, with such thoughts for the future, I wouldn't keep my emotions under strict wraps. I'd reach for the object of my affection and stroke him tenderly, but I don't have those feelings for Wendice—or anyone else. Never had, and most likely, never will. It's not in my nature.

I suspect Maman guessed that about me, that mine is not a romantic heart.

When we return to the inn, me grinning, both with the foolishness of Frederick's actions and his earnestness, I am showing off a bouquet of daffodils that he picked for me. The tavern is filled with commercial travelers drinking and reciting tales of adventure and male prowess. The news has spread about the County that Georgie is dead; Maman, too, and I've fully recovered. I imagine my neighbours are craving the delicacies served at our table. Pa has let them know that the Devil's Stone is up and running once more. Friday night will be my first performance preparing a grand dinner for Maman's followers.

Griselda is lurking around in the corners of the scullery, stuffing calves' skins with sausage. When I scream at her for having pork in the kitchen, she just laughs in my face.

"The days of you ordering me about are over, missy, now that your Ma is dead."

I could cause a great ruckus, but I must remember to pick my battles carefully. If I do eventually join Mr. Wendice at his manor house in Holsworthy who will be the wiser when the inn's kitchen is reeking with pork? If Maman is looking down disapprovingly from heaven, surely she will forgive me and if she does not, I suppose I shall find a way to live with the guilt.

## - II -

My cooking is a great success. Within days, not only is Mr. Wendice bringing his quality friends to my doorstep, but he's also inviting his political associates, the Fabians, to drop by on Friday nights when I prepare my long table. If only Maman could witness the splash I'm making. I have discovered what I do best and it is cooking. Not even all the force of the Tilleys combined, not husband or lover or king or potentate will be able to take me away from what I love doing. If I'm different from other women, preferring to invent new methods of braising lamb shanks or duck, rather than dwelling on the joys of matrimony, so be it.

I stick as closely as possible to Maman's French menus, but I can't say that I haven't experimented with a few new concoctions, like Escoffier's newly invented *Peche Melba* and another highlight of French cuisine, a dish called *Oeufs Careme.* It was canonized by Marie-Antoine Careme, who cooked for Talleyrand, George IV and for Czar Alexander I. Maman always said that Careme's five-volume encyclopedia of French cuisine was her Bible, but to my knowledge she never tried stuffing an artichoke with an egg and spreading sweetbreads and pickled tongue overtop. Now that I am the inn's cook, I spend hours pouring over the recipes in the encyclopedia. Just before serving tonight, I plan to spoon a bubbling sauce of veal stock, butter, flour, cream, lemon juice and egg yolks onto the pink tongue. The toffs won't be able to get enough of it.

The trouble is that Frederick interrupts my work at noon, just as I'm placing my pots and pans on the stove to begin brazing the sweetbreads for dinner. It is Friday night, just a little more than two weeks since Frederick arrived at the inn to court me.

"Put down that pan, Cordelia!" he orders in a voice more stern than I've heard before.

"Why, for the love of God?" I inquire. "It's my big night. Your friends will all be scrambling for a seat at my table and a taste of my *Oeufs Careme.*" I take a quick peek at myself in the bar's mirror and notice there is flour in my hair and my apron is covered in blood.

"You must announce that the inn is closed until further notice," he asserts. "Dinner is cancelled. Typhoid is spreading throughout County Devon."

"I beg your pardon. This is my establishment and I'll do as I please."

Frederick looks at me most strangely. "Everyone who is sick and dying has eaten at your table or resides with someone who has."

"So what?" I am seeing another side of Frederick Wendice and I don't like what I am witnessing. "What has that got to do with me?"

"I'm not entirely sure yet. But it cannot be a coincidence. The fever must be spreading from a miasma at the Devil's Stone Inn." He points his finger at me.

I'd heard the term miasma before, but never paid it any heed. Country folk believe in them and some uneducated city folk, as well, but similar to the superstition surrounding the Devil's Stone, Maman always claimed that blaming sickness on a miasma was pure, unabashed ignorance.

Frederick is adamant. A miasma, he explains in the pedantic way he has, spreads from piles of garbage to circulate into the air. Eventually it winds it way down the lungs of the unsuspecting, who promptly fall ill. "The miasma is here and it's causing typhoid."

"Are you completely barmy?" I ask him. "You won't be watching me disappoint my customers. Not on a Friday night."

"If people are falling ill, you must not cook tonight or any other night, until we discover the true source of the contamination," he states firmly.

In my life, I've never heard anything so silly, so I just turn on my heel and begin peeling the little red and white potatoes for the *Pommes Anna*.

Frederick stands at the entrance to the kitchen. The windows are covered in steam. Baskets everywhere contain mounds of vegetables ready to be peeled. He looks at me, covered in flour, with my wild hair, and my hands red from slicing freshly butchered meat. I can tell that he is considering what he will say next.

"Until you are mine, I suppose I can't force you to do anything." He says this next bit oddly, as if the words are popping out of his mouth and he can't control them. "I love you, Cordelia. I can't help myself."

At once, Frederick slumps into the chair beside the entrance to the scullery. He looks so out of place at the Devil's Stone Inn, I almost laugh, but I daren't since he immediately begins his confession.

"Even to myself, I can't quite explain it, this love, this obsession I have with you," he confesses. His voice is dripping with emotion. "I can barely stand to be out of your presence, Cordelia. I must have you, you must be mine."

"Are you completely dotty," I respond. "You've just accused me of spreading typhoid, of causing an epidemic right here in my own kitchen. Why on earth would you wish to have me, then?"

Frederick looks up at me with his eyes red. He is squeezing his temples with both index fingers. "Can't you hear me, woman? My intentions toward you are beyond my control!"

Just when it looks like he will break down in tears, he asks in a hoarse voice, "Don't you understand that I am the only one who can save you? I can convert you. I can cleanse you of filth. Filth and disease."

---

As Frederick babbles on, I wonder what it would be like to feel that way: feelings out of control. I can't imagine. If he thinks I am dirty why does he want me? I have sworn on my mother's grave, I will never convert to Christianity. More so, it's ridiculous that he believes me tainted. It's all connected to the idiocy surrounding the turning of the Devil's Stone and my birthday being on that very day. The inhabitants of the West Country, even the wealthy ones, are too superstitious for their own good. Maman believed riches released people from the chains of irrationality, but she may have been wrong. I shall call Frederick's bluff.

I look him square in the face. "Is this your way of asking me to be your wife?"

Frederick agrees that it is.

"And the typhoid? My Jewish faith? How will you square that with marrying me?"

"I am a good Christian man; I believe in salvation and I shall find a way to save you. If we Reformers can save the ladies of the night, surely we can save you, a respectable young woman from the country."

"Ladies of the night. How would you know anything about them? You're a gentleman, aren't you? " I am trying to get under his skin. Every one takes it for granted that a Victorian gentleman, no matter how prudish, enjoys his night on the town. Yet Frederick's desires appear to be obsessive.

Frederick looks at me quizzically. "Surely you must understand that my first duty is to you, Cordelia. You are my lady love."

"Surely, but what will your mother say? Your lady love is a cook. A Jewish one, at that! Aren't you marrying far beneath your station? How will you square that?"

"Mater will accept you, Cordelia. She will support my decision. Your religion intrigues me. Jewish women are believed to ..." he stops himself. "In time she will come to understand my plight."

"Your plight?"

"My need to have you and to heal you at one and the same moment."

"I'm not sick."

"Not outwardly, but you are of the Hebrew faith ..."

"You must believe me, I shall never convert to Christianity," I tell him bluntly.

"We shall see," he pauses and adds, "The Jews are adept at commerce. At making money."

"So are you, good at making money," I retort. "I know nothing of the mechanics of business."

"You shall be able to advise me on my business ventures." It is as if Frederick is measuring my bad and good points on his pudgy fingers and is not listening to a word I am saying.

"The Jews have special powers when it comes to usury." Frederick makes this statement without shame. "It's common knowledge: the Jews are better at it than anyone else."

What can I do but giggle at his outlandish pronouncements? I look at him and shake my head. My expression is one of condescension. His ideas about filth and usury and Jewish women are utterly ridiculous. To utter such superstitions, he must be daft. I must force myself to believe that he is half mad with love for me and no matter who I am and what I do, he will always adore me.

Truthfully, I, too, am silently making a list of the reasons to accept Frederick as my husband. It is a legal agreement, isn't it? I am searching for any reason to marry him since the alternative for me is becoming unthinkable. Perhaps it is a failure of imagination not to see clearly what Frederick's pronouncements foretell. Perhaps I should try harder to envision a future at the Devil's Stone Inn that would include me. Perhaps I could convince brother Albert to fight for my place here, among my family. But I can't muster the courage to do it, to believe in a future that would be anything but constant drudgery and abuse. As for Frederick and his dotty ideas, surely I will be able to dissuade him of my inherent "dirtiness" and his more spurious superstitions about Jews and our mystical money-making rituals. After all he is a gentleman, accustomed to the finer things in life, not just wealth, but art and music. Does not a love of the arts make people more humane? He often speaks of Turner and Beethoven, as his favourite painter and composer and art does release the goodness in the soul; it erases the need for ghastly superstition and unkind behaviour. I believe it to be so. I shall embark on changing Frederick more than he could ever change me.

As Frederick observes my expression softening, he gets down on one knee to ask me properly if I will marry him and I, oddly enough, accept. Just like that, I say "yes" and the deal is sealed. He appears to be relieved. "Mater shall be pleased," he says as he heaves himself back to standing.

As for me, it is my only way out, away from the Devil's Stone Inn and the Tilleys with their crass, untutored ways. It is my only chance to be surrounded by art and ideas and finely bred friends! Last night, Pa was encouraging me to spend more time with Mr. Wendice. My own father wishes me out of the way; his plan is to hand over the kitchen of the Devil's Stone Inn to Griselda. I see them talking to each other while looking surreptitiously in my direction. But that is not my only reason for accepting Frederick's proposal, if reason is a word you would use in this instance. It is that tincture of fear, the fear of what would become of me if I stayed at the Devil's Stone as the unmarried sister and resident drudge. And curiosity. Yes, curiosity. With Wendice as my husband, I would be the wealthiest woman in County Devon. Revered and obeyed. I would be the lady of the manor and experience a life I'd never dreamt of having. Romance is a luxury I can ill afford. Not in my position. If I am making a mistake, if I wait for romance, I might wait all my life. Worse, I might end up like Maman, toiling from morning to night, butt of the jokes of an uncivilized man I've been forced into marriage with.

I recall Maman insisting that we don't always act in character. "People do inexplicable things," she would say. "What a dull place the world would be if everyone acted as expected." I suppose I am proving her point and so is Frederick.

Later that night Wendice secures Pa's permission to take me as his wife.

***

The air smells of the raw sea. Gusts of salty air lash the slender trees near the inn. Along the northern coast of Devon, during night storms, pirates, by the light of their lanterns, guided foreign ships onto the wild, craggy rocks. The sailors were praying for a safe place to anchor, but the ships split into pieces upon dashing the rocky coast. The innocent sailors drowned in the roiling sea while the Devon blackards watched from atop the jagged precipices until the waters turned to calm. By morning, these long-bearded ruffians, tied to ropes, would shimmy down the rocks to the beach to board their little boats and fish for the goods floating in the sea. Anyone still alive, who washed upon the shore in the storm, was bludgeoned to death. When in his cups, Pa revels in these stories.

They are among his favourite tales and he swears they are true. In fact, Pa claims that if you root into the nooks and crevices of the caves at Merlin's beach, the skeletons of the drowned sailors can be discovered. He keeps a near-perfect skull in his butcher's shed beside the inn. It is his prized possession. Along with his pigs, of course.

***

After closing the kitchen for the night, I walk to the churchyard to stand at Maman's grave. She is separated from the rest—in St. Michael's abandoned corner for sinners and suicides. Since Maman was never baptized, it is supposed she is now burning in hell. Looking up at the stars, I inform her of my impending marriage to Frederick Wendice. And beg forgiveness for not lighting the Sabbath candles on this Friday night.

I cannot discern if her joy at learning of my engagement to Mr. Wendice outweighs her disappointment with me for not observing the Sabbath and others to come. I am beginning to recognize why Maman was so harsh, so unforgiving. With her sophisticated taste, her sense of high style and her well-educated mind, it is no wonder she found the Devil's Stone Inn intolerable, here in the remote English countryside, at a superstition-ridden place she would consider the tag end of worldly civilization.

I can see her now, as she was when I was still a little child, dressed in her organza gown, drenched in sequins and feathers, sewn from a pattern that she studied in a French fashion catalogue. She is attempting to engage the customers seated at the long trestle table with sparkling repartee as they stuff their mouths with her delicate creations. Not a soul responds to Maman and from the corner of my eye I can see Pa, too, his shoulders heaving in laughter. His wife is coming undone. What I do know is that I certainly must acquiesce to this betrothal: the only path to avoiding her ignominious end.

## – 12 –

Frederick is right. Typhoid is taking its toll on the inhabitants of our village and the surrounding countryside. At least half the cottages in the village display the sign of the typhoid cross on their front doors. Albert reports that the fever is spreading like wildfire and that young men are the most dreadfully affected by the disease. "They're not lasting a week," he says, and I can see the fear in his dark eyes.

---

Although I'd wager that Frederick Wendice is essentially a coward, he is stalwart enough to remain by my side. He doesn't actually touch me or kiss me. Instead he keeps watch over my every move in the kitchen. And, although I have agreed to wed Frederick Wendice, he must wait until the ceremony to try to stop me from cooking in my own establishment. Once I'm ensconced in Wendice Manor, I shall be the lady of the big house and I, and only I, will decide when and how to cook. Not Frederick. I shall give grand dinner parties and invite only Quality. I shall be the talk of the County Devon.

"Wash your hands, Cordelia. Before each and every utensil you pick up, carefully wash your hands. You must be certain that conditions in your kitchen are sanitary." He implores me to agree.

On the stone wall in the kitchen, I've preserved Maman's display of cooking instruments, the way any proper French chef would, and not in the sloppy way the English hide their implements, out of sight and bundled in a drawer.

"My hands will be raw to the bone if I do that." I am busy trimming the fat and gristle from a side of stringy beef. I'm fixing a brown stew and measuring the fat for pastry dough. If it's just local farmers appearing for dinner tonight—with Frederick frightening away the Quality and the churchmen—I'll only be offering plain Cornish pasties for supper. Perhaps I should throw in a few peas and carrots to give the filling some colour. Sure enough, it's common food, but even so, I enjoy giving the farmers a taste of my savoury pies. My fingers knead the dough, stretching the malleable forms and then packing them into hefty balls. It is the most satisfying feeling in the world, making a gorgeous pastry.

Frederick is devoted to my cooking, but since I agreed to be his wife, he travels to and from Shebbear and Holsworthy, bringing his own repasts with him in a basket prepared by Mrs. Bullbrook, the housekeeper at his manor house.

"Are you ever going to taste my food again?" I ask him, "I can't see what my cooking has to do with the typhoid epidemic. Look at me, Frederick Wendice," I demand. "I'm as healthy as a horse."

"Yes, I can see that. It just doesn't make sense. Here's the rub: everyone who comes down with the fever reports a connection to The Devil's Stone and to you. Is it this place or is it you?"

"I hope to God you aren't going around collecting information about me and my customers, then, are you?"

"Not exactly."

"I have work to do and this kitchen to run. As long as I'm here cooking for the inn, everyone depends on me."

"I must confess that I am keeping a record of every death from typhoid in the County."

As he speaks, droplets of white spittle squirt from the corner of his mouth. Sure enough, he has been carrying a black-leather lined notebook along with him wherever he goes. I notice that the moment he learns of a new death by typhoid, he balances the notebook on his stomach, while scribbling down the deceased's name with pen and ink.

I ask him why he is keeping this notebook, but he does not provide me with an honest answer.

"Did you cook for Farmer Leatherby?" Frederick inquires, wiping his brow. "He died of the fever today."

"And if I did? What of it? I'm not living a life of leisure, keeping lists, as you do, of those I cook for and if and when they fall sick. What's got into you?

Frederick is clutching his notebook and staring at the pages of the names of the dead. Of late, he has begun to mumble openly to himself. "I will succeed. Eventually, she will listen to me, she will see what I am saying is true."

"Who are you speaking to?" I ask him. Frederick clamps his mouth shut, as if I have caught him being a naughty boy. Next thing, I'll be washing out his mouth with soap.

"Marry me now, today. We could go at once to my church in Holsworthy. The Vicar will conduct the service. I'll take you away from all of this, Cordelia, from this sweltering kitchen and this unhealthy little village. You can live as a lady should, in the manner your Maman dreamed."

For once, I do not know how to respond. When Frederick asked Pa for my hand, the old fool immediately responded, saying yes, without even inquiring if I actually wanted to become Mrs. Frederick Wendice. Clearly Pa longs for Frederick to take me off his hands. But I don't want to give him that satisfaction. I work like the devil. If the typhoid hadn't spoiled everything, I would be doing better than Maman, after all her years of cooking at the inn. It was never my intention to depart the Devil's Stone so quickly, no matter what Maman wished for me.

Although I am not of a romantic nature, I am not without aspirations. If there is anything I desire, it is to live life on my own terms.

That's why I adore the kitchen, where all things tend to run amuck unless they are managed properly. The pot is boiling over, the butter is melting too quickly or the meat is roasting to a burn, but it is I, or any other cook worth her salt, who must keep conditions orderly if dinner is to be served. The kitchen is where I control what is prepared and when and how. The kitchen is my world. It suits my nature, even if Pa calls me bossy and overbearing.

"Give me time," I say coyly. "I need to consider what you are offering me."

I'll admit that I'm not a bad looking woman, with clear skin and an ample figure that I'm not afraid to show off. The customers declare that I could sell spice to the Indians. Yes, I play on my looks, with Wendice and the other blokes bursting through the door of the Devil's Stone Inn. Why shouldn't I? Most women do—since it's all we've got in the end, isn't it? Our looks and our God-given talents.

***

As I'm learning every day, my true talent is for cooking. I am more certain of that with each day that passes. Just as some women are Florence Nightingales, drawn to the battlefield, I am drawn to the belching stove. If the life of a cook is one of hardship and servitude, so be it. Above all, I relish the imagination—and the precision—it takes to fix the very finest of meals. I'd go so far as to say, food artfully prepared, heals the soul, and that counts just as much as slapping a dressing on an open wound. Perhaps I have agreed to marry Frederick without considering my alternatives. What if I went to London and found my own way as a cook for hire? The thought terrifies me. I'd be entirely on my own, without any protection. And what would Maman think of me going into service? My thoughts are interrupted by Frederick demanding my attention.

"There is no time for you to consider anything. More people are dying every day that you continue to cook."

"I don't see what that has to do with marrying you."

"It does. It has everything to do with it," Frederick is stammering. "You are a stubborn and obstinate girl!"

"If you say so, but I won't be pushed into marriage so quickly. Folks will say I'm with child."

Frederick looks up from his notebook. "There's that. We wouldn't want anyone to think we've ..."

"We've what? Oh Frederick, just say what's on your mind."

I am not entirely convinced that life as Frederick Wendice's lady of the manor will make me content. If I hold my ground, the fever will blow over eventually and trade will return to normal. I could remain at the inn as cook, as I've always wished to do. Customers will come pouring back to the inn. Now that I've established my reputation with the better sort, I don't actually need Frederick to send the Quality my way. What if a bloke more suitable to my taste walks into the dining room of the Devil's Stone Inn tomorrow and instantly falls prey to my charms? A man of letters, let's say. If I consent to marry Frederick before the New Year, I'd be giving up the opportunity to find someone more suitable to my taste than he.

"Go home, Frederick. Get a good night's sleep in your own bed. We'll both give this serious thought. Possibly you're rushing things. We've decided to marry at Hartland Abbey next spring. We wouldn't wish to disappoint your mother, would we?"

"Mater would understand if I explained the situation to her. About the fever."

"Would she now? Are you planning to tell your mother that I'm the cause of the typhoid epidemic? What if I have nothing to do with the typhoid epidemic, you silly goose? I can't see how I do. You have absolutely no proof except that wretched notebook of yours with the names of the farmers and traveling men who've perished of fever. Of course, they've eaten here. Everyone in County Devon does. Your notebook proves nothing."

"Nothing scientific, I must admit." Frederick is almost apologizing.

"Why would you wish to marry a woman who you are accusing of spreading typhoid? A criminal! Have you thought about that? Perhaps I am infecting you with my filthy ways." This man exasperates me. "Perhaps it would be best if we delayed the wedding indefinitely."

At that moment, Frederick, who's been studiously avoiding contact with me, grabs me by the waist. He is absurdly strong for a toff who has never in his life done an honest day's work.

"I can't imagine living without you," he wails. "Can't you understand that you have infected my entire being?"

He is kissing me and then shaking me like rag doll. I don't relish the thought of one day soon having this man in my bed. Putting off the marriage might be best for both of us.

"Dearest, Cordelia, what was I thinking?" He hovers on the verge of tears while holding me close to him. "If a disease as dreadful as typhoid emanates from your lovely self ..." He kisses me again, more passionately than before. "Yes, that's it, if it does; I shall save you and re-make you sweet and pure. First I shall heal the mind and then the body." But his expression betrays more lust than compassion.

"Yes, well, we all lose our heads from time to time but now is not the time for me to lose mine." I pull him from me to shove him out the door and straight toward his carriage.

There's no longer any doubt, I must re-consider if I will be able to tolerate the u-n-c-t-u-o-u-s Frederick Wendice as my husband. The thought of being blamed for the typhoid epidemic is despicable. Why ever he accuses me so unjustly, makes me think he is half mad. It is his taste for the wicked that stokes the fire of his ardour. Whenever he approaches me a kind of hunger strains his face. Yet what he finds attractive about me are the very things he wishes to change.

Everyone who has succumbed to the disease has, indeed, eaten at my table or resides with someone who did. But, that doesn't mean a thing, does it? This obscure notion of his: that a miasma at the Devil's Stone Inn is responsible for the epidemic unnerves me. What he actually means is that I am the miasma. How can I be expected to love a man who thinks I am rubbish? As for the grand dame, his mother, I can't imagine why she would allow our union. Surely, there are better bred young woman in the West Country, good Christian girls, none of them born on the day of the turning of the Devil's Stone, or from the loins of a rough publican and his despised Jewish wife?

But I must remind myself that love is the last reason I would marry Frederick Wendice. Nor am I marrying his mother. She will live at Hartland Abbey. Far to the north of us and unable to affect me. In the end, what choice do I have?

## – 13 –

I glance up from my chopping board. Trade at the inn has dwindled to next to nothing. To complicate matters, Frederick is bringing his valet to dinner tonight. He claims he wishes to treat his manservant to my cooking, but I believe that Frederick wishes me to practise in front of the man. Jeremiah has been with Frederick for years and will tell him honestly if I am ready for society. He will observe me like a specimen writhing on the surgeon's table. To discern if I am ready to be introduced to Quality.

Frederick wishes for me to begin circulating with the better sort before our marriage—to ease my way into society before taking my place as the wife of a prominent industrialist and social reformer.

For this occasion, I'm preparing tripe with jellied vinegar sauce, a perfect dish for the pinch-nosed and squeamish valet.

Since Frederick accused me of spreading typhoid, and I, in turn, threatened to reconsider our marriage, he, himself, has been on his best behaviour. He does not blame me openly for the epidemic for fear that I will put an end to our arrangement. Instead he smiles at me, with a fraudulent grin on his face, and keeps his incriminating notebook out of sight. Whenever I ask him why he does not bring his mother to dinner, he pretends to not hear me or changes the subject.

"If you believe my cooking is so grand, why don't you invite your Maman?" I ask querulously.

"Mater disdains travelling." He has not glanced up from his folded hands. He is intent on making little circles with his thumbs.

"Are you certain you've cleared our engagement with her, Frederick?"

Frederick rolls his eyes upwards. "Yes, my dearest. I've repeated many times over that Mater approves of our union. She views you as the perfect mate for me."

"I cannot imagine why. I have neither blood nor wealth nor the proper education. You will be marrying a Jewess and still she does not object?"

Frederick has closed his eyes and is breathing heavily by now.

"There are reasons, dearest, that we believe make you suitable. Now, let's leave it at that. Isn't my love and devotion enough for you?"

"If you say so," I reply. What strange beings the gentry are. Secretive. Thank goodness, I don't believe in all this nonsense about the Devil's Stone or I'd be pondering that they want me for some hellish reason.

***

As the afternoon proceeds, I can see that our conversation has made Frederick anxious. He stalks the kitchen and the scullery, running his white handkerchief along the wooden surfaces. Finally he breaks down. Carrying a huge pot of boiling water, he moves cautiously towards me.

"What on earth are you doing now?" I ask him. I fear the blighter is going to pour boiling water on my head.

"If you wouldn't mind, my dear, I'll scrub you down with a little soap and water. Just for good measure." The expression on my fiancé's face is a mixture of lust and trepidation.

In Maman's old bones pot, is a bar of green carbolic soap, floating atop the steaming water.

"Can't you make yourself useful?" I ask him. "Pour the water into the cistern for the dishes."

"What if my valet falls ill?"

"From my cooking?"

"Yes," Frederick admits with a guilty expression crossing his face. "Please don't be upset with me. Taking a few precautions never hurt anyone."

Although Frederick is not mentioning the miasma at the Devil's Stone Inn, clearly he still imagines it exists.

"You actually believe that by scrubbing me down with soap and water, you can stop the typhoid epidemic and rescue Jeremiah? Well, try it, Frederick Wendice!" I am incensed by his determination to blame me. Whenever I begin to feel the slightest flame of emotion for the man, he has a way of dousing the spark.

Frederick bundles me into the scullery to wash my hands and face. He asks me to open the top buttons of my blouse, which I do. He is staring at my breasts, which are popping out of the top of my camisole. He cannot resist. He drops the soapy brush, to kiss my chest and neck and face. I feel his tongue, which is wet, licking my ear. I return his kiss and he sighs a great sigh of relief.

Falling to his knees, breathing heavily, Frederick places the side of his head against my stomach. "You will carry my baby, dearest. Eventually we will have children. Healthy, perfectly formed children." He reaches for my breasts to caress my nipples and then to suckle them as they tumble from my camisole. I begin to crumble to the floor, where I collapse in his arms. For the first time, I sense the fire in him and it moves me. Could this be love? But abruptly, when he feels I am returning his ardour, he stops, as if afraid that we will slip beyond the limit of what is sanctioned.

***

When he is done, I button up and return to the chopping board. Frederick stumbles to his seat at the bar and acts as if nothing peculiar has occurred. But it has. Something inside me has erupted. It's true, I can't approve of all this superstitious nonsense about me as a miasma spreading typhoid throughout the West Country, but I do trust his emotions for me. How can they be anything but sincere? The man wishes to give me his seed.

What I do not understand is that if he is so desperately attracted to me, why does he not bed me? Today, in my scullery, I would have let it happen. What harm could it have done if we are to marry presently and start a family immediately? That's how it usually goes in the country. But for Frederick, this obsession with me is something I do not fully understand. He admits he wishes to save me, to purify me, as if I was a common streetwalker and he was Prime Minister Gladstone himself out on a mission of good deeds in the east end of London. Yet at the same time, he wishes to preserve my innocence. Why not just get it over with? I must admit that I am curious, what it would be like to have him take me completely. I want him to have me.

When Frederick finally vacates the kitchen, as an experiment, I put my fingers in my mouth and straight into the pan to pull out the tripe for the valet. Then I wash my hands and pull out the remainder of the meat for Freddy. Let's see what happens. What if he is right: that I can infect people with a lick of my finger? What then? But the thought of it terrifies me. I must hold my curiosity in check. If they both fall ill or neither, it will confirm that Frederick is mad. But this game is too risky!

I have allowed Frederick's foolish misgivings to confuse me. I shall ignore them. Our romantic frolicking has transformed me. Made me bold in ways I couldn't imagine. I could no more harm Jeremiah than I could turn the Devil's stone by my own strength. I steady my hands to throw the dinner in the rubbish and begin preparations again. Supper will be more than an hour late tonight.

***

By the next day, with Frederick and his valet on the county road to the coast, I'm beginning to envision a life with my intended that could bring me happiness and fulfilment. Myself as the beloved and Frederick as my heartfelt protector, wife and husband locked in a union of graceful comfort. How can I resist this image of besotted domesticity? Before departing yesterday, he recited a poem from Coleridge in a clear voice, neither stammering nor affected:

*Is the night chilly and dark?*
*The night is chilly, but not dark.*

---

*The thin grey cloud is spread on high,*
*It covers but not hides the sky.*
*The moon is behind, and at the full;*
*And yet she looks both small and dull.*
*The night is chill, the cloud is grey:*
*'Tis a month before the month of May,*
*And the Spring comes slowly up this way.*

*The lovely lady, Christabel,*
*Whom her father loves so well,*
*What makes her in the wood so late,*
*A furlong from the castle gate?*
*She had dreams all yesternight*
*Of her own betrothed knight;*
*And she in the midnight wood will pray*
*For the weal of her lover that's far away.*

I am not immune to the cadence of the lines and the words hold me in a dream-like trance. I feel the pangs of a new pleasure tinkering with my insides. It makes me wonder what Polly was on about when she and Frederick collided. Surely Mrs. Turney is too shrewd by half and overplayed her hand with me. She tried to trick me into believing that Frederick is deranged when he is lonely and wishes for a lively wife at his side and rollicking children at his knee. Surely, I am nothing like the creation she wishes me to be. I shall expel Polly from my mind and belong entirely to my intended. If Frederick was about, I would reach out to cup his face in my hands, to stroke him and make him blush with aching desire.

Later tonight I will assure brother Albert that he has nothing to fear; Wendice is the husband for me. We have swum across the river to an inviting landscape where he will cherish me from this time onward.

## – 14 –

I attend three more funerals today. The churchyard at St. Michael's is fresh with newly dug graves. At the inn, Pa and the brothers, except for Albert, afford me a wide berth, acting as if I am responsible for the deaths. Although I am their flesh and blood, they treat me like a pariah. How has it come to be that so soon after Maman's death, I am the outcast, the untouchable?

After the service, Pa suggests we ride in the dray to the Morwellham Quay Copper Works. I have never been to the Quay and I wonder why he has chosen today to show me Wendice's holdings.

Along the way, Pa utters not one word to me, nor does he touch me. The Devon air smells sweet with the blooms of summer. The heat is overwhelming for June.

Everywhere along the path to Morwellham are stalks of Queen Anne's lace and purple lavender. I jump down from the dray to pick a bouquet of wildflowers, which I rub against my cheek. The leaves are prickly, but the petals feel like finely-woven silk. A deer races through the forest.

Just outside the Copper Works, I catch a first glimpse of the half-naked bodies scattered about the forest floor. This compound, the mine, the distillery and the shops, all belong to Wendice. He sells arsenic and manganese from the Works.

"Why are there no physicians to help these people?" I ask Pa. "They are sick from the fever epidemic."

"Too far gone. What good would it do?"

A young man is lying in the dirt up the hill from the factory. Our dray winds around the path, passing him by. His arms and legs, covered in black matted hair, are as thin as a spider's. He is wearing a white sheet tied about his middle, as a baby's nappy would be. The sheet is soaked in blood and shit. A young woman, a girl really, sits beside him, caressing his hand and staring up at the blue sky. Her expression is blank. The young man's eyes are bulging with pain, but he makes not a sound.

Untended children are racing through the woods. Some are naked. White army tents are staked among the tall trees. A woman with blue-veined, yellow-skinned breasts is trying to coax her baby into latching onto her shrunken nipple. The tiny baby is crying loudly.

"It's hungry," I say to Pa. "Shall I try to feed it the milk I brought with us?"

"Leave it be," Pa says firmly. "You'll do the babe more harm than good."

"How can you say such a thing?" He wounds me deeply.

"Do not touch the baby," Pa orders.

---

As I reach into my hamper to retrieve the bottle of milk, Pa puts his hand on my arm to stop me. Although it is spring, he is wearing gloves.

"Your Mr. Wendice, the proprietor of these works, claims it is you who is responsible for the typhoid epidemic." Pa bites his lip and his beady eyes won't meet mine. "It's high time you married your fine sir and left the kitchen to Griselda and Albert."

I ask Pa what Albert thinks about his plan.

"Albert is soft on you, missy. That's why you are asking."

"I'm a much better cook than Griselda."

"No matter. Griselda has nothing to do with it. The villagers say it is you, the Jewess, your mother's daughter, who is the cause of the sickness. Everything you touch goes rotten. The villagers agree with Frederick."

"Agree that I am the reason for the typhoid epidemic?" I ask in a quivering voice.

"Have you not noticed? No one dare come within fifty yards of the inn. Our usual trade has disappeared and if we don't retrieve it soon, I'll be sure to die a pauper. Everyone believes that they'll catch the fever by breathing in the bad air circulating at the inn and spread by those who have eaten at your table. That's why the sick are scattered about the forest floor, out in the open, here at Morwellham. They are trying to outwit the miasma by dissipating it into the pure forest air."

"You couldn't possibly believe that," I say.

"I do. You will agree, daughter, that most of the sick have eaten at the Devil's Stone Inn. Mr. Wendice has ordered his workers out of their houses and into tents to try to save them.

"The tents would be stifling in this heat," I assert.

"Your Mr. Wendice says that the copper mines are operating at half capacity and that the Works, where the women extract the ore, has closed. So say, he must find a quick method of getting these people back to honest labour."

I'm bewildered by Pa's condemnation of me and his approval of the hell that Frederick has forced upon these unsuspecting folk. How can my own husband-to-be blame this catastrophe on me? I believe his real concern is that he is losing money at the Works, not the welfare of his people. When he mumbles about recreating me, making me over into the ideal wife, all ivory skinned and pure of heart, I must always remember his people at the Works and how he treats them. Although Frederick appears to be of mild manners, I wonder if there is a brutality to him. It shocks me; it unlocks a well of resentment deep inside me that I did not realize I had. I wonder what the Reformers would think of Morwellham Quay today? False charity. If Maman were alive, how would she counsel me in light of what I am witnessing today?

On the drive back to Shebbear, Pa does not deign to speak with me, nor will he take a morsel of food or a drop of water from my lunch basket. The sun beats down savagely on us. With no bed for the night, Pa drank until dawn with the men beside the waterwheel at the mouth of the Quay, while I tried to sleep on a blanket beside the dray.

Although I cupped my hands over my ears, the shrieks of the dying kept me awake. I have not washed in two days and I am covered in sweat and mud.

My choices are diminishing by the hour. If I remain at the inn, it will be as Griselda's work horse, be it that I'm allowed to enter the kitchen at all. Before the summer is over, Pa will bribe a widowed farmer with a dozen children to take me off his hands. Who else would agree to have me, after all of this? If I go ahead and marry Wendice, even after what I've seen at Morwellham Quay, I will be rich—and immune to the vagaries of life. If only I were brave enough to investigate Polly's offer. She appears to be a seductress. Frederick fears her, but I might be judging her superficially. On my own I am not able to sort out the contradictory thoughts in my tired head.

## - 15 -

Frederick Wendice and I are to be married today, Whit Sunday 1881. Only seven weeks since Maman died yet it feels like a lifetime ago. According to Frederick it is fitting that we marry on the Pentecost, since it is the day the Holy Spirit descended upon the Apostles. Frederick describes Whit Sunday as the Birthday of the Church and assures me that I am being welcomed into a life inside the Church and Christian morality. In my books, and according to the Jewish faith, this day symbolically commemorates God giving the Ten Commandments to Moses at Mount Sinai, but what I believe matters little to him.

At the last moment I refuse to be baptized as a Christian, to confess my sins and take Jesus into my heart as my saviour, so the service must be moved from the church to the manor house. Frederick insists that the Reverend marry us, no matter if I am baptized or not.

Olympia, his mother, won't look me straight in the eye. I suspect, if I dared to touch her, she would recoil. She is a grand woman, slender and stately, with hair that shines like polished silver. Her bright blue eyes condescend to all those who surround her. She is a woman who has been well served for all of her life. If Frederick had his way, he would turn me into the mirror image of his mother. Might he believe that by placing me in contact with Olympia and the better sort, I will join the righteous?

On her end, Olympia avoids me, not even wishing to share memories of Frederick when he was a child. I have inquired on three occasions if he was a happy little boy, wishing to know if our children will resemble him in temperament. Although I try to soften Olympia's heart toward me by speaking of grandchildren, she remains strangely aloof.

"There were children before and after me who did not survive. It unhinges Mater to discuss my youth. Best to give her time." Frederick always apologizes for her.

"But you claimed she was accepting of our marriage plans?"

"She will be ... she is," Frederick prevaricates.

"No, she will not. She cannot look me straight in the eye," I retort. "Why won't she reminisce about your childhood? You survived and did not die as her other infants did."

Frederick turns silent. His face is crimson.

"I'd so much like to know about your previous friendships with women," I continue, unsettled by his intransigence.

Frederick looks at me aghast. "That is none of your business!" he states emphatically.

"It is, if I am to be your wife."

"My friendships with the opposite sex have not been terribly successful, if you must know." Frederick is vexed by my interrogations.

"Why not?"

"I cannot assume. Drat! Each and every Emily and Beatrice, the privileged girls of the County, didn't seem to ... I have not been successful with them."

"So you chose me? The publican's daughter. I was bound to accept you particularly with my father wishing to get me off his hands and with all the speculation about typhoid and the Devil's Stone Inn. Why ..."

But Frederick cuts me off sharply. He squeezes his thumb and forefinger together, as he does when he is overcome with anxiety. "Why must you ask so many questions? What does it matter at this point? We are to be married."

***

A few days ago Frederick decided that Mr. Ealing, the village physician and not Pa is to give the bride away. "I thought you and Pa were as thick as thieves," I remind him.

"Mater does not wish to have Mr. Tilley in the wedding party."

"Why not?"

"She thinks it would be unseemly for a man of your Pa's station to walk you down the aisle."

I can feel my heart flutter as Frederick explains that my father could never pass the muster with the Wendices. It's not that I care so much about Pa's feelings. He's never bothered to show me anything but contempt, but what this says about my future as the daughter-in-law of Olympia Wendice is unnerving.

Since agreeing to marry Frederick, I have been fretting about the huge differences in our stations of English society, our difference in ages, our religions. How will I ever fit in at the manor when I am hardly accepted by my own people in Shebbear? For as long as I can recall the Tilleys and all of our neighbours treated Maman and me as if we were exotics: poisonous flowers, too strange to ignore, too deadly to touch. I fear that Frederick believes that Jewish women have special sexual powers. Or powers of procreation. Why else would he be constantly talking about hybrid vigour and what he is eventually expecting from me in the matrimonial bed?

I must remind myself, as well, that it was Pa, the old satyr of the Devil's Stone Inn, who pushed me into this union, as if he harboured a secret hatred for me in his heart. What I cannot fathom is what I have done to him.

Apart from the physician and Frederick's housekeeper, Mrs. Bullbrook, only Wendice family members, my brothers and their wives are invited to the wedding. Mr. Ealing is exceptionally grateful that he's been asked by Mrs. Wendice to give me away. I beg Frederick to allow me to invite Polly Turney, as she is my only friend. At first, he forbids it but when I begin to cry, he softens, and allows me to send her a telegram asking her to be my matron of honour.

Without Frederick's permission, Albert and I walk over to the station to meet Polly's train. Albert and Polly greet each other like long-lost friends.

---

"It's not too late to get out of this marriage," Albert declares, taking my hand in his own. "No one is forcing you. You have nothing to prove to Pa or anyone else."

I am shocked by Albert's words. "Pa will be happy to see the backside of me, and so will you, Albert. Everyone at the inn wants to be rid of me."

"I don't," Albert says softly.

"He hates me, Pa does."

"Don't take on so. Pa sticks to his own ways. It has more to do with Maman than with you."

Polly grabs my other hand, as we walk toward the big house. "Listen to Albert. It is not too late. I'll tell Wendice to send everyone home. What does it matter what your Pa wants? You are a free woman."

I am afraid to look Polly straight in the face. It does infuriate me that my own Pa shuns me and that my brothers, except for Albert, feel the same. Life at the inn could become intolerable, while at the manor, I would be in charge.

"Why do you think Pa treats me so?" I ask Albert. "I am his only daughter."

"Don't go sticking your nose where it shouldn't be." Albert pulls at his collar to loosen its grip. "What happened between Pa and Maman is no concern of yours."

"What did happen?"

But Polly has no patience for these private family matters. "If you are going to wiggle out of this marriage you'd best do it now, my friend."

"Make up your own mind, my girl!" Albert shouts. He is my older brother and it is natural that he is concerned only for my welfare. "Follow your heart, girl, and you won't go far wrong."

Albert looks to Polly for affirmation. He is captivated by her. Any fool could see it, but he has no better idea of what fuels my friend than I do of what motivates Frederick.

When I was a little girl, not more than five, I was lost in the forest. I'd wondered past the graveyard skirting the inn and ran toward the ruined castle on the hill above Shebbear. Hours later, it was Albert who came for me. I was leaning against a great oak tree crying when he gathered me in his arms. Me, covered in dirt and sweat and tears. My frock ripped by brambles. Handsome Albert of the Levantine features, the olive skin, the voice of velvet. To this day, it amazes me that he wed Griselda, but then, I must recall what Maman said about people embarking on inexplicable paths. "If life was predictable, all the charming women in the world would be happily married to men who adored and cared for them." And then she'd wring out yet another rag of black washing up water. "I reckon that handsome men often marry homely women because they believe they will be unchallenged. This ungainly creature of the good heart could never hurt me, they assure themselves. But they are fooling themselves and Griselda is as mean as she is unbecoming. The plainest women find ingenious methods of imprisoning their husbands." Their jealousy recognizes no bounds, according to Maman.

"You don't need all this," Albert says pointing to Wendice Manor. "Go to London; make your own way as a cook." He reads my mind, does Albert. We are like two trees planted closely together. Above ground, our trunks and branches appear disparate, but underground our tangled roots are intertwined.

"I would, if you'd come with me," I reply, mocking him.

My eldest brother belongs in a painting crowded with red and purple flowers and dancing women cavorting beside a desert oasis. He could have been so much more than he is now. Maman's intention was for Albert to attend school in Bristol, but Pa wouldn't hear of it. His first-born son was destined to work the farm surrounding the inn, as the Tilleys have been expected to do for generations.

I run ahead of Albert and Polly. Every bride gets cold feet before a wedding ceremony and I am no different. I shall go through with my plans as any good woman would. I have given Frederick my word. Pa may have tried to convince me since I was a little girl that I am a rascal, dishonest and untrustworthy. But I shall prove him wrong. I shall take the straight and narrow path ... to everyone's surprise.

***

A few hours before the ceremony, as Polly is fixing my hair for the veil, Frederick enters our room without knocking.

"It's bad luck for the groom to see the bride before the wedding," Polly exclaims. Since offering me her unsolicited advice, she has been acting strangely, avoiding me whenever possible or, at other times, clutching at my hands, as if she is dressing me for the gallows.

"Jeremiah is dead," Frederick shouts. "Ealing has been tending him in his own home. The fever took him."

"I liked him." I appear not to notice that Frederick is in a state.

---

"You murdered him, Cordelia."

Polly and I stand at attention as if Frederick is the drill captain and we are his benighted foot soldiers.

"He ate at your table, most recently. The jellied tripe, if I recall correctly. Did I not ask you to wash yourself thoroughly before cooking? Am I not correct?"

"You are correct, Frederick. You ate it too," I reply, removing the veil from my head. It is a long gossamer affair, with inlays of delicate lace, billowing down my back and onto the floor. Before he entered the room, I was enjoying my reflection in the mirror. I look rich and pampered, not at all like the brides in Shebbear, who wear their mothers' ill-fitting gowns sewn from rough cloth. Why must this man spoil everything for me?

"It is not too late to end this charade," Polly says abruptly, looking directly at me.

"You must not submit to this degradation, to his wild accusations. I will call for your brother Albert. He is with me, that you mustn't marry this man."

"Call for Albert? Why on earth?" Frederick looks affronted and alarmed all at once, but Polly holds her ground. She cares not what Frederick thinks of her.

"Albert will explain why your father is cruel to you. There is no need to be pushed into this unfortunate union by Thomas Tilley or anyone else," she says to me.

"Albert would actually put a stop to this marriage?" I ask. Polly's admission frightens me. Originally, my brother's note of caution seemed to be natural, a simple act of affection. Does he truly not trust Wendice to treat me kindly? If Frederick's display at this moment is any indication, I am, indeed, making a grave error.

Frederick stops shouting. He stands between me and my friend and glares at her. "She is mine," he says defiantly.

I sit down upon the cushioned divan in the morning room. The room is small, but glorious, like no other room I have ever been in. If I marry Frederick, this room will be mine. The floor to ceiling windows are covered in thick royal blue velvet drapes, the desk constructed of the finest mahogany. On the polished wooden floorboards are exquisitely designed Persian carpets woven of persimmon red and cornflower blue yarn. Olympia has laid out gilded ivory combs and brushes for me. An ornately painted Oriental urn filled with white camellias sits majestically on the mantelpiece. The scent of the flowers is enchanting.

Frederick walks towards me. His steps are mincing. His hands are trembling. He is fearful to be so near to me, but embraces me at this moment, whispering. "You are so beautiful."

"Are you certain you wish to marry me?"

"I am the only man on earth who can protect you now." Frederick's anger has subsided. He grows meek as he usually does whenever he fears that I will leave him. "I give you my solemn word, as a gentleman, that I shall keep you safe, here with me, at Wendice Manor." Frederick speaks as if he has rehearsed these words many times. "However, if you desert me today, on this our wedding day, I can assure you that you will be on your own. I shall never agree to take you back."

I ask Polly to leave us.

"But if your accusations are true, if you believe that I infected your valet," I insist, "how can you make this promise, no matter how deep are your feelings for me?"

Although Frederick does not explain—cannot explain—he does kiss me with such utter abandon that I am surprised by his ardour. "I cannot imagine living without you," he whispers. "Please, please, Cordelia, allow me to save you."

Is it possible that this creature is so devoted to me that he would place me above his own welfare and the good name of his family? Above life and death?

I nod my head in agreement. "I will marry you, Frederick." He holds me in his arms as I weep.

***

Descending the staircase, I can hear the vicar's wife pounding out Felix Mendelssohn's "Wedding March" on the piano, which is ever so slightly out of tune. It is the music he composed for *A Midsummer's Night's Dream*. I am wearing white, of course, a princess sheath frock. My ample figure is outlined by the tight-fitting cuirassed bodice, reaching down to my thighs. I am encased in the armour of this dress. Polly is right behind me, bearing the formidable train.

As I keep pace to the music, my white slippers barely touch the ground. I am floating. I am real and I am unreal. This moment is happening to me and yet it is happening to a projection of me. I stop for just a moment and turn to look back at Polly. There are tears in her eyes, so I glance away. Why is my friend crying at my wedding?

I might only imagine what Polly is thinking: that Frederick is a poor choice, he will hollow me out, prevent me from living the life of my choice. She is wrong. The marriage will be a happy one! Of that I am certain. She cannot possibly understand the place where I am coming from. There will be children, many of them and I need never worry about my role in society. I shall be one of them now. I am safe.

Mother-in-law, Olympia Wendice, is splendidly attired in azure blue. She hired a dressmaker from Plymouth for both of us and our dresses are not dissimilar. Before the French doors leading to the flagstone garden terrace, she has created an arbour, the Reverend's perch and a flowered enclave for Frederick and me, filled with white freesia and larkspur. Mother-in-law hands me my bouquet, the very last of the white Narcissus of late spring.

On one side of the aisle are the Wendices and on the other, the Tilleys. Olympia would never want them to mix. How different they are in costume and in demeanour. Albert and Griselda are sitting in the front row. Griselda in her high-collared brown muslin and Albert in his Sunday collar and tie. He, too, is crying. Griselda catches my eye and mouths these words:

"Jew bitch."

I cringe; and then the Reverend begins the simple ceremony.

The pure words of commitment overwhelm me. I could be this wife and Frederick could be this man, the kind of good people envisioned in our vows. Frederick, who displays little emotion in public, is dreadfully agitated. I can tell. He struggles to slip the ring on my finger. We kiss gingerly, his lips barely touching mine, and the thudding chords of the wedding march sound.

The party following this solemn ceremony is held at twilight. My husband has commandeered a violinist from the seaside resort of Bude and the musician accompanies the vicar's wife, who looks exhausted, but bravely plays on. Frederick grabs me by my waist and we begin to dance, exuberantly, to one Viennese waltz after the other. He holds me close as we circle under the emerging stars in the darkening sky.

"If the stars were mine," Frederick whispers, "I would pull one down from the heavens and pin it, glimmering, to the bodice of your wedding dress."

"You are a poet, Freddy," I say. I have never called him Freddy before.

"You have no idea, dear girl, how I wish to be able to worship you freely, and to raise you high on a pedestal, as a man should his delectable bride."

Although we are on display and Olympia is watching our every move, I take Frederick's face in my hands and kiss him on the lips. "Try not to be so earnest, darling," I tease. The champagne has gone to my head. "I'm only flesh and blood. And try to stop staring at my breasts, your mother is watching. You'd think you wish to consume me!"

"I do," Frederick says seriously. "Why else would I have married you? I wish to rip you apart and put you together again. To recreate you as my ideal."

"One who refuses to convert to Christianity? Who loves to cook, who itches to poke her fingers into every pie?" I tease.

"No! None of those things."

Frederick is waltzing no more. The fiddler puts down his violin. While I remain in my husband's arms, I assert, "That is who I am: the red-headed Jewess, the Devil's Stone Inn's cook, the lowly publican's daughter. Can you adore me still?" I am speaking out of turn and much too loudly. The others stop their conversations to listen.

Frederick is silent. Mrs. Bullbrook, who came from Hartland Abbey, where she served as Frederick's long-time nanny, approaches. She will preside as both housekeeper and cook at the manor. For the wedding, she has pinned her greying hair in a bun rather than wearing the braids she usually twists into a cap for her head. She is an ample woman, more square than round and her hands are stained with tobacco. Last night, I saw her smoking a pipe beside the kitchen stove.

She can tell that Frederick is distressed. They are so bound together, these two; they hardly need to say a word to each other to be understood.

"Would you be wanting me to fetch your valise, Master Frederick? It is time to catch the night train to Plymouth."

"Yes, please, nanny Bullbrook," Frederick says. "The party is over."

***

My husband and I travel by rail to Plymouth. We are to cross the Channel to France the next day by steamship. I would have wished to spend one night in our home together, but Frederick forbids it. He reminds me that he must whisk me away from all the trouble I have caused and might yet cause if he is not careful. My imprudent words uttered on the dance floor have broken the spell of the wedding. Polly is not allowed to accompany us to the station, but she insists on taking a seat in the same train as Frederick and I.

Our first-class private sleeping compartment is luxurious, all leather upholstery and brass fittings. The gaslights, shaded by flowered glass sconces, are turned down low, befitting the occasion of our marriage. The porter arrives before we have a moment to settle. Frederick still wears his top hat and his cravat is crooked from the exertion of climbing into our compartment. The bustled skirt of my glen-plaid honeymoon suit is so stiff, I can barely sit. We both stand in silence as the porter delivers the hot milk and biscuits that Mrs. Bullbrook has arranged for us in advance. Under one arm, the junior porter carries a folding Bombay serving table and in the other, a silver bowl of shiny green apples. He is wearing white gloves.

"Leave them," Frederick orders.

We sit down; careful not to touch, me perched upon the bustle of my skirt, Frederick removing his boots. I notice that his enormous big toe is poking through a sizeable hole in his hosiery. I cannot stop staring at it.

From one perspective, we must look the very portrait of civility, of marital expectation. Frederick rises to open the compartment window.

"Fresh air. I need some air. It's like a miasma in here."

I wish for him to take me in his arms, but he does not. I imagine he is considering what a dreadful mistake he has made by marrying me.

"Please Frederick. I apologize for speaking out of turn on the dance floor. It was a gaffe. It's not necessary ..."

"A gaffe? It was an outrage. Everyone could hear you."

"It is not necessary to accuse and humiliate me."

"Whatever it takes to stop you, to stop the typhoid epidemic."

***

The porter knocks to turn down our beds for the night. The mohair-wool coverlets are trimmed with silk-ribbon borders and the starched-linen sheets are warm, freshly ironed and smell of rose water. When the porter congratulates Frederick on his marriage, my husband simply hands him a few shillings and tells him to go away. I was hoping for a nightcap, but Frederick says he's tired from the festivities and must regain his strength for the battle.

"Now the real work begins, Cordelia," he announces.

---

I am to sleep on the upper bunk and Frederick on the lower one. He instantly begins to snore as soon as he lays his head upon the pillow. The train pulls out of the little Holsworthy station and begins to pick up steam. I, who have never boarded a train before, wish to see and feel everything, but the curtains are drawn so securely I can only imagine the moonlit moor flying by our compartment's window. But I do feel the movement of the train, rocking me, as if I were a baby in a cradle. We are moving so quickly. What would take a day by horse and carriage, takes only hours by train. The glorious sound of the train whistle resounds in the midsummer night. I pull the mohair coverlet under my chin and dream of my future life as lady of the manor.

***

When we arrive at Plymouth, Polly and I say a restrained good-bye. She kisses me delicately on the cheek and I return the favour. Frederick is watching us and I don't wish for him to get ideas in his head about my liaison with Polly. He is wary of her, frightened by her presence. She knows about Frederick in ways that I do not. In my heart, I know she is my only friend. After I tell her, *sotto voce*, about last night she says, "If you wish to leave him before the marriage is consummated, now is the time."

"Frederick is my husband," I lower my eyes and withdraw my hand from hers.

At the port, the merchant ships crowd the harbour. The docks are laden with crates and barrels overflowing with the natural riches of Victoria's Empire. In one crate are elephants' tusks from Africa; in another leopard skin hides. In an open casket, rubies and emeralds the size of hens' eggs sparkle in the sunlight. The gems are guarded by a Nubian slave dressed in pink-satin pantaloons and wearing a necklace of black pearls. Royal Navy men are climbing up and down the gangplanks of the vessels, too occupied to notice me, dressed in my most fetching honeymoon attire and trying to smile brilliantly. Frederick points to a press gang on their way to the Australian bush. He is a knowledgeable guide and appears to know many of the merchants who are counting their goods as the barrels and crates are loaded onto dollies for transport to London. The air is tinged with spice and sweat and salt water. I am excited for our honeymoon journey. I assure myself that our second night together will be better than the first.

# - 16 -

The ship is silent except for the soft caress of the waves on the portholes of our elegant cabin. The air is close, as it is in Devon, before a thunderstorm. Frederick has booked the most elaborate stateroom on the ship, with its own private loo. Inside sits a round, porcelain receptacle, which the French call a bidet. An elaborately carved, wooden bedstead and frame, designed to resemble a sailing vessel, fills the cabin. I light a candle in the dark waiting for Frederick to return.

There is no doubt that I am eager to consummate our nuptials since we'd dutifully waited until the wedding to test our love. My husband appeared so intoxicated with me before we married; he could not take his eyes from my person. But now that our ship, The Griffin, has left England his behaviour has changed radically.

Once we are settled into our sea cabin, I dart to the WC to change into my nightdress. I emerge wearing a most seductive bride's chemise, all pink frills with an inviting décolletage. Sitting under the wool covers is Frederick, bare-chested, with only a purple fez atop his head.

"Forgive me, my dear, but Mrs. Bullbrook neglected to pack my night shirt. How strange, she is usually so fastidious."

Frederick's chest and back are covered in hair and he looks like a blonde furry beast. When he turns to remove his fez, I see the blood warts on his back. I close my eyes, gulp hard, and climb into the bed.

Instead of embracing me, Frederick addresses me formally: "Now is not the optimal time to launch our life together as man and wife."

"Why not?"

"Two words, Cordelia." He pulls the blanket over his protruding belly. "Birth control. It's a slippery slope to reproducing before we are absolutely certain that our union is meant for the procreation of normal healthy children. We must discern when it is safe to indulge. Ahem!" Frederick clears his throat while straightening the bedclothes.

I recall Maman counselling me to insert a kitchen sea-sponge sliced in half before commencing intercourse, as is the custom for French women, but in England these matters are never discussed. I also recall what Maman once said to me about her marriage: "A crow flies high until she lands on a pig."

"In addition," Frederick continues, "I have not decided whether to leave my fortune to my heirs, or to the Fabian Society, to my comrades Beatrice and Sidney Webb. They would know best how to aid the poor and destitute."

I am shocked. "Why did you marry me, Freddy, if you do not want me? If you don't wish to have children with me?" Tears are pouring from my eyes. Just two days ago, he could not keep his hands off me.

"Marriage is about trust and loyalty, not desire." Frederick passes me a handkerchief inscribed with a wavy "W".

"I've always believed that marriage is about love," I cry. Although this is not exactly true, I was hoping for the best by marrying Frederick and now I am facing the worst: that Frederick cares for me even less than I care for him.

"We must be stalwart, dearest." He is drawing the black-leather notebook from below the covers. "As you are aware, I've been recording the names of the dead souls of County Devon—since the typhoid epidemic broke out. I now have irrefutable evidence that the great majority of the dead supped at your table before they fell ill."

Snatching the notebook from his hand—while Frederick leans back with a smug expression on his face—I began reading the list of the victims of the fever.

*D. Bailey & wife*
*A. Leatherby*
*R. Hindsmith & two children*
*M. Tartt*

There are twelve pages of the names of the dead—all inscribed in my husband's precise, small-lettered, round hand. Beside each name is the exact date of death, with another date beside it, recording when the man of the house stopped at the Devil's Stone Inn. What an intrepid sleuth Frederick has turned out to be.

"I thought we agreed that this was nonsense," I utter, trying to control the fear rising in my chest. "I thought you would destroy this book. Didn't we agree before I married you that you would forget about all this?"

"No, not at all. You threatened to postpone our wedding date if I continued to question you about the dead and so I kept my investigations to myself. Now that we are married, I can do as I please with you and what I wish to do is to ensure that you never serve another unsuspecting soul a morsel of food."

Pulling a shawl about my shoulders, I shrink toward the door. "How can you utter such wretched words, Frederick Wendice? Why would you marry me? To bar me from having children? And why would you wish to stop me from doing the one thing that I love to do, to cook? Why could you not leave me alone? I am better off an outcast than the object of your derision."

"Calm yourself, woman." Frederick appears surprised that I am taking his accusations to heart. "For the greater good, my dear. Think of the lives we'll be saving, you and I, just by keeping you out of the kitchen. And, if I control my urges," he adds, "I will be cleansing my soul before God. Undoubtedly, He shall notice that I am sincere, that I am making up for past offenses."

"What past offenses?"

"I've always enjoyed the ladies, you might say. Now, I have vowed to give all of that up. You and any others that might play to my weakness. Small price to pay."

"It is not a small price for me to pay! Do you not owe me something as my husband? Do you not love me at all?"

"From the moment I set eyes on you again that night in April at the Devil's Stone Inn, with your Maman making such grand gestures, trying to show you off, I was re-assured that you were the woman who would become my wife."

"Again?"

"I've been dreaming about you since the first time I saw you, when you were just a girl, before these fully developed," he says reaching over to pinch my bosom through the cloth of the pink nightdress. "You and your Maman reckoned I had forgotten about you, but that would be impossible. You were such a lovely, innocent, straight-backed child that I could never forget you. So fulsome you were, Cordelia."

"Why didn't you admit that you remembered me?"

"I didn't wish to spoil your Maman's fun."

"Then why did you wait four years to come calling?"

"I suppose I wished for you to grow up, to become the beautiful woman you are now." Frederick is speaking as though his intentions are those of a sane man's. Once again, Frederick is staring at my cleavage while motioning for me to sit beside him on the bed. "With your mother's clever, Jewish brain and your father's muscular, Christian physique, you are the perfect specimen of hybrid vigour."

"You married me because I am an example of hybrid vigour?"

"Yes, in part. Bi-racial marriages have produced some remarkable results. In the end it could bestow a distinct advantage on any children we might wish to propagate."

"So you agree, there will be children?"

"Possibly."

"And what about these possible children? Are they to be objects of your bi-racial experiments?"

Frederick begins to twist the gold band on his ring finger. "Over time, I will make that decision. We must determine whether isolating you in Wendice Manor will stop the typhoid epidemic. First things first, before we consider children."

"And ... you imagine this will take how long?"

"Who can say? Together we now have a mission in life and down the road we must hobble. It's a three-legged race for you and me, my girl. A marriage is like a three-legged race down the obstacle course of life," he explains, while coaxing me to re-enter the bed. "I shan't touch you, don't fear, not until this dastardly sickness has passed from our midst."

With his promise, Frederick hastily dresses and leaves the cabin. It is the middle of the night. I cannot sleep. Frederick has left to speak to the Chief Mate, Mr. Rich. He wishes to know what time The Griffin will dock at Roscoff. He claims he is eager to show me France, but I imagine he cannot stand being in the same cabin as me.

I light a candle waiting for my husband to return. My hands are shaking.

***

By the time Frederick returns to our stateroom, the ship is pitching violently.

"The waves are washing over the bridge," he reports. Frederick is soaking wet and his hair falls in fuzzy, blonde ringlets, destroying the fine white-silk scarf wound around his neck.

At this very moment, if I had my way, I would will the ship to go down. Instead I curl myself into a ball beneath the covers. Frederick disrobes, dons the fez and drapes a dry towel about his chubby shoulders. I have no idea what he expects from me.

"You might have mentioned all this to me before I consented to marry you. Now, not until I'm bloody well good and ready for you, will you have me," I blurt out.

"Try not to be a contrarian, wife," he snaps with a look of fatuous satisfaction on his face.

We both spend a wakeful night trying not to bump into each other as the ship pitches from port to starboard in this angry channel storm.

# Book Two

HOLSWORTHY, COUNTY DEVON

1883

# - I -

IT IS NEARLY TWO years since I came to live as Frederick Wendice's wife at the big house in Holsworthy. My brother Albert insists he cannot recognize me, I've grown so slender and still. Other than Albert and the servants, I see no one. Not a soul is allowed to call on me without my husband's permission. Frederick describes me as subdued.

Most days I spend reading. Anything and everything I can get my hands on. The stories I read alter the voices in my head so what I am imagining is beginning to sound like a novel. It's easy to compare the people in my daily life to the characters in books. Even the postman and the chimney sweep take on the colours of imaginary characters. Each is capable of outlandish acts. The course of my characters' lives might change direction at a moment's notice, the way they do in novels. However, my own circumstances never alter. What I do understand about myself is that I am not the Esther of *Bleak House* or the Dorothea of *Middlemarch*. It is left up to me to imagine who I might become.

On my darkest days, I do not move a muscle. I sit numbly at the escritoire in the morning room dreaming of the children I fear I will never bear. I derive what little pleasure I might from things, objects of my feeble desire. Much of the day I consider how I will decorate the manor by browsing through merchandise catalogues arriving from London or abroad. In Paris, at a precious little shop on the rue Saint Germaine, we purchased this ornate, extravagantly priced desk at which I sit. In France, during our honeymoon, not once did Frederick attempt to bed me. Strolling along the Left Bank, we slipped into a dance hall. I sensed that Frederick was aroused by the can-can girls' antics, but his exuberance dissipated long before we returned to our Hotel, Le Meurice.

---

I returned from France a virgin and unbelievably I remain one today. My husband is convinced that he is helping me by insisting on our continued state of celibacy. After two years, he promises that "in good time" he will re-consider if I am fit to carry his children. Or if it is safe for me to travel beyond the confines of the manor, or if I may invite friends to visit me. Since my arrival at the manor, he has forbidden me to enter the kitchen, let alone cook in it. Mrs. Bullbrook dictates the lunch and dinner menus and all the marketing and preparation of the food, as she does most everything else in the house.

She rarely bothers to consult me, the lady of the manor, in case I was to contaminate the kitchen and make more people sick. Frederick is now entirely convinced that he has been correct about me all along. Since our marriage, the typhoid epidemic has been slowly subsiding and he reckons it is because he has isolated me in his home.

Wendice Manor is only a close block by the high street in Holsworthy. It is a four-storey Georgian mansion, with a red-tiled gabled roof. Below stairs is the expansive kitchen, washing tubs, wine cellar and most of the servants' quarters. Mrs. Bullbrook's room is on the third floor next to Frederick's private study.

The big house is painted a pale fern green, allowing it to blend in discreetly with the willow trees and hydrangeas surrounding the structure. The shutters are white. Beside the manor is a small stable for the greys, a manicured vegetable plot, and a stately wooden swing where Frederick sits when he is deciding upon a course of action that concerns my future. The house is surrounded by an eight-foot high wrought-iron fence with little black-iron pineapples adorning every sixth stake. Ivy cascades over the bars, making it impossible for the villagers to see in, or for me to see out.

People like Frederick, born with a silver spoon in their mouth, often do the oddest things under the guise of helping others. I've never met a do-gooder who doesn't derive a vicarious thrill from observing the lower orders squirm; and in this respect, Frederick excels. If anyone bothered to ask me, I would claim that charity does more for the giver than the receiver.

## - 2 -

Mother-in-law is visiting this spring and she plans to stay with us for a fortnight. We are sitting silently in the morning room when she suddenly remarks, "When two years pass and there is no sign of a child, something is amiss."

I shake my head in disagreement. "Nothing is wrong, Olympia," I advise, trying to sound undisturbed by her obvious observation.

"Are you unwell, my dear?"

"Actually, I'm fit as a fiddle."

"That is rather difficult to believe. You have lost weight and you are so deathly pale."

I remind myself that Frederick prefers me rosy cheeked and on the plump side, but my appetite has disappeared since residing in Holsworthy. It isn't just our peculiar arrangement, but also the smell of the slaughterhouse, spreading throughout the entire village, day in and day out.

"Frederick has his own peculiar likes and dislikes," I say.

Olympia observes me closely. Her silver hair is artfully combed to enhance her high, Patrician cheekbones and then back and up into a swirling chignon effectively concealing the wrinkles on her face. The high collar of the blue-satin morning gown conceals the sagging, crepey skin of her throat. "Turkey neck," Maman called it.

"You can confide in me, my dear. I was a married woman for more than forty years and Mr. Wendice was not always ... the most understanding man. There were many pregnancies, one after the other. I cannot bear to talk about my dead infants. Freddy was the only child who survived. Perhaps that is why he is so precious to me."

"Precious."

Mother-in-law's fingers grasp the handle of the teacup so firmly, I suspect it will shatter. "My son is a gentle soul. You knew that when you agreed to marry him."

"Perhaps you should discuss this matter with your precious son," I say. It is easy enough to raise Olympia's ire.

"You do not understand how fortunate you are, Cordelia, do you?" Olympia's eyes are boring into mine, so I turn away. "Look at me, girl," she orders. "You are his wife and you must encourage him. He is the quality of man who requires inducement. Be kind to him." Around mother-in-law's neck is a sapphire-studded lorgnette, which she brings close to her left eye.

"Frederick can be stubborn." I owe her no more response than that.

Recently I'd ordered drapery from the Liberty's catalogue and I can tell that it is not to Olympia's taste. She points her lorgnette to the window to inform me that the pattern of plumed birds on the embroidered silk "does not flatter my red hair or freckled skin."

I am dying to laugh in her face.

"How little you have changed, Cordelia," she says, once again directing her critical gaze to me. "Entirely the country girl from top to bottom," she remarks cruelly, while diverting her attention from the game of Patience spread before her on the little, gold-inlaid folding table. "You wish to be ravished, to be taken, as any plain country maid might. But you have married above your station and you must be the one to make the effort, not my son. You must pay, one way or the other, for your ambitions. You must bear my son's children!" Her withered cheeks are turning orange with rage.

I fold my hands; they are a cook's hands, sinewy from working in the kitchen at the inn. I can only imagine how foolish I look in the ruffled georgette tea gown Olympia has brought me from Hartland Abbey. I say nothing. But I do imagine Olympia violently choking on a grape from her silver bowl. She has become a character of dubious moral fibre in my make-believe world. The skin of a purple grape is caught in her throat. She throws herself against the desk, but the grape is not dislodged. Olympia's face turns to blue.

"Do you actually believe that you, a plain, unsophisticated publican's daughter are able to make my son happy?" Her words pull me out of my reverie. "At the very least you must attempt to be inventive."

Before mother-in-law can excoriate me further, Mrs. Bullbrook bustles into the morning room. Her skin, in daylight, is almost as creased as Olympia's, but more coarsely. Under her eyes, are brown pouches that resemble discarded tea bags. I smell gin on her breath. Housekeeper ignores me to ask Olympia for her approval of tonight's dinner menu.

---

They discuss alternatives to parsnip soup while I sit silently, spurned in my own home.

***

The next day Frederick and Olympia return from church renewed. No one dare mention that I am never invited to accompany them to mass at St. Peter and St. Paul's, the Anglican Church sitting directly opposite the manor house. Although I spend hours wandering among the gravestones in the churchyard when Frederick is not about, I have never entered the stone building, or the manse. Olympia believes it is because I will not agree to be baptized, but of course, it is because my husband thinks I will contaminate the vicar and his parishioners with typhoid.

"Where was your mother born?" Olympia asks me once we are settled in the dining room, Frederick at the head of the immense table, immersed in *The Sunday Times*. "In England or in Eastern Europe?"

"Neither," I respond, sullenly. What business is it of hers where Maman was born? "She was born and raised in France, in Angers."

"Really! I'm surprised. I didn't think there were any Jews in France. Only here in England, where we are terribly broad-minded, or in the farthest reaches of Eastern Europe, where, I suppose, everyone is quite odd." Olympia fans herself, acting miffed that Jews could possibly be born in France.

"There are many Jews in France—and in high places. In the military, in law and in politics. My own grandparents were prominent citizens of Angers before the Catholic Church accused them of poisoning the well water at the monastery just outside town."

"And did they?" Olympia inquires. "Did they poison the water? Your family, did they do it?"

I can hardly believe what she is asking me. She can't possibly be serious. I feel I am living in the dark ages.

"Yes, they did it. Doesn't every Jew wish to poison the Christian's well?" I reply, rushing from the room. I can't help but think about my jellied tripe that Frederick claimed poisoned his valet. Preparing mother-in-law a plate would serve her right, but I am barred from the manor's kitchen. If only Frederick's fears were founded on reality and not on superstition. Perhaps, then, I might find a way to rid myself of this odious woman.

## – 3 –

Olympia has finally departed for Hartland Abbey and Frederick is off to Tintagel to quell the spirits of his rambunctious quarrymen. I have decided to completely re-decorate my morning room. I gaze about the semi-circular room. It is my favourite in the manor, reminding me of Catherine de' Medici's little writing room at Chenonceau. During our honeymoon in France, Frederick escorted me to the Loire Valley where he discovered the crumbling chateaux of French royalty, many of them being refurbished by wealthy merchants. I loved the tidy, stone-walled writing room of the little Queen, with tall windows on three sides, overlooking the lush Loire River and the chateau's geometric gardens. It was in that very room where Catherine plotted the demise of the King's lover, her rival Diane de Poitiers. In comparison, my life is dull.

***

Days later when Frederick returns from the slate mines, he appears pleased to announce that the quarry will make a goodly profit this year, the best since the slate trade began to dwindle. All of Devon has suffered from the meagre demands for slate and in my books, Frederick has suffered least of all.

"Your mother is encouraging us to present her with a grandchild," I blurt out, not caring a half penny about the profits at the mine.

"Has she spoken to you about that?"

"Yes. She is growing older. She desperately wishes to have at least one grandchild before she dies. Surely, you would not deprive her?"

If this is my only inducement to get Frederick interested in procreation, I will not ignore it; but true to form, Frederick admits that he's encountered similar entreaties from his mother without bothering to mention the subject to me. "I blamed you, of course," he reveals. "You haven't displayed any interest at all in me since that first night on the ship to Roscoff."

In his heart—if that is what is buried under his ribs—he must know that it is he and not I, who has delayed the consummation of our marriage.

***

The same evening, Frederick carts a dog-eared issue of *The Westminster Review* down from his study to our parlour. He wishes to read to me from W.R. Greg's essay, "Prostitution" which appeared in the magazine in July 1850. My husband believes that the ideas in the piece are as fresh as they were thirty-three years ago.

"All women including prostitutes know no desire until they are exposed to exciting causes." Frederick reads laboriously now, having gained so much weight since our marriage that he's become a mouth breather.

It is after dinner and we sit before the grey, marbled hearth in which a low-burning fire smolders. A breeze rustles the pleated, silk drapes. Frederick's piano legs—his bare feet without boots, braces or stockings—are stretched out on the green-leather divan. As he reads, he interrupts this diatribe to implore me to trim his yellowed, curling toenails.

"How can I reach them myself?" he complains, patting his stomach after ingesting three helpings of Mrs. Bullbrook's leg of mutton. On the platter, the meat was swimming in grease.

I resist, saying that my nerves are too frayed to hold the scissors without nicking him. The putrid odour of overcooked mutton and Brussels sprouts invades every inch of the house. How I loathe Brussels sprouts and over-cooked meat. At the Devil's Stone Inn, in the spring, Maman would make creamy watercress soup, with roast chicken drenched in tarragon butter.

Sepia paintings of dead Wendice family members peer down at me from above the mantle. Bits of hair, pressed flowers and onyx jewelry decorate the inside of the bevelled-glass frames.

I miss the Devil's Stone Inn. On clear nights in the heart of summer. In the sticky heat. Me, with my white-cotton gypsy shirt pulled low about my shoulders, a paisley scarf tied tight at my waist and a torrent of black skirting falling below my knees. A woman knows when all eyes are on her. I know, with me swishing among the card tables under the moon, serving brown beer and golden cider. I wipe a wisp of red hair from my glistening face: that is all it takes to make the men sit up and take notice. Or, if I offer a slow-eyed downward glance at the gamblers, sweating and eager in the impossibly bright light of the moon.

***

The following evening, Frederick reads to me once again from Greg's essay on prostitution. Tonight Mrs. Bullbrook sits with us in her spindle-backed rocker. Frederick treats her as a member of the family. I wonder how much control she actually has over him; does he confide in her about the state of our marriage, about his conviction that I spread typhoid?

He reads aloud in a voice reeking of righteousness: "If the passions of women were ready, strong and spontaneous even remotely approaching the form they assume in the coarser sex, there can be little doubt that sexual irregularities would reach a height, at which, at present, we have no happy conception."

I am no longer able to suppress my anger. "It can't be that wrong to enjoy spontaneous acts of love or there'd never be a child brought into the world," I cry.

My words awaken Mrs. Bullbrook, who has been dozing. Her head emerges from her shawl like a turtle's, poking out from its shell. Her gaping mouth is immediately snapped shut.

Frederick is amused by my anger. "I can't discern how your idea is, in any manner, connected to Reverend Greg's." His supercilious smile sickens me.

I rush from the parlour, out the open doors and across to the churchyard. It is impossible for me to imagine how I can submit to this life with Frederick for one more day. It begins to rain, lightly at first and then with more determination. I remove my shoes to run down the hill toward the railway bridge. The train to Plymouth will be crossing momentarily. I can hear the call of its whistle. If I were to climb up to the railway bridge now, I could put a stop to this endless humiliation.

---

Standing under a giant oak, I ask myself if there is any reason why I should live.

Then in the drenching rain, I see Frederick loping toward me, an open umbrella in one hand, my rain jacket in the other.

"Come to me, Cordelia," he implores. I run into his arms, clinging to him. I am such a broken thing, yet he kisses me with the same abandon he did on the day of our wedding. "Do you love me, my darling girl?"

"I wish for us to be man and wife, as we should be, as normal couples are. I wish to have a child of my own. Can you grant me my wishes?" I beg.

"With Jesus' help, by denying myself, I've prayed I could save you from yourself. Finally, the typhoid has disappeared from Devon."

"Are you saying we can begin?"

"It is time," Frederick puts my rain jacket about my shoulders and covers my head with his scarf. "You'll catch your death. Come back to the house with me." The huge, black umbrella protects us from the downpour.

Inside the manor, there is no sign of Mrs. Bullbrook.

Frederick leads me up the stairs to our bedroom where he removes my rain-drenched clothes. I stand naked before him. "You have grown too thin, dearest," he says, as if seeing me for the first time in months. I continue to stand before him as he dries me with warm towels. Perhaps he does love me, after all.

"We can begin now, but you must first agree to my terms," Frederick says, once I am completely dry and fitted into my muslin nightdress. My hair is wrapped in a towel like an Indian man's turban.

"You must agree to map out your menstrual cycle every month if we are to be as man and wife. I must know the exact start and end day of your bleeding."

"Why?"

"It is still too early to risk a pregnancy."

"But I want a child. Didn't I say that just now?"

"Indeed, you did. However, what if you were to inflict typhoid on our unborn fetus?"

I am silent. Will this madness never end?

"Four days in each month we can be ... uhhmm ... together. Do you agree?"

"I agree, for now."

"Come with me, then. Tonight is safe, is it not?"

How would he know that I've just ended my monthlies if that old bat housekeeper was not spying on me? But I acquiesce. "Yes, tonight is safe. I've just stopped bleeding, if that is what you want to know."

Together we climb the narrow stairs leading to the third floor of the manor and Frederick's private study. He pushes me ahead of him and fondles my bottom. Once inside the room, he closes the door and locks it. From his trouser pocket, he hands me a key and in a manly voice, orders me to unlock the top-right drawer of his desk. "Remove the collar and padlock and return the key to me."

Frederick removes everything from my hands and roughly strings the collar around my neck. Next, he clamps the padlock shut and locks it with the little key, which he returns to his pocket.

"Climb onto this table," he orders, pointing to the slim metal gurney in the corner of the room. I shudder. "Climb onto the examining table," he insists. "Do as you are told."

I hike my nightdress above my knees to climb onto the gurney and then to lie still on the table. My head is spinning. Frederick pulls a screen from behind the examining table and places it between us. It is constructed of linen sheeting secured tightly on an iron frame. I can see his silhouette against the light. He is changing into another topcoat.

"Get on all fours," he orders, more softly this time. I do as I am told.

In a few moments, Frederick enters the little space behind the screen dressed in a surgeon's white canvas topcoat. He is wearing a linen mask and blue rubber gloves. He speaks officiously as if he has never set eyes on me before: "What can be the problem tonight, miss?" I am silent, but Frederick instructs me to say this: "Please help me, Doctor, my bleedings ended and my cunt is so dry it's on fire."

"Ah, let us take a look, then," he replies most professionally. "Let's see if we can put out the fire, Miss." Frederick mounts me like a dog. Six or seven thrusts and the deed is done. Afterward, he is panting heavily and tells me to wash myself in the water basin beside the table and return to my own bed. He will join me when he is restored.

---

When he comes to me, it is well past midnight and I am wide-awake. The rain has passed, but the air remains sultry. The cloying scent of climbing roses, clinging to the outside shutters, wafts into the room. The haunting whistle of the midnight train punctuates the stillness.

"Settled in, then, are we, dearest? Frederick asks. He smells of disinfectant and tobacco.

Shall I mention that Frederick has not kissed me, not once during this entire performance? Shall I also mention that Frederick has neglected to remove the padlock and collar from around my neck?

## – 4 –

After being married for four years, Frederick is allowing me to pay a visit to Polly. It is 1885 and I am seated in the first-class compartment, travelling on the afternoon train to Plymouth. Since I am stopping with Polly, I have been given leave to remove the collar and lock from around my neck. It is the first time I have left the manor, or its immediate surroundings, without Frederick or Mrs. Bullbrook at my side, watching my every move. Frederick has consented to this trip because there has not been a recorded case of typhoid in north Devon for two years, not since I have succumbed to "his terms." He believes I am cured of my malady.

At the station, Frederick cautions me, "You may be shocked at what you witness at Mrs. Turney's lodging house, but I daresay, you are now strong enough, in body and in mind, to resist the temptations of the flesh. Remember that I love you and that I trust you, good lady wife," he says, shutting tight the door of my little compartment. From my window I watch him disappear as the station platform recedes from view.

For the first time in four years, I am absolutely alone. Frederick has given me his permission to travel. For appearances sake, Frederick is pretending that this holiday is my reward for succumbing to the rules and regulations of our marriage. But we both know differently. I have reminded him that in her recent letters, Polly writes how certain she is that Frederick visited her lodging house.

"Mrs. Turney recalls that you appeared regularly, boasting about your shipments of slate to the Continent."

For weeks before my trip, Frederick attempts to ignore me.

"How could she know that you ship your slate from Plymouth?" I ask him repeatedly. Eventually I force his hand.

Frederick holds *The Times* high above his nose at the breakfast table. He deems not to look at me.

"Another letter from Mrs. Turney," I comment, talking over the top of his newspaper. "She remarks that one of her lodgers swears she saw you in Plymouth just last month, standing in a place called Bragg's Alley. Is that true, Frederick?" I ask.

Frederick slowly folds the paper to look me in the eyes. "What exactly are you getting at?"

"Since you've asked," I reply obligingly, "I'd like to visit Polly. It's been years since we've been together. Would you allow me this one time ... a small vacation?"

He considers my request. The thought is mounting in his mind that Polly knows much more about him than she should. Unless he allows me the small freedom of a vacation, my friend might divulge all to me and possibly, to others much more important than me.

A few days later at the breakfast table, Frederick surrenders. "It will do you good, my dear, to see the world beyond the confines of our little manor. By all means, why shouldn't you enjoy the company of a friend?"

***

Travelling alone is a most glorious state of being. I remind myself to treasure every moment, to commit each sight and impression to memory, so I may envision everything in detail when I am back at the manor with Frederick. When I first took the train with him, after my wedding, I was too overwrought to relish the experience of train travel fully.

Today I am different, not at all the innocent young woman, who still imagines she is embarking on a most expeditious union and a superior life. No matter how cleverly and judiciously Maman plotted my future, how could she have known what kind of man Frederick would turn out to be? Maman, as Frederick does, only saw what she wished to see. Maman was clever and assiduous in her scheming, but as bad luck would have it, his machinations were much more devious than hers. Her taste was all too selective; she saw position but ignored character.

Turning to view the valley, deep and green beneath the rail track bridge, I cannot help but consider how closely we define our worlds to suit our own purposes. Only a few years ago, I was prepared to end my own life to escape the one that Frederick had created for me. No more. He has not broken me, although he believes he has. Not since the night when I considered laying my body upon the railway track, have I conjured up such black deeds of self- immolation. Yes, he tricked me, at that time, into believing he would give me a child, but that was the last trick Frederick Wendice will ever play on me. It no longer matters to me how long it will take; in the end, I will outwit him and on my own terms.

I imagine, of a future morning, Mrs. Bullbrook bent with work.

"Yes, ma'am and how would you like your eggs prepared this morning?" I can imagine old Bullbrook asking me, the lady of the manor, as she scrapes and bows before me—once I am in control of the manor. At breakfast, I intend to send her back to the stove twice, no three times, to prepare the eggs precisely as I wish them to be. Soft and runny.

"For dinner, Mrs. Bullbrook, you are to attempt a cheese soufflé," I add coldly as she shuffles from the dining room. "Could you, at the very least, attempt to make the soufflé fluffy? The last one was as flat as a pancake." That's how I will repay her for her kindness, if I am given the chance. One day.

I have grown strong, despite my demeanour, not by avoiding temptation, as Frederick believes, but in my own peculiar way. It is vengeance I seek—and that alone—although by looking at me not a soul would dream it. I am a vision of the dutiful village wife, in lock step with her husband, my only interest being to please him and keep our home safe from ungodly intrusions. I wear a plain round-collared ivory blouse with a black fitted gabardine jacket and matching straight black skirt, grey stockings and matronly oxfords with the laces tied tightly in a bow. My hands are gloved, although it is summer. Frederick insists that I carry with me, at all times, a large handkerchief, to cover my mouth, in case anyone comes too close. What if I were to contaminate an innocent soul, me being the dirty, dirty girl that I am?

With nothing on my hands but time at Wendice Manor, it is no wonder that my thoughts turn to a deadly proposition. My mind is clouded by waking dreams. Fantasies. What if it is true and I am able to contaminate at will, as Frederick claims? What if the source of the typhoid epidemic did spring from my kitchen and my cooking? However unlikely it seems, I cannot convince myself to entirely rule out the possibility. I imagine Olympia, sitting prim and proper at my dinner table, her eye on the juiciest cut of roast beef, the fluffiest slice of pudding, the sweetest morsel of brandy trifle. Relishing the thought, I spit on my hands and rub them together. If my life continues on this path, what choice will I have other than to twist the course of my actions in deadly directions? But, of course, it is only my ever-fertile imagination, playing tricks with me once again: the persistent fantasies that have become my only escape from my incarceration at Wendice Manor.

***

From my passenger's seat, I am taking in the English countryside in high summer: the manicured farms with their fresh-cut haycocks neatly stacked beside the hedgerows. Near to the houses and barns are ancient, low stonewalls with every description of wildflower peeking out from between the rocks. Farmers and their children stroll along the towpaths and sheep are grazing in the afternoon sun. Along the route, glistening streams meander through the shady woods. Everywhere the rich, velvet green of Devon's forests abound.

When I pull down the compartment window, I wish to reach out and touch it all, to be inside this fertile, glowing, verdant world. But I have grown cautious. If I have learned anything during the last four years, it is that I ought to protect myself.

What if my arm were to be caught in the bramble bushes beside the railway track? I, alone, am responsible for my welfare, for I am the only one who can rain down havoc on Frederick Wendice's head—and in one way or the other—that is exactly what I intend to do. If he does not allow me to carry his child, Frederick must face the consequences of his decision to marry me.

***

As the train approaches Plymouth, I am mesmerized by the grandness of the city. On my honeymoon, Frederick obscured the view. His constant chatter distracted me as he attempted to impress me with his knowledge of the merchant marine and the Royal Navy.

Today, and for a short time, I am rid of him. From the train window, I can see the entire Hoe with its flotilla of war ships anchored in the outer waters of the sound. From this distance, it's possible to see the round holes in the ships' hull where the cannon guns will poke their long black noses.

High above the harbour is the Promenade. It is a humid summer night and all of Plymouth is out, walking along the grand pathway or settled on the grassy expanse of lawn. I can see the couples strolling arm in arm or sitting side by side on the manicured green. Sailors are carousing with the girls dressed in party frocks. A brass band is enthusiastically playing a bold military march. Across the sound is Drake's statue. I recall Maman telling me about Sir Francis and how he defeated the Spanish Armada in 1588. When she was tutoring me in geography and the sciences, she also spoke of Captain Cook and Charles Darwin, who both sailed from this port. The feeling of being overtaken by a great city thrills me. The scent of hops and malt from the whiskey distillery mingles with the sea air and for the first time in years, I inhale deeply and do not smell the stink of death from the slaughterhouse. I believe I am destined for better things than being held prisoner at Wendice Manor.

Polly meets me at the station. She is as beautiful as ever with her raven-black hair falling in ringlets from her scarlet bonnet. Her eyes are green as a budding leaf. The moment she catches a glimpse of me, she heads straight toward me, waving madly, and then, clutching me close in her arms. "I've missed you, terribly," she whispers. I notice a tear in her eye.

"I've missed you, too." Isn't this what I am supposed to say, however little I actually feel? Since residing at the manor, I must admit to feeling almost nothing for anyone. Nothing except resentment and fear. She observes me carefully. Her expression, usually lively, grows still and gloomy.

"Have you really missed me?" she asks with a distinct note of alarm in her voice.

For a fleeting second, I reach out to touch her pink cheek and suddenly I do sense an unfamiliar catch in my throat. It feels dangerous like a fish bone: unexpected, explosive and razor sharp. This might be how it is to experience love. All I can do is sputter. I cannot catch my breath. Polly slaps me hard on the back. Although the coughing fit does not subside, she motions for me to raise my arms high above my head.

The choking subsides and we laugh at the severity of my attack as we walk together from the railway station down into the lower town toward her lodging house. Polly slips her hand inside my arm. My hair is dishevelled and cascades from the clasp holding it up. Polly gently tucks a wisp of unruly red curls back under the brim of my hat.

What if life could always be this way: tender and forgiving? "I have missed you, Polly. Truly I have."

## - 5 -

When Polly first came to stay at the Devil's Stone Inn, Maman was dying from typhoid and Frederick was beginning his courtship of me. How strange that she appeared so predatory to me and so foreign. She is neither. I was an innocent then and easily frightened by anything outside my experience.

Although most women dare not mention it—or perhaps never allow themselves to entertain the notion—I'd bet my last penny that many are confronted with the conundrum that faces me now. If I allow my instinct to guide my actions, rather than my head, would I choose to share my days with Polly, as her "beloved," as she now calls me?

***

On the night of my arrival, as dusk turns into night, Polly and I meander through the mean passageways of Plymouth's lower town, past Adelaide Street and Bragg's Alley, on our way to Polly's lodging house. Not far from our destination, I spot an old synagogue.

"We could go in," Polly offers. She is trying to make me feel comfortable. How could she understand that I have removed myself from my own community and have not the nerve to re-acquaint myself with it?

"Another time." Despite a few rushed visits to the temple in Exeter with Maman, I am ignorant of the rituals inside a Jewish house of worship. I wouldn't know what to say to the rabbi. What if the rabbi asks me if am Jewish? How would I answer? How could I begin to explain who I have become since Maman died?

As we stroll past the synagogue and through the lower town, I can't help but notice the ladies of the night leaning against dripping wet alcoves in the dark tunnels scattered along the Hoe. Bragg's Alley is the dirtiest place on earth, I fear. Steam is rising from the sour drains, rats are scurrying up from the sewers and the girls are hardly afforded the time to pull up their knickers before the next blighter takes aim.

"I want you to observe the street walkers and compare them to the girls who work from my house. I want you to make up your own mind which is preferable." Polly is determined to win me over.

The Purple Peony Lodging House sits at the corner of Cross and Granby Streets. Although sailors roam these streets, there are gentleman congregating about as well, prowling through the seamy neighbourhood. Polly's brothel is obviously a favoured spot, with hansom cabs lined up around the block, presumably waiting for a fare. The outside of her house is painted a delicate yellow with the woodwork outlined in white. Forest-green awnings shade the expansive windows on the second and third floors. Lining the windowsills of the third floor bay windows are lush baskets of multi-coloured flowers. The steps leading up to the entrance are decorated with fancy bricks and clay pots of miniature palm trees. On either side of the purple-painted door, burning gaslights shielded by milk-glass sconces illuminate the way.

Inside the black and white tiled vestibule, a girl of about fourteen greets us and takes our jackets and hats. Polly instructs her to hurry round back to the servant's entrance to collect my cases and carry them to her private quarters.

"Mrs. Wendice will be sharing my bedroom."

The girl, not blinking an eye, treats Polly with deference, but not fear, as she opens wide the landing door leading to the second floor parlour. Navy men in full regalia, Quality in their finest collars and ties, and a few lucky sailors dance with the girls. Placed strategically around the exquisitely decorated room are older-looking women holding trays of crystal flutes bubbling with champagne and heart-shaped plates stacked with sugar-coated strawberries. Each employee gives a short bow to Polly as she enters her domain. Their expressions are neither mean nor slatternly. More bored than anything.

The parlour is so splendid, I can barely catch my breath. Enormous reproductions of classical art in three-inch wide gilt frames adorn the walls. Potted ferns grow in rosewood planters. An ebony grand piano occupies the northwest corner of the room. Atop the piano are vases of heavily-scented flowers with huge, purple blooms. Photographs of the working girls, encased in extravagant mother-of-pearl frames, line the rim of the gold-threaded shawl protecting the piano. The customers, I see, are invited to make selections from the pictures. Everywhere, men and women, reclining on the plush, red divans scattered throughout the parlour, laugh and drink and fondle each other with abandon. It brings to mind how I imagined a certain side of Paris would be, the side I didn't see on my honeymoon with Frederick.

"The parlour is where my ladies commence their work. Shortly after ten, the gentlemen arrive," she explains.

My watch says 10:30. "Business is thriving."

"My employees are clean, well-fed. Each has her own private bedroom, access to a physician, who visits the house when necessary, at my expense. One day a week they are completely free. They can do whatever they like on their day off. The older women who you see are raising families without husbands. They and their offspring would be in the workhouse or worse, begging on the street if it were not for me."

Beyond a doubt, Polly's trade is of a superior sort than Maman's was at the Devil's Stone Inn. In England, there is strict social stratification among whores and their customers. My husband enjoys crossing that line. It is what he lives for.

The prettiest girls are dressed in flimsy gowns of black organza and Spanish lace. The youngest are in pink and white. Most wear their hair down, partially covering their bare backs and shoulders. Legs are exposed. All are heavily adorned with white peonies and heaps of sparkling costume jewelry that make them appear dramatic and foreign, as if they are posing for a portrait painter at a masquerade party. One woman displays her large breasts, which hang freely outside her corset. Alluring Levantine music plays on the gramophone. The air smells of sandalwood and wine and for a moment I breathe it all in, imagining I've entered a world even more delightful than the ribald side of Paris. With Polly as my guide, I've stepped into *One Thousand and One Arabian Nights.*

At the Devil's Stone Inn, Maman ran her trade in milkmaids in a catch as catch can way. I've witnessed the look on the men's faces in Polly's parlour before, but not the expression on the girls' faces. Polly's women are certain of themselves, in ways I have rarely witnessed. I can't help but wonder if the whores' lives are superior to mine. At least they are paid and have a day of freedom every week. If I were to share my tale of indignity with a whore's, how could mine compare favourably?

***

Upstairs in Polly's bedroom, she undresses me. But before she begins to unwrap my clothes, she points to the skylight above her boudoir table. The moon and stars are shining brightly.

"Let's pretend we're sailing the heavens on unicorns made of glass and feathers," she says.

"Or flying on a magic carpet."

We don't require a candle; the room is illuminated by the night sky. Under the skylight we stand face to face. First she removes my starched, white shirt and the black, gabardine skirt. I pray she cannot make out the markings on my skin from my collar in the dim, opaline light. She kneels to undo the laces of my black-leather oxfords and I kick them off. Polly then slips off my cotton stockings, and then more carefully, my crinoline, muslin slip and camisole, lastly my knickers. Without speaking, she gently kisses me once between my legs, where she applies a puff of scented talcum from a small, china box on her dressing table. Gracefully, she rises to dab cologne between my breasts. No one has ever been so kind to me.

---

We collapse on the bed together, half laughing, half gasping with excitement. Polly kisses me everywhere, my shoulders, my breasts, my stomach, the place between my legs, even my knees. I feel as if I am encased in a bubble of sweet, undulating liquid, until the slow spark inside me catches fire and I shake with a burst of inexplicable pleasure.

When finally I grow still, Polly lights a single candle and I lay my head on her shoulder where her arm is outstretched to enfold me.

"You could live with me at the Purple Peony," she muses, her watchful eyes taking in all of me, the pulse of my fast-beating heart included. The same feeling I'd experienced at the railway station catches in my throat again, but I force myself to push it back down into my chest, as best I can.

"I want children, Polly."

"Can't you see that it's possible to be happy without them? Try not to be so conventional, darling."

If I could see it, I would. Polly and I, the Purple Peony, happiness, even love. But I can't. Instead for the all the degradation I endure at Wendice Manor, for all the isolation and ignominy, I remain the lady of the manor. My place in society is secure, as Maman wished it to be.

Yet, I'm not keen on discouraging Polly entirely. She brings out the best in me and I'm fearful to let it go. If I say the wrong thing, burst the bubble, as I did with Freddy at our wedding, I'll ruin everything: this visit, her love for me, an opportunity to escape someday if life with Frederick becomes unbearable. If I remind Polly that I am the lowly Publican's daughter, the French Jewess' daughter, the cook who even she suspects spreads typhoid, it is bound to wind down the same avenue as it did with Frederick. Maman always claimed that you could never tell with the English, "their charming manners often hide their baser thoughts," she warned. Perhaps Polly would not accept me for who I am, if she actually knew me. It could easily end as it did with Pa, rejecting me, or as it is now with Frederick. She might come to see me as a debased creature unworthy of her love.

It is always safer to conceal my true identity. Above all, I must decline from falling prey to the emotions of the moment, as I did when Polly collected me at the railway station.

"Can't you see how much more complicated it is than that?" I force her to sit up straight. "Wendice would never give me a divorce."

"I suspect not," she reluctantly agrees. "Does it matter that much to you that you would not be legally divorced? Many women decide to live on their own leaving their husbands behind."

"You of all people should understand that I am a *femme couverte*, as Maman would say. I am an invisible woman, a ghost, who haunts her husband, only to become half solidified when he is no more."

"Forgive me, but your Maman filled your head with outdated notions. Why, the world is changing! What does it matter, beloved? We shall live in sin. I rather like the idea of thumbing our noses at polite society."

"English law forbids it. Two women together in this way," I counter.

"How painfully bourgeois you are! Whose business is it anyway?" She grabs my face. "We've nothing to be ashamed of."

"It's unthinkable. We should be doomed to exist outside the farthest margin of society, as disgraced women. Do you expect me to live in a brothel with whores?"

As soon as the words escape my lips I know I've revealed too much. But I can't help considering Maman's teachings and all that she did for me. She wore herself out preparing me for society and a judicious match with a gentleman of considerable means. How could I spoil everything so late in the game? Being with Polly makes me long for the security of the manor. At least I am not required to be constantly explaining myself there.

"What is the alternative?" Polly asks me incredulously. "That I give up my establishment so we may live in disguise as spinsters, in rural penury, accepted by society for our piety? Shall we live in an isolated cottage on the moor? I've experienced poverty and I never wish to know it again. After all, I have my work, helping the girls, and my friends, Adela and Daphna, to whom I am devoted. I wouldn't give up any of it for the world."

"But I am to give up my place in society as lady of the manor, and destroy my one chance at becoming a mother?"

Polly does not respond to my question. "You must meet my friends. They are independent women who earn their living by keeping a lodging house. Much of the time, we concern ourselves with charitable causes. We know who we are and are little concerned with public approval."

"Yes, of course, Polly, I will meet them, but could you grant me a little time to consider your offer, to sort things out?" I beg, and with that a magnanimous Polly nods and kisses me gently on the forehead. She holds me tenderly in her arms as I drift off to sleep.

# – 6 –

Before elevenses, we meet Adela and Daphna on the Promenade. Nannies are pushing their charges in huge black prams. It is summer holidays and I can see the lower-town urchins climbing down the slippery steps of the wharf to jump into the waters of the Pool. Polly's friends sit on a bench surveying the expansive view of the sea with the Royal Navy's fleet of warships proudly gathered in the commanding harbour. There are many four-masted vessels scattered about the outer harbour. Their giant sails are furled.

Adela is stout and tall with blazing, blue eyes and thin salt and pepper hair. Her expression is formidable without a hint of cruelty. I'm certain she would take me under her wing if I allowed it. She keeps her large hands in her lap clasping tightly to today's edition of *The Plymouth Mercury*.

Polly opines that sooner or later there will soon be a second all-out war with the Boers in South Africa. Adela declares that a prosperous-looking man who tips his homburg to us is actually a warmonger, intending to make pots of money whenever and wherever war is declared. Without even lowering her voice, Polly says she is a Pacifist and the other two nod their heads in agreement.

Daphna is Jewish and attends the synagogue, the one Polly and I passed during my first night in Plymouth. Around her neck is a silver chain with the Star of David. Her house skirts Bragg's Alley where the streetwalkers share their beds after working all night in the tunnels beside the Hoe. Bragg's Alley is the place that my husband favours when he visits Plymouth. Daphne, God bless her, has confided to Polly that she has observed Wendice in the alley after midnight, on his knees, imploring the whores to take Christ into their hearts.

---

In certain respects, Daphna reminds me of Maman. She is tiny with a delicate, aquiline nose and thick, chestnut hair surrounding her heart-shaped face. Although she greets me politely, she is distracted. I can tell that she does not approve of me or of my marriage to Frederick Wendice. How could she?

Adela's bordello is on Central Street and although not as fancy as Polly's, it is not as low as Daphna's. We are to walk there to take our morning refreshments. In Adela's kitchen, I listen to the three friends discuss their prodigious charity work. They are alarmed about the women picked up last night by Inspector Anniss of the Plymouth Metropolitan Police.

"Thrown into the Black Maria to be carted off to the Royal Albert Hospital, they were. The girls were stripped down naked, and checked for the clap," Adela declares.

As we sip tea and nibble on the saffron cakes that Adela offers, Polly plots how to spring the girls from hospital. It is the first time I have been inside a kitchen in four years. The smell of fresh, baking bread invades my senses. I am about to inquire if I could prepare a meal for the women of the house, but Polly interrupts me.

"Shall we get ourselves over to the Rescue House straightaway? I'll find us a solicitor, that's what I'll do," she says assuredly. "As a civilized society, we can no longer tolerate incarcerating women because the military suspects that they might be diseased—or because the sailors cannot control their masculine urges."

Adela and Daphna agree. "That evil Inspector Anniss plays his own game," Adela says sharply. "The thieving bastard is squeezing money from the Navy to round up the corner girls while blackmailing the poor dears for a share of their nightly bank."

The women click their tongues and shake their heads in unison. I scrutinize Daphna carefully. She appears to be one of them, no matter that she is a Jewess. I follow the friends to the Rescue Hall where Polly, indeed, commandeers a solicitor to help the streetwalkers. I am amazed by how forceful Polly and her companions are: in command of themselves and others as well. The dollymops respect them, but so does the man of law. They are considered women of means and good judgment by those who volunteer at the Rescue Hall. If I do decide to stay at the Purple Peony, I cannot think how I would fit in with this illustrious group, these domineering, forceful madams or how they could possibly accept me. If Frederick hadn't agreed to remove the dog collar from around my neck, I'd be wearing it now.

At breakfast the next morning, Polly announces that she is taking me to the Royal Albert Hospital to see where the dollymops land when Inspector Anniss plucks them off the street.

Everyone from the guard at the entrance to the nursing sisters knows Polly. We walk the halls until we reach steep steps leading to the basement. The sister at the desk nods to Polly, allowing us to enter the quarantined zone. The contagion ward is small and dank with locked windows covered in black shades.

"Shall we get right to the point, then?" Polly inquires.

Although I'd assumed that Polly would take me to the ward where the dollymops are held captive, at the last moment she has changed her mind and now directs me straight into the typhoid ward.

I can barely see, with only the low gaslights burning from the wall fixtures. Without special permission, no one is allowed in and no one is allowed out of this place. The ward is steaming hot. Sisters, in their starched collars and caps, wear harried looks on their tired faces, as they march between the patients' cots, closely arranged along the air-less rows. Blood and vomit stain their prim white aprons.

"Nothing to fear. You've had it already and so have I," Polly affirms.

Inside the public typhoid ward, the stench of death is so strong that I am tempted to turn on my heel and run from this place. Patients lie supine, some in cotton nightdresses, some only in their undergarments. It is on the scantily dressed ones that I see the telltale rash across their chest signifying typhoid fever.

"The fever can burn as high as 105 degrees," Polly informs me. "It can rage for weeks, sometimes even a month, before the sick are brought to the hospital. By then it's too late. They are dying of pneumonia." She snaps her fingers and motions for us to continue our investigation of the ward.

Sisters are dousing the sick with cold compresses, but Polly re-affirms that once they enter hospital with typhoid "most are turned out in a hearse rather than on their pins."

I tell Polly that I would rather spread my legs on Bragg's Alley than tend to the sick and dying. I can't bear to look at the lost souls calling out for their mothers no matter how old they are. "I wish to leave. I can't bear it here ..." The words stick in my throat.

Outside the Royal Albert, Polly does the talking as I gulp mouthfuls of fresh air. "No one is asking you to spread your legs, Cordelia. Try not to be so dramatic. Or act the part of the naïve maiden."

Polly understands me in ways I thought impossible. "You could cook for me, manage my kitchen. Weren't you going to ask Adela if you could prepare something in her kitchen yesterday?"

I croak out: "How did you know?" but Polly gives me a knowing look.

We walk in silence until I ask, "What are you suggesting?"

"I'm suggesting that if you take proper measures, wear gloves and keep your hands where they should be, I can't see any reason why you shouldn't be able to return to your profession, to the kitchen, doing what God intended you to do. I've sampled your cooking in Shebbear, if you recall. It was divine."

But I am stunned by her pronouncements. "Why don't you and Frederick wrap me in bandages like a Mummy and stick me in the British Museum?" I cry. "That's what you both want, isn't it? To treat me as a freak of nature: a living, breathing miasma that spreads typhoid wherever she goes. Why on earth do you bother with me?"

"Don't be childish. Listen to me. There is a scientist in France, Louis Pasteur, who has discovered that disease is spread by tiny, little, living creatures called germs. They are so small that we cannot see them with the human eye, but only with a microscope, a kind of magnifying glass. We pass them along unwittingly, one to the other, when we are ill. No one does that purposefully."

"But I am not ill. Frederick claims I'm dirty and that I spread typhoid just by breathing when I'm near food or drink."

"Nonsense. Frederick is monstrous. I've already recounted Daphne's sightings of him in Bragg's Alley, carrying on with the lowest girls in the Hoe."

Polly's words are neither false nor affected. She speaks plainly to me, full of good sense and possibilities. Yet, for all he has done to me, it is impossible for me to consider Frederick a monster. I have not come that far.

"Why won't you leave the blackard, live with me and run the kitchen at the Purple Peony? The customers would adore your French cuisine.

If you employ the precautions I've described, no one will end up in the typhoid ward."

"And when Frederick comes for me? What then?"

"I promise to protect you, if he does."

"Oh, most assuredly he will. He will fight to have me back."

"You think so? Perhaps he has already done all he can to alter your character."

"He's not changed me as much as you might imagine. Not inside. Inside I'm still Cordelia Tilley, daughter of the raw publican and his wife, the Jewish witch.

"I don't wish to change you, Cordelia. People are who they are."

I stop to look closely at Polly. She is bossy; there is an overbearing quality to her nature, however much she adorns it with good intentions. I wonder whether I would be simply trading one master for another.

"But you don't know how determined Frederick is. He believes it is his duty as a Christian gentleman to make me over." For a moment, I consider revealing the truth about my situation with my husband, but I am ashamed about the dog collar and the monthly sojourns to the gurney in his study. "I can't, Polly. I wish to have children. It means everything to me."

"Does it?"

"Everything. You don't know what it is like to want a child and be denied. You have no idea."

On the pavement where we speak, young mothers are wheeling their babies in prams. What I take to be sisters, walk arm in arm, in the pungent salt air baked by the sunshine.

Polly leads me into a teashop on Plymouth's high street. We sit at a small, oval table beside a window adorned with lace curtains. She removes her gloves, but I leave mine on.

"Why on earth did you agree to marry him in the first place?" Polly's face is red with disappointment. "Didn't I try to warn you who he is, the brute? And sweet Albert, too. Albert had the measure of Wendice from the beginning. Why will you not listen to reason from those who love you?"

I'm terrified that she knows more about my life with Frederick than she admits. But who could inform her? Only Albert has an inkling of my bizarre existence and that is because he has observed the dog collar peeking above my shirt.

I try to save face, recalling my days with Maman at the Devil's Stone Inn. "Think back, Polly, to what my life was like slaving in the kitchen of the inn and what it would have been like for me after Maman died, if I had stayed on. How could I not accept Frederick's offer? Surely you must see that I had no other choice."

"You might have accepted my offer, to be my companion." She is mad with me now and who can blame her?

"When Frederick began to court me I believed he wouldn't hurt a fly. He appeared to be so gentle and concerned with my welfare. Compared to the Tilleys, his manners never faltered. I can see him now: spreading his napkin neatly over his belly while holding his knife and fork properly. How he tucked into the sumptuous repasts I'd conjured up especially for him! My heart melted, witnessing the true gentleman shine in him. It tickled my fancy when my future husband rose from his seat whenever I entered a room—and in that way I am my mother all over again. Hankering after Quality while holding a greasy cooking spoon in my hand."

"I, too, was under the thumb of a man once."

Could Polly be generous enough to understand my predicament? Her determination to keep me by her side surprises me.

"Maman dreamt of better things for me. She wanted me away from the Devil's Stone, away from Pa, and into society, the society of gentlemen and ladies."

"Does it matter that much to you?"

"It mattered to Maman and so I suppose, yes, it matters to me."

"And wealth is the only measure?"

How can I respond to Polly's question when I hardly know the answer myself?

"Manners. Good English manners count as well. Gentlemen's manners. Not a soul could ever mistake the Tilleys for gentlemen—or so I thought before my marriage."

"And now?"

"Unfortunately I must agree that manners, however pleasant, are not the only characteristic of a gentleman, though it's taken me four years and thousands of tiny disappointments to comprehend this immutable fact."

"I suspect your brother Albert is a gentleman, in his own way. He drove me to the rail station in Holsworthy just after your mother died. We had a good, long talk."

I try to smile, to reach across the table to squeeze Polly's hand, but she is reserved and pushes me away. She is beginning to accept that I will return to Frederick no matter what the cost.

As she rises to leave the tearoom, a tall man in a stained raincoat enters and heads directly for Polly. He shows no hesitation as he places his long-fingered hand on her shoulder. His familiarity surprises me.

"So good to see you out and about Mrs. Turney," he says, showing a mouth full of crooked teeth.

Polly, who is usually so inviting, recoils from his reach and moves to sit close to me at the table. "Inspector Anniss, I understand you are harassing the girls once again."

His full lips curl into a snarl. "It's the law."

"The Contagious Disease Act is about to be repealed," she retorts.

"Not in my domain, it won't. A whore is a dangerous woman." He looks squarely at her and then at me.

"Miss …

"Mrs. Wendice," I reply.

"Not Frederick Wendice's wife! I'll be damned. In Plymouth, cavorting with the madam of the Purple Peony."

I'm about to defend Polly when she whispers in my ear to be still. This is the first time I've witnessed my friend fearful of anyone.

"Frederick Wendice's lady of the manor, out with a whore. Now that's something to remember." The Inspector, who backs out through the tearoom door, tips his hat to me.

# Book Three

HOLSWORTHY, COUNTY DEVON

1892

# – I –

*FOR SEVEN YEARS I have been drawn across the cobblestones of Holsworthy by a raging horse. My skin is shredded, my fingernails torn to bits. Every bone in my body is cracked as I'm displayed before the butcher's shop, the cheese monger, the tearoom near the city square. Dragged all the way to the abattoir, high with the stink of dead flesh. The good people of Holsworthy come out to watch me; I am their only sport and spectacle. The flesh on my face is entirely gone so that my cheekbones jut straight out from my bonnet. It remains strangely askew on my head, covering my red curls. Curls of the devil. And shining white bones. Skinless. My eyes are blinded by the blood dripping from my skull.*

*For seven years this is who I become whenever Frederick sits me down for a lecture. I am the sole audience for his pronouncements on the malignancy of Jewish ritual. The Ripper is a Jew. Frederick knows who did it. A Socialist and a Jew. He is hiding in the underground warrens of Whitechapel that harbour my people, the demons who applaud the murders of the five whores of East London. Frederick is fearful that the Jews, hungry for blood, will rob the whores' graves. He writes letter after letter to the London Metropolitan Police imploring the peelers to install a sentry, from dusk to dawn, to watch over each dead girl as she rests. He sends flowers to their graves. White, white lilies.*

*Frederick is most alarmed that the Jews are carrying Continental socialism to our fair isle and infecting the unknowing poor with their lies and incitement to revolution. European socialism is controlled by Jews, as is the international banking system. Two sides to the same coin. He wishes to have that devil Marx's grave in Highgate Cemetery exhumed. He believes it is immoral for a man to be buried between his lawful Christian wife and his mistress. That his mistress was an English servant, he considers particularly deplorable.*

*Among his other abiding interests, is the one about diseased children born with deformities. My husband consults medical encyclopedias filled with illustrations of peculiar children, some born with a crooked spine or with-*

*out limbs, or brought into the world dead, without heart or brain. He asks me if deformities appear in Hebrew children or our rituals guard against such horrors.*

*This is how I exist, until now, until I end it with my very own announcement. I jump atop the rooftop of our tall house at cock's crow. I am playing a fiddle as I dance and serenade the waking village with my wondrous news. My music travels down country to remind the slumbering hermit exposed to the savage wind of the Bodmin Moor that he is human; it travels across country to the unsettled souls of the sailors who drowned on the rocks at Merlin's cave, to tell them to fly home. The sound of my fiddle travels far enough to rouse the solitary poet in his rat-infested warren in Whitechapel, so on this very morning, he recites from memory all the songs of Solomon, reminding him that he is forever a Jew.*

*I am starting over. I have been given a chance to turn evil into good. This is my fantasy.*

## - 2 -

Life at Wendice Manor unfolds more prosaically than in my dreams. After turning down Polly's offer to live with her at the Purple Peony, it did take me seven long years to become pregnant, but now I am with child. Each day my breasts, sore to the mildest touch, grow fuller. Before long I will clutch my newborn baby to my breast to suckle. Mr. Ealing, who is pleased to deliver the baby, says he will be born on the summer solstice. How extraordinary! How lovely! Since announcing my pregnancy, Frederick has ceased his lectures about the Jews. He has stopped consulting his medical encyclopedias about deformed infants. My nightmares have ceased. The pregnancy is giving Frederick and me another chance even if I had to cheat to accomplish it. I am brimming with hope.

In August of this year, Frederick neglected to mark his calendar, the one that he keeps locked in the desk drawer of his study. For years I'd watched him as he tracked my monthlies, but I'd never had the gumption to pick the lock. However, in his fever to mount me that month, he forgot to order me to return the key to him.

---

As soon as he departed the manor, I grabbed the key from my hiding place, beneath the potted aspidistra on the second floor landing. Now it was in my hands, so without hesitation, I snuck up to his study and turned the lock to his desk. What I found was a bottle of Hardwick's Vigour Pills and the green bottle of chloroform, which contains the nauseating gas Frederick presses to my nostrils to calm me when my nerves get the better of me. The key to my dog collar was there, too.

In the end, deceiving Frederick was as easy as pie. He'd not marked in pen and ink my bleeding days in August, probably assuming that he'd misplaced the key. Naturally, I switched them. By mixing the right days up with the wrong ones, I found myself quickly pregnant. I could tell immediately because my breasts began to feel sore, like overblown balloons, and it was then, within a very few days of the deed that I knew a baby was coming.

## – 3 –

The long, sweet days of my pregnancy were surely the best of times for Frederick and me. They blossomed into another chance for us to rekindle our marriage vows and turn our union into something grand instead of something sordid.

In the early spring, before the baby is to be born, I implore Frederick to allow me to accompany him to Tintagel and the quarries, where his business interests reside. To my amazement, Frederick agrees.

"Why not, why shouldn't my dear wife tag along?" he says. His look is indulgent.

I am wearing a white-cotton nightdress with tiny, lace pockets along the neckline. Frederick occupies himself examining my skin, my freckles peaking through the eyelets of the lace.

"How fetching," he declares.

Ensconced in our great four-poster bed, with the plush, red pillows, I tie back the damask curtains so the robust, west wind will cool my skin. It is the warmest spring in memory, with the sun's heat oozing over the countryside. During the night, I swear I can smell the salt air wafting across the Devon countryside. The scent of the sea is a relief and I inhale deeply. Usually all I can smell is the stink from the abattoir.

"You are my witch," says Frederick, following the pattern of lace along my shoulders with his fingers.

"And you are my magician, making me do things I would never dream of doing without you."

"Such as?" Freddy asks.

"Such as this, you and me. Most married couples abstain during the confinement."

"But not us." A cloud passes over his face. Frederick is wearing a grey-striped nightshirt that rises high above his dimpled knees. "If the baby is born healthy, we could start afresh, as far away as Scotland, in Glasgow or Edinburgh. A bustling metropolis where no one would know you. I could found a Mechanic's Institute for Christian workingmen. What do you say, girl?"

I sit bolt upright on the bed.

"Pardon me? *Know us,* you mean! You're just as much a part of this now as I am. You've covered for me all these years. Otherwise the typhoid epidemic would be blamed on me—guilty or not—and that's for certain. Who else could they blame?"

"So you admit to it, spreading typhoid!"

I pull myself out of the bed and away from Frederick's reach. "Of course not. I'm just saying that pointing a finger at the Jewess, the cook, the red-haired witch, is always in order."

I expect Frederick to become angry, but instead he stretches out his arms to pull me close. "Why you judge our countrymen so harshly, I'll never understand. Come to me ..."

"You saved me from them," I murmur and for a moment I believe he did. I lie on the bed beside him.

Frederick presses himself to me, as near as my ballooning belly will allow.

"Maybe what I do to you is black magic," I tease.

***

For this short time of my confinement, we are as devoted as any couple could be. Frederick no longer forces me to climb the stairs to the gurney in his study. It is both the anticipation and the fear of what will come in June that binds us together. While the child is in my womb, my husband accepts me. And so, nightly I turn to him, with my wanton ways and coy words. He always responds. As I grow larger and larger, feeling the baby kicking inside me, rousing my blood, I do see some long-forgotten goodness in Frederick.

Perhaps his motives for marrying me were as pure as he claims, however strange. Perhaps he did love me enough to risk marrying me, impregnating me and protecting me from harm, no matter how high the cost. For my part, I believe in a small corner of my mind that a healthy baby will absolve me of my sins, a wager most pregnant woman share, I believe, in one way or the other.

***

The air is ripe with planting when we set out in Frederick's carriage for the coastal slate mines. We are flying across the countryside to Bude, then down the coastal path and straight across the Bossiney Road to Tintagel. From how my husband talks, it sounds as if he owns Tintagel and everyone in it.

It is the clearest of days, no drizzle or fog. High above the sea, the salt air quickens the beat of my heart. How can I not recall Pa's tales of shipwrecks along this shore? The drowning sailors ripped open upon the rocks.

Today is calm and I banish dark thoughts from my mind. The Atlantic is on one side, my husband on the other and my darling unborn baby in the middle, snuggled deep inside me.

"If only Maman could see me now! Her own daughter, sitting on silk cushioned seats, her gentleman beside her, is travelling to Tintagel to inspect their business interests."

"How happy you would make her," Frederick agrees.

"Shall we visit Merlin's Cave? Maman always wished to explore it and never did."

Frederick turns incredulously toward me. "Merlin's Cave is the most danger-ridden quarry on the coast. Will shall certainly avoid it in your condition."

"Just for a moment, dearest," I plead. "I vowed to try to do all the things that Maman never could. I so wish to see the ships towed into safe harbour at Tintagel Haven. I have heard it is a sight to behold."

Frederick indulges me, but makes sure that the hours we spend together in the carriage are not frittered away. As the time for the baby's birth draws closer, he is demanding that I keep accounts of my spending.

"Never took you for a spendthrift, Cordelia," he remarks, "but Nanny Bullbrook reports that money flows through your fingers like water."

"Does it distress you that I appreciate beautiful things? After all, we are hardly poor." I stretch out my hand to cover my husband's sausage fingers.

"Nevertheless, it would be instructive for you to, at least, attempt to keep accounts. You can be profligate, as your mother was, an extremely unbecoming trait in a woman."

"How do you know what my mother was like?" I ask.

"Your father imparted many stories to me. Are you surprised?"

"Indeed I am. What business was it of his? Or yours for that matter?"

Frederick pulls my hand from his and looks uncomfortable. "Have you ever considered how little my miners survive on and how their good wives make do?"

"That is because you pay them a meagre wage. If you paid them properly, what their work is actually worth, they would be rich like us."

"Where do you get these strange notions?" Frederick asks, looking more and more distressed with each comment I make.

"*The Communist Manifesto.* It's been translated into English. You have it in your study." It's always a joy to shock Frederick.

"You are not to enter my study without me, or Mrs. Bullbrook at your side."

For a moment, I fear I will give it all away and Frederick will put two and two together to figure out how I became pregnant. If only I could learn to keep my mouth shut.

"You're a great Reformer," I say, trying to get him off track.

"Yes, I am. Our movement will change the world. A time is fast approaching when all the world, rich and poor, will exist in harmony. The twentieth century shall be the most peaceful, the most fair-minded in human history. Inequality between men shall disappear. I can assure you of that."

I wonder if Frederick is correct. "Then why don't you share your wealth, not the pittance you give to your saintly charities, but your real money? Give it to the miners. Once I visited Morwellham Quay and it was obvious they have next to nothing."

"May I inquire when you were at Morwellham? Have you been slipping out of the house, without me knowing?"

"It was years ago with Pa. I never disobey you, Frederick. You must realize that by now. But I can't agree with you about a harmonious world looming right around the corner. Polly says there will be other wars in Africa and India, that people don't fancy being under the thumb of the Empire. She says there are growing tensions between England and Russia."

"And she should know. A woman, a brothel keeper." Frederick clamps his lips together as I realize I am in the soup once again. Why can't I keep myself quiet, why must I speak out boldly when I know it will get me into terrible hot water?

"A time is approaching in the affairs of men ..."

I interject. "I certainly pray so. For my people."

"Your people?" Frederick is surprised.

"The Jewish people. Our child will be Jewish since he will be born of a Jewish mother."

"I suppose."

"You suppose."

"What I was going to say, if I may be permitted, is that presently it won't matter. Jew and Christian shall live together in peace. In the next century, we will abolish war and discrimination. The twentieth century will be like no other," Frederick concludes, folding his hands together.

"Possibly you could begin this impending rush to equality by raising the quarrymen's salaries by a guinea each week? To help the Fabian movement along?" I suggest.

"Don't be ridiculous! They wouldn't know what to do with it."

"But you claim the miner's wives are so thrifty, I should be emulating their ways."

Frederick's expression changes from irritation to avuncular concern, a stance he often assumes when he attempts to avert a row.

"Let's not argue, dear," he says, attempting to pacify me. "It isn't good for the child." Frederick pats my protruding belly as we travel in our plush carriage to Tintagel.

## – 4 –

My husband's intention is to head straight to the Vicar's house, nestled safely below the high rugged cliffs of Tintagel, but I convince him, following his lecture about the frugality of the quarrymen's wives, to visit the terrace row near Merlin's Cave. I wish to inspect the poorest miners' hovels and I refuse to let go of Frederick's promise to allow me to observe his men, crawling like monkeys, up and down the ropes leading to the cliff tops from the caves.

"Don't get too close to anyone, or touch anything or breathe on them," Frederick insists. "The last thing my men need is another typhoid epidemic."

No matter how long the County has been free of typhoid, Frederick will never let me forget that he blames me for the epidemic. Not even today. On judgment day, my husband will have me quarantined from all the rest, shouting up to his God, that I am untouchable.

With all my heart, I try to ignore him as we approach a row of knobby dwellings rubbed raw from the salt air engulfing them. Neither a blade of grass nor a flowering bush grows in the postage stamp yards. Children dash about without shoes. Two down, two up are the Wendice company's rows, each with the slate hearth in the big room downstairs and the children, no matter how many, packed into one bedroom upstairs and the parents in the other. The stench of the row's shared outdoor privy wafts throughout the compound. Frederick pulls a handkerchief from his pocket to cover his mouth and nose.

I refuse Frederick's offer to cover myself. I've smelled just as bad in the kitchen at the Devil's Stone Inn. Smells and rotting matter are part of life as far as I'm concerned.

The long ride from Holsworthy has left me parched so I ask a boy if I might drink from the water pump outside the row of houses. "Might you have a cup for me?" I ask him. The inhabitants maintain a single outdoor water pump and the night soil, I notice, is dumped at the back end of the garden in the earth closet or heaved out the front window before dawn.

The lad is about fourteen. His face and neck are entirely covered in encrusted boils. He smiles at me although it must pain his face to do so. Without hesitation he leads us toward the first dwelling in the row.

"Who are you, then, grand missus?" the lad asks. "You look like me Mum just before she pops out another one, but much more splendid you are."

No one, not even a young lad, has called me splendid for a long time. I can discern that he is handsome, under the red, bulbous eruptions and the look in his eyes is one of native intelligence. I reach out to pat the lad's blonde curls when Frederick shouts, "Stay away, do not touch!"

"The boy needs medicine," I insist, observing the stricken expression on the lad's face. "What's your name, son?"

"Jack is my name, Jack Livesay. I am the eldest son, and head of the Livesay family since my Pa passed." He holds down his miserable face to avoid Frederick's condemning gaze.

Inside the row, the only shard of light emanates from a soot-soaked glass pane at the rear of the room and it is curtained off to conceal the stone scullery and a cot where a small girl is sucking her thumb while half asleep. A mangy cat dives at the black beetles surrounding the dried bones and curdled milk by the hearth. Jack's mother has wedged a tiny suckling baby between her hip and bosom, while she kneads the dough for bread.

"By what stroke of luck do I deserve this visit?" she asks. "Who are these fine folks, Jackie?"

"It's Miss Cordelia and Master Frederick. Mr. Wendice owns the quarry."

"Does he now?"

While not shaking Jack's mother's hand, Frederick does step through the entrance and immediately hits his forehead on the low ceiling beam.

"Be careful, sir, or you'll knock your block off," Mrs. Livesay advises.

Under her oily hair, black as coal, I can discern the lines of a beautiful woman, still young with high colour and good bones. Suddenly she appears alarmed.

"Is it trouble in the pits, then?" I've just lost my man, but the others …

"Not at all … we're ttttripping today, my wife and I wwwwish to see …" Frederick is stuttering now.

"You wish to see how the other half lives," she says grimly. "I should know better. Where were you when my own man plunged to his death hauling your slate down the cliff, Mr. Wendice?"

"Shall we go?" Frederick says to me.

"Mrs. Livesay, I wish to apologize for my husband." I move toward her.

The woman gives me a knowing smile and we begin to talk, she offering me a seat, in my advanced condition. Frederick continues to stand by the entrance, shifting his weight from one foot to the other.

When she offers a cup of tea, I accept although Frederick tries to weasel out of it. I sip the strong, black liquid from the household's best crockery while conversing with Mrs. Livesay. Cockroaches escape from among the floral cups and saucers.

"Jack needs medicine to fix his face," I urge, trying to ignore the steady profusion of bugs roaming among the dishes. "Would you object if we took him to Holsworthy with us, to our doctor, Mr. Ealing? He will make him right as rain."

"Are you mad?" Frederick's voice is high-pitched as he takes a few more steps toward the hearth.

"It will only be for a few weeks, until he is better," I say confidently.

"Not now, Cordelia, with the baby due."

"I can't see why not."

"If it's not too much of a bother?" Mrs. Livesay questions, a slight smile of expectation crossing her face.

"Why me, missus?" Jack inquires.

"I like you. Something about you reminds me of myself," I reply honestly. The expression in his eyes is one of cleverness and I am trying to tell him that he deserves a chance at a better life than the one fate has dealt him. We need a stable boy at the manor. Why shouldn't it be Jack Livesay? There's no saying he must return to Merlin's Cave after he recovers. Surely, his mother struggles with enough mouths to feed without Jack.

As we depart for Tintagel, Frederick demands that Jack ride up on the box. Jack agrees, holding on for dear life. My husband has relegated the lad to the category of untouchable, a place usually reserved for me. Jack is tainted and must be contagious, according to Frederick.

Heading for St. Materiana, Jack sings in a husky, melodic voice. His song drowns out the sound of the wind. Brave boy that he is! Although he is not quite a man, he is taller than I, slender with muscular arms. His mother told me that he's already worked at the slate quarry for two years. He's agile and quick of mind, so the boss has Jack climbing the ropes, like a monkey, carting slate down from the cliff to the shore at Merlin's Cave. One false move and he'd be crushed on the rocks.

The lad is ambitious, however. I recognize it in him. When Frederick begins to snore, I stretch my head out of the window to see that Jack is sitting comfortably beside the driver. I must admit to being captivated by his boyish beauty, but there is something more shocking that I see. Beneath the nut-brown tan, the sun-bleached curls, green cat's eyes, I discern the ruin of Jack. I can see what he will look like when he is old and sour and chewed up by disappointed ambition.

We are stopping at the vicarage overnight. When Frederick retires for a nap before evening tea, I slip out to roam about the church's ancient graveyard. It is high atop a cliff of windswept, craggy rock, the parish church of St. Materiana. The foursquare bell tower joins to the squat, Norman structure. As I climb, the little village recedes from view and I am wandering among the clouds, in the territory of the Roman invaders and the Spanish pirates who once plundered these shores. The buttressed gravestones tell the story of the dead from the many centuries before us. But today the graveyard is still except for the haunting whistle of the wind bringing sounds of battles long past. If only Frederick would let go of his obsession with typhoid, if only the baby would be born healthy, if only I could love my husband as a wife should.

In the vicarage's kitchen, Reverend Kinsman's housekeeper is washing Jack's clothes in lye. She's offered him a soak in her copper tub.

---

As she removes the lice from his head, I pour myself a spot of tea and lather some raspberry jam on her freshly-baked scones. No one orders me to leave the kitchen, as they would in my own home.

When the Reverend enters the kitchen, he is quick to shake my hand. He explains that he has been visiting the infirm in his parish.

He tells me he's fascinated by the Roman lineage of his church and offers to accompany me back up the hill to the graveyard. Reverend Kinsman speaks with a slight lisp that is more affection than physical impediment. His lush, grey hair falls in waves to his shoulders. Standing more than six feet, he wears his black suit well. Before I can answer, he rushes out to his library and then returns with a book detailing the Roman occupation of Britain.

"There's a milestone serving as a coffin rest in my graveyard," he says with great pride. "Did you happen to notice it?"

I admit that I did not.

"On close inspection, I've recorded that it bears the inscription of the Emperor Caesar Gaius Valerius Licinius."

"You don't say," I respond enthusiastically. Recently I've been reading about Heinrich Schliemann's digs in the Orient. To pass the time of day at the manor, I am reading more voraciously than ever.

When I mention my readings to Reverend Kinsmen, he is impressed and invites me once again to hike with him to the craggy ground high above the vicarage. I decline, politely, although I'm fascinated by his discovery of Roman ruins.

The Reverend pushes his hair from his face and looks at me closely. Mischief dances in his eyes. "I would never have guessed you'd be too meek to embark on a new adventure." I demure once again, lowering my gaze to my protruding belly. On this day, there is no point upsetting Frederick further. He would be apoplectic if he knew I was straining my limbs, in my condition, by climbing the precipice twice. I am trying to please my husband, whatever it takes.

What I would do, however, if I could, would be to bake a brioche, flakey and rich, with a hint of orange rind and brown sugar sprinkled on top; but I dare not upset Frederick in that way either, by asking it of the kind housekeeper presiding over the kitchen of St. Materiana's vicarage.

Putting my hands in my pockets I retire to the parlour while waiting for Frederick to rise refreshed from his nap. From the corner of my eye, I can see the Reverend observing me. He appears amused. What a mismatched couple, this Frederick and Cordelia, I imagine him thinking.

I close my eyes to compose a story in my mind about a young woman, not unlike myself in temperament, who springs from noble Roman birth. She is forced, by her evil father to marry a Celtic king, a barbarian, whose brutal rule disgusts her. She flees to Merlin's Cave, where she is rescued by a Roman warrior. Handsome, young, younger than I, in fact, black-haired and nimble, he steals her away to Italy. I am imagining the Roman warrior taking me in his arms when the dream is interrupted by my husband's drowsy voice, beckoning me to the adjoining library where he is reclining. Quickly I return to ground, where I fear I shall remain forevermore.

## – 5 –

The late spring of 1892 is so uncommonly hot, that I am left with nothing to wear except a faded yellow, linen shift with its seams stretched to the limit. I have taken to wandering outside the gates of the manor house and over to the churchyard across the way. The moon is full and sharp in St. Peter and St. Paul's graveyard as I stand alone in the night, a rotund figure, my face turned to the white moon. It is so luminous, I can make out the mountains of the moon. I can even read the inscriptions on the tombstones engulfed in the salubrious spring night air.

The world is such a gorgeous place, with fragrant, violet wisteria blooming over the churchyard's ancient stonewall. Nearest to the church are the oldest gravestones. Some congregants had lived such long lives—well past three score and ten—that it's possible to discern that certain husbands and wives, who are laid to rest side by side, were wed for more than half a century. Panic at the thought of being married to Wendice for that long or lying beside him into eternity engulfs me. I am overwhelmed by the thought, collapsing under the weight of it.

When I return from my walk, Frederick is waiting for me, with a poem in his hand:

> *This independence, which you prize so High?*
> *What is it? Solitude and Apathy!*
> *Like some dejected Vine near which is found*
> *No sheltering Elm to raise it from the ground.*

My husband's little recitation so enrages me that I offer to pour him another glass of port, which I mix with forty drops of laudanum, a tincture that I keep hidden in my knickers' drawer for such occasions. The thought of entertaining him tonight in my bed is inconceivable. After administering the drug, I escape the house once again, my feet so swollen with pregnancy that I cannot go far. I am alone under the moon, resting on the garden swing.

Only Jack provides me with agreeable company in the final few days before the birth of my child. He is young and beautiful, unlike Frederick in body and soul. As soon as he arrived at the manor, I fetched Mr. Ealing, who mixed a steaming paste of ground meal, witch hazel and boiling water. I apply it to his face nightly and although I can see the tears in his eyes, he consents to allowing me to heal him.

My mind turns away from pleasant thoughts of Jack to the dark thoughts that have been plaguing me recently. I am finding it difficult to concentrate, to read or write letters. As my confinement draws to its conclusion, I am more ill at ease than ever before. What if Frederick is correct about me, what if the typhoid epidemic was my fault, what if I pass it onto the unborn child? Fear clutches at my throat. In Polly's letters, she writes again of the French scientist, Louis Pasteur, who has isolated the exact germ responsible for typhoid. Soon, she assures me, the disease will be fully understood. Progress is being made on the Continent. But if the germ lives inside me, wouldn't I be ill, as sick as Maman and Georgie became, or the dying souls at Morwellham Quay or in the typhoid ward at the Royal Albert in Plymouth? Polly has suffered from typhoid and no one accuses her of contaminating others. Why me? Although I am nine-months pregnant, I am as healthy as a horse. None of this makes sense to me.

When I return to the manor, Frederick is expired on the divan, snoring so loudly I would swear the figurines on the mantle are shaking. While I was outside, Mrs. Bullbrook must have thrown a coverlet over him.

She is sitting next to the stove in the kitchen, drinking nettle tea, when I approach.

"First thing tomorrow morning," I order her, "I want you to go to market for blood pudding, smoked mackerel and a pig's head. I'm famished."

"Yes, ma'am," Mrs. Bullbrook's eyes bulge suspiciously. "Anything else, ma'am?" Her voice quivers with insolence. Her bonnet of grey braids is coming undone. It falls about her thick, wrinkled neck. The skin on her hands is peeling with dryness. Her nails are bitten to the quick.

"Nothing else. Go to bed."

"Master Frederick says I must remain in the kitchen until you are in your bedroom."

Her words enrage me. Who does she think she is? No matter how hard she pushes at me, I must remember that she is the servant and I am the lady. I imagine her as a character in a penny novel. Poison is placed in her water dish. She laps it up like a parched dog until she begins to choke and sputter. Until she lies dead in a pool of her own vomit.

But in truth, at Wendice Manor, there is nothing for me to do but acquiesce.

When I pass the floor-length glass in my bedroom, I inspect my bloated belly and bursting, apple cheeks. All the years I have longed for a baby, from the time I was a girl in Shebbear, I have imagined something cozy and sweet smelling with wispy tufts of red hair, the same colour as mine, and with a guileless smile, unlike mine. Now my breasts are vein-lined melons and my abdominal skin is stretched so tight that I feel as if I will explode. I slip into a light, cambric nightdress, turn the key in the lock and climb onto the four-poster. Should my husband awake from his drug-induced slumber before dawn, he will not be able to enter.

# – 6 –

The very next night I go into labour with little William. Mrs. Bullbrook and the parlour maid are in attendance, as is Mr. Ealing. Our doctor has objected to the presence of the midwife, who he claims will impede my labour.

The contractions go on and on. I try to keep my mind on Jack, the only soul at the manor who cares if I live or die. I call out for him and by morning, no one objects to his presence in the birth room. Having witnessed his own sweet mum in agony nine times, he ties a sheet around the pillars of the bed. Jack shows me how to tug at the sheets when I am straining to push out the baby. He gives me the strength to go on after I believe I am done for and will perish expelling this baby from my body.

By the second evening, the birth room has gone awry. I am shrieking in pain. The child's head is stuck in the birth canal and I cannot push him out no matter how hard I try. This must be how it is when a typhoid child is born; he is broken from the start. All I can think about is that I am cursed. Pa saw through me from the beginning and that is why he never cared for me, never cared to love me.

The windows are wide open. Housekeeper has left them that way to dilute the air, so the miasma, the dirtiness I carry inside me, won't spread to the baby.

"I can't anymore, I can't ..." I scream in terror at the ferocity of the pain. The baby's head is tearing my insides from stem to stern. A cold, sea wind is rattling the windows. I am shivering, but Mrs. Bullbrook refuses to close the windows.

"Push, push," Jack Livesay's voice rings out. In my extreme pain and exhaustion, I'm terrified that if I rip wide open during this ordeal, no one except Jack will mourn me. Finally Ealing cuts me open with a surgical instrument. The incision, long and deep, allows the baby to emerge and for me to rest. If I bleed to death, so be it.

Although I am falling in and out of consciousness, I can hear my husband's voice, as if he shouting from afar. "Is the boy healthy? Why isn't he crying?"

Ealing swaddles the baby in a blue, receiving blanket and hands him over to Mrs. Bullbrook. There are tears in Frederick's eyes.

"What is the matter with the boy's head?" he pleads. "Is he like her? Does he look as he does because we are being punished for Cordelia's sins? Is it the typhoid inside him?"

"Don't take on so, Wendice," the doctor remonstrates. "You must understand that miasmas do not pass from person to person in the way you are suggesting. Disease spreads from sewage, from bad air circulating about filth and decay."

"Not so," Frederick cries. "Disease is inside of her."

I open my eyes to peer up at Frederick. "Hand him to me," I beg.

My husband is openly weeping now, crying out: "Dear lord, forgive us for our sins. I knew this would happen. I should have never allowed you to become pregnant, never risked it."

Housekeeper passes the child to Frederick who has uncovered his head and is staring at the swollen protrusion.

No one bothers to look down at me or give me my child to hold. Instead Ealing remarks, "I've seen one or two like this in my time."

"How can you blame the child's sickness on me?" I murmur. "Why didn't you allow me to throw myself across the tracks years ago, as I wished to do?"

Frederick is not able to bring himself to look in my eyes.

"I truly believed I could save you. Cleanse you of your diseased spirit. Do the best deed a true believer can do. Save a fallen woman and restore her to the righteous arms of our Lord, Jesus Christ."

Upon hearing the utter madness of Frederick's intentions, the room tilts and I am drowning in darkness.

***

I do not regain consciousness for a day. When I do wake all is silent and I realize I have been left alone to wallow in dried blood. The sheets, my nightgown, even the sheets thrown around the bed have not been removed. I promise myself that however long I live, I will never go through the ordeal of childbirth again, not if there is the slightest chance I could produce such as child. A child with a bulbous malformed head that ripped at my insides with such excruciating sharpness.

Although I finally do make an attempt to nurse, the poor boy won't suckle and I am much too weak to hold him properly to my breast.

Around my leaking breasts, Housekeeper Bullbrook binds wide swaths of rough-woven muslin to force my milk to evaporate. I cannot tell what hurts more, my swollen breasts bursting with milk or the incision Ealing cut to get the child's enormous head out of my body.

***

The fever rages inside of me for a fortnight. Just as Frederick claimed, I must be diseased. At some point, Mrs. Bullbrook and Jack heave me up and out of the four-poster and into the spindle bed in the sickroom where the windows are now shut tight with small sandbags laid along the frames to keep out the draughts. Frederick, who has not visited me since the day of the child's birth, has hired a wet nurse to replace me. From afar, I watch, bathed in fever and pain. The wet nurse places my boy's malformed mouth in her well-formed tit and his crying subsides.

"I wish to hold my boy," I cry out to the wet nurse, but she says she has her strict orders. I am to look at William but I am not allowed to touch him.

"A little birdie told me that you are the Jewess who started the typhoid epidemic years ago in Shebbear. Better safe than sorry," she advises me.

William's head looks as if it will burst. "What's wrong with my baby?" I ask her. No one, not Ealing or Frederick or Housekeeper will tell me what's wrong with William. No one will be truthful with me.

Against Wendice's rules, the wet nurse places the child's head close to my face.

"It runs in families, this sickness," she says coldly. "If you offer me a fair sum, I could put some drops on my nipples. Sleeping drops. It will soothe him."

I'd heard of this trick before. In London, unwed mothers abandon their babies in nurseries where they are fed soothing drops to stop their crying. Eventually the potion dampens their will to suck.

"You wish me to pay you to murder my son?"

"I didn't say that, did I?" the wet nurse cringes, pulling William away from me. We never speak of her offer again.

***

---

My convalescence lasts for more than a month during which time I miss the sweetest days of summer or any comfort my boy and I might have given each other. Most of the time, I am alone, but occasionally I hear voices speaking just outside the sickroom door. Today I overhear Frederick conversing with Mrs. Bullbrook before she brings me my supper tray of porridge and tea.

"It shames me to keep her locked in here," he says sheepishly.

"Don't blame yourself, Master Frederick. It's her fault," replies Housekeeper Bullbrook.

My head is swimming.

"Yes, but doesn't William's affliction remind you of someone else?"

"We never speak of that."

"But what if William's affliction has nothing to do with Cordelia? What if it's in my family, this crooked spine?"

I attempt to sit up, to move to the door to better overhear what Frederick and Housekeeper are discussing, but I am too weak. Mr. Ealing is treating me with laudanum, to help with the wicked pain of the incision, so I'm unsure of myself, even to the point of not being certain whether I am dreaming their words. They continue to speak of a sickness about which I am ignorant.

"Don't talk nonsense," Housekeeper says. "There is no inherited sickness among the Wendices. Why you are practically royalty."

Frederick accepts the compliment easily.

"Best she stays out of sight, at least until she can fend for herself." Housekeeper's voice is singsong and happy. "It's time you consider pitching her out of this house. All she's done since coming here is bring sorrow into our lives. I recall the good days before she snared you into marriage."

"I don't recall being happy. I was lonely."

"That's why we sent you off to Plymouth, for female company and comfort."

"Yes, but it was evil, the company of loose women. Worse than anything Cordelia has done."

"Worse than spreading typhoid?" Housekeeper demands.

"I suppose not. If only I could be sure the fault is hers," my husband whimpers. "Nothing is worse than that. Nothing is worse than what she has done to my son."

"Nothing!" Mrs. Bullbrook assures him.

***

After being confined to an invalid's diet of milky oats and sugared tea for forty days and nights, I am weak-kneed when Ealing finally pronounces that my innards are sufficiently healed for me to walk on my own. I leave the sickroom, a prison inside a prison.

Once I depart, Jack reports that the room is sealed off from the house and sulphur rocks are burned in an iron dish over top a water bucket for six hours.

"Mrs. Bullbrook insists that the room will be disinfected of your sick spirit," Jack relays. "She is going to take down the drapes and boil the bedclothes in carbolic acid. She says this is the only way to cleanse your illness from the house. I don't know much ma'am, but you'd think we're living in the Dark Ages."

I exist, frightened and ostracized, in my own home. Everyone except Jack blames me for William's disfigurement and I am helpless to prove them wrong. I am the scapegoat for all that goes wrong in this blighted house and it is not possible for me to convince anyone that I am innocent. Why the burden of proof resides with me, William's mother, I will never comprehend. Worse still, I am beginning to believe in their lies.

# – 7 –

On William's first birthday, I experience a glimmer of hope: the boy might survive, no matter how broken he is. Frederick sees it, too. William is smiling a crooked smile and his cry is more robust, his actions more deliberate. He is not just "a vegetable with a heart" as the fancy doctors at the Royal Albert described him when we paid dearly for their sage opinions.

Frederick is a devoted father, unlike my own Pa in every way. Although William cannot sit or stand, Frederick carries him around the manor, into the garden and plays with him on the swing. Today Mrs. Bullbrook has made a huge white cake with boiled, chocolate fudge icing. Together we sing happy birthday and William smiles his crooked smile as Frederick holds him. When housekeeper leaves the room to plate the cake, I touch Frederick's hand with mine. His face turns red.

"If William is happy, what does it matter to us that he is not like other boys?" I ask.

"You are right. It does not matter. If we three can be a happy family."

I am surprised by Frederick's words.

He puts the boy on his back on a blanket and takes me in his arms.

"If God Almighty can forgive, so can I," he says.

"Turn the other cheek and all that, you mean?" How Frederick struggles to be a good man! I feel a renewed fondness for my husband. Other men would turn their back on a son such as a William.

"Maybe I believe in second chances," he says grinning.

Frederick stoops to tickle William's belly and the boy begins to giggle.

I wonder how Maman would have treated my son? What I do know is that I don't wish to end up bitter and alone, as she was, fearing all around her, envisioning all as her enemies, at war with her own flesh and blood. The worst might be over between Frederick and me. As I watch him playing with William, down on the carpet beside the boy, I recall that once I had feelings for Frederick, once I must have cared for him. I try to recall the times when he was courting me and when he read poetry to me. In the bright light, I notice how pockmarked his skin is. When he was a child he must have suffered from the pox, although he never speaks of it.

"Were you terribly sick with a childhood illness?" I ask him running my finger down his cheek.

"Cordelia," he says earnestly, "Mater gave birth to another child, after me, one that lived for ..."

"Enough of that, Master Frederick." Bustling into the parlour, Mrs. Bullbrook cuts him off. "Today is a day of celebration, not of mourning," she says.

"Of course, Nanny Bullbrook. How right you are, as always. It is time for levity. Now William look at me and say Papa."

Although William cannot spit out much of a sound, he adores Frederick and me, for all the attention we lavish upon him. All we must do is to enter the nursery, to make him gurgle with joy.

Yet, no matter how hard I wish to believe it could be true, William is not like other babies. His twisted spine and great, bulbous head pin him to his crib so that turning over remains a feat forever beyond him. As the months pass, we begin to accept that he will never crawl or walk or manage any of the other milestones that mark a baby's happy progress. By the time our boy is eighteen months, it is just misery, puke and pain for him. Frederick and I attempt to remain kind to each other, but as William's health deteriorates so does our civility. Our affections, already stretched like pulled dough, turns sour enough to curdle milk. In the end, as William collapses, so does our marriage.

# – 8 –

On the day of our son's funeral, Frederick blames me for the boy's death. Broken as our boy was, he never did fall ill with typhoid, as my husband always feared he would. But Frederick is muttering about the way William tore out of my womb, claiming he was suffocating in there, and that it was his difficult birth which made him deformed, that and the miasma lingering inside my belly.

On the day of the funeral, as I don my black veil, Frederick once again reverts to accusing me of infecting the village of Holsworthy with typhoid, and before that, Shebbear. The funeral is bringing out Frederick's mad side and I have no inclination to try to sooth him. All I can feel is how I long for my boy. His misshapen, waterlogged head might have cast him as a monster to some, but I was his mother and I loved him dearly from the pit of my stomach, as much as I have loved or ever will love another living creature.

Before our boy departed this world, Frederick stood beside Mrs. Bullbrook as she wailed. He was patting her fat, dimpled hand. I was too exhausted to move. All of Frederick's pity was focused on the servant and not on me, his wife.

"Mustn't cry," he said softly to the old woman, keening with grief.

It was me who held William in my arms as he expired, sputtering and choking, unable to take in another gasp of air. There was nothing I could do to help him. Later came the death rattle that continued for an hour, after which he slipped away forever.

"Our beloved boy will ascend to heaven, he will leave behind his earthly woes ..."

I wished to cup my hands about my ears so I could block out Frederick's feeble words meant to comfort the meddling, old woman and not me.

William's faded, brown, stuffed pony lay on the floor beside the crib. Housekeeper covered my son's head with the nursery sheet, the one she was to sew into his shroud.

"If you had obeyed me from the first, instead of threatening to do away with yourself, the boy never would have been born," Frederick said to me, his eyes pierced with pain. "Why bring a child into this world, to make him suffer?" He tore off his spectacles to dry his eyes. "William perished just as all the others have perished at your hand."

I stood frozen to the floor of the nursery. "The boy's death is your fault," I shouted. "How dare you accuse me of harming my own baby?" I dissolved into tears, too fierce to control.

Frederick turned away from me to leave the room. I could hear his heavy footsteps descend the winding staircase to lumber out the manor's entrance. Standing up and peeking out the nursery window, I watched him stride awkwardly along the cobbled path to the lane and on into the churchyard. He had always been a ponderous man, heavy of foot, with ungainly arms swinging out of step with his plodding gait, but on the day of my son's death, the very look of him offended me. If once there was a love between Freddy and me, it was over. All of our sharp disagreements with each other have culminated in this moment when I wished him dead—dead as my poor, innocent boy.

At the graveside, three days later, my husband and I avoid touching each other. I cannot look into his eyes. I have not the stomach for it.

It is a huge procession walking back to the manor. All of Holsworthy has turned out for the Master's boy's funeral, unlike Maman's funeral, when no one appeared. As our entourage moves away from the freshly dug grave, I watch the brown squirrels burrowing for nuts. The pond, which divides the church from the ravine below, is congealing with ribbons of ice. It winds around the brown plant stalks rising above the water like a carnival man's legs on stilts.

The path home takes only minutes and for the first time in eighteen months, I concern myself with something other than William's struggle to live.

Olympia is holding onto Frederick as she picks her way through the ice. "It is we two again, you and I, my son," I hear her remark. "We two against the world."

On this dreadful day, Olympia does not deem to speak to me, not once. I fall behind with my four brothers, each one dressed in his Sunday collars and tie. The pitch-black earth from plowing under the autumn field stains their nails. Their ruddy tear-stained faces are turned against the bitter November wind. Griselda does not bother to attend. Pa, crippled with arthritis, walks with two canes. His mincing steps annoy me.

"It's a blessing your mother never lived to see this day," he mutters. "Her grandson dead and buried before becoming a proper man."

I have absolutely nothing to say to Pa. The platitudes uttered during William's funeral, the false feelings, the utter audacity of the grieving performances of the townsfolk, astound me. During William's short life, not one of these people came to visit him. They were afraid to look at him.

Only my dear brother Albert is a true comfort to me. He takes my hand in his as we approach the manor.

"It is not your fault sister," he assures me. "All the money in the world, all the doctors, all your care, could not keep this boy alive. God knows, you tried your best."

From the corner of my eye, I see Polly trying to keep her boots out of the ice-encrusted muck. Frederick pretends that he does not recognize her.

"She's been a good friend to you," Albert says. "I like her ways. She's strong, like Maman was."

"Yes, like Maman. Albert, do you think Maman could have loved William, the way he was? She wanted everything to be perfect?"

"Wanting everything to be perfect gets folks into trouble."

"Polly is more practical than Maman was. She accepts the hand that fate dealt her. She makes the best of things."

"When I drove Mrs. Turney to the station, long ago, after Maman died, she tried to convince me to stop Pa's plans for your marriage to Wendice. She said she'd seen Wendice in the alleyways of Plymouth ... with the whores. He was on his knees begging them for forgiveness. I suppose she expected me to warn you."

"Why didn't you tell me?"

"Pa wanted you out of the inn, away from the family. He blamed you for the typhoid epidemic, he still does".

"Do you?"

"You are my sister and I love you."

"Answer me, do you blame me?" I want to know the truth about how Albert thinks of me. He is the only one of the Tilleys who I care for, with my attachment to Albert surprisingly strong. There is a winsome quality about Albert. He always appears to be waiting for good news even when there is none. Today his face is entirely bleak.

"Sister, I don't wish to hurt you. Lord knows, you've suffered enough."

But I insist. If there is a grain of truth in Frederick's suspicions, I must be aware of my chances of infecting others. "Tell me the truth," I beg Albert. "I deserve to know the truth."

In my heart, I've always felt that Maman and I were different from the rest and not just in our family, but different from the village of Shebbear and the County. A person knows when there is a gaping hole between yourself and other folk.

By nature, my brother is a kindly man, with a sweet voice and a soft step. At home, at the Devil's Stone Inn, he would steel up behind me without me hearing. It was a game we played. He scaring the living daylights out of me and me, loving the thrill. "You and typhoid are connected in some way, but for the life of me, girl, I can't figure out how."

"And William. Do you think I killed him, too?"

"No, I don't. I've seen other babies like him. It happens in families."

I look over to Frederick. "Not in our family, Albert, but maybe among the Wendices. There is a secret about mother-in-law's dead children, but no one will tell me. Frederick almost revealed it to me once, but Housekeeper stopped him and he hasn't allowed me to question him about it since."

---

"Best forget the past and get on with the future," Albert says, suddenly confident. Soon it will be the turn of the century, 1900. Everything is changing. Progress. The world will be a better place."

Just then Polly catches my eye and brings over a ragged looking couple for me to meet.

"Gerta and Rubin Stollman knew your mother." Polly forces the two to stand directly in front of me. They are as different as chalk and cheese.

The man, who is tall and lanky, with soft, brown eyes that crinkle when he smiles, takes my hand in both of his. He expresses sorrow at my loss, speaking in a heavy Germanic accent. The woman who is tiny, tinier than Maman was, with a hungry bird demeanour, does not outstretch her hand to me. Instead she curtsies as if I am royalty.

"Your mother was a loyal friend to us," the woman declares.

"When you are ready, you must come to visit us. We run the Café Demel on the high street, just in town," the man adds.

"I've never frequented it," I admit.

"We would have recognized you from your red hair ..."

Rubin interrupts his wife. "Never mind about her hair. With your Maman, we debated the merits of Viennese versus Parisian cuisine. She was a great cook."

I had no idea that Maman maintained true friendships in Holsworthy. I knew there were some Jewish people she visited, more like charity calls than social engagements, but I had no idea they operated the local café.

"You wouldn't remember, but years ago your Maman brought you to the synagogue in Exeter. We met you there; you were still quite young. It was years ago," Gerta says.

***

Once we are inside the manor, Mrs. Bullbrook, her eyes swollen with tears, sets out the tea for the mourners. Composed of sliced leg of mutton, roast potatoes, bowls of carrots and turnips, and platters of freshly baked rolls and sweet cakes, it is decent English country fare, the kind of food Maman and I deplored. If I'd been allowed to prepare the meal, it would have been splendid, perfect, but I'm not allowed to enter my own kitchen.

Nevertheless, it is a fine affair. Gentry from across the West Country have gathered to pay their respects to the Wendice family.

---

"Blighted from birth," I overhear one matron, dripping in emeralds, remark to her heavily pregnant daughter. The daughter's yellow hair is caught up in a bun and her cornflower blue eyes are lively. The older woman wears black crepe, surely the frock she reserves for funerals. The bodice of interwoven ruched satin ribbons strains tightly around her stout middle, flattening her bust. If she drops onto all fours, her udders would scrape the floor.

"Thank the Lord that you and Papa would not allow Frederick to court me," the younger woman whispers. This is the daughter's sixth pregnancy. Her five healthy children now populate the County.

The matron's voice is low and so I inch closer, standing behind the massive fern arrangement where I am disguised by its green tendrils. "It runs in their family, sickly children, maimed from birth. Who would marry Frederick, no matter his wealth? It is the Wendice curse."

Around my head, the room is spinning as I clutch the platform holding the ferns. It teeters. If I don't straighten up, the entire arrangement, me, the plants, this façade of simpering grief, will fall apart. I must attempt to put this out of my head, remembering that there is nothing County Devon adores more than a vicious rumour. People here believe that the turning of the stone keeps the Devil at bay. And yet ... what if the dowager is right?

Unsteadily, I gather myself together as I hide behind the ferns, watching the mourners feast. Everyone is famished after the lengthy church service, and while the Vicar hypothesizes on why a child's death is God's divine will, my guests eat with abandon until there is nothing left, nothing except a heel of dried cheese.

Stuffed to their gullets, the crowd disperses and Frederick and I are left alone. Only Olympia remains in the house. I imagine she is conferring with Mrs. Bullbrook on how to get rid of me, now that my son is dead. I collapse on the bench beside the bay window of my morning room, the room I've adored from the first moment I entered the manor. The gas lamps are buzzing softly in the dimming light of the cold November afternoon.

'You were a proper lady today," Freddy assures me.

"I behaved myself, did I? Didn't contaminate the goddamned mourners?"

"Don't blaspheme," he warns.

Moving from the bench to the chair at my writing table, I am irritated that my taffeta mourning dress with its crispy crinolines is needling my thighs. The corset cinched tightly at my waist leaves me gasping for air whenever I attempt to bend. I undo the dress and begin removing the whalebone stays from the corset. Next I pull the crinoline out from under the skirt.

"What on earth are you doing?" Frederick shrieks. "Get dressed." But I do not. I will never do what my husband orders me to do again, if I can help it.

"Olympia said not one word to me today, not at the graveyard, nor at home after the service."

Olympia remained imperious on the day of my boy's funeral. Her lush, grey hair caught in ebony combs under her veil, her eyes alert, perfect pearl tears falling in tidy order down her vellum-white, crinkled complexion. Even her hands, ungloved, are white, with only the liver spots to betray her age.

"Mother is distraught. She is heartbroken."

"And I am not?" As I ask this question, Mother-in-law slips into the room. Most likely she has been eavesdropping outside the door. At this very moment, if I did, indeed, hold the power to kill in my hand, I would poison her.

"So it's finally ended," she says, once safely seated beside her son on the divan. Neither of them can bear to look at me. They are happy to blame me for little William's death, but there is something else in the air. A look of ... could it be relief? Do they imagine that now there's proof I cannot produce a healthy child, they are done with me? Perhaps I will leave them of my own accord. But why should I? After all, I am Frederick's legal wife and the lady of the manor.

"You mean now that the death watch has ended?" I inquire. "I don't recall you spending much time with your grandson."

"If you wish to hurt me, Cordelia, you will." Olympia is exasperated with me. But it will be more bothersome to get rid of me than she supposes. "I suspect you'll desire to return to your home in Shebbear." She speaks without a hint of compassion in her voice.

"You surprise me, Mother-in-law, and here I imagined you would like me to console your son. I am his wife."

Olympia does not bat an eyelash. "I only thought you must miss the Devil's Stone Inn. Your father; your brothers. Albert appears to be a decent chap. Do you celebrate Jewish feasts together?

"Yes, Passover. At the Devil's Stone Inn we eat little Christian babies for dinner on the first night of Passover." I feel that my brain will explode: the sound pounding in my head drives me to cover my ears with my hands.

"Stop immediately!" Frederick squirms, uncomfortable in his seat.

But I will not stop, I will never stop now. "Do you think I am not human, that I cannot hear what others say about you and your dead children, Olympia? They call it the Wendice curse."

I am screaming now, so loudly that Frederick, greatly perturbed by my outburst, stumbles across the room to tightly lock the window. God forbid if one of the mourners is lingering on the terrace and overhears us.

For the first time today, Olympia, herself, appears to be truly disturbed. My accusation has touched a nerve.

"You are thinking you can dispose of me along with your grandson?" I erupt again. I am spinning around the room. "I'm beginning to see that you hatched a plan long ago." I could spit in their faces. "Who else but me, the Jewess' daughter would consent to marry Frederick?"

Olympia, who is quicker than Frederick, raises herself from the divan. She puts both of her hands on my shoulders and her long fingers dig into my flesh. Olympia has never touched me before. She turns me to face her and looks straight into my eyes. The old woman is strangely strong.

"My dear Cordelia, that is not at all what I mean. What a silly girl you are. So dramatic! I am not attempting to dispose of you. What nonsense. You are one of us, the family. I am only encouraging you to spend time with your own people, who are so different from us in every way. Perhaps it would be best for Frederick to recover at the Abbey, with me, at his home. In a few months' time, we shall all be recovered and life will continue on as it was."

"I shall never recover from my boy's death and life shall never continue on as it was. Never." I wrench her fingers from my shoulders and retreat from her menacing grip.

"How you constantly twist my words. I am only attempting to help. Have it your own way, Cordelia. You always do." Olympia fixes her bejewelled lorgnette to her eye and clutches at the newspaper on my escritoire to read the announcement of little William's death in *The Times*. "I arranged for the obituary. Someone in this family must do the proper thing."

I turn away from her sharply to open wide the window that Frederick has locked. Let them overhear us, let all of Holsworthy learn of our secret troubles. Outside on the terrace, I listen for the sound of the wind in the trees, the rustle of the forgotten leaves of autumn. Beside the last remaining potted palm, the one that will be left outdoors to tolerate the winter chill, I see my brother Albert. He is smoking and I discern the lit tip of his cigarette, glowing in the deepening November twilight. His cap is sitting raffishly on his head, a blue and red wool scarf is wrapped around his neck, concealing most of his chin. He has thrown a green hunter's jacket over his mourner's suit. He stays on to protect me although he cannot possibly understand the catastrophe of my life and how impossible it is for me to escape this room or to invite him inside.

## – 9 –

After William's death, Frederick travels continuously, either to the mines on the coast or to the copper works at Morwellham Quay. He cannot bear to be in the same room as I. If before, my husband attempted to save my tainted soul, now I imagine he views me only as a source of contagion. Jack informs me that often he walks the moor at Dartmoor, not far from the prison.

It's said that a man can bury himself in his work, but for me, there is nothing to occupy my mind, nothing but thoughts of William and how terribly he suffered. My mind is littered with strange thoughts. When I close my eyes, swollen from crying, I can see little insect-like creatures, little bugs living under my skin.

I can barely lift my head from the pillow as one day follows the next. Mr. Ealing suggests that I might bear more children, but whenever he claims so, my mood darkens further. Frederick thinks it wise that until I regain my former self, I remain in the sick room, away from the normal hustle and bustle of the manor house. So I am isolated in the room I swore, after William's birth, I would never return to. It is a simple room with a single bedstead, a night table with a pitcher of water and a milk-glass bowl for washing. There are no pictures on the wall and the drapes are thick and grey, dark enough to shut out the light.

Dutifully Mrs. Bullbrook knocks on the sickroom door with a tray for each meal, but invariably I demand she leave it outside. Washing has become a chore too complex to accomplish and although my nightdress is stained with brown tea and sweat, I cannot bring myself to bathe or to fix my hair. My red locks fall in long, greasy streaks down my back so I have hitched them up with a paisley cloth to cover my head. I look like a woman suffering from typhoid fever. The few times Frederick has entered the room, I can tell that he thinks the same.

Jack is the only soul who visits me. His reading and writing have improved greatly since coming to the manor. From the first, I insisted he attend the local Mechanic's Institute. He is a remarkably able scholar. Regularly, he brings me notes from his young teacher alerting me to his abilities. According to the teacher, he will be ready to attend a proper school presently. Miss Staples, that is the teacher's name, wishes to inquire if I would consent to sending him to Bristol for a time, to train in the Classics and in the Sciences. Apparently, he is gifted. But how can I let Jack go? Without him, I would be entirely alone.

Through the haze of my melancholia, I am concerned that Jack, clever lad that he is, reads Miss Staples' notes before I do. The teacher is most likely girlish and pretty, with a clean conscience and an innocent smile.

"There is a school in Bristol where boys like me are taken in on charity," Jack remarks, trying to sound nonchalant. I cannot say that I did not see the Protean shadow of ambition cross his countenance; from the start, the same sense of yearning I once held in my own mind. How did I dare to ignore it?

"Miss Staples could visit the manor to discuss my schooling with you and with Master Wendice," Jack says now looking at me urgently, but I brush him away, his eagerness for a taste of the world making me tired.

After the horses are stabled for the night, Jack reads to me from Wilkie Collins. These mysterious tales calm my nerves and for a short time, I am able to forget about the death of my only child, and that I will have no more babies, no matter how long I survive.

***

Today, I am too weak to even stand so Frederick, who is at home, summons Mr. Ealing to my bedside.

"She barely touches her food," Mrs. Bullbrook says.

"I suggest a change of scenery," Ealing asserts. "Nothing that a small vacation won't cure."

---

He pokes at my ribs, while listening to my chest. Housekeeper stands next to the bed, holding a sheet across my naked torso, as Frederick, red in the face, turns away.

"I can't see travel being in the cards right now," Frederick says. "No, indeed. Until Cordelia can stand on her own two feet, she must remain, here, in the sickroom, where Mrs. Bullbrook can care for her, and ensure she doesn't stir up more trouble."

At that, I begin striking my head against the bedpost until my forehead becomes a bleeding well. Housekeeper, at Frederick's request, ties my hands to the sides of the bed until my self-immolations subside. Ealing prescribes laudanum for my splayed nerves. Now I can sleep more than ever. In the end, what has this disastrous marriage to Wendice come to? I am no more a part of society than Maman was. I can't say that Polly did not warn me, did not offer me another way. Even Albert made an attempt to deter me from marrying Frederick. But the prospect of living outside the bounds of proper society frightened me. Now I am alone, in a dark place, where no one can know me or the deranged thoughts scourging through my brain.

When I sleep I dream of the night of little William's birth and how I have failed at everything. At becoming an established cook, a devoted wife or a protective mother. Surely there must have been something I might have done to save my boy! Anguish and defeat are my constant companions.

# – 10 –

I am fast asleep when Jack brings me the day's post. In it is a letter from Polly, which he reads aloud to me in his clear, husky voice.

"Look, ma'am," he says, trying to rouse me from my lethargy. "It's done up on a typewriter. My teacher talks about these new machines during class. Look! Miss Polly says if her lodging house should fail, she would consider becoming a typist."

At first I refuse to open my eyes, objecting to Polly's optimistic ideas about the future—about typewriters and bicycles and all the other new inventions she waxes poetic about—but as Jack reads, the letter becomes more enticing.

> *'There is a doctor named Murchison. And another one named Budd and the two have been arguing for thirty years about what causes typhoid fever.*
>
> *Dr. Murchison claims that exhalations from sewer drains are the culprits, but last year another medical investigator, Dr. Alessi jumped into the fray. Alessi believes otherwise. He put rats, rabbits and guinea pigs in a box with a perforated bottom communicating directly with a sewer. Then, and this is the most amazing part, he inoculated the rats with a very small quantity of a very slightly contaminated cultivation of typhoid bacillus, but only forced half of the inoculated vermin to exist on sewer air.'*

"Do you understand what this great doctor is attempting to prove, ma'am?" Jack is delighted with his insights.

I reply that I can't possibly see what his experiments have to do with me.

*"Everything,"* Jack exclaims." It means Master Frederick is entirely wrong. Can't you understand that?"

I consider telling Jack to mind his mouth, but I'm too exhausted.

"Those rats that were inoculated with typhoid germs survived. Yes, they became sick, but they did not succumb," he says and then continues to read Polly's letter in a solemn voice.

> *'Dearest Cordelia, you will be overjoyed to learn that the results were rather similar for the guinea pigs and rabbits exposed in the same manner. Every one of the eleven rabbits exposed to sewer gas died, but not one of the inoculated animals, which were not exposed.'*

Jack reads on, sounding out the most difficult words, clever lad that he is. He wishes me up and about, able to speak with his teacher, sponsoring school fees in Bristol and convincing Frederick to do the same. He has grown up quite different from the Tilley brothers. Ambition drives him while they ponder only day-to-day affairs. Jack is stuck on his future. He believes he can overcome his birth. But how can any of us do that?

I can't say that Frederick didn't warn me. "Why do you encourage the lad?" he inquired one evening after I'd pushed Jack out the door to the Mechanic's Institute.

"Why shouldn't he learn to read and write properly?" I countered.

My husband and I were seated at the dinner table, he at one end and me, at the other. From where I sat, I could see Mrs. Bullbrook listening at the partially open door.

"The path of Jack Livesay's life was set at birth." Frederick dug his fork into the lamb. "His place is at the quarry."

"You, the great Reformer." Accidentally I knocked over a glass of the claret, giving Housekeeper her opportunity.

"What do you think?" Frederick asked her. "My wife believes there is merit in sending young Jack to school."

"It will only put ideas in his head and when he fails, his spirit will be broken," she muttered, sopping up my spilt wine.

"Some things are set in life and can't be changed," Frederick said, looking indulgently at Mrs. Bullbrook. "Some things never change." But I ignored them both. It was weeks before my baby was to be born and I was alive with enthusiasm and brimming with hope.

Now, months after William's death, what good are these doctors' findings to me?

"Stop!" I beg Jack. "I do not care."

"But you should, please ma'am," he says. "I can hear the Master and Housekeeper talking above stairs, about you and the typhoid fever."

"I suppose you do."

"Dr. Alessi's experiments might also prove that those who come into contact with the disease might become resistant to it."

R-e-s-i-s-t-a-n-t! Such a good word! Jack is following in my footsteps, catching on to the fancy words that Quality uses.

Jack places his hand over mine and although I know I shouldn't touch him, I reach out to grab his. I am so desperately lonely and he is beautiful. Miss Staples must be fond of him, picking Jack out of the group, choosing him as the one to go for schooling in Bristol.

"Don't you see what this means?" he asks again and before I can answer he explains. "It means you aren't the evil witch they say you are, that you aren't able to murder the innocent with a substance breeding in your insides. It means the reason you aren't sick is because you've become used to them, the typhoid germs, when your own mum died. Remember? You told me about that, nursing her when she was ill. And how you came down with the disease, but you never got really sick or died. Same as the rats in the doctors' experiments."

"It would have been better if I had succumbed."

"I wouldn't have wanted you to die, missus."

"Yes, but my husband claims the miasma, the sewer gases and the rotting garbage, are inside of me."

"Well, I might not know much, but I know that's daft. Here," he says boldly and shoves Polly's letter into my hands.

Jack is quicker than I could have imagined. If Dr. Alessi's experiments are correct, I am not the source of the typhoid epidemics.

Perhaps progress will be made in the new century as doctors come to understand the nature of disease and illness. But I must remember that half of England believes that the stone in the middle of Shebbear was dropped from Satan's pocket and the other half that the twentieth century will bring with it the eradication of all disease and war among men. I am too exhausted to think about any of this and so I turn my back on Jack to find solace in sleep where no one might disturb me. Where nothing might disturb me, not even my dreams.

## – II –

It turns out Jack's ambition knows no bounds. After receiving Polly's letter, he has the audacity to write to my brother, Albert. I watch him do it, the little blighter. Jack assumes I am sleeping, but I am awake with my eyes open just a crack. He sits beside me in the sick room with his books and his chalk and slate, paper and pencils. Where did he find the money to buy the paper? Could Frederick have relented, deciding that the good fortune in Jack's life should be encouraged, or is it Miss

Staples, herself, making exceptions for the beautiful, bright boy in the front row? The one who puts up his hand each time she asks a question. The eager student who keeps all the correct answers stored at the back of his throat.

Jack writes, laboriously, holding the pencil awkwardly in his left hand, his plush lips twisting with the effort as he makes his round letters on the page. Folks in County Devon would swear the devil was in him if they saw him writing with his left hand. When Frederick beckons him, Jack leaves the scribbled letter on the table beside my bed.

*Dear Mr. Albert Tilley,*

*I am sorry to bother you far away at the Devil's Stone Inn. I am sure you are busy with the inn and the farm. Missus has described the Devil's Stone Inn to me many times and I hope some day to see it with my own eyes.*

*For now I must inform you that she is gravely ill. She will not eat and cannot raise her head from the pillow. All colour has drained from her face.*

*Please do not be mad with me, but I do not know who else can help her but you.*

*Your faithful servant,*
*Jack Livesay*

By the next morning, the letter has disappeared.

## – 12 –

I would have given anything to see the expression on Housekeeper's sour puss when the Plymouth Ladies Brigade arrived unannounced at the door of Wendice Manor. Jack tells me that each lady, Polly, Adela and Daphna, demanded entry to the house and to be shown to me directly. Each lady carried an overnight case, a hamper of groceries and a satchel bulging with novels.

It was Jack, of course, who'd tipped off the ladies to my pathetic condition. Once he decides that he is too good for his natural-born station, his ambition is boundless. Unfettered, a living entity, true only to itself. After reading Polly's last letter to me, I reckon that he wrote back to her himself, informing her that the effort of putting pen to paper was too much for me in the maelstrom of my melancholia. In no time, Jack will be everybody's pet.

What a difference the ladies make as soon as they enter the house! The ladies call themselves free thinkers but, in effect, what they are, are free spirits. Not in the organized sense like those toff Fabians and Mrs. Beatrice holier-than-thou Webb, who Frederick is enamoured with, but in the sense that they encourage everyone to speak their minds, even if their thoughts are not commonly considered right and proper.

The three friends barge into the sickroom and emit a collective gasp. Polly sees through me immediately, that I have given up all hope, but when I look at Polly's lovely smile, her pink tulip lips turning up at the corners, perfect little dimples and that tiny nose that wrinkles when she winks at me, trying to disguise her horror, I am overcome with sentiment. I have missed her so!

Immediately Adela holds up the glass to my face. My skin is sallow, my cheeks sunken. Dishevelled hair falls from the kerchief tied around my head. The black circles under my cloudy eyes actually frighten me. I have become the evil witch that my husband accuses me of being.

"Now look at the mess you've made of your beautiful, red hair!" Adela shouts, releasing my greasy locks from the kerchief.

Skinny as I am, without an ounce of meat on my bones, she grabs me from under my arms as Adela straightens me out with my feet touching the floor for the first time in weeks. Jack has been bringing me the night pan. Faithful Jack.

"Put your feet on the ground, Cordelia," Adela orders and to my surprise, I do as I am told.

Polly takes charge. She strips the soiled linen from my sickbed and replaces it with fresh sheets from the hall cupboard. When the tangles in my hair prove too much for her comb, she hauls me right out the door to the porcelain tub, where she instructs me to hang my head under the waterspout. Briskly, she rinses my hair with vinegar before applying the soap.

"I'm not ready," I cry. The soapy water on my skins feels like pins digging into my flesh.

"Nonsense!" Polly forces me to soak my entire body in the hot, bubbling water. Drying me, she sets out a clean nightgown, hair ribbons and lamb's wool slippers. I am then moved to the four-poster bed in the master bedroom. I sink into the luxury of the soft sheets and the satin covered eiderdown. It feels so good to be back in my own bed.

***

That same night as the ladies rescue me from the prison of the sickroom, Polly plucks one plump orange from her hamper and peels it methodically. The orange's sumptuous skin reminds me of Maman's carrot pudding, the one she taught me to prepare with sugar and rum-soaked raisins. I have almost forgotten how to bake, it has been so very long since I have been inside a kitchen, feeling the dough in my hands, whisking an egg sauce bubbling on the stove, or stuffing the duck with sausage and fennel and freshly baked breadcrumbs.

"Eat this, now." Polly will brook no nonsense. After I manage to keep the orange down, there is breaded liver, leeks and dark green spinach. Adela declares that this dinner will put the colour back in my cheeks. And it does, almost immediately.

By next morning, a defeated Mrs. Bullbrook, who cannot muster the stamina to bar the ladies brigade from the kitchen, shoves Jack out the door with a missive, reporting my transgressions to Frederick. After all, since William died I am not allowed visitors and I am not allowed to leave the sickroom, not without permission.

But Jack is jubilant. On the way home, he stops at the village café for berry pies and scones. Daphna, with a twinkle in her eye, pours a droplet of Bristol Cream into my morning tea and I can't say the brew doesn't taste the better for it. After breakfast, Polly and I slowly walk onto the terrace.

"You need to get your strength back," she says, "if you are to depart this deplorable situation with your life. There should be a law!"

Polly assumes I will leave Wendice Manor with the Plymouth Ladies Brigade, but I can hardly think into the next day.

"Why, oh why, did you consent to marry him in the first place?" she asks sadly.

"Don't interrogate me, Polly," I implore her. "We have discussed this before. If you could have witnessed the mean look on Pa's face every time I came within striking distance of him, you would understand why I married Frederick."

Polly stops our exercises and turns to me. She holds my hands in hers. "There is something you need to know about your Pa, but I cannot be the one to tell you. You must visit the Austrian couple, the ones who attended William's funeral. They will be able to answer all your questions about your father."

"What could those two know about Pa?"

"Quite a lot, if you bother to ask."

As usual, Polly confounds me. What could the Stollmans tell me about my father? Surely, Maman relayed to them the same dreadful stories about her removal from Angers that she'd been telling me since childhood. Some would call it airing her dirty laundry in public. What more is there to know?

"You've always assumed I married Frederick because I am a social climber, but that was only part of it." Confessing to Polly is a relief. "I wished to show Pa that I could move up into Quality, even I, the Jewess, could rise higher in society than all of the Tilleys. It gives me great satisfaction to have done so."

"Pity you," she says with an exasperated sigh.

## - 13 -

By the time Frederick returns from the quarries at Tintagel, I am propped up against silk pillows in the master bedroom. Polly is beside me, reading in her perfect honeyed tones from *Middlemarch*. Earlier in the day, the ladies dispensed with the medicines that Mr. Ealing prescribed. In the background, Caruso is singing *"Ich Liebe dich"* which plays over and over again on the gramophone. Each time the song concludes Polly rises from the bed to the turn the crank on the music machine. Music and literature fill my senses, as do the lavender candles she is burning on the nightstand.

When Frederick abruptly intrudes on this small moment of happiness I am experiencing, I turn angry. How dare he? He is wearing a pinstriped waistcoat adorned with a flowered, yellow cravat and he looks as awkward as ever.

"Leave this room immediately," he shouts to Polly, who gracefully gathers her books and recordings without so much as uttering one word.

"She's my friend," I protest.

"I don't give a monkey's toss about your friend."

"Clearly, but there are some who enjoy my company."

Frederick stops shouting and closes his eyes. Oddly enough, he sits down beside me on the eiderdown. His face is changing expression faster than a West Country storm.

"Your friend, yes, I see." Frederick is holding his head in his hands. "You must be terribly lonely," he whispers and without a dram of guile asks, "What have I done to you, dear girl?" From his pocket he removes a silver flask and begins to drink.

"When did you start drinking?" I inquire. "What would Mrs. Beatrice Webb think? Isn't she a teetotaller?"

Frederick swallows again from the flask. "Beatrice swills more champagne than a French can-can girl."

It has been such a long time since Frederick has actually looked me straight in the eye or spoken to me with anything but complete disdain that I am taken aback.

"Why are you here, Frederick?" I demand. "Talking to me in this way."

"We've made a great mess of things, haven't we? Don't suppose we might sort it out."

Just as I prepare myself to rid him from my life, Frederick, as always, makes a bid for my affection, or at the very least, my loyalty.

"We've tried before, Freddy, and it never works. Something always goes wrong, something terrible and spiteful."

"It's the typhoid inside of you, Cordelia. I was only trying to protect you, you and the boy."

What he will never understand is that contagion is our natural condition. When one human being touches another, we change, for good or evil. In Frederick's perfect world, everyone would be isolated, dark planets circling a disinterested sun.

I have learned the hard way to turn my heart to stone each time this man comes near me. "There are many theories, new ideas that would absolve me and prove you wrong. You have always been so eager to apportion blame to me. What if I'm innocent? In my entire life, I've never hurt a fly."

"Don't be disingenuous, Cordelia."

My husband rises from the bed to pace the room. At this very moment I see clearly the folly of our marriage: Frederick, in his lust for me, believed he could cool the fires of his desire by turning me into his charity case, his receptacle for good deeds. He needs me to be evil. My transgressions, however imaginary, comfort him.

"When we married, I believed I could protect you from the wrath of the County. Sooner or later, people were sure to discover it was you infecting their lives. I set for myself a superhuman task, I will admit to that, but once on course, I could not cut out or give up on you. That would not be worthy of the Wendice name or my status as a gentleman."

"No matter what your superhuman task did to me, your wife?"

Frederick clasps his hands together in prayer. "If I could save you, I would do anything."

I rise from the bed to pull my dressing gown about me. "I am not one of your charity cases."

Frederick returns to recline on the bed. "No, I suppose you are not. But if I could make you love me, I believed we could defeat the infection growing inside you, spreading out like an evil flower."

"You must stop saying such things."

"If only you'd loved me."

"I have loved you, Frederick. Perhaps not as much as I should, but in my way, I have tried to be a caring wife to you. Recall when I was heavy with child, remember how we were together?"

"It seems like a century ago, before the boy was born and all went wrong. How unfortunate, but now my zeal to do good has all but disappeared. If I had my way I would lock myself into the prison at Dartmoor to spend the remainder of my days in penitence for aiding and abetting what you have done."

---

"What I have done!" I shriek. In a sudden rush, I recall the words of the dowager at my boy's funeral. "It is the Wendice curse," she said in her doughy voice, filled with superstitious dread. I tried to push it out of my mind after William's funeral, but no longer shall I allow myself to bury this truth deep inside me, so deep that it is the real infection destroying my soul. The truth of the matter is what I must permit myself to accept. The truth is pounding inside my head until I believe it will explode! I throw a goblet at Frederick. My rage is uncontrollable. When the glass shatters against his cheek, I begin to pummel his chest. If I could murder Frederick, I would, at this very moment.

The need for revenge is engulfing me.

"William was born broken and it wasn't the typhoid that twisted his spine and swelled his head until he looked like he would burst. It wasn't me, it was you!" I step back and point my finger at his incredulous face. "You had a younger brother who died. And there were other children, too. I've heard you speaking of this with Housekeeper. Your brother had the same disease as our William. You've known all along. It is the real reason you married me: if a child was born with the swelling sickness you could put the blame on me. Recall how Olympia reacted after the funeral. She knew I was telling the truth."

Frederick begins to weep, but I care not a fig for his humiliation. The side of his face is dripping in blood. Let him bleed. Bleed to death.

"You planned it from the beginning, you and your mother." My voice is low and in control now. "As soon as the epidemic in Shebbear broke out and I did not die of typhoid, while others around me did, you intended for me to be your scapegoat. Who better than a Jewess, the proverbial poisoner of wells, the witch who spreads typhoid while remaining healthy herself? You counted on the worst superstitions of the County, the backwardness and intolerance of country folk who were certain to believe your falsehoods. And you counted on your own kind to remain silent."

Frederick shakes his head wildly, denying everything. He is pretending that I am mad and he is the perfect English gentleman, caught by circumstances entirely beyond his control.

"No other woman would marry you. Your sort knows about the curse; the toffs don't speak of it openly, not in polite company. But one old, nattering matron did at William's funeral. I overheard her. You must realize that the gentry are aware that you and your mother carry this curse in your blood. That's why you chose me. If our child was born with a twisted spine, you could pin the blame on me. No wonder Olympia allowed our marriage. She was involved in this deceit from the beginning. You both knew if I bore you a child, he could be dreadfully deformed. You both knew it and yet you ..."

Instantly as soon as the words escape from my mouth, I feel an icy resolve descend on me. "Things will be different now, Frederick. I am setting down new rules and unless you wish the entire County to know about your nights in Plymouth with your whores and the disease your family carries, you will abide by them. I am done forever taking the blame for the Wendices." I have said enough.

This is the moment my marriage ends. I fully comprehend how terribly the Wendices have used me: unforgivably so. There will be no more chances for Frederick.

I look outside into the moonlit night and see the first shoots of spring narcissus bursting through the black earth. There are tiny, green buds on the elm trees beside the house. It is the same delicate world, the same bucolic English countryside as it was before I became melancholic; but I am a different person, no longer hopeful or accepting. Maman was wrong; I could never have become a Wendice, no matter how hard I tried. Frederick did not marry me because I was beautiful or because he loved me. He dissembled. If I could tell her now that he, not she, plotted our marriage, before she even considered it, would she sanction what I am about to do next? "Maman, he took me because he needed someone to blame in the case that his child was born malformed," I whisper inside my head. His lust for me, his so-called desire to save me, camouflaged a darker secret. I am entirely vindicated. William did not die because of me!

At last, I have awoken from my long sleep to two choices: to end my life or to continue on in a different way, one that experience has taught me will be more suited to my true station. Although I was the best mother I knew how to be and I certainly had nothing to do with William's illness, no one, not even Frederick, is able to explain the rash of typhoid deaths of those who ate at my table in Shebbear.

---

I cannot catch my breath. My chest is rising and falling uncontrollably. Indeed, what if I could kill by cooking? What if in some strange way and for all the wrong reasons, Frederick is onto something. What if the doctors' injections of typhoid germs into the rats are the key to the puzzle of infection? It is not in my purview to analyze the findings of these medical men and their fancy experiments but, somehow these high and mighty masters of Science have neglected to insert a revealing piece of the puzzle, and it might be me. Otherwise, why did the valet Jeremiah, who supped at my table at the Devil's Stone Inn so many years ago, die, even if it was by accident? And so many others neatly catalogued in Frederick's notebook. While I remain in perfect health. Why was Maman felled by the disease while I survived? As in my worst fantasies, I could be the murderess. The miasma. What if I can infect and kill with a flick of my cook's finger. I carry typhoid, but it doesn't harm me, only others.

I shall test the hypothesis. Discover, once and for all, if I am a person with the power to poison, to maim and to kill. Not by tainting the tea and scones with arsenic, as any frantic murderess would do, but by spreading what's inside me to the insides of others. By eating, they shall make themselves sick. *Naturally*, you could say. I could become the purveyor of a living experiment with people standing in for rats or guinea pigs or rabbits. Why shouldn't I use my natural-born power, if that is what it is? Mind, I'd never wish to harm the innocent, whoever they might be. No, I shall concentrate on those who deserve to die, or at the very least, to fall dreadfully ill. Who better to launch my experiment with than Olympia and Frederick Wendice standing in for rats?

It sounds harsh, don't I know it, but with William dead, and the Wendices making use of me unconscionably, all feeling of compassion has disappeared from my soul. I might have loved Polly once, but that was a long time ago, so long ago, it feels like another lifetime, before my son died, and before tonight, when I finally accept that Frederick tricked me into believing it was all my fault. Why should anyone be content, when I shall never have a moment's peace again? Why should the guilty not suffer at my hand?

Again I find myself in the dream. I am drawn across the cobblestones of the village by a raging horse. It is blackest night and the spectators swing green lanterns to observe me. The flesh is ripped from my bones as they cheer my demise. The difference is that this time I fight back. Screech and claw against the leather ties that bind me to the great bay's saddle.

Why shouldn't I despise them and seek my revenge on this place? So many knew about why Frederick proposed marriage to me. It would have only taken one person to speak out, to tell me the truth about the blighted family. After I was ensconced in the manor, it would have taken only one voice to warn me about the danger of producing a child with this man. But no one spoke out. Nanny Bullbrook, the old crone, she knew it all, but she kept her secret secure. No one dared tell me the truth and now I have lain in bed for many months, first burning with fever and then with a remorse no amount of repentance could quell. Until now, I blamed myself for my boy's illness and death while not one soul from Holsworthy bothered to rescue me, to tell me the truth. Surely Ealing knew. And how many of the gentry, too hidebound or stupid to speak up? I also imagine that some observers saw the situation clearly from the first, watching and waiting to see what might befall me or any child that I might bring into this world. How the toffs must have laughed at me: the spectacle of the common Jewess rising above her station. The lady of the manor, indeed!

It is like committing suicide, deciding to become a murderess. And like suicide, there is no turning back. The only questions are whether I shall be successful or not and if I happen to hit my mark, will I get away with it?

Of course, while I plot my next move, Frederick in his ponderous, affected manner, continues stammering, spouting one ridiculous platitude after the other. I loathe him. He, with his yellow cravat and his waistcoat stretched over his protruding belly, is at the root of my despair. He is sweating profusely and pouring the last of the whiskey down his gullet.

"For all those years, I reckoned if we waited until the end of your monthlies, when you were cleanest, we could avoid infecting the fruit of our loins." He looks up at me, longingly. "You must understand, dearest, that I would have bedded you each and every night, if it were safe. My precautions were only meant ... you are still so very lovely."

---

The lascivious expression on his face would normally upend me, but I reside in another land now, far beyond Wendice's lame excuses or his conjugal predilections.

"You are a fraud and a dissembler," I say bluntly. "If you'd been truthful and told me about your malformed siblings and your fear of this swelling disease, we would have found a way ... But you preferred to create a witch-like creature, one who you could desire and fear in equal portions. You found me tucked away in the darkest corner of England where superstition reigns. Where not only the common folk, but also the clergy and gentry believe in ghosts and Satan's direct hand in the daily affairs of mankind. You surmised that Pa would agree to the marriage straightaway. Even a fool could see he blamed me for the fever and if he didn't do it wholeheartedly at first, you could always convince him, as you surely did. You coaxed him into taking me to Morwellham Quay. You wanted to frighten him and me. Did you bribe him, Frederick? Offer him money to take me off his hands?"

After many minutes of sitting on the bed silently, Frederick finally says, "If only the boy had lived. None of this would have come out. I only wished for a healthy child, one who could walk straight like other boys, who could talk, smell, taste. A boy who would realize how much I loved him."

"William knew how much you loved him. He knew everything."

Frederick sits limply and weeps.

Although I cannot bring myself to touch him, I do say, "You must see that it is over between us. It is too far gone to repair."

He looks up at me imploringly, his eyes bloodshot from tears and drink. "I beseech you to stay on at the manor. We will confine ourselves to separate rooms. I won't lay a hand on you. I give you my word as a gentleman."

As always, Frederick has got it all wrong. He is only concerned about how it will look if I were to leave him. After some consideration, it will dawn on him that it would be preferable for him if I left or died. Then he might be able to lure another unknowing woman to the manor. Why not try to impregnate a new wife, younger and more compliant? One without family or friends. Certainly Olympia and Mrs. Bullbrook would be game to have Frederick try again.

Quickly, however, I have caught a glimmer of opportunity through this darkness.

My own comet bursting across the sky. "I might be persuaded to stay, but I must have the run of the house, to cook to my heart's content, to roam the village and countryside at whim and without you or Mrs. Bullbrook."

It is, indeed, my opportunity to put my experiment to work, to test it on humans rather than on rats, as the good doctors of science conscientiously do.

"How can you ask this of me?" he says, bewildered. "To risk everything."

"These are my terms," I repeat.

"I implore you," he begs. "You may come and go as you please, but the danger in allowing you to cook is too great."

I present Frederick with my most angelic face. "But you must allow me to cook in my own home. If you agree, I shall stay on as your wife. If not, I shall leave tonight."

"Where will you go?" Frederick asks earnestly.

"That is my business. What I wish from you is your permission to hold a grand dinner party, to invite your friends and mine, to open the house to the best people. Show the world that we, as a couple, have weathered the storm."

Frederick stammers while pacing around the room. "Do you agree to take every sanitary precaution I prescribe? You must agree to wear rubber gloves, a surgical mask, you must wash your hands whenever you touch garbage or refuse. You must promise me or I will not allow you to enter the kitchen. That is my final word."

"I promise. I shall be as cautious as a surgeon carving a fresh cadaver. Whatever you wish, Frederick, I will do."

Frederick looks at me slyly. For a moment, he is weighing the odds, calculating how far I might go. He decides to chance it with me, as he has done so many times before.

Frederick gives me an odd look, but strangely enough, he extends his clammy hand to me and we shake to seal the deal. As if a handshake might overturn all the wrong he has inflicted upon me.

It is high time for me to pay Frederick back.

Olympia tried to convince me to give her a grandchild. She was in on this scheme from the very start and she must pay the consequences for her duplicity. Who else but the Devil's Stone Inn's daughter, the outcast, would be foolish enough to marry into a family such as this?

The daughters of the landed gentry of County Devon would have known better. Tales of Olympia's tainted children would have circulated among their mothers, as they did to the one at William's funeral. But not to my mother; no one spoke to my mother.

For so many years, I have acquiesced to each of Frederick's demands, no matter how humiliating and demeaning. Now I can see that Frederick must own up to what he has done to me. I must devise a plan to make him and his mother suffer for their deeds. From today, I will inhabit the four-poster bed and he will sleep on the divan in his study.

***

I will begin to make preparations for my plans for a grand dinner party, the celebration to end all celebrations, but I will bide my time. First I will produce a series of scrupulously prepared meals. I will follow Frederick's direction to the letter. I will clean myself, as he wishes me to be clean. I will cook as he wishes me to cook. I will feed him as he wishes to be fed.

Then, one meal, my way.

If illness befalls, I know I am the murderer he has always thought me to be and he and Olympia will suffer the fate they deserve. If all should survive, then I will have proved that I am unblemished and I will remind him every living day that his family's lies and secrets killed our son and that those lies and secrets are at my disposal. Either way, I will finally have the power to be free to live as I wish to live.

I call for Polly, who no doubt, has been listening on the other side of the door. I hear Frederick, excusing himself to her, as he leaves the upstairs hall.

"I suppose you overheard every word?

"Every word," she affirms. "I remained at your door in case Wendice became violent." In jest, she pulls an imaginary sword from her belt and begins to shake it in the air. "Villain."

"Frederick is concerned that I will tattle to his toff friends, inform them that his brother was a crooked back with the same bulbous head as our William. He would no longer be able to blame me for his misfortunes," I confide to Polly.

"Leave the blighter straightaway and come away with me."

"I shall stay until I can make a proper farewell."

"As you wish," Polly says, lowering her eyes and pulling out her copy of *Middlemarch*. She is not assuaged.

"It is remarkable to me that a nation of cold hearts has written such an astonishingly wonderful literature," I remark.

"The English only show their true emotions in fiction or on the stage," she replies unhappily. And with that Polly begins to read exactly where she left off.

## – 14 –

Before entering the dining room, I hear the Plymouth Ladies Brigade conversing noisily at the breakfast table. The smell of fatty bacon, buttered toast and smoked kippers invades the hall, but my friends bring their own variety of fresh air to this stuffy, old house.

"You would not believe what I found in an old journal in Wendice's library," declares Polly.

"Do tell." Adela and Daphna speak in unison.

Polly bites into a scone slathered in Devon cream and strawberry jam before launching into her rant: "Dr. Maudsley fears that educated women can turn into men if they do not exercise their organs."

At this, Adela rushes from her seat to Polly, planting a rough kiss on her neck. Polly pretends to swoon, but manages to continue, "When a woman is notorious for her mind, claims Dr. Maudsley, she is generally frightfully ugly, and it is certain that great fecundity of the brain in woman usually companies sterility."

"Wouldn't our lodgers love to hear that? Getting properly educated as a sure fire method of contraception. Why would Wendice keep such nonsense?" Adela clutches at her sides laughing as I approach the dining hall.

"Come sit down, dear," she says. "We apologize if we disturbed you."

---

"Not at all. It is refreshing to hear new voices in this house, to hear laughter." Suddenly, I do need to sit down. Although I am able to descend the stairs cautiously, I remain weak as a kitten.

"Adela, Daphna, a word with Cordelia, if you please," Polly says with a look of grave concern crossing her face.

Adela and Daphna do not appear surprised by Polly's request.

The morning sun, gentle as it is, breaks through the lace curtains in shards of dappled light. Green buds of climbing wisteria are circling the great floor to ceiling iron-latticed windows of the dining room and a swallow perched on a slim branch twitters a delicate song. It is spring.

"Have you made up your mind? Will you leave Wendice?" she inquires before I have had a chance to take a single sip of my tea. "I can't just abandon you here."

Where would living with Polly put me? In the end, would it be any different from residing with Frederick, attempting to placate him, pretending to be someone I will never be. Would it offer me the freedom that I crave?

"In good time, I will leave him, but for now I have set my terms for remaining here as his wife and he has agreed to them. I have my reasons for staying and I'm planning a party. A beautiful dinner party to display the skill he has demanded I keep hidden for so long."

"Yes, well, the dinner party. I've been thinking about that. Why bother staying, to impress Frederick's friends? I don't understand you!"

I dare not look up from my plate of eggs and kippers. Polly reads me like a book.

"You mustn't succumb to your basest notions no matter what a brute he is," she cautions. "What the Wendices inflicted upon you is unforgiveable. You can flee this place with all its dreadful memories and begin afresh. You owe Frederick nothing."

"Nothing, in a matter of speaking."

"You must understand that it is impossible to undo the wrongs that were done to you?"

"Impossible."

"We have so often come to the aid of women in circumstances similar to yours," she pleads. Rational, kind-hearted Polly. But it is too late for that. There are no similar circumstances.

"Whatever I can do to help you, I will do. Anything."

How could she possibly understand where my thoughts are taking me? I am wearing a Japanese, flowered kimono and it is wide open at the neck to display my gown of French cambric, gauzy and revealing. Without giving me time to protest, Polly stands behind me, placing her fingers deep inside the folds of the kimono. She cups my breasts in her hands.

Although Polly is a woman of the world and I am considered the naïve country mouse, I cannot imagine that my intentions would be safe with her. After all, betrayal is all that I have known and no one, not even Polly, is immune from betraying me.

"You must give me time," I assert, removing her hands from my chest and moving toward the door.

Slowly I climb the stairs to my bedroom. Polly regains her composure and announces that she will hike to the high street for her daily constitutional.

I am alone to plot my course.

***

Safely settled in my bed, for a fleeting moment my heart softens to consider Polly's invitation when Daphna knocks sharply on my door.

"I thought you'd appreciate seeing these," she says.

She drops an old edition of *The Telegraph* onto my lap. "Dreyfus Convicted of High Treason," the headline reads. The paper is dated 1894 when I was too absorbed with my boy to take notice.

"What does this have to do with me?" I ask.

"Dreyfus was convicted for offering up French military secrets to the German Embassy. He was sentenced to life imprisonment on Devil's Island," Daphna informs me. "You believe," Daphna blurts out, "if you impersonate them, you will become one of them, but that will never happen." Daphna has never had much time for me. "No matter how hard you try, you will never be good enough. Poor Dreyfus. The Jew, who tried too hard, who overcame his reach, and must now be punished. He will perish on Devil's Island."

I motion for Daphna to sit upon the bed, but she declines.

"I must catch the train if I am to reach Plymouth before sundown. Today is Friday, the eve of the Sabbath, if you have forgotten."

Adela will keep her company on the journey while Polly elects to remain at the manor.

After she departs, I cannot help but think about Dreyfus. Maman believed life might be different for Jews in England; but it is not. The fear and suspicion is just less vocal, concealed by society's good manners.

For so very long, I have been hiding my Jewishness. Maman's scheme to have me married to Wendice and safely wrapped inside the warm embrace of English society has turned into a farce. As for Polly, she imagines she wants me with her, but she has no idea what ill will would rain down on her head if I were to share her life in Plymouth. She has no idea who I am inside, what it is like to dissimulate your Jewishness in a world that loathes Jews. I am both victim and villain, the hated and the hater. Just as Frederick transformed from ardent suitor to callous incarcerator, Polly would slowly come to loathe the sight of me, the touch and smell of me. After all, I am the ultimate coward, afraid to present myself as I truly am.

I cannot bear the thought of Polly turning against me, which she will surely do if she watches her beloved companion become a murderess. How could Polly possibly understand that I am only matching Frederick's expectations, fulfilling his worst fears about me? Polly must become a stranger to me. It is the only way now that I have embraced my fate.

***

"Cordelia, I went to see the Stollmans this morning," Polly says bounding into my room after her constitutional. She is ever beautiful, her complexion in high colour, her hair pouring down her shapely back in perfect, black ringlets.

"They are looking for sympathetic company, just as you are."

Oddly enough the Stollmans do not disguise their religion although they operate the café on Holsworthy's high street. Certainly they are subject to the vilest notions about our race.

"Why don't you visit them? They have fond memories of your Maman. Apparently they accompanied you to a Hebrew temple of worship when you were a child." Polly is trying desperately to raise my spirits, to untangle me from the mess I am in.

"I don't recall," I tell Polly, but in fact, I do. The synagogue was an enormous red-brick structure and we climbed a multitude of stone steps to enter the sanctuary. Inside the heavily-bearded rabbi and the cantor were standing before the cloth-covered lectern upon an elevated platform. Behind them was the Ark holding the Hebrew Bible, the Scrolls of the Torah. Above them was a hanging lantern holding an oil flame. Maman called it the eternal light and said it was never allowed to burn out. The ardent sound of the Hebrew incantations and the swaying movements of the men dressed in white prayer shawls enthralled me.

We climbed the steep wooden steps to the balcony where the women sat. Maman, Gerta Stollman and I found three seats in the front row of the balcony. The ritual of the Sabbath service was dazzling. Although I was only a girl, I felt uplifted, as if I were floating high above the balcony. If only for a short time, I was transported, looking down upon the worshippers swaying in the dimly-lit sanctuary and across to the beams of light streaming through the stained glass windows. I squinted, so the light meeting my eyes would be splintered into thousands of gloriously hued shards. It was a moment that would never leave me.

Before the prayers concluded, I saw Maman press two fingers to her pink lips. She had removed her white, silk gloves. A red-haired man was looking up at her from the sanctuary floor, smiling sweetly. He placed his hand on his heart as Maman held her hand to her mouth. Their small gestures were redolent with meaning. I had never seen Maman so radiant.

Of course, Maman never returned to the synagogue in Exeter, nor did I. The trip from Shebbear was arduous. Pa complained for weeks afterward that he couldn't do without Maman in the kitchen. Before long, she gave up and we reverted to our secret prayers, apart from the community of worshippers, and for me, apart from the sight of God.

Polly interrupts my reverie. "You do remember, don't you?"

"Yes, I do remember something."

***

In the interest of restoring my health, Polly suggests we gather on the lawn for tea. "You require fresh air and sun," she advises. Polly, too, has taken a shine to Jack. He is invited to join us after he sets out the table and lawn chairs. I give Mrs. Bullbrook orders to serve our afternoon repast on the front garden.

"Master Wendice has given me strict instructions that you are to remain indoors," Housekeeper answers belligerently. "He's off to the slate pits again. Works hard does our boy."

It is Polly who dares to disagree with her. "Mrs. Bullbrook, your mistress is recuperating from a dire illness and she requires fresh air and healthy food. Do you wish to see her wither away to nothing?"

Housekeeper stamps away on her thick legs, mumbling that tea will be served on the lawn, as requested. "Master Wendice will hear about this," I hear her repeating to herself. Without stockings, I see the bumpy blue veins standing out on her table legs. On the way, she bumps into Jack who is running out with another chair. Housekeeper is growing more close-sighted by the day.

Outside the thick walls of the manor house, the weather is fine. The sun is hot. The blooms of white hydrangeas are flowering against the sun-drenched walls of the stable. Jack has set our table under an arbour of vines. Trellises of unfolding pink climbing roses surround our little tea circle. Adela has departed with Daphna for the train for Plymouth so Polly, Jack and I sit together peacefully. For a short moment, I am tranquil.

But as Polly is about to pour the tea, there is a flurry of activity from the road. I make out a man fast approaching on a tall horse and as he moves into focus, I see that it is my brother, Albert. From a distance, he is unmistakable: Maman's son, the dark Levantine. When my brother dismounts, he explains that once he received Jack's missive, he set out for Holsworthy as soon as he was able.

Albert gathers me in his arms. From the expression on his face, I realize that my appearance alarms him. "Sister, my sister," he repeats. "Why did you not write to me earlier?"

Polly explains that I have been indisposed, but that I am now on the mend.

"Thank the Lord for Jack, here, that the lad took matters into his own hands."

"Such a bright boy," I add. "A prodigy."

---

Albert puts his hand on Jack's shoulder and Jack beams. "He tells me that you are being held prisoner in your own home."

The sun moves to the west, as the sky turns from pink to purple. Grey clouds wisp across the heavens. We four sit in this circle of friends, talking for hours. There is so much to say. I attempt to explain my illness to Albert. Polly and Albert rekindle their friendship sealed long ago at the Devil's Stone Inn, before I was married. From the look on their faces, they are enchanted to be in one another's company once again. Jack is quiet, only interjecting when he offers to bring a blanket to warm me, as the air turns chilly.

"Wendice is a brute," Polly states. None of us bothers to disagree.

"We warned her, can't say that we didn't." Albert's voice is kind rather than accusatory.

Finally Jack, eager to help, pipes in. "I hear things, below stairs. Housekeeper talking to whoever comes to the door, the postman, the chimney sweep, the gardener. She blames my mistress for everything, for young William's death."

Albert's face turns red. "How can I assist you, Cordelia? Shall I speak to Wendice?" Albert clenches his right hand in a fist.

"It won't help, brother." It is much too late for Albert's intervention. Albert's or anyone else's.

Albert unfurls his hand and brings my fingers to his mouth. By nature, Albert is an affectionate soul. Unlike Maman and me, who find love exhausting.

And yet, as we sit in the failing light, I catch a fleeting glimpse of another world. There are no barriers between the four of us. We touch each other gingerly on the hand, or on the arm. We edge closer and closer to each other as the night draws near. We are fireflies fluttering on the lawn. Our conversation is meaningful, laden with understanding. We four are of one heart, one mind. At least for tonight, I am inside the circle. Is this what life is like for some people, inside, rather than always looking in, from afar? I wonder if Jack feels the same?

"I beg you, all of you, do not try to take me away," I say finally, when I hear that Albert wishes for me to accompany Polly to Plymouth. To quit this place forever. He offers to hire on Jack as a hand at the Devil's Stone Inn. Clever Jack, always winning over those who matter.

"Do not attempt to save me. It is not what I wish," I say truthfully. "You must trust me and honour my request to be left alone for a time."

It is my hope that none of them could possibly imagine what I have in mind.

***

With the help of my circle and my newfound resolve, I regain my strength after some time. To finally understand how I have been used by the Wendices and to know I am not responsible for the death of my beloved William has lightened my heart and lifted a heavy burden. To pass the time as I recover, I occasionally drift into the kitchen, despite the angry glares from Mrs. Bullbrook, and create with my scrubbed and gloved hands, meals reminiscent of those Frederick once devoured with such gusto at The Devil's Stone Inn. He consumed the first of these with the look of a condemned man, but as he has not displayed the slightest of symptoms, he now indulges without reservation. Jack tells me he has even seen Frederick write to Olympia of the magnificent meals he now consumes at the manor, although he has spoken not a word to me about my cooking. No matter the circumstances, he will always believe my passion for the kitchen to be beneath my station as the lady of Wendice Manor. Still, it is as though he believes that things may be permanently mending between us. Having agreed to my terms does he think I am now resigned to become the dutiful wife? I cannot know the disposition of his mind as we barely speak to one another, but I realize this is my moment and I send out my invitations for the dinner party. The notes, on blue embossed stationery, will arrive in the post for my guests a full two months before the party. No one need decline or pretend previous commitments. The last Friday in August will be my night. Nothing shall deter me now.

## – 15 –

In my reinvigorated state, I have decided to visit the Stollmans at the Café Demel in Holsworthy. If Polly is correct, they are privy to information about my Pa and it will be useful for me to learn of it before I depart Holsworthy. Perhaps they know of the red-haired worshipper with his hand to his heart.

The Café stands at the rounded corner of the town square. There is a large plate glass window, which displays cakes, tortes, buns, scones and breads of all sorts. Inside are nine little tables, each with a green-checkered cloth, a vase of daffodils and a menu. During the day, the Café is busy so I time my arrival for just before closing time.

Rubin greets me warmly. "Polly informed us you were ill," he says in his heavily accented English.

"Thank you, I'm much better now."

"She looks fine to me," Gerta says to her husband.

Rubin invites me to join them for coffee. The thick, black liquid is mixed with whipped cream and shards of chocolate are sprinkled on top. We sit and talk of village affairs. Everything inside the Café is the complete opposite of everything outside the shop. The air is warm and aromatic. Along with the English scones and jam cakes, the Stollmans also bake rye and pumpernickel bread. Apple struedel with almonds and honey, rugelach and poppy seed cakes adorn the shelves lining the wall behind the counter. The pastry is splendid. Afterward Greta offers me a cigarette, which I accept.

"I understand that you knew my mother quite well," I finally say, getting down to business.

"We knew her well ... very well," Gerta responds, not meeting my eyes.

"And my father?" I ask.

Gerta and Rubin look at each other at the same time and say, "No, not your father."

"But Polly told me you knew my father ..."

"Your Maman made us promise that we would never tell anyone, not even you," Gerta says.

"Tell me what?"

"Tell you about your father."

"I'm not certain there is much to tell. You needn't be concerned about what Maman disclosed. I'd overheard them arguing since I can first remember. It was not a love match. Of that I am fully aware."

"Well, yes, your Maman was not satisfied with her husband," Gerta adds caustically.

---

"And that's it?" I ask once again.

Rubin clears his throat. "Not quite, *shayna maidele*," he says, reaching out to touch my hair.

Whenever Maman had something important to relay to me, she also spoke in Yiddish. I understand the language a little, although Maman discouraged me from speaking it.

"Your father is not who you think he is!" Rubin exclaims after a long pause.

"You know how your mother felt about Thomas Tilley," Gerta adds. "It should not come as a complete surprise to you that for a short time she found her true love elsewhere."

"What are you telling me?"

In the end, it is Gerta who is willing to reveal the truth. "Your mother, she met a man before you were born. They fell in love. He was Jewish, a pedlar, who hawked his wares from his cart and horse along country roads. He was married, as of course, was she."

"A pedlar!"

"You need not be alarmed," Rubin says gently. "He is actually a learned man, from the East, a small village on the Russian border with Poland. His Hebrew is exquisite. He attended *Cheder* in the *shtetl* Nesvicz. Unfortunate circumstances brought him to England where the only way he was able to put bread on the table was to be a rag and bones man. *Farshteyn*?"

"My mother took a lover."

"Yes. You saw him once. He was at the Sabbath service at our synagogue. It was a long time ago. You were only a child, how could you possibly remember?" Rubin asks in a kindly fashion.

"But I do recall. The man with the red hair. The one with his hand over his heart staring up at Maman in the balcony."

"Yes, him."

"My real father."

Gerta and Rubin sit with their hands in their lap.

"We weren't going to tell you, but Rubin feels you deserve to know, after what you've been through."

"Thank you," I say. "Thomas Tilley is not my father."

"No."

"Pa, does he know?"

Gerta speaks before Rubin has a chance to open his mouth. "I do not believe so."

"Does my father, my real father know?"

This time Rubin speaks first. "He knows, but Madeleine made him promise that he would never reveal this fact to you. She was afraid for you, what Tilley would do if he found out, what he would do to both of you."

"I understand." Could it be possible that Pa disliked me because he did know about the red-haired man?

Before I depart, the Stollmans invite me to visit often, everyday if I wish. They claim it is to keep them company, to stop them from bickering with each other, Rubin says good-naturedly. But I know differently. They feel sorry for me. I am not accustomed to being in the company of strangers, but it is a tantalizing offer, one that calls to me. Being with my own people, it's difficult to imagine what that could be like. I have been so alone for so long. So isolated.

In the middle of the next night I turn up at the Café Demel. Rubin begins his baking in the early morning hours so his bread and cakes will be ready for the first morning trade. He and Gerta are surprised to see me, but I explain how interested I am in cooking and how, after Maman died, I wished to be the cook at The Devil's Stone Inn. Rubin asks me why I didn't stay on in Shebbear and I can only say that Pa wouldn't have me. He lowers his head and mutters to himself. Maman surely would have told him about Pa and his rough ways.

There is much to do, and before long Rubin, who baked at the Café Demel in Vienna, is teaching me how to make a Sachertorte. "I'm only too happy to have some company," he says again to save me any embarrassment. He reminisces about the famous coffee houses along the *Ringestrasse* and how the artists and writers sat in the cafés for hours at a time, arguing about politics and aesthetics.

In the meantime, I observe Rubin carefully. He is an expert baker and I dream of the day, when I, too, shall be able to get my fingers submerged in dough, to knead and stretch and to primp various floury mixtures into copper baking pans. I am thinking about what I shall bake for my dinner party.

---

I become a regular visitor to the Café Demel. Jack often walks with me to the Stollmans in the middle of the night. He claims he fears for my safety, a woman alone, in the town in the dark. He is the only one who knows of my nightly excursions since I'm careful to leave the Café Demel before the morning clients arrive at the shop.

When Gerta rises at four-thirty, she also shows me how to grind the fish for gefilte fish, and how to make the round matzoh balls for chicken soup, in case I wish to celebrate the Sabbath. I am always careful not to touch the ingredients.

Before long, I also find myself embroiled in their early morning arguments. Rubin and Gerta often discuss the Dreyfus affair.

"Your Maman predicted that it would happen this way," Gerta says, "that the Jews of Europe would drown in their complacency." She is staring up to the heavens and waving her spindly arms for what I believe to be Maman's approval, or is it God's? When she stands likes this Gerta resembles a malnourished pelican swooping aimlessly in the air for prey.

"Now, now, Gerta, you're going to frighten our young friend." Rubin is careful not to upset me since I confided to him that I was bedridden for a time after William's death.

The Stollmans do not agree on politics. She is a budding Zionist, while Rubin remains true to his Socialist ideals. The couple was deeply engaged in revolutionary actions in Munich and Vienna, actions that they are wary to describe to me.

"If Socialism is so wonderful, why don't you join the British workers' party?" Gerta says, taunting him.

Rubin's answer is always the same: "The workers' party in England is milquetoast." His pronunciation is as green as if he had departed Leopoldstadt yesterday.

"The Fabians are the worst. Dreamers! If the Socialist Party failed against the iron fist of the Hapsburgs, this bloodless British socialism is doomed." Rubin prefers revolutionaries such as the young Rosa Luxemburg and V.I. Lenin to our Fabians, Beatrice and Sidney Webb. Rubin explains that Lenin is from Russia and Luxemburg from Germany and that they believe the proletariat must fight for its rights by armed struggle and insurrection.

"Rosa is Jewish and Lenin has Jewish blood in him," Gerta adds. "Neither can see the forest for the trees." She is proud of herself for using this English expression.

Gerta and Rubin push each other to extremes; he into the revolutionary camp and she into the Zionist one. When I arrive in the darkness of night the café is silent, but by first-morning light, the Stollmans are arguing about Socialism and Zionism. When I prepare to sneak out the back door, just as the earliest patrons arrive at the café, I overhear them worrying about the old Queen's health. Two different worlds.

From the little table in the kitchen where Gerta does the accounts, she says, "If it can happen to Dreyfus in Paris, it will happen across Europe: Moscow, Berlin, Amsterdam, Rome, Warsaw, Budapest and Prague, every city where there are Jews. Unless we build our own homeland, we are doomed."

"Stop already!" Rubin shouts at her. "Use your *kop*. The twentieth century is upon us. The days of random persecution of the Jews are over. A Socialist Europe will be different. Lenin will ensure it."

"Rubin Stollman and Vladimir Ilyich Lenin. What a pair!" Gerta says disapprovingly. Pew, pew, pew ... you can have him. Lenin won't admit to being partly Jewish. He will never do anything for our people." Gerta spits on the knuckle of her thumb as she figures out if this month they might make the rent.

I depart by the back door, draped in my black cape and hood. No one would guess it is me, the lady of the manor, Frederick Wendice's sickly wife. The dupe of the entire county.

A single gaslight still burns in the gloomy village square. White rain rips across the airy gloom, pouring onto the brown cobblestones in a straight, comforting pattern. This is England, I assure myself, while the Stollman's concerns are a faraway fantasy.

***

For the next month, I often visit the Café Demel as Rubin and Gerta argue about Zionism or Socialism. According to Rubin, Lenin has been arrested and exiled to Siberia with Krupskaya, his wife. "The comrades plan to bring him to London, when it is safe," he says. I must admit to wishing to meet this man. If he really could free the downtrodden from their oppressors, he must be a magician. All for one, and one for all. Perhaps he could cure me of the contagion sickness, too!

***

At the manor, I make my presence in the kitchen known. Mrs. Bullbrook gives me the cold shoulder whenever I enter her domain, but as I remind her, I have Master Frederick's permission to cook. As is her way, Housekeeper mutters under her breath about her Freddy being a "forgiving soul."

As Mrs. Bullbrook curses under her breath, I prepare a White Ladies Pudding. Maman would make this for the hired girls who worked in our kitchen at the Devil's Stone. Desiccated coconut, thickly buttered white bread, milk, vanilla, salt, eggs and sugar. The farm girls adored it, gobbled it down in one sitting. I would offer it to the Stollmans, but I do not wish to put the couple in harm's way. After my dinner party, when the entire village will be searching for scapegoats, it would be easiest to blame them. I am thinking of the villagers who even now will not enter the café because the proprietors are Jewish.

First I butter the pie dish and sprinkle it with desiccated coconut. I remove the crusts from the white bread and cut them into neat little squares to arrange at the bottom of the dish. Heat the milk and add the vanilla. I prefer to double the vanilla essence since it gives the pudding a more exotic flavour. Next a pinch of salt. Never forget the salt. Beat the eggs with the sugar and pour in the milk to stir. When Housekeeper leaves the kitchen I remove my awkward gloves. This is a dish that requires the most reliable of tools, my hands. No one to tattle to Frederick. I strain the milk mixture over the squares of bread in the dish, and pat it down. I love the next part. Place the pie dish in a *bain-mairie* of boiling water and bake for an hour. Each pudding serves six, according to Maman's calculations. Afterward, I smooth fresh butter on my fingers and spread it on top of the pudding.

I offer it to Jack to present to his teacher, to Miss Staples, the one who is enamoured with Jack's progress as a student at the Mechanic's Institute.

Before heading to the Café Demel, I pack my lovely puddings, many more than Miss Staples could possibly eat on her own, in layers of muslin, more like bandages than napkins. Next I tie French silk ribbons around the packages. I can only imagine how Miss Staples will be delighted by Jack's gifts and how the wrappings will be shed, like a multi-coloured snake unravelling its skin.

By the time the typhoid epidemic of 1895 befalls the town of Holsworthy, I have handed a baker's dozen of carefully wrapped puddings to oh-so-clever Jack to give to his adoring teacher. At the Café, I'm particularly careful not to touch the food with unwashed hands. When Gerta inquires if my husband is curious about my middle of the night excursions to her establishment, I simply tell her that Frederick is a busy man, occupied with his business interests at the quarry or at Morwellham Quay.

Indeed, when my husband is at home at the manor, he never leaves his bed until after eight in the morning, so I make time to wash and fix my hair before joining him at the breakfast table. Most days, he ignores me, holding *The Times* before his imperturbable face while spooning a soft-boiled egg into his mouth. When he does fold the wrinkled pages on the table and looks directly at me, we have nothing in the world to say to each other. I feel that the house is inhabited by ghosts. Not surprisingly, Frederick hasn't noticed that I am absent from the manor between three and six in the morning, but then how could he know? Assiduously, Frederick remains true to his promise not to press me in the bedroom. He hasn't come to me since before William died and if I have my way, he never will again. I can't bring myself to imagine him touching me.

Sadly, fewer and fewer customers are frequenting the café as the village succumbs to the fever. Business has wound down to a trickle. To lure more customers, I have Housekeeper polish my best silver plates and goblets from my Catherine de' Medici room, and present them to my friends, the Stollmans. I insist that their baked goods will appear more enticing displayed on silver platters and I even have Jack carry dozens of my Limoges plates to enhance the Café's tea service. When Gerta notices me laying the table with my Limoges, she shakes her head in disbelief.

"Why give them your best china? They will nick it," she says confidently.

"How do you know?"

---

"We are hardly human to them, we are foreigners, worse, we are Jews. Why should they not steal these beautiful plates?" she asks and during the next few weeks I discover that she is right.

# – 16 –

As the time for my dinner party draws near, excitement begins to radiate throughout the big house. Mrs. Bullbrook, the parlour maid and the scullion are scouring every nook and cranny of the manor. I instruct the gardener to trim the ivy and move the irises from one garden bed to another. The flowers must be perfect.

Even Jack, who has been promoted to both valet and footman to Frederick, is caught up in the fever. Against his better judgment, my husband is growing increasingly fond of the lad. He calls upon Jack to sweep out the odorous barn and lay fresh, sweet-smelling hay for the greys. For his effort, he flicks Jack a shilling, patting the boy's head and tussling his yellow curls.

As we descend into the golden, final days of the summer, other than the shared meals I prepare for him, which he consumes silently, Frederick avoids me entirely. He spends time bantering with Jack and makes it appear like a guilty pleasure. My husband is aware that I watch them conversing beside the stable door.

I sit in the old swing by the flower garden. The evening sun is a ball of white fire, burning out the view of the church's graveyard across the road. Isn't it odd that there have been so many funerals at St. Peter's and St. Paul's this summer? Frederick, who is at the quarries most of the time, hasn't noticed the black hearses and funeral processions descending upon the church.

The menu I have devised for the dinner party is splendid: *Terrine de Lapin,* roast shoulder of mutton, braised eels with prunes, *Pommes de Terre Anna* and stewed green onions with a rich, creamy butter sauce. Before the main course, I shall serve cold potato and leek soup and freshly dressed perch. Dessert shall be *Peche Melba* with handcrafted chocolate *bonbons* on the side.

I wonder how Frederick would react if he actually knew that I have accepted his point of view and embraced it. He remains in rude health despite the many meals I have cooked for him. Now I must conduct my own experiment, for I am like the rat in Dr. Alessi's laboratory, the one who survives. The rat that gets sick but does not succumb. If it is inside of me, the typhoid, the fateful germ will force others to fall ill and even to die.

I have become ill in my mind. I imagine a scenario I cannot yet know will occur and cannot truly understand.

"Beyond a doubt, Olympia will go first. She is older and much frailer than vigorous Freddy," I say aloud. Lately, I notice that I am talking to myself. No one pays me any mind. I recall Frederick mounting me in his study, me naked and on all fours, he in his surgeon's white coat. It's remarkable, that he's lasted all these years, I must admit.

I remind myself to stop talking aloud and to keep my thoughts to myself. My plan, should it proceed as hoped, is to ensure that the Wendices are the only two at the table of my dinner party to risk infection. No one need suspect me, not of Olympia and Frederick's death. The fever is raging in the village. Anyone is liable to become ill. If there are others at our party who survive, how can I, or my meal, be blamed.

Another note arrives in the post from Albert. He demands to know why I haven't left Frederick. The summer is all but over, he writes. What are you waiting for? If I told him that I am plotting the death of my husband and his mother, I wonder if Albert would believe me? Would he believe his sister capable of such acts?

***

At Frederick's command, Mrs. Bullbrook continues to leave me alone in the kitchen. It is one day before the party, and I am making the chocolate *bonbons*, except that the gloves Frederick insists that I wear are constraining my work. I cannot shape the little halos for the angels' heads. I struggle with the first two dozen, surely enough for my innocent guests and then I remove the gloves, put my fingers in my knickers, and then begin to squeeze decorative halos from the layers of sugar and congealing chocolate for another six *bon-*

*bons*. Three each for the Wendices. That surely will be enough to do them in.

"Why does he make you wear those gloves, Cordelia?" Jack asks, surprising me in the kitchen.

Jack's impudence is growing worse every day. I slap him on the head, a little harder each time he calls me by my Christian name. Frederick was right from the beginning. It was a fatal mistake to bring the boy to the manor. He knows too much.

"You know perfectly well why he does. His Lordship's strange ideas," I declare, spinning my index finger around my temple.

"You think he's barmy?"

"He can't let go of the notion that I transmit typhoid. Can you imagine, Jack?"

Suddenly Jack's face turns mean when he asks, "Why did you keep it from me, Cordelia, when me mum passed?"

"Your mother? I'm so sorry. How?" I am truly surprised. Is it possible that because Jack is a servant no one bothered to inform him that his mother had died?

"She perished of the filthy disease, less than a month after I came to the manor."

"I'm sorry, Jack. I didn't know."

Jack's eyes are red with the tears he is trying to hold back.

"You're upset. Of course you are, lad," I say, walking toward him to comfort him. "You should have been told much earlier, about your mother, that is."

"Don't be fooling me, Cordelia. Pretending you're surprised. It was you who spread it to me mum. The Master is right about you. You spread the filthy disease to others."

He must stop calling me Cordelia. What will our dinner guests think of me, the lady of the manor, being called her Christian name by the stable boy? I reach out to slap him, but instead push a lock of yellow hair from his face. "Don't you be getting any silly notions in your head, Jack. Why would I wish to strike down a lovely woman like your mum? She died long after I visited her and met you. Many have died of the disease, my own Maman. Have I killed them all?"

Jack shakes his head, as if to imply, he couldn't say.

"Here are some fat cuttings from the mutton. Throw them to the dogs and then come back to the kitchen. I'll make you a cup of chocolate, with whipped cream, the way you like it."

I watch Jack as his scoops up the mutton fat in his hands.

"Don't let Mrs. Bullbrook catch you, or she'll skin your hide." Housekeeper sticks to the ancient custom of rendering fat for tallow candles, which she insists on burning, no matter how foul the smell.

***

I slump down in Housekeeper's stool beside the stove. Knowing what I know now, I suppose it is entirely possible that I passed the typhoid onto Jack's mother, but if I did, I certainly didn't intend to. The guest list for the dinner party is in the pocket of my apron. I pull it out to peer for many minutes at it.

My husband demanded that I invite the Webbs, Beatrice and Sidney. The couple have recently published *The History of Trade Unionism* and he's invited Beatrice to make a small, but pithy after-dinner presentation about unions in Britain.

I am allowed to have Polly, much against Frederick's wishes, but I tell him I must have at least one friend at my own party and who else has he permitted me to know? He insists we avoid any acknowledgement of her vocation. Reverend Kinsman, from the Tintagel vicarage has accepted, as has Thomas Glassock, an American chum of Frederick's who is recreating the court of King Arthur near the slate quarries at Tintagel. He and the vicar will ride by coach together to Holsworthy and have readily agreed to share one of our guestrooms. Mr. Ealing, the pestilent physician, as always, is happy to oblige.

Holsworthy's Barclay's banker, Mr. Salt and his young wife Nancy, fresh from London, will also be joining us. Beatrice Webb has suggested that the prominent orator and Jewish playwright, Mr. Israel Zangwill, who I'd met briefly when he visited the Café Demel earlier this summer, also be invited. They are interested in conversing with him and so he has agreed to travel by rail from London to sit at my table along with the others. Of course, Olympia will be in attendance. The Queen, reigning over her subjects. Mother-in-law has not visited since William's funeral. She is to stay in the sick room.

It is the perfect combination of business contacts and intellectuals. It cannot help but appeal to Frederick's vision of himself as benevolent magnate and his pretensions as a philosopher and social reformer. While he sees the sense of it in the end, it did take some persuasion on my part to present the logic of the list.

I am not certain what misguided mischief prompted me to extend a special invitation to someone unknown to us all.

"I have also asked Mr. Wiseman, a German phrenologist to treat our guests to an exploration of their skulls. Mr. Wiseman claims that he is able to analyze a person's character by the shape of his skull," I inform my husband.

Frederick walks away shaking his head. He is defeated. "What will Mater think?"

***

On Friday afternoon, Beatrice Webb is the first to arrive. Next appears Olympia, drowning in yellow diamonds and black pearls, exhausted from her travels and requiring silence and rest until dinner is announced. Frederick pecks his mother on her withered cheek. Her mouth is turned downward in a perpetual frown. "Not now, Mater," he says, informing her that he must speak privately with Mrs. Webb about the Fabian movement.

"Fabian movement, indeed. Why don't you join the Tories and be done with this Socialist nonsense?" Mater inquires.

Mrs. Webb and my husband pretend not to hear Olympia and they retire to his study. I chortle to myself imagining what it might be like for Beatrice to become Frederick's patient on the gurney. His woman in distress. Sidney Webb is suffering from a migraine so he has chosen to remain at home, at their seaside villa in Bude. Frederick insists that Mrs. Webb be given the master bedroom for the night and so we are relegated to a stuffy guest room on the attic floor. I would rather die than share a bed with Frederick. I'll sleep on the divan, in my morning room. Before dressing, I escape there to rehearse what I must do following the dinner party.

After the deed is done, I will need to disappear, for a time. I'll miss my little Catherine de' Medici retreat where I've composed letters of affection to Polly, Reverend Kinsman, and anyone else who had captured my fancy for a short time. This is the only room in the manor where I could listen to my own beating heart and find some release for my emotions. If I had allowed love to rule my life, perhaps I would not be on the precipice of what I am about to do. Calculated murder. If Miss Staples is down with typhoid, is it my White Ladies Pudding has felled her? If so, the sad truth is that my plan will work.

I try not to face the possible consequences, but I must. The only unknown factor is what if Frederick and Olympia live to tell the story? Not everyone dies from typhoid fever. Could I cheat the hangman's noose, if one or the other survives?

I recall the afternoon of William's funeral, when I'd sat on the window box, all prim and proper in my black mourning taffeta, with mother-in-law Wendice tearing my heart out, one chamber at a time, and not a contrary word from Frederick to show the old bitch that I am his wife and that I come first. My own dear son, not in the ground three hours. I shall never forgive them for that; how could I?

I search through the letters in my escritoire before pitching them onto the grate. Here it is, the letter I'd considered saving as a memento of the kind of man my husband really is. This letter was composed a few short months after our marriage.

*Dear Mater,*

*I confess I am confused by the turn of events in my marriage. I married Cordelia thinking her so kind and affectionate that I might influence her as I chose and make of her just such a wife as I wanted. I am grieved and disappointed at finding I cannot change her, and she is humiliated and irritated at finding she cannot alter my character.*

*I must confess to making the gravest error of my life. Cordelia is unreformable.*

*Her low birth makes my wife impervious to my lamentations. What am I to do?*

---

My husband, in his usual rush to depart our home for Tintagel, had forgotten the envelope, addressed to Hartland Abbey, on the vestibule table. He'd already stamped it for Her Majesty's Post, so I snitched it before Housekeeper could pass it to the postman, figuring it would contain naughty things said about me. From that point on, it never stopped, his desultory letters, complaining to his mother about me, and my uncouth, unpredictable, dangerous ways.

These are among the things that make it impossible for me to forgive Frederick Wendice. These are among the things that make me certain that Frederick and his mother must die.

As for Mrs. Webb, Frederick's favourite, she is only a few years older than I, but acts the grand dame with her imperious voice and demeanour. I can't understand why all Frederick's Fabian associates are wealthy, well-educated toffs who write revolutionary treatises or dabble in timorous watercolours. Some of the Socialists write poems or design furniture. Olympia and Mrs. Webb share much more in common than I do with either of them. When Jack rushes into the drawing room to alert me to the arrival of the next guests, Beatrice doesn't deem to even look at him. He is invisible to her.

Although it is August, I've dressed Jack in livery to resemble a toy soldier with white gloves and a red-feathered fur headdress. I wish to show him off. He sinks under the helmet's weight, but he does not falter, ushering our friends through the expansive foyer and up the baroque staircase, which curves toward the dining hall and the drawing room. A twenty-four foot mahogany dining table with sixteen matching Queen Anne green-striped silk chairs adorn the room. In the drawing room are matching lounge chairs, covered in green velvet. Two pewter candelabras preside over both rooms. I've selected African Marigold and Daffodil wall coverings for these rooms.

For my party, I have chosen a red satin frock, low about my shoulders, with tiny rhinestones on the bodice and leg of mutton sleeves. My waist is cinched so tightly, I can hardly exhale, but this is the fashion of the day. After today, I will no longer need to be concerned with frocks sewn with hard bustles or billowing sleeves or tiny waists which make me gasp for breath. After tonight's dinner, I will choose to exist outside the realm of what is fashionable and what is not. I will do as I please, dress as I please, speak as I please, cook as I please. If I get away with it ... anything is possible.

***

Mr. Wiseman, my phrenologist, enters the drawing room with his diagrams and instruments, just as Polly arrives. Polly takes one glance at Mr. Wiseman and says quietly to me, "I am expecting you to behave."

The party games are about to begin. Polly is radiant in midnight blue. If I could love another, it would be her. But what she offers is another cage, more brightly coloured, but a cage nonetheless. Fine netting from which I could never escape. Polly's rules, Polly's concept of right and wrong. Help the sick, the infirm, the unfortunate. Do your duty, Cordelia. But what is my duty?

I notice Beatrice Webb taking Polly's measure and deciding that my friend is not worth knowing. Beatrice is about big ideas that ought to change the world—no matter how savage. She is the high priestess of English Socialism. With her lush chestnut hair, clear blue eyes, fine pointed chin, dimples on both cheeks, it is no wonder my husband cannot resist her abundant pre-Raphaelite charms.

Israel Zangwill appears next. Zangwill has brought a copy of *The Jewish Chronicle* for Mrs. Webb. He wishes to convince her that the Jews are people, too, and that they should be included in her landscape of big ideas. All I can think about is Maman, buried and alone in the outermost regions of the graveyard in Shebbear. And little William, who will never, ever attend a dinner party where the conversation will turn to how to change the world.

"How delighted I am to finally meet you, Mr. Zangwill," Beatrice says, stretching out her hand for him to shake, or is it to kiss? "How is it possible that we have not met in London?"

"I suspect we travel in different circles," Zangwill responds graciously. He is a short and wiry man with great ears that stick out like an elephant's. His expression is without guile.

"Will you be the first, then, Frederick?" I implore my husband. "Mr. Wiseman reads our minds by studying the indentations of our craniums. Your head is certainly the largest in the room, dear."

---

It is my hope that Mr. Wiseman and his prognosis of my guests' dispositions will serve as a silly distraction from my darker plans for the night.

No one will suspect my intentions. Not Cordelia, who, after all is said and done, is lady of the manor. Who will remain to recount tonight's story? Mrs. Bullbrook, a lowly housekeeper, who can barely discern one face from the other. Of course, Polly could betray me, but she loves me. I am trying not to think about Jack. Clever Jack. As he steps from the drawing room, the look he shoots me chills me to the bone. Mustn't underestimate Jack. I could show him the door, but now that Frederick has taken a shine to him, it might cast suspicion on me. Who knows what Jack might say? Best to keep him close.

Frederick cannot bear my attempt at clever entertainment. He finds it cheap and tasteless no doubt. "One of our guests ought to go first," he says with false gallantry. He abhors party games. Frederick is a serious man.

Polly volunteers just as the Salts enter the room. Nancy Salt is hanging on the old banker's arm. What a strange and disparate couple they make! He ungainly, gnarled and grey; she, fair and beautiful, but with the pallor of a fading Easter lily.

"This is Mr. and Mrs. Salt. Mr. and Mrs. Salt ..."

Everyone in the room stands silently waiting to be introduced by name.

"For goodness sakes, Cordelia," Frederick remarks, "can you not manage a proper introduction?"

He tries to restrain himself in front of Mrs. Webb while the young Mrs. Salt launches into an immediate apology.

"It's my doing that we are late. Harald was convinced I should wear the chartreuse, but I was certain the lilac was more flattering. He made me change into this dress," she explains lifting her skirt quite high. Her legs are long and shapely. All the men in the room take notice. I notice that she is wearing a fussy, lime frock with ruffles up to her chin, the affect of which is to make her appear like a timid child in a grisly nightmare.

"What an enchantingly shaped head you have, Mrs. Salt," Herr Wiseman observes, holding his callipers in one hand and his map of the brain in the other.

"Please no," she says meekly. "I've been examined from stem to stern by doctors from Bristol to Plymouth since marrying Harald. Mr. Salt thought the foul air of London was the reason for my collapsing health, but since we've moved to Devon, I've become much worse."

"Herr Wiseman, why not try Mrs. Turney?" I suggest. She's the bravest woman I know and she's volunteered."

"You shan't hurt me, shall you Herr Wiseman?" Polly inquires coyly while sending me a disparaging look.

"Wiseman wounds no one," the little man declares. "Everyone has twenty-seven areas of the brain organism," he explains. He begins to enthusiastically remove the pins from Polly's dark locks. "By measuring your head, I will search first for the instinct of reproduction, Frau Turney. It can easily be discovered in the cerebellum." He is pointing to the back of Polly's head. "I shall also explore your faculty to imitate, your firmness of purpose; and lastly, your instinct for affection, for love!" A giant hubris is emanating from the little German phrenologist.

"Is that all?" Polly questions glibly.

Everyone laughs out loud except Beatrice and Frederick. Although she is pretending to be disinterested, I can sense that Mrs. Webb is intrigued. Frederick inches closer to her as the examination begins.

In the meantime, Polly remains still as a statue.

"Very good. Yes. Very good. Ahha!" Herr Wiseman is busily measuring Polly's head with his callipers in one hand and scribbling notations with the other. When he reaches the spot above her right ear, the indentation responsible for affection, he stops cold.

"How odd!" Wiseman pulls at his salt and pepper goatee. He appears to be distressed.

"Don't forget that this was your idea, Cordelia." Polly is pulling back from the phrenologist.

"Shall I ring for more whiskey? Where is Jack? He is supposed to be mixing American-style cocktails, spirits, sugar, water, and bitters with ice. Where is the ice?"

More drinks, what a stellar idea," Frederick adds, nervously glancing from Polly to me and then to Mrs. Webb, who is sitting upright with a stony expression on her Patrician face.

"I say, shall we eat?" Frederick suggests.

---

My husband is once again attempting to thwart me by spoiling my fun. "We've hardly begun," I shout, much too vociferously. "Try not to be such a spoil sport, Frederick, just this once."

As I am scolding my husband, Nancy Salt, who's been leaning heavily against the grand piano, swoons.

"Sit down, wife!" the banker orders. "She will not eat, just tea and toast and not much of that. Everything that goes down comes up again."

Herr Wiseman, deep into his calculations of Polly's phrenology, ignores the careening Nancy. "What we have is a droll woman, intelligent, forceful, not to be undone or out maneuvered by anyone, man or woman, and yet she exhibits no desire to bear children. A total anomaly! Mrs. Turney, are Herr Wiseman's calculations correct? Do you not wish to propagate the species?

"How right you are, old man," Polly says, excitedly. "There are too many mouths to feed on this little island and half of them retire without food in their bloated bellies. Mrs. Webb surely you must agree that ..."

But Frederick interrupts: "That is why Mrs. Webb founded the Fabian movement."

Looking squarely at Beatrice Webb, I say, "I hardly think so."

Mrs. Webb pretends not to hear me. I am a social climber of the worst sort.

In the corner of the room, Nancy Salt looks as if she might faint. "My dear Mrs. Salt," I say over the tumult in the room, "allow me to guide you to my morning room. You need to be observed. Come along, Mr. Ealing. This poor woman is in need of a physician."

Ealing, who has only just arrived, is more than happy to oblige, but I have ruffled Herr Wiseman's feathers.

"Do you not wish me to proceed with the analysis of Mrs. Turney's cranium?"

"Perhaps another time," Frederick says.

But surprisingly Polly interjects. "Now! I want to know everything!"

"Of course. I'd be delighted Mrs. Turney, what an enigma you are to Wiseman." The little German is leering at Polly in a most indelicate fashion. "As I was about to proclaim, you are more comfortable in the company of the gentler sex, no?"

---

Zangwill is chortling softly to himself. His eyes are alight with mischief.

Polly smiles into the middle distance, as if chastising me and silently saying, I told you so!

Olympia, having no idea what might be swirling in the undercurrents of the room, nonetheless senses the discomfort.

"Really, Frederick." She pulls her lorgnette to her eye to examine Polly.

I do not wish for Mother-in-law to excuse herself from the party and so I surrender my hope to provoke Frederick's genteel guests.

"Shall we get you off your feet, then, Mrs. Salt?" I inquire. I turn my back on Polly and the other guests while rushing Nancy from the drawing room and across the hall to the morning room. Ealing, clutching his medical case and a tumbler of whiskey, trails behind us eagerly.

"Now what seems to be the problem?" inquires Ealing of the prostrate Nancy Salt.

I shut the door of the morning room behind us. "Tell the doctor everything," I urge.

Nancy begins to cry, "I miss London and my family and the draper's shop where I worked.

"I see," Ealing says gravely.

"Harald, Mr. Salt, that is, assured me that the country air would cure my neurasthenia, but I'm worse.

"How so? " I inquire.

"Every time I eat something, I bring it up.

Ealing is busily unhinging the hooks and eyes of her frock to listen to her chest with his ear.

"Harald, Mr. Salt that is, likes me slender and I tend to fat if I'm left to my druthers. With nothing to do out here I was getting thick around the middle. Mr. Salt says my arms were looking like the smoked hams hanging in the window of Mr. Perkins' butcher shop ..."

"So you stick the feather down your throat, don't you girl?" I ask.

"Yes, yes. I admit it." Nancy is sniffling. "When I was at my draper's, Packer-Jones Draper on the Marylebone High Street, I was good at picking colours and patterns for the fine ladies who frequented our shop. They preferred me waiting on them to the other shop girls. Here there is no one to talk with. Just my maid-of-all-work and Mr. Salt won't abide me getting chummy with her ..."

While Nancy Salt continues to complain to the doctor, I return to the kitchen by the servants' staircase to ensure my special, six chocolate angels are resting undisturbed. Blessedly, they are safe in a corner of the highest cupboard where I've hidden them. Mrs. Bullbrook is standing before the oven, watching over the sauces that are beginning to congeal. She says not a word to me or me to her. If I'd made more special angels, it might be a thought to offer one to her at this moment, but I shouldn't wish a change of plans this late in the game.

By the time I reach the drawing room, Mr. Ealing and Mrs. Salt have already returned. He is kneeling beside her and patting her dimpled hand. She looks flushed as if she has just been kissed by a stranger.

Suddenly he is struck by a thought. In a whisper he asks, "Might you be in the family way, my dear?"

Less discreet, she blurts aloud, "The family way! I daresay no! Harald is always so busy with the bank these days."

As a muffled guffaw breaks out among the guests, it is apparent that even Mrs. Webb cannot conceal her amusement, but Olympia's visage grows more thunderous.

My attempt at smart entertainment has failed as all the guests demure when Herr Wiseman offers to examine them. In desperation he turns to me. Eagerly, I recline on the Persian chair and cross my legs in the modern fashion while the phrenologist measures the dimensions of my head.

"All my secrets are sequestered deep inside my head," I announce. "I cannot imagine they might be read on the surface."

"What are you hiding from me?" Frederick attempts a comic delivery but it is clear to all that he is growing concerned and that he feels the evening is catapulting in an unsavoury direction.

Wiseman is mopping his brow while puffing excitedly on a Turkish cigarillo. I ask him for one, which he lights with continental flourish, although his hand is trembling. The rules are being broken.

"What are you hiding?" Frederick repeats, more insistent now, dropping all pretence of a joke. "I must know. I have the right to know."

"I would prefer not to say." The German is stubborn.

"I don't give a monkey's toss what you'd prefer. He who pays the piper calls the tune!"

"As you wish. I shall oblige you. Frau Wendice's cranium suggests a firmness of purpose, perseverance . . . less politely, obstinacy."

"Undoubtedly," Frederick says. "Continue."

"She is full of guile," Herr Wiseman reports, looking from me to Frederick, who is holding his ground. "She exhibits the carnivorous instinct."

The room goes still. Mrs. Webb rises to stand beside Frederick. A-g-i-t-a-t-e-d, c-o-r-p-u-l-e-n-t Frederick.

"How amazing you are Herr Wiseman. So accurate. I'm feeling particularly carnivorous at the moment. Is anyone else hungry? Shall we go to dinner?" I say as breezily as possible. I am done with Herr Wiseman. It was to be an amusing party game, but as with most of my endeavours it has turned sour.

And by now everyone is terribly hungry and most are tipsy with my deceptively potent aperitifs.

After Wiseman's too candid comments, I expect Frederick to be apoplectic, but he is attempting to control himself in front of Mrs. Webb. She, like Mr. Zangwill, Reverend Kinsman, Thomas Glassock, and the Salts are oblivious to the danger they might be in. It is only a party game, they assure themselves. Cordelia, the publican's daughter, is attempting to be droll and has failed miserably. I imagine, they wonder why Frederick married beneath him.

In an effort to move the evening forward, and perhaps end it all the sooner, Frederick asks the doctor to say grace.

"For what we are about to receive ..."

Blah, blah, blah.

"And for our friends and neighbours in our village who are sick with the typhoid fever, may God have mercy on their souls."

At this point, Frederick is unable control his rage. "What do you mean?" he cries. "I have not been informed of another typhoid epidemic."

"You are away so often, Frederick, how could you have known?" I respond, perhaps a tad too quickly. My husband lives in his own head. He imagines only sinners and saints and ignores the life revolving around him.

"No matter!" he shouts.

"When did it break out precisely?" Polly asks. Her face is stricken.

"During the last month," Ealing volunteers. "Many have perished, but I dare not speak of it in polite company. The contagion." He covers his mouth with his hand as if he has just burped.

"It is so-called polite company that is most vulnerable to the fever," Polly volunteers boldly. "Did you know that more numbers of the upper classes perish of the fever than do the lower classes?"

Mrs. Webb finally deems to acknowledge Polly. "Is that true, Mrs. Turney, and if so, how would you know?"

Polly glares directly at her. "Scientists are doing ground-breaking investigations in this field, as we speak. There is an interesting experiment with rats ..."

Frederick cuts her off. "Enough, I wish to know precisely the date of the first incidence of typhoid in Holsworthy, how many have died, and where they resided?"

"Shall we discuss something more appropriate?" I suggest.

"No, we shall not," Frederick shouts. If looks could kill I would be dead.

"I must know immediately who has succumbed."

The table grows silent as the guests inspect each other, looking for the tell-tale signs of a rash or a fevered brow.

Ealing whose hands are still folded in prayer closes his eyes: "So many it is hard to account for all. Today we lost the school teacher, Miss Staples. She is in God's hands now. I did whatever I could to ease her suffering."

Jack, who is preparing to serve the wine, turns so violently he loses his livery hat with the motion. "You gave me puddings for her; you dressed them in pretty little packages. You killed her!" he screams as he points his accusing finger at me.

"Not again." Frederick rises from his chair. "I want you all to leave, to go straight to your homes until this is sorted. Do not touch a morsel of food on your plate. Jack, bring the carriage around for Mrs. Webb," he bellows.

"But I don't wish to leave tonight," Beatrice cries. "I have my presentation on trade unions to deliver. After dinner."

"We're all so hungry," Thomas Glassock adds. "Couldn't we eat before you cast us out?"

"I'm not casting you out. I'm trying to save your lives." Frederick's face is flushed.

But my guests demure. They are famished. Neither have they spent years convinced, or attempting to convince others, that I am the cause of an epidemic that is ravaging Devonshire. It is past ten o'clock and they haven't been served a morsel of food.

I chastise Jack for his insolence but cannot bear to banish him and my delicious repast cannot be served properly without him. I instruct him to pour the Gewürztraminer for the fish and soup courses. I am his mistress, I rescued him from the pits of Tintangel and he must do as I command.

"Darling, Frederick," I say before he can stop Jack, "the drink has gone to your head. No one is going to succumb to typhoid in my house. And Freddy, think of Mrs. Bullbrook, working her fingers to the bone preparing the manor for our guests. You wouldn't wish to disappoint her, would you?"

Olympia lists like a great ship toppling in the wind. The conversation has unnerved her. Only she and Beatrice have remarked, if silently and through glances and stares, how bold Jack is. Everyone else is too hungry to think of anything but their empty bellies.

"Mind your manners, Jack. Please pour."

Frederick holds his head in his hands. "You're putting your lives in Cordelia's hands! Shall I take you upstairs?" he asks his mother.

If Olympia leaves this table, months of planning will be for naught. But to leave her own table, or what she most certainly still considers to be her own table, would be the epitome of unacceptable behaviour. Will she allow her insistence on social grace to trump her son's outbursts?

I must take action quickly. I rise and ask quite simply. "Who, at this table has already survived a bout of typhoid? I know I have, so I am safe."Polly raises her hand obediently. Herr Wiseman as well.

"Reverend Kinsmen?"

"Not I, but my housekeeper fell ill when the disease swept Tintagel and so did many of Master Wendice's workers succumb. You'll remember ma'am, you and your husband visited at that time. Poor creature, she fell into a dreadful state. When housekeeper departed this world, I imagined I was to follow, but no, the good Lord is protecting me. However, she has left me alone to care for my flock."

"How troublesome of her to inconvenience you in that way," snipes Polly.

"So you have had close contact but remain untouched, Reverend," I say closing the matter. "And our American friend, Mr. Glassock?"

Glassock takes his turn.

"Doesn't appear to be an overly risky situation, to me. Even your Prince of Wales, Bertie, caught it and that scoundrel survived. I've just hired away the head chef for the Rothschilds. I'm paying the man three times what those Jews pay him. If I trust him, I trust you."

"Mr. Ealing. I don't suppose you've ever come down with a fever? You are a cockroach and cockroaches never fall ill."

Ealing, who is busily inspecting Mrs. Salt's bosom, doesn't much notice what I have called him. "I say what, cockroaches, nasty beasties."

Having remained silent most of the evening, expressing her displeasure only with her eyes and her frown, Olympia finally speaks. "We live clean, Christian lives, as do most of your guests, Frederick," she turns to briefly glance toward Polly. "Typhoid has never touched the Wendice family."

"Splendid! And I'm quite certain that it will not touch you tonight," I interject. "Mrs. Webb, you must be in the same category as Olympia. Immune from contagion."

"If you wish to put it that way, but, no, I've had the good fortune never to come down with typhoid. I don't see what the reports of typhoid have to do with delaying my presentation on trade unions."

"It has to do everything with your 'cause' Mrs. Webb," says Polly, clearly angered by the superciliousness of the beliefs and conversation represented at the table. "I work closely with those who are disenfranchised, those you claim to fight for; those who do not have the luxury of living clean, Christian lives, as they must fight every day just to stay alive and to feed their children by whatever means possible. I have seen for myself that those who have suffered from the disease cannot catch it again."

What Polly really wishes to say is we all are capable of carrying the contagion no matter our station or race.

"Mr. Zangwill, as a fellow Jew, you and I are generally considered to be the cause, not the victims of the filthy disease," I interject.

"I don't like to say, not here in mixed company," Mrs. Salt interrupts, meekly, at first. She appears to have recovered from her unsteadiness. "In my draper's shop in London, the girls, well, we watched out for the Jews even though they spent a lot of money. It was rumoured that they spread it, typhoid that is, the Jews bring it over from Europe and from India and Africa, too."

"Do they, indeed?" Israel Zangwill, who has avidly been listening to the conversation, finally joins in.

"Yes, Mr. Zangwill," she says. "But they say many Jews, present company excepted, carry it on their skin, with that peculiar odour they have, and when they don't favour someone, they can strike down an unsuspecting, Christian soul immediately."

"And yet all of you in this room have had contact with Jews, but remain in good health. Is it simply that you have not met the right Jew? Otherwise you would be dead by now. Mr. Salt and Mrs. Salt, have you experienced this plague of the Jews?" I inquire.

"Neither of us has suffered from the disease," he says. "But I don't much care for Jews."

Just then the first course arrives.

"Here comes the fish, shall we begin?" Mr. Glassock asks enthusiastically. And with that, he plunges his fish fork into the de-boned perch.

After such provocative conversation, the table settles slowly and somewhat uncomfortably into conventional pleasantries and exchanges that appear to soothe Frederick and his mother. I have managed to rescue the evening and my plan. I will guard my tongue and refrain from agitating my guests any further. The dessert course is my goal. I will stifle my publicly proclaimed inclination to obstinacy. It is Cordelia the well-mannered hostess for the rest of the evening.

After the last of the main courses, I rise to gather the chocolates myself. The infected ones are pushed slightly to the side of the silver serving plate and I keep them by my right hand to wait until the main dessert is served. The uncontaminated *bonbons* assuredly will not harm the innocent, if my calculations about the spread of typhoid are correct. I understand contagion in ways more subtle than anyone else possibly could.

---

Mrs. Bullbrook presents the *Peche Melba* and it is by far the tastiest I have ever prepared. It is composed of eighteen large peaches, ten cups of sugar and five teaspoons of vanilla. It is firm, sweet and luscious. Each of my guests is served this concoction in a silver dish with a thick layer of vanilla ice cream that Jack and I had churned in the back garden under the willow tree in the morning.

In the centre of each bowl sits the perfect half peach dusted with granulated sugar and topped with whipped cream. And hovering there on the cloud of cream are the chocolate angels, one per dish. I have carefully ensured that only Frederick and Olympia receive the tainted chocolates. Everyone eats with unchecked relish, even Frederick. His sweet tooth has got the better of him.

Finally Olympia deems to speak to me. A spurt of cream is seeping through her teeth. She is eating greedily. She stops for a moment and lifts the *bonbon*. Inside it goes, she chews and a tiny droplet of chocolate falls from her mouth to the bodice of her maroon satin frock.

"Excellent," she whispers, begrudgingly. She has never tasted anything like it, Escoffier's *Peche Melba,* set off deliciously by my chocolate angels. Sanguinely, I believe, she never again will taste anything like it.

"No one can make a dessert as you can," Frederick admits, licking his spoon clean. I observe him as he stuffs one little chocolate angel into his gluttonous mouth.

I slip into my favourite reverie of escape as the others continue to talk.

I shall leave the manor by Monday morning. No one will be sick as early as that. According to my calculations, it might take up to a fortnight for Olympia to fall ill and perhaps more for Frederick, who has always been a sturdy soul and miraculously escaped the filthy disease for all these years. No more! Within eight weeks, they should both be dead. If I am lucky no one will suspect me since I shall be away, at home, at the Devil's Stone Inn, when typhoid strikes the manor house. In the meantime, I need to borrow a few sovereigns from Frederick's secret stash, to tide me over, while I am travelling. There are two paintings I wish to take with me as well: both by J.M.W. Turner, both of which Olympia presented to us before William was born. The paintings will look glorious on the walls of the Devil's Stone Inn. Maman would appreciate my gesture.

---

When my sated guests depart, I am careful to return the remaining tainted chocolate angels to the cupboard high above the sink in the kitchen. Only two tainted *bonbons* remain since Olympia and Frederick each requested one more before leaving the dining table. "Your wish is my command," I declare to Frederick and then to mother-in-law as the angels are consumed.

I could destroy the infected *bonbons*, but I do not. Not quite yet, but there is no use infecting the scullion who is only fifteen. I wouldn't wish to make the innocent suffer, if there are such people in this world. Unfortunately, Mrs. Bullbrook, who was in her cups tonight, has passed out, snoring in her rocker, and isn't expected to wake until dawn.

# - 17 -

I have chosen to return to the Devil's Stone Inn and afterwards to carry on to London for my first glance at the capital. By my reckoning, out of sight is out of mind. No doubt, it's best for me to be nowhere near Wendice Manor until the epidemic blows over, although I must admit to a gnawing craving to see mother and son suffering with the filthy disease. With so many townsfolk sick and dying, who could pinpoint how those two caught the plague? At least for now, I vow to keep my curiosity under control and stay the course. I will know soon enough. Tragic news travels fast enough in the West Country.

In the meantime, it is only right that I make amends to Pa, the brothers and their wives. Other than Albert, I have ignored the Tilleys for too long. For the occasion of my homecoming I shall concoct a *Pot-au-feu*, almost as Maman prepared it, packed with short ribs and veal shanks and all the savoury vegetables, leeks, parsley root, carrots and cabbages, in green and in purple. I shall salt it heavily so the stew will pickle during the journey to Shebbear.

***

On Saturday morning, Jack and I walk together to the High Street to purchase the ingredients. I'm no longer fearful of Wendice and what he might inflict on me if he discovers me out and about, acting as a normal person might. The damage, on both our parts, has been done.

Together, mistress and servant head along the towpath to the village and towards Perkins the butcher. I'll add beefy marrow bones, pounds of them, since I believe they are the heart and soul of a delicious *Pot-au-feu*. Jack has dug out four bottles of preserved cornichons from the cold room, and five jars of Dijon for the Tilley family.

Recently, Jack discovered Maman's old red kettle that I'd carried with me from Shebbear long ago when I'd still assumed Freddy would want me showing off my culinary talents for him every evening—before we retired to the privacy of the nuptial room. How wrong I was! Now I'll be bringing the fine, old kettle back with me, home to the Devil's Stone Inn where it rightfully belongs.

"There's his Lordship," Jack says pointing to a tall, portly man in the barber's chair. Frederick is having his goatee trimmed. There he is, with his imperturbable expression. As we approach, I can see his face reflected in the glass. My husband resembles a boiled egg with a patch of scorched grass springing out of the top of his head.

If only Jack were not a mere seventeen years old, I might consider taking him with me to Shebbear and on to London. But he is too green. People would be sure to take notice, just when I wish to become invisible.

Saturday is market day so the shoppers are pouring into the street. The dressmaker, the greengrocer, the ironmonger and the lending library are open for business. The typhoid has not dampened Holsworthy's commercial urges.

Housewives and housekeepers alike scurry round the farmers' stalls, selecting the freshest onions, the greenest parsley, the firmest potatoes. I glance at the newly churned tubs of butter, the canisters of fresh cream, the buckets of brown eggs and the terrines of sausages and liver. The fishmonger is selling oysters wrapped in newsprint and ready to swallow raw.

After our trip to the butcher, I suggest we visit the Stollmans to see how they are faring. Then I notice Olympia Wendice standing tall, her arms akimbo, before the farmers' stalls. Surprisingly she has deemed to mingle with the town's people this market day. More surprisingly, she is shouting out something about the Café Demel.

"It is your fault," she yells to Gerta who has just stepped outside the entrance to the café.

"It is these Jews who have brought the filthy disease to County Devon. Under the light of the morning sun, Olympia resembles a dinosaur. Her head is small and although her neck is slim where it meets her hair, hers is an elongated neck, widening out at the back to give her the look of an ancient creature. She has this fearsome way of talking, staring straight into one's eyes, demanding obedience.

Gerta is white as a sheet. "We are innocent!" she cries.

"It's the pies and buns we buy from your window," a matron shouts.

Jack sends me a look. "Is that true? You infected the Café, too?" Only he has known about my middle of the night visits to the Café Demel from the beginning. The grey sky is reflected in his eyes. I expect his eyes to be hard, but no, it is something else. Jack's green eyes are wide with excitement. He is enjoying this. He intends to get his own back.

"Of course not," I say. "You should know better . . ."

As I speak, Frederick, partially shaven and without his waistcoat, emerges from the barber's.

"Now my good friends, people of Holsworthy, this is an old wives' tale. Typhoid is spread by miasmas, which spring up in the air around filth and garbage. I can vouch for the cleanliness of the Stollman's establishment. How about a slice of your famous torte?" he asks Gerta.

Rubin is now standing by his wife's side and shaking Frederick's hand.

"In my life, I've never known such narrow-minded fools." Rubin is trembling with rage. "You line up for my tortes, my sweet buns, accept my credit, and with never a pleasant word to myself and Gerta. My God, you steal the china from our tables and then you claim we are spreading typhoid."

"You are responsible," mother-in-law says with conviction.

"The Stollmans are good, kind people." I finally join in.

"Jews spread typhoid," Olympia repeats in a voice louder than my own and staring into my eyes.

Before I can respond, attempting to defend my friends, Israel Zangwill comes racing into the square. He has stayed on, after my party, to visit his friends the Stollmans. He is wearing a skullcap and a prayer shawl since it is Saturday morning and he is saying the ordained prayers.

---

"How can you suggest that Jews spread disease?" he cries. How can you suspect such a thing? It is 1895 and this is England."

But Olympia stands by her words.

Zangwill is beside himself. "In the Bible it is written thou shall not bear false witness against your neighbour. What about Christian charity?" Zangwill puts one of his arms around Rubin's shoulders and takes Gerta's hand in his.

"We have chosen to live among strangers. What can we expect?" Gerta wails.

The three turn toward the café, but Frederick stops them. For the moment, all attention moves away from me. It is the three self-confessed Jews, the brave ones, walking together, who arouse the villagers' deepest suspicion. I am the lady of the manor and Wendice's wife, Olympia's daughter-in-law. By habit, it is much more difficult to denounce me.

"Oh please, don't accuse Mater of neglecting her Christian charity." Frederick pushes himself into the middle of the square while brushing me aside. "No one is bearing false witness against her neighbour. Mater is an old woman who has recently lost her only grandchild."

How can he, I think to myself.

"When typhoid breaks out, people are frightened, horrified; they repeat old superstitions from gone and forgotten eras that they would normally never utter. We must look to our own hygiene. If we rid ourselves of garbage and the foul smell of decomposing materials which circulates around refuse, we shall defeat the fever."

Upon hearing my husband's words, Rubin turns back to shout at the crowd.

"You English pretend you are so superior. There is garbage everywhere. London is worse, the sewers, the stink from the Thames. Why blame us, make us your scapegoats? Look to yourselves for the source of the fever and leave us be in peace." He slams shut the door to the café.

I can't help but remember the tales Maman told about her family's business in Angers and how it fell into creditor's hands after being accused of poisoning the well water. Purveyors of fine food and wine, destroyed, overnight.

By this point, Frederick moves back toward me and reaches out to clutch my arm.

"Get into the carriage with me, now, Cordelia," he orders. He is determined that the townsfolk of Holsworthy will not discover that it is me who is to blame.

"Mater, the carriage now, please. You do not look well. This outburst is no doubt more than the result of simple fatigue. We must get you home to rest."

Beside our carriage is a pedlar and I want to look more closely at him. An ancient mare is hitched to his heavily laden, broken-wheeled cart. The pedlar is on his knees, repairing the bent wheel while talking gently to the mare. He is speaking to the horse in Yiddish. His hair is tangled in long red ringlets. It is exactly the same colour as my hair, flaming red, not in the least like the pale ginger of the Tilleys. His beard is full and it brushes his barrel chest. His eyelids are furled downward, like a Mongol's. Although it is summer, he is wearing a mismatched, wool suit, with brown trousers and a blue topcoat.

On the cart are piled bolts of nubby cotton, copper pots, stone crockery, cases of tin cutlery and boxes of soap and candles.

I turn to inspect the pedlar further. No doubt, he is a Jew from inside the Pale.

"You see, there's another one making trouble," Olympia shouts, running toward the pedlar. "He's stealing trade from our own merchants."

The mangy pedlar turns his face to the shouting woman. Although I can discern that he is of an advanced age, his skin is unwrinkled except around his eyes and mouth, where there are deep worry lines.

"Are you a Chinaman or a Hebrew?" Olympia inquires.

The pedlar rises to his feet and extends his hand to her. "I am a human being, just as you are," he says softy. His English is accented.

Mother-in-law stumbles back. Under no circumstances will she shake this man's hand. He is hardly human to her.

"I won't say it again," Frederick shouts. "Both of you. Get into the carriage this minute."

We leave the pedlar behind, but I know who he is. He is my mother's secret lover. He is a rag and bones man selling tawdry goods from a broken-down cart. He is poor beyond anything I have experienced. He is also my father and he exists beyond the furthest boundaries of English society. But there is the look of a questioning intelligence in his face. We are people of the book. Rubin Stollman told me he'd studied at a good school, in the Yiddish language. He must have been a handsome man once, long ago, with his chiselled nose and brilliant blue eyes. I can understand why Maman cared for him, why she needed to have a child with him.

I think him brave to stand his ground with Olympia Wendice. He does not flinch.

"Under no conditions are you allowed to the leave the house without my permission." Inside our carriage, my husband is seething. "Look at me! There will be no more visits to the Stollmans."

I believe that Frederick will strike me. I meet his glare, inviting him to give me the excuse to finally leave him. He bunches his hand into a fist; he cannot do it. I have defeated him.

If he is correct, if Olympia's uncharacteristic public scene signifies illness, then soon he will fall ill with the filthy disease himself, but not before he watches his mother writhe in fevered pain.

## - 18 -

It is Saturday evening before dusk and Frederick is hiding in his study. I am perched on the window seat of my morning room looking down upon the flagstone path that winds toward the graveyard. Perfectly staked blue cornflowers and pink delphiniums line the walkway. I'd ordered purple and yellow painted China lanterns from Fortnum and Masons to brighten the garden outside the dining room, but in haste to prepare for my party, I'd forgotten to have Jack string them up. I can't begin to calculate when I will hold another dinner party at the manor. For years to come, I may be dining alone. Alone with the servants. Mrs. Bullbrook and Jack. I must keep a watchful eye on Jack. His freshly acquired learning at the Mechanic's Institute could stand him in good stead with the law, but no, mustn't worry. In the end he is only a stable boy, an orphan from the slate pits of Tintagel.

I hear voices downstairs and Mrs. Bullbrook trundling up the stairs to fetch Frederick. I am surprised since no one ever calls on us. Banker

Salt wishes to speak with my husband so I bolt down the stairs before the Master can reach the old man. He is looking green around the gills so I offer him a chair by the open window in the parlour.

"Harald, man, you look poorly!" Frederick announces as soon as he enters the room. I must admit that my husband's face is colourless, too. "Are you feverish?" Frederick asks the banker, forever suspicious.

What if I poisoned his food by mistake? I'm certain I didn't confuse the *bonbons*. Clean angels to one side and dirty, dirty angels to the other.

"I haven't been myself all day," Salt admits. "Last night's conversation disturbed me."

"Most likely you drank a teeny weenie too much last night," I offer, knowing I am being churlish, but I cannot contain myself.

"That's enough!" Frederick commands. He has not said one word to me since this morning in the carriage.

I leave the room but keep my ear pinned to the keyhole of the parlour's door.

"Feeling disgruntled are you? Then let me pour you a whiskey. A stiff one before dinner," Frederick suggests.

Salt accepts the drink. "May I be frank with you, Wendice?"

"By all means."

"Your wife is a bad influence on Mrs. Salt. Nancy is a simple girl and I don't wish for her to get ideas in her head. Why, Mrs. Wendice and those friends of hers, they are outrageous."

"You think so, do you?"

"That Polly woman, now there's a good looking piece," Salt remarks. "Yet the German phrenologist claims she does not wish to propagate the species. What kind of woman is she, I ask you?"

Frederick is sweating and looking uncomfortable. "With her green eyes and black hair. She is the snake in the garden. I've told Cordelia as much, but she never listens." Frederick stares into the middle distance and allows the banker to continue.

"How many marriages are anything more than mutual forbearance? I despair. Perhaps there ought not to be such a thing as enforced permanence in marriage."

"Do you think not?"

"If you don't mind me saying, Wendice, I noticed that your wife never looked you straight in the eye, not once last night. If a woman cannot endure a direct, searching gaze, must it not imply some enormous wickedness?"

It is now my turn, so I push open the parlour door. "Would you agree, dear Frederick?"

Frederick remains silent. I have brought a small Limoges candy dish with the two remaining tainted chocolates from last night's party.

"*Un petit bonbon*?" I ask.

"Assuredly yes, Mrs. Wendice." The banker smiles his thin, listless smile.

Mr. Salt pops the chocolate in his mouth.

"Another? It's the very last one."

"Don't mind if I do."

"It's all this talk about Jews that troubles me," Salt says. "In the carriage ride home, this Israel Zangwill fellow chastised Nancy for blaming the Jews for spreading typhoid. However, we've known from the days of our Lord Jesus Christ that the Jews are poisoners of well water. I believe Nancy may be onto something."

"Onto what?" I inquire.

Salt looks at me disparagingly. "We should investigate this foreign couple in the village, the ones who operate the Café Demel. Could they be the cause of the typhoid in our village?"

"Have you spoken with Olympia Wendice today?" I inquire.

"Leave Mater out of this," Frederick mutters.

"As I said last night, I'd rather not do business with the Jews. Or have them in my home or sit down to dinner with them. The Jews are a sneaky lot. Shylock and all that, ahem. I've never allowed the Stollmans to trick me into advancing them credit. " Salt clears his throat and I leave my husband and his banker to their own devices.

Frederick is leaving for Tintagel after early morning church services tomorrow. I must stay until after he departs. When Olympia falls ill, he will be called back to the manor. Assuming she succumbs to my poison before he does.

***

Throughout the sleepless night, I consider taking Jack with me. The orphan is such a bright penny! Why not give him a chance? Would it be prudent to keep him by my side? But, no, I cannot afford to keep him with me, not until I am absolutely certain that Olympia and Frederick perish of the disease. What I must do before departing is to walk along the path to my William's grave. I visit at least once, each and every evening when Mrs. Bullbrook is already in her cups and Frederick is snoring on the divan. Today I shall try to explain to my boy that I won't be returning to visit him for a time, but he will live in my heart every minute of every day and no one will ever replace him.

I also confide in William that his Papa must die of typhoid fever, so he must not worry himself if Frederick is absent. What I do promise William is that I shall return to him. As I should, I tell William that I have decided to stay at the Devil's Stone Inn in Shebbear until the storm blows over. There is unfinished business at the inn that I must attend to. If am lucky, perhaps I will run into my true father before I depart Holsworthy. William understands. My true father is strong of heart. He is not afraid to declare who he is. He is not like me, pretending to be someone other than who I am. Always concealing.

On Monday morning, I am packed and ready to go. Jack watches from on high in the barn's loft as I pull on the greys' reins and direct the mares out the stable doors. I look up at his face, but he has turned away.

"I'll find you, Cordelia, wherever you go. I promise, you'll not get away with it," he says. "Miss Staples died that same way me mum did."

His ambition has got the better of him. With teacher Staples no longer able to help him advance, I am his one and only chance and he bets that I will capitulate to his demands. It's true, he knows too much, but I can't allow his threats to interfere with my plans.

But there is something else I see in his face, a look of fear, even regret. Jack and I have been together for a long while now. If I abandon him, who will he have left? He's much too clever to count on the benevolence of Master Frederick.

At the last moment before I pull away, I'm stopped outside the barn by a stranger. I have no initial idea who he is. The man is tall, wearing a stained-tan topcoat although it is late summer. His brown hair falls in strings down his neck. His lips are full, slightly snarled and his eyes are sharp. He could see through darkness.

"Mrs. Wendice, I'm Inspector Anniss of the Metropolitan Plymouth Police. You must recognize me."

"Indeed, I don't and why should I?" Remain calm, I tell myself.

Jack jumps down from the rafters and I see the same look of excitement in his green eyes that I saw the other day when I was in trouble.

"Oh we met years ago, with Mrs. Turney, I believe."

"At the tearoom in Plymouth," I am faltering as I hold the reins in check.

"See, you know it."

"Yes, I was her guest."

"Just so. No idea you were the lady of the manor." He speaks gruffly through his thick lips. Then a quick, fatuous smile. Any fool could see he remembers that I am Frederick Wendice's wife. He is dissembling.

I recall the Inspector and the disrespectful way he addressed Polly. She and I encountered him in the tearoom in Plymouth, after visiting the typhoid ward in the hospital. Anniss was the menace that Adela spoke of, harassing the girls, working for both sides, the law and the whores, and stuffing loot in his pockets as he went.

When Olympia emerges from the manor, the Inspector makes a courtly bow. She has called upon him to investigate, he explains.

"Investigate what? There's been no crime here as far as I know."

"Mr. Salt, the Barclay's banker, believes there is tomfoolery going on in town. Certain types are spreading typhoid," says Anniss.

Olympia will not let this go. She and Salt have already exchanged notes by first morning post, I fear.

"Certain types," Anniss repeats.

"Could you be more specific?"

Olympia dares to look squarely at me, but even Anniss cannot imagine that I am guilty of a crime such as this. Poisoning the townsfolk.

"And so a national epidemic is due to a murderer? I'll be off, then," I say. I am holding my breath. "Off to town. Mother-in-law knows everyone, anyone who might be guilty of this improbable and impressive crime. "But Olympia, I fear Frederick is right. You do not look well. You do seem greatly fatigued. It might be best to rest rather than concern yourself with such tawdry affairs. If they are in anyway real and not imagined."

It is up to Mother-in-law to advise him that I am Jewish, that I am responsible for the contagion.

Anniss sticks out his arm, intending for Olympia to walk to the manor before him. "The servants. They'll be the ones I'll interrogate first," he declares.

Olympia is standing still. This is her moment. She looks at the blanket I've used to cover my belongings in the dray.

"Of course, Inspector," she says. "The servants and the Hebrew couple in town who operate the bakery. The Café Demel, they call it, these Stollman people, Austrians, Socialists, I understand from Mr. Salt. He wouldn't contemplate advancing them credit. I'd speak to these foreigners if I were you." She refuses his arm.

Anniss follows her, like a dog, into the big house.

***

With me in the dray is the *Pot-au-feu* that I have prepared for certain members of the family, and a hamper filled with leftover delicacies from Friday's supper, my portmanteau and the two paintings by John Turner that I nicked from the parlour. My hands are trembling as I steer the greys out of town and onto the road to the Devil's Stone Inn.

# Book Four

SHEBBEAR, COUNTY DEVON

1895

# - I -

IT IS SUPPERTIME WHEN I arrive at the Devil's Stone Inn. Horses and wagons are hitched to the red painted post, the flickering lights of the oil lamps are burning brightly inside the dining room and from a distance of more than fifty feet, I can make out the farm hands regaling each other with tales of work and women. The familiar smell of cider and sizzling fat hits me squarely in the face as soon as I cross the doorstep.

I leave the *Pot-au-feu* in the dray. I could throw it to the pigs. Not a soul notices me as I take my seat at the bar of the Devil's Stone. If that isn't enough to put me off, the look of the room nearly knocks me senseless, hardly resembling the place I'd left fourteen years ago.

When Maman ran the inn, the mahogany bar was glowing with spit, elbow grease and lemon oil polish. Chairs and long tables for the customers were neatly lined up in rows near the blue painted, wooden shutters encasing the windows. The floorboards were always swept clean before supper and Maman would have her hot table loaded with the finest food in all of County Devon.

My hand floats across the cool dark surface of the bar. With my fingers I find my initials, C.T., carved into the wood. I'd done it with the tip of Maman's butcher knife and Pa had given me a royal beating for defacing his property. Maman cried out when he pulled his belt from his trousers, but he pushed her away.

"I'll teach you a lesson, young miss," he said swinging the leather belt across my buttocks. Sweat dripped down his face. I felt the leather cut into my skin, but it was Maman who fainted and not me. There are things a child never forgets.

Tonight the sight before me is of a dilapidated drinking hole, neither clean nor tidy. Many after me have carved their names into the wood of the bar. The tapestries that Maman brought with her from Angers, which adorned the hall's walls, are missing, as are her copper pots that hung from the ceiling beams. Even the blue and white Limoges plates that she displayed along the broad, black beams of the rear wall are chipped and covered in grey soot. I shan't bother sharing the paintings I nicked from the manor house with this lot.

What doesn't surprise me is that sister-in-law Griselda is behind the bar, dishing out harsh words to the farm hands, who are holding out their plates in anticipation of their supper. "You think you deserve to be fed, do you now?" she squawks at the hungry men.

Griselda's hair has turned to grey since I saw her last at my wedding in Holsworthy. Two of her front side teeth have blackened. She is wearing a brown muslin shirt with the sleeves rolled above her bony elbows and a brown, faded skirt to match. As I glance around the room, I see crockery and caste-iron pots and roasters piled sky high in the washing tubs, and baskets of corn and ripened tomatoes spilling onto the floor. Through the passage to the scullery, I notice hens and their chicks lurching in and out of the garden door, pecking at the grime on the flagstone floor.

Finally Griselda deems to greet me. Without looking up, she says, "Look what the cat's dragged in."

"Good evening to you, too," I reply as politely as is humanly possibly.

Griselda calls for Albert, who must be sitting out in the back garden nursing his ale. "You'll never guess who's shown up at our doorstep? Your long-lost sister. The lady of the manor, herself."

The farm hands peer up at me from their plates of pork sausage and fried potatoes. No one cares who I am. No one except Albert, who kisses me and embraces me.

"I've done it; I've finally done as you've demanded and left the blighter."

"It was your idea for her to come here?" Griselda asks incredulously.

Albert wipes the sweat from his brow with his brown, knuckled fingers and looks to his wife in whom a storm is visibly gathering. I should offer Griselda a bowl of my *Pot-au-feu* and be done with her.

"Don't think you are welcome here!" she declares. "We don't want your kind of trouble. We have enough of our own."

Who is Griselda to tell me what to do?

"This is my place as much as yours—"

Albert cuts me off, before I can launch into a full-blown tirade. "Hush, you two. We'll need to consider—"

"Consider what?" Griselda asks. "She's won't be stopping under my roof, I can tell you that for free. Get her out of here, Albert. Why would you tell her to leave Wendice? She was the cause of the typhoid fever that raged at the time your mother passed and I won't have her scaring away the customers. Folks around here have long memories."

"If I remember correctly, your people were tinkers—"

"Stop it the both of you!" Albert sits down.

Albert confesses that the news of the typhoid epidemic in Holsworthy has spread to Shebbear.

"Is anyone sick here now?" I ask Albert.

"No," he replies with a worried look on his face.

"Where's Pa?" It strikes me that Pa is not sitting on his usual stool at the bar, telling ribald tales and drinking Scrumpy.

"Go ahead, ask your Pa if you can stop here," Griselda says. "Let's see how pleased he is to see you." Griselda is as spiteful as ever.

"Mind your own business!" I say.

Albert moves to a table near the corner window. "He's poorly, Cordelia. Mostly he rests out in the garden or we keep him upstairs in a room at the inn. You haven't seen him for going on two years. He's changed."

Perhaps Pa has softened in his attitude towards me. Perhaps I might convince him that I'm not the bad apple he always thought I was. "Could I see him, now?" I ask Albert.

"Not tonight. The old man hardly sleeps and I won't be having you wake him." Griselda answers for Albert.

"I need a place to stay. You said I should leave Wendice. I want to see my Pa."

"The inn's full up," Griselda states. "It's too late. You're not welcome here!"

I look out the window to the thatch cottage where I was born. Griselda's words never fail to wound.

The roof needs repair. The once neatly trimmed garden has turned into an abundant patch of weeds and wild flowers. In the western corner of this patch, the pear and the apricot trees are in full bloom. It's canning season. The picked fruit would be luscious and it brings to mind the jam and jellies that Maman showed me how to boil up with sugar and a hint of rum. I imagine smelling the heady fragrance of boiling fruit wafting throughout the inn's kitchen, as it did every harvest in Maman's time.

While I'm reminiscing, Griselda is scheming. She instructs Albert to make up a straw pallet for me in the stone shed where Pa still keeps his guns, butchery knives and pipes. "He won't notice," Griselda claims.

In the old days during times like this, the barn would be spilling over with the harvest's hands, many more than were eating from Griselda's kitchen today. I used to carry the workers their tea in wicker baskets while the farm girls eyed the well-muscled lads forking hay into golden pyramids. Albert and I walk out to the stone shed. It is where it always was, right beside the pigpen. And there they are, Pa's prize pigs: droopy eyed, mottled pink and black with huge bellies and long snouts burrowed deep into the oozy stink of the sty. Albert throws a pail of slop and corn husks inside the pen, rousing the snorting creatures from a blissful lethargy. Pa always cared for his pigs more than he did for me.

"What's happened to Pa?" I ask Albert. "Why didn't you tell me he's so poorly?"

"He's old and he's angry. Nothing you can do about Pa. He's still arguing with Maman."

"She's been dead for fourteen years."

"Doesn't seem to matter; he has a bone to pick with her, dead or alive."

Is it possible that Albert knows about the red-haired pedlar? I recall my brother saying something. "Do you know about my real father?"

Albert, who is walking with his arm about my shoulders, moves away. "I know."

"Why didn't you tell me? Why do you keep so many secrets from me?"

"Maman made me promise not to. She reasoned that it would only hurt you and if you blurted it out to Pa, he would take it out on you."

"How did you find out?"

"I'm the eldest. I can remember. Maman was dashing into Holsworthy every second week, spending more and more time with her friends the Stollmans. Pa was furious that she wasn't at work in the kitchen. When she started to show, she was gloriously happy. I knew the baby wasn't Pa's."

"And you truly believe Pa doesn't know?"

"How could he? Maman went to her grave with that secret."

Albert pushes open the double door of the shed. He hands me a bar of soap and a towel and makes me promise to wash up before leaving the shed.

"Griselda made me promise that you would stay away from the kitchen."

In truth, I wouldn't wish to harm my brother or his children. Griselda is another story. I can easily imagine her in the same condition as Frederick and Olympia. "And you agreed, as you always do with her?"

"What do you expect? Granted, leaving Wendice is all for the best, but you can't stay here with us. Not now, with typhoid breaking out again. You'll have to make your own way, sister." He can barely look me straight in the eye.

"Who's told you about the epidemic in Holsworthy?" I ask my brother.

"Your lad Jack keeps me informed. Quite a letter writer, he's turned out to be."

"What will Jack look like when he's chewed up by ambition?"

"What an odd thing to say," Albert says innocently.

***

If I run back to the dray and offer Griselda a bowl of my *Pot-au-feu*, I realize now she would turn me down. Why would she eat from my hand if Jack's news of the typhoid fever has reached Shebbear? But I can always try.

"Give me a minute to get my bearings," I ask Albert. "I'm starved. Could I, at least, grab some cheese and bread from the kitchen?"

Albert is dubious. "Best I bring something out to you."

I cover my ears with my hands. "Albert, I just want a bite; I haven't consumed a thing to eat or drink since morning. I'm parched. You can't believe I would contaminate the kitchen tonight, my first night back at home? I just want a bowl of my stew and to make a cup of tea."

Albert, trusting soul that he is, agrees. He has not the temerity to oppose me as I am storming about, making wild motions with my arms.

He passes into the stone shed with my bedding while, out of his sight, I return to the dray for the French stew. The kitchen is deserted when I enter with Maman's old bones pot. There's soup simmering on the stove, filled with hens' necks and goose fat that's skimming the surface. Peppercorns are floating atop the yellow grease.

I see it instantly, Griselda's bowl brought from the tinkers' encampment when she came to the Devil's Stone as Albert's wife. Her only possession along with a doll made of blue and red yarn, with brown buttons for eyes. Although it is difficult to imagine, Griselda was a child once.

Only one ladle of my stew is what I pour into Griselda's wooden bowl, mixed with more than a cup of her waxy soup. When sister-in-law enters the kitchen at dawn for her porridge, she will spoon the soup down her throat, and then clean the bowl. Waste not, want not. That is her motto. She will never allow the soup to go to waste. She will never suspect.

If she'd only been a little more welcoming, offering me a room to share in the inn, a seat at the table with the family, I swear I would have dumped my potion in the trough for Pa's pigs. Instead Griselda's getting what she deserves.

What I'm wondering is who will fall first, Olympia or Griselda? Frederick next. I'd prefer to see them all in agony.

***

When I enter the stone shed, I see hundreds of dead blue-bottle flies blanketing the floor. They'd been feasting on the smoked pig trotters hanging from the rafter below the sloped ceiling. Along the wooden benches lining the walls are legions of more dead flies and moths. Everything in here has failed at escaping the suffocating heat of this mummified shed.

Pa's cluttered worktable is littered with pouches of tobacco, racks of pipes and, surprisingly, sepia photos of Maman when she was young and beautiful. In one photo, she is wearing a pale-coloured frock with beaded sequins. Her hair is wrapped in an elegant chignon and she is smiling. It must have been taken on her wedding day. It appears that he holds this photo to his eye since it is tobacco stained and the edges are furled from handling. In another photo she is heavily pregnant. My brothers are gathered around her in this family portrait, so she must have been big with me. Pa is also in the photo, although he is standing to the side, with a mystified look on his face.

***

*In my dream, I am playing the fiddle while dancing on the roof of the inn. I am lighter than air. This time I am not celebrating the impending birth of my child. No. The taste is bittersweet. I am flying above Shebbear, caught in the serpent's tale of the west wind. My heart's a furry sharp-toothed thing that charges out whimpering. My wrath recognizes no bounds. The music of other fiddlers, those who have searched for love and acceptance, in vain, serenades me. We are an orchestra of unclaimed hearts.*

*Floating downward, I tiptoe upon the devil's stone, laughing. I slither over its smooth surface in my velvet slippers. Appearing in many disguises, tonight I am the mottled-green snake. The angel of death cloaked in ruby-red feathers. I am the plague. Splash the blood of the sacrificial lamb on your door for tonight I am the witch on the road to chaos.*

## – 2 –

My first morning back at the Devil's Stone Inn, I lie in until eleven. Although I'm sleeping in the shed, I must admit to having the best rest I've had in years. There is no one to disturb me. The only sound is of the snorting pigs next door. By now the poison is doing its work inside Griselda.

Last night before falling asleep, I did sweep out the dead insects and all the dust mites from the shed so it looks half decent in the morning light. Swinging open the top half of the door to the shed, I listen to the cicadas chirping, a sound I missed hearing at the manor. I pull bits of yellow straw from my hair. I feel as if I've been dancing in my sleep.

---

In the overgrown garden, I see raspberry canes rising above the weeds. Gone are Maman's Tigeralla and Sweet Million tomatoes, her purple kale and white leeks, her butter beans, dark orange carrots, nubs of garlic, sweet and sharp sprouting onions. No one has bothered tending this garden in years.

Looking toward the horizon, I see three carriages with two chestnut ponies pulling each one. I can make out a bride dressed in mauve and stepping spritely between the haystack-lined fields. Her groom is catching her up from behind. It should have been me in this picture, but it never will be.

Under an ancient pear tree, Pa is balanced on a three-legged stool. He sits alone in the corner of the ancient garden. His face is blank.

When he waves a hand in my direction, I move eagerly toward him. Will he recognize me? Or would it be best if he couldn't recall a thing about me and we tried to begin afresh. Children, even bastard children, expect their parents to forgive their sins, no matter how horrendous. If he'd lived, I could have forgiven William anything.

"Pa, it's me, Cordelia!"

The old man rises to hobble toward me, but even with two canes he cannot properly support his weight.

"Sit down Pa," I say running to meet him. "Here, I'll give you a hand."

"You've never given me a hand before. Why would you start now?"

Pa remembers me. He turns his face from me while attempting to land solidly on the wooden stool. I reach out to aid him, but he pushes my hand away. "Leave me be."

"Griselda won't allow me to sleep in the cottage or the inn," I inform him. "She's forced me to sleep in your shed beside the pig sty."

"Ha, you've always hated those pigs of mine, Madeleine," he replies.

He is confusing me with Maman. I wish to discover if he knows if I am another man's daughter, but he cannot even distinguish between his dead wife and me.

"Madeleine, Pa? It's me, Cordelia."

Pa grunts in reply, sounding more like a pig than a man. "Cordelia." He screws his face into a half grin, but he keeps his distance from me.

"Do you want to know why I came back to the Devil's Stone Inn?" Would he care no matter what the circumstances? "Wendice did horrible things to me, Pa. I can't stand it anymore."

"Why here?"

"This is my home. Where else would I go?"

Out of nowhere Griselda appears. "You two becoming reacquainted?"

"You could describe it that way." Perhaps the old man isn't as daft as he acts. He doesn't appear to fancy Griselda any more than I do. "You've put Cordelia in my shed, have you?"

Before she's able to respond two scrubby urchins appear. The boys, who are twins, carry frogs in their hands.

"What, Ma!" Their voices were exactly the same. They wear short pants, rough cambric shirts rolled up at the sleeves and they are barefoot. Their heads are shaved down to their scalps. Their bright eyes shine with merriment when they see how distraught their Ma is.

"Put us in the shed with the pigs," they both say in unison. "We love the pigs."

Pa lets out a belly laugh while Griselda shoos the boys away like flies.

"Settled then, is it daughter-in-law? The twins move to the shed while this one moves into the inn." Pa is delighted to cross Griselda.

"We'll see about that," she says, stamping away and crying out for Albert, who no doubt, will take her side over mine. I cannot yet detect a change in her countenance.

Although my marriage is dreadful, I can't see much in brother Albert's to commend it. Frederick's idea of the perfect world is my vision of hell, but then it might be like that for married folks in general. Holding opposite visions of heaven in their heads. After Wendice is dead, I promise never to enter into the state of holy matrimony again and I pray that Albert will imitate me after his wife is gone.

My stop at the Devil's Stone Inn is not turning out exactly the way I'd planned. Pa can hardly remember his own name, let alone Maman's indiscretions of more than thirty years ago.

Later that afternoon I dump the remainder of my *Pot-au-feu* in the trough for the pigs. It has gone rancid with the heat and no one would dream of eating it now.

***

For two weeks, I live alone in the stone shed, waiting for Griselda to fall ill. Lately, I am unable to sleep, What if I am entirely wrong?

---

If Griselda does finally fall ill, I wonder if she will resemble Maman when she was dying or will she look more like the unclaimed bodies in the contagion ward at the Royal Albert hospital? Maman went quickly while the hospital patients were burning for weeks, so long that they no longer resembled human beings. They became feral, looking more like ailing, shelterless dogs than men or women.

During the day, there's more than enough time to consider how my life has reached this place. In the evening, as soon as the sun sets, Albert visits me. We light the oil lamp and sit together on the stoop of the old shed. The air is a cornucopia of sweet smells that I can taste on my tongue.

With Griselda out of sight today, I was able to sneak into the kitchen earlier to steam a Chester Pudding. Equal amounts of flour, shredded suet, breadcrumbs. Caster sugar, egg and milk mixed into the dough. I let it steam for three hours and then carried it back to the shed for Albert and me. In a preserving jar, I transported the sauce: blackcurrant jam flavoured with sailor's rum. It's Albert's favourite pudding and I've taken special care to keep my hands clean and where they should be.

We talk about Maman.

"You could have told me about the red-haired pedlar," I say, reproaching him mildly.

"Polly introduced you to the Stollmans and they confirmed it. The deed needed to be done by someone outside the family. I couldn't betray Maman, not even for you."

"Knowing who my real father is wouldn't be a betrayal," I say.

"The Stolllmans are good people. Polly thought they were the right ones to tell you about him."

"Polly." I look at Albert, tanned and gaunt, in the flickering oil light. "Why didn't you just up and grab her?"

Albert doesn't seem surprised that I know. "I couldn't leave Griselda."

"Why not?"

"Because I made a promise when I married Griselda."

"But you don't love her anymore."

"It's a different kind of affection. You wouldn't know it ... and, it's not me Polly loves. It's you."

"Where is your missus today? She hasn't been wagging her finger in my face."

Albert's eyes are points of light. His lips quiver. He no longer loves me. He already knows. "Griselda turned poorly yesterday," he says. "The fever is laying her low. You deliberately contaminated my wife. It's only a matter of time. We both knew it would come to this."

I dare not meet his eyes. "Everyone else, the children, the farmhands, are safe." I pray to God that I am right, as he dips a spoon into the warm pudding.

"Let's hope so, but you best be on your way, sooner rather than later, before more are infected," he says plainly. "You are no longer welcome in Shebbear."

***

The next morning, I'm leaning on the bottom ledge of my half door, watching the sun, high and hazy, burning down on the parched, yellow field when I hear: "Farmers could use some rain."

"If you'd been raised in the country and not beside Wendice's quarries, you'd know that dry weather is best for threshing."

It is Jack. The lad has figured out that I'd gone home to the Devil's Stone Inn. Clever boy, he knows something about how my mind works.

Without asking about how I am faring in Shebbear, Jack pulls a letter addressed to me from his shirt pocket. "It's from Master Frederick," he announces.

I see the wavy "W" inscribed on the back of the blue envelope. The contents of the letter are not a complete surprise:

*27th September 1895*
*Wendice Manor, Holsworthy*

*Dearest wife Cordelia,*

*As you intended, I fell ill twenty days after you deserted me, indicating to me—with a menacing sense of finality— that you care not a crumb for the long years of our marriage or the tragic death of our only son. His death ought to have bound us together for eternity. If you truly respected me, or I dare-say, the memory of our benighted boy William, I believe you would have remained at my side to nurse me through this terrible ordeal.*

*How achingly slow time lingers when one is critically ill and one's wife has deserted one. Cordelia, do not dissemble when you read this missive, do not prevaricate by shaking your fair face or directing your invidious smile into the middle distance—or by pretending that you meant not to destroy me forever.*

*As you can surely imagine, the fever is burning the inside of my mouth & nostrils. Although Housekeeper has opened wide all the windows, as I instructed her to do, the manor is stifling with humidity and the fetid smell of decay. The worst of the headaches, when I expected my brains to explode, have passed, but I cannot keep even a dollop of soup in my belly, nor can I defecate. A miasma is rotting inside me and it reminds me of you, dear wife.*

*On my skin, hideous boil-like eruptions are congealing as perforated wounds across my body. I no longer have the strength to lift my sodden head from the pillow & it is only due to the kindness of the banker Mr. Salt, to whom I am dictating this letter that I am able to convey my admonishment to you.*

*Mater died seven days ago from the fever, just as I was showing the first signs of the illness and although I could not attend her funeral, I watched the burial from the window of your morning room. As you imagined I would.*

*By the time you read this, I suspect I will already be dead and buried beside our dear son and mother. Although you belong to me –you are my wife and it is your duty to care for me now that I have fallen under your unfathomable curse—you abandon me when I need you most. Know you not that we will be reunited eternally as man and wife in the afterlife? It is remarkable to me that, after all our years of concealing your secret, you actually believe that you could escape unscathed. As the scriptures say,"Watch, for ye know not what hour your Lord doth come."*

---

*Without me, you must admit, you would surely have been exposed, but instead of matching my loyalty, you throw me to the wolves with this intolerable fever. At her death, Mater knew perfectly well it was you who poisoned her. Mrs. Bullbrook and Jack know it, too, but they demand that I give it my all & fight for my life. If I succumb, as I anticipate I will, Inspector Anniss will be relentless in his hunt for you, of that I am certain. Mater told him everything before she perished and how could I stop a dying woman's last wish? I remain in this life and the next,*

*Your devoted husband,*
*Frederick*

"If I was to bet, I'd say he'll be dead before the week is over," Jack states with a sneer on his face. "Compared to him, Madame Wendice went easily. I've never seen a body suffer worse than Master Frederick."

Frederick is going the hard way, as he deserves.

"Master Frederick, is it? Not his Lordship, the way we referred to him between ourselves?"

"He's not exactly the villain you made him out to be, ma'am."

I'd always hoped that Jack would be on my side.

"You cannot know all that has passed between my husband and me. There are such things as crimes of omission. The Wendices have set out from the start to deceive me."

"They'll come for you. They know it was you who did it to Master Frederick and his mother and to the banker Salt, too. The banker is back on his feet so he's strong enough to sit with the Master. It's him and Mrs. Bullbrook who are with him during his time of need."

"Are they now? Mrs. Bullbrook and the banker Salt. What a fine pair they make," I respond. "They'd be better off calling for Polly. At least she knows what she is doing."

"They did. Polly knows."

"Pardon me. Has Polly turned against me, as well?"

"That's for her to decide. She knows that the Master is very sick. It's Inspector Anniss of the Metropolitan Plymouth Police, who suspects you. On her deathbed, your mother-in-law begged Anniss to track you down and bring you to justice. Miss Polly confirmed that the Inspector did meet you in Plymouth years ago. Inspector Anniss remembered you; said so when you crossed paths just before you left the manor and you didn't deny it. You recall how he looked at you. Claims you were up to no good back then in Plymouth when you visited the typhoid ward at the Royal Albert Hospital. He says he could detect the shadow of the devil on your face. He says all whores are diseased and that it figures that you are as well. Now he knows you are a Jewess. Olympia told him when she was dying. She said the Jews use black magic to make Christian folk sick."

"Inspector Anniss. He's frightfully ugly and not at all refined. Didn't you notice how deferential he was around me?"

"That's what you say, ma'am, but the Inspector claims differently. He claims you propositioned him."

"What are you going to threaten me with next, Jack?"

"All I need do is inform them of me mum, the way she passed and Miss Staples, too. The Master's mum dead and buried and himself on his way to an early grave. They've all gone the same way! Why'd you do it?"

It is difficult for me to take this all in. I'd always depended on a certain bond between Jack and me, no matter how strained things became, one that could transcend our difficulties. But he's turned on me, my Jack. The demise of his Miss Staples has affected his head, stopped him on his road to success. If Jack is telling the truth, Inspector Anniss would be eager to charge me with Olympia's death and Frederick's murder, too, if my husband dies, that is. And now there's Griselda. But what hard proof does Anniss have? A raving tinker's daughter claiming I poisoned her with typhoid fever? Would Anniss take Jack's word against mine? How could Jack's mother or Miss Staples be traced back to me?

'*Incroyable*!' as Maman would say. And me, healthy as a horse. I threw the *Pot-au-feu* to the pigs and they've all survived.

Jack begins to walk toward the inn, but before he sets out, he informs me he will ask Albert for work in the barn until I make up my mind.

"Make up my mind about what?" I inquire.

"Make up your mind, if you'll turn yourself in," he says without emotion, "or I'll be forced to lead Inspector Anniss to your doorstep."

---

Before leaving me, I make Jack promise that he will not tell Albert about Frederick's illness, not just yet; and he gives me his word that I have two days to decide whether I'm going to do the right thing or not.

"Remember that if not for me, Jack, you would have been left there in Tintagel with your mum. Left maybe to share in her fate. You cannot say I have not given you a better life."

He thinks on this. "Two days. After that, whatever I do is fair game," Jack insists.

## - 3 -

Jack enjoys the work at Shebbear. And for today, he keeps to his word and stays far away from Albert, who is otherwise occupied with Griselda. At night, Jack sleeps in the old milking barn with the other hired help, but after the first night with the men, he visits me. From a far distance, I think I hear Griselda pleading with God to forgive her, her sins. I should leave this place before Albert throws me out. Once his wife is dead he will see to it, that I never return.

Autumn is fast approaching and the darkening sky is clear with a pumpkin moon above us. We leave the stone shed and walk along the path beside the River Torridge. For a long while, we say nothing, but when we are far from the inn and I see Jack's face clearly, the same sculpted cheekbones that I'd noticed on his mother that first day in Tintagel, the same nut-brown skin, the same yellow curls swirling about his ears, I cannot hold my tongue any longer.

"Why did you follow me here?" I inquire.

"So you would own up to what you've done."

"What else?" I've never known exactly what Jack is onto next. "How can you hate me so?" I ask him. "I was the one who rescued you, who took you away from the quarry. You have a chance at a decent life now. Otherwise, you'd be dead before you turn forty, buried below a pile of slate."

As we meander beside the trout-filled stream, I can sense Jack trembling. Under the moon the willow trees are gleaming in the white light. The green leaves are sparkling with night dew.

---

At that moment, he takes me in his arms and kisses me on the lips. He is fearless. And although his kiss is wet and sloppy, it is full of genuine emotion. He is young, Jack is, inexperienced with women and he is entirely alone in the world. His moods change as fast as West Country weather. No one can deny that there is an attraction between us, no matter how stormy the sky. He struggles against it, but it's always engulfing us, a hand on a shoulder, a slow-eyed look of his green eyes. Like humid, restless air on a summer day with rain clouds travelling from the east, too ominous to ignore.

"You could report to Anniss that you'd not found me. That I'd left the Devil's Stone Inn before you arrived," I say, stepping back from him.

"That would be a lie."

"Then, tell Anniss I've snuck off to London. It's impossible to find someone in London. Just give me a chance to get away."

Jack kisses me again. "Take me with you to London and I won't tattle on you."

We sit on a fallen log beside the river. The moon remains bright and I can see the flickering candlelight from the inn peaking through the willow trees.

"I would if I could, Jack, but I can't. They'd find us in no time. A woman on her own can disappear into the crowd, but an older woman with a fresh young lad like you, why they'd have us. You'd be blamed for tipping me off and you deserve better than that."

Jack's face is stone. I fear he despises me now.

"With me, you could end up in Newgate, just as I'm sure to do if you shop me to the Inspector."

I spend the remainder of the night gathering my few belongings, ensuring the Turners are covered in burlap bags and that the jewels I'd taken from Olympia's travel case are sewn into the hem of my skirt. I'll need something to keep me going once I'm in London.

I'm still wearing the same clothes I arrived in: my crimson shirt with a blue-checked dirndl skirt and a straw bonnet with dried cherries on the brim. There is no point in saying good-bye to anyone; it is best to disappear or they will rat me out, as Jack will probably do. I can no longer trust the lad. No matter that he needs me.

---

I cannot bear to think about Albert. What will happen when Jack shows him Frederick's letter? Would he testify against me in a court of law, my own flesh and blood?

If only I could sleep, but the frigid night air keeps me awake. I'm shivering and contemplate running to the inn for more blankets when I hear a noise outside the stone shed. I raise my head to peer out the window and it's Inspector Anniss I see. Jack must have sent him a missive before we met earlier tonight. He knew when he kissed me that Anniss was on his way. He'd expected that this would be our last night together unless I'd agreed to run away with him before morning. It was Jack who led Anniss directly to my door or the Inspector might have waited until dawn.

Anniss is circling the shed in the dark. The moon is hidden by clouds. It's the middle of the night with only tiny wisps of light to show him the way.

I open the half door to the shed and stick my head out to talk with him.

"You can take me now, if you'd like." Offering up myself is the only chance with Anniss.

"Hello, Mrs. Wendice," he says placing his hand inside the open half door, unpinning the latch and pushing himself inside. "Appears you've come down a step or two in this world since I ran into you last."

"Take me or shoot me, cut my throat. I'd rather die than being brought up before the court by you."

"How dramatic you are tonight. When I met you in Plymouth long ago, with Polly Turney, you wouldn't give me a second look. I was beneath the lady of the manor, wasn't I?"

"That was many years ago, before my son was born and before he died."

"If I recall you sneered at me."

I'm beginning to undo the buttons of my nightdress when Anniss inquires of me, "How do you know I'm still interested in you, Mrs. Wendice?"

"There's money, I have. Take it all," I say proudly, pulling at my handbag filled with Frederick's coins. And the paintings, too. I have two Turners. They're worth—"

He cuts me off. "Paintings aren't what I'm looking for," he replies, smirking.

"What are you looking for?"

"First off, for you to wipe that snooty look off your guileful face. You're no better than I am. You'd sell yourself to the highest bidder. In fact, you did that years ago when you wed his Lordship and look where it's got you."

My face closes down.

"Second, to admit to me that you're a murderess and a bleeding whore. You've killed them all, haven't you?"

I remain silent.

"The unlucky folks in Shebbear, when your mother died, you poisoned them, just as Wendice accused you of doing, and now in Holsworthy. Teacher Staples and her friends died because of you. Why you've murdered your own mother-in-law."

I am waiting to hear if Frederick is dead, but Anniss doesn't say, so I'm left with my doubts.

I could run, but he'd give chase. I light the lamp.

I tear open the buttons of my nightdress so he can see my breasts. He grabs me by the hips and pushes me down to the floor. He rips the cotton nightgown in two. Over and over, he enters me before exploding inside me. I am left bleeding and raw.

Before he departs, Anniss warns, "When your husband perishes, I'll have you. I'll come for you with my evidence in hand. We've sent his spit to a laboratory in London and now I have your blood on this slide." He holds a small rectangle of glass in his hand. It's smeared with blood.

There is red patch of liquid staining the floor near where I lie curled in a ball.

"Don't think for a moment, you'll get away with all this," he warns, tipping his cap. He doesn't bother to shut the shed door behind him.

***

At dawn, I set out for the rail station in Holsworthy. My hope is that no one will recognize me. If I can forget this night with Anniss, I might survive. Wipe it from my memory. Push it away or I will dissolve in its brutality. It is Jack I must keep top of mind forever. Let it be on his head the injustice that has befallen me. He betrayed me as no other could have done. I tie a paisley kerchief over my hat and pull a ragged, black shawl around my shoulders. Without much effort, I am beginning to resemble the pedlar's daughter.

And yet, I could outsmart them all yet. My blood and Frederick's spit might not be the match Anniss is searching for.

What I am facing now is a long stretch in London. At least for the time being, I will be entirely on my own. Until the typhoid blows over, which it should in the next few months, if my calculations are correct. There is still a chance, I tell myself over and over, that I will beat them at this game and that I will once again be the lady of the manor.

If things go according to plan, I could be at the manor to roast the Christmas goose. In the meantime, I have no resources, except a few sovereigns and trinkets and the paintings I swiped from Frederick and which Anniss would not accept. What I do have, I keep reminding myself, is my rare talent in the kitchen and although I have no character to ensure me a place in a good establishment, I can always forge one. By the time my mistress discovers I'm a fraud, I should be on my way. Once I overheard Adela speaking about a missionary hall in Soho where girls new to London could apply for work. I don't mind how low the work is as long as I am away from here.

As I set the greys on course, a fierce wind begins to blow, followed by a razor-sharp downpour. The rain cuts into my exposed skin. The greys are skittish so I drive them harder toward Holsworthy. Anniss' red face appears before my eyes. He is panting hard; I smell his sour breath but I wave it away. The evil sight of him, the stink. Bury him deep inside where no one will recognize the pain on my face, bury him in the silent place where I collect the great injustices done to me. They make up my personal museum, relics behind glass, the broken pieces of my heart that will never mend. I reckon, if I can make it to London safely, no one will be able to find me there with all the other lost women prowling the city streets. No matter how hard Inspector Anniss searches for me, I will find a way to elude him.

# Book Five

LONDON

1895

# - I -

LUCKILY, NO ONE BOTHERS with me at the railway station in Holsworthy but then why would they? The villagers have more important things on their minds, such as the typhoid epidemic that hasn't subsided since summer. If I had the guts, I would have inquired how Master Wendice fares, but I thought it better to keep to myself. Eventually, someone will take notice of the dray at the station and call Jack to collect the greys. I wouldn't wish the horses to suffer.

London is another world. I arrive at night. From the moment I poke my nose into the foul air of Paddington Station, I begin to tremble. I had absolutely no idea it was so huge and so crowded. For all my good intentions, it instantly becomes evident to me that I could be done for. Not a soul gives two hoots if I live or die. The buildings, reaching up to the sky, are lit up inside and out with hundreds of gas-fired globes of light. When I emerge from the station, the fog is so dense, it doesn't much matter if it's day or night, which is disconcerting to a country girl like me. I peer up at the stars, to get my bearings, except in London you're blessed if you can breathe, let alone catch a glimpse of a shining star. On the street, I cannot see any farther than the grim face next to me, skittering like a rat through a maze.

On my first night in London, since there is no one to approach for a bed or a bowl of soup, I decide to head for the Servant's Registry in Soho. Here I stand outside the great Paddington rail station with my black shawl, checkered skirt and the straw bonnet with the dried cherries on my head. Under one arm, I carry the two Turner paintings wrapped in burlap and in my other arm is the portmanteau.

All my worldly possessions are in my hands. Although I must look a sight, no one bothers to turn their attention to me.

I tramp along the Edgware Road toward the Marble Arch where a pedlar with a cart takes pity on me and offers me a lift to his market stall. He assures me it is not far from Soho. Much too late, when we have long passed the turn off for Soho, I end up in his rookery in Holborn. The smells from the corner market hit my senses hard. Refuse from spoiled fish and scraps of meat line the alleyways. The drains are overflowing with filth. They are spewing up black clouds carrying a fetid odour so rank, I must protect my nose with my shawl. A high wind, gusting from the south and carrying the putrid smell of the River Thames makes the air even dirtier.

Although it is after ten at night, when I approach this market, it is bustling with crowds of what must be London's shabbiest folk. The costermongers are hollering to the lucky souls who might have a few pence in their pockets. There are stalls for women's capes, another for nightcaps, shirt-buttons and pin-cushions. Boot and stay laces and ladies' garters are most in demand along with yards of taffeta ribbon. Printers and glassblowers covered by makeshift awnings display their curious creations. As I walk with the crowd, I see that in one corner of the market, there are chemical potions that I've never even heard of before: one for blacking, another for removing grease, another for poisoning spiders and yet another for lighting cigars. One swaggering costermonger is shouting to the crowd, extolling the virtue of his birdcages, spectacles, dog collars and key rings. A woman, without any hair, grabs me by the arm and asks me if I'm in the market for a red-herring toaster or a gridiron.

"The finest in all of London," she squawks.

Another woman in a soiled chartreuse frock is hawking bloomers, camisoles, silk stockings; and waist-cinchers made of black lace and red satin. Her business is brisk with fancy men queueing up to buy from her pushcart. I'm not so innocent that I can't tell that the men are buying gifts for their dollymops.

In another corner of the market, a group of Frenchmen are singing *La Marseillaise* to an appreciative audience. Across from the Frenchies are coloured folk, probably from the Spice Islands, chanting their own rollicking melodies.

I feel as if I have landed half way across the globe, in Calcutta or Madagascar. The surroundings are so strange to my eyes, the sounds so new to my ears that I grow dizzy with these remarkable sights and sounds. It is getting late and I'm afraid I am far from Soho and the missionaries who will offer to help me.

Just as I am about to sit on the curb and try to get my bearings, a well-dressed fellow begins to holler from his perch on a soapbox. He is a short little bloke, with pale skin and tiny hands and feet. As I draw closer to him, I see that his face is moon-like with almond-shaped eyes, and that he has a tiny mouth with a thin upper lip and downturned corners. He is not as corpulent as Freddy, but he appears soft and flabby, like a fluffy stuffed toy.

"I beseech you, my co-religionists, do not forsake the faith of our fathers and their fathers before that. Socialism is a false God. Do not be fooled!"

Beside the Patterer kneels a screever, who is drawing a chalk picture of a Menorah on the pavement, and a blind man who is reciting verse in Hebrew about Jerusalem. A large circle of men and women, some in traditional Jewish garb, crowd around. The women are wearing kerchiefs over their heads and some of the men sport long, corkscrew curls cascading around their cheeks. They remind me of the red-haired pedlar, my real father. Many are wearing huge fur hats, although it is early autumn. The men stay to one side of the Patterer while the women circle around to his other side. Everyone is dressed in black, even the young boys, who clutch their fathers' hands.

Farther from the Patterer are other groups, which are taunting him. They are speaking in Yiddish and holding up placards. In these groups, the men and women mingle together. They are shouting out slogans about workers rights.

"Down with capitalism!" they assert. "Down with religion, the opiate of the people!"

In one corner of the yard, a tall bloke is reciting poetry. He has the face of an intelligent man. A group of his co-religionists are applauding and nodding their heads in agreement.

I am aware that many Jews make London their home, but I had no idea I would run into my own people on my first night in the city. How fortuitous!

Perhaps they can help me to get settled in the great metropolis. All I need do is to explain that I am a Jewish woman who has fallen down on her luck. If a kind-spirited family would take me in for a week or two, I could establish myself and pay them back for their generosity. Possibly one member of this crowd is acquainted with Israel Zangwill. I'm certain he will remember me from my dinner party of last month ago in Holsworthy.

Before I can approach the Patterer, a young man begins to play the harp. The music is sweetly melodic and the crowd, dressed in black, begins to chant along with the harp player, while the demonstrators continue to chant, "Down with religion."

No one is particularly interested in what the Patterer has to say. I am the only one who is listening intently to him. He peers down at me from his soapbox.

"Who might you be?" he asks me after he concludes his rant.

"I am Cordelia Tilley from County Devon and Mr. Israel Zangwill is a close friend of mine. He's invited me to visit him in London."

The Patterer looks at me through his almond-shaped eyes. His skin is as white as a peeled onion. "And here you are!" he says joyfully. He jumps down from his soapbox to stand very near to me. "May I introduce myself? I am Otto Shiner of the Inns of Court, mine being Furnival's Inn."

I stretch out my hand to shake his. Mine is larger than his and he grimaces as I grip his hand.

"You're a lawyer, then, are you?"

"Indeed, a man of law, at the Chancery Court."

This man is Jewish and a lawyer. If he is a good man, he might come to my assistance.

"May I inquire how you came to be acquainted with Israel Zangwill?"

The answer to his question is more complicated than I wish it to be. "Mr. Zangwill is an associate of Gerta and Rubin Stollman. They were kind enough to introduce me to him when he was visiting their café in Holsworthy."

"Their café?"

"Yes, the Café Demel."

The lawyer laughs and I notice how his thin upper lip twists into a grimace. "Named after the famous establishment in Vienna, is it?"

"Rubin Stollman baked Sachertortes at the Café Demel."

"Did he, now? How fascinating. And what do you do, Miss Tilley? I assume, it is Miss Tilley?

Although I'd removed my wedding band on the train to London, out of habit, I check my ring finger. The lawyer hardly neglects to notice.

"Right! Well, Miss Tilley. My quarters are not far from here."

"Where's here?" I am completely lost.

He looks at me oddly. "Why Leather Lane, of course. The market in Leather Lane. Have you never been to London before, Miss Tilley?"

"This is my first visit. I intend to settle here. To find employment and a room in a respectable lodging house."

"Aha! I guessed it. You are starting over. Most people believe that London will provide them with a second chance. Are you of that opinion, Miss Tilley?"

"I am."

"I see. Well, look around you, Miss Tilley. My audience has decided exactly the same. To begin life afresh in London. They come from across the globe. Spoil our great city, they will." The lawyer is working himself up into a fevered lather. "What do you think about that?"

His question unnerves me, but I reply by saying everyone deserves a second chance even the poor and disinherited. The rabble, as the lawyer refers to them, do not resemble Mrs. Webb or any of Frederick's reforming colleagues. These people look terribly poor. They are angry.

"I wish to work, to establish myself as a cook in London," I affirm.

"Fine. Well then, suppose I offer you a place for the night and we arrange to contact Mr. Zangwill in the morning. Would that suit you?"

I have no reason to imagine that this man is dishonourable, but then again, I have no reason to believe he is honest. If I take him up on my offer, I might be signalling to him that I am a loose woman, and that would be untrue.

"How awfully kind of you," I say attempting to imitate his manner of speech. "However, I intend to stop with friends for the night."

"I see. Where do your friends reside?"

"In Soho," I remark confidently.

"Soho," the lawyer says softly. "If you wish I could drop you there in my carriage. You are carrying a great many parcels and the night is all but over for me."

At this time the young poet shouts directly to me, "Beware the strangers you meet in London, my girl."

I am confused and uncertain who I should listen to in this jumble of languages, voices and noise. It is easiest, though, to rely upon myself.

"No thank you, sir, I prefer to walk. Might you point me in the proper direction?"

"It is very late, Miss Tilley. Are you absolutely certain I cannot be of service?"

"I am certain."

In my mind, I have no clear idea why I am turning down the lawyer. He is Jewish, and a man of the law. He must be wealthy and secure. How could I go wrong with him? But I demur.

The lawyer continues to smile and points his index finger toward the heavens. "You will discover that it is a long walk to Soho," he remarks and turns away from me to the harp player, who holds up his palm to be paid.

The market crowd is thinning. There are only drinking men loitering about the street and the odd gentleman in top hat and tails roaming the alleyways. The costermongers are covering their wares for the night. The pushcarts are deserting the market. In the lifting fog, I can make out women dressed in gaudy frocks leaning into the doorways. They call out to the gentlemen. I believe I am not safe among these people of the night. The drinking men whistle at me and shout out nasty words as I rush from this place. I am entirely out of place, with nowhere to rest before beginning the trek to the Soho.

## - 2 -

The lawyer is right. It is a long walk. With my luggage and the paintings, I struggle through the filthy, twisted lanes of the grandest city in the world. Only my black shawl and straw hat protect me from the elements. A wild wind is blowing as I cross Holborn Street and step past the Charing Cross Road to Soho.

In smudged hand-painted letters, I see written: "Soho Rescue Hall for Women." I wonder if this is the establishment Adela recommended?

Matron is locking the iron padlock on the great wooden gate encircling the hall when I approach. An enormous key ring, hanging on a thick, black rope, is slung around her neck. I am parched and breathless. Matron takes pity on a poor country mouse and allows me to enter the dormitory although it is past midnight.

She leads me into a gigantic rectangular room, which is locked from the outside. One of the keys from her ring fits into the lock. Inside I see instantly that the women are all whores, tarts of the foulest order, ones who no self-respecting gentleman on any street in London would want, at least as far as I can tell. They look even worse than the whores did in Bragg's Alley in Plymouth.

I push into the dormitory, lugging my belongings. The heavily-painted creatures are already asleep in their creaking cots. The whores resemble giant babies lined up in rows in an orphanage's window. Matron shoves a yellowed sheet and a piss-stained blanket at me. I see that none of the whores are undressed so I keep my clothes on under the filthy cover.

If I thought the air in the streets of London was foul, I hadn't had a chance to breathe the air at the Rescue Hall. It is fetid with the aroma of cheap perfume circulating among the women. I can smell the scent of men on them, these whores with tomato-red rouged faces, sickly ochre skin underneath and orange painted lips. A few have kicked off their rough blankets. Their legs are skinny, like chicken legs. Most appear to be short, underfed; and when I look closely, toothless. They are old, these women. At the end of their careers, I daresay.

Being cautious, I stow the paintings under my cot and tie my small reticule, containing my sterling coins, to my right foot with a double knot. I am half done for, starving, thirsty and frightened out of my wits. Before I fall asleep, I watch an old whore foundering in her own saliva, coughing and spewing, like an ancient cat. Her sunken eyelids are flapping up and down as she dreams of adventures I pray never to experience. I think back to Rubin Stollman arguing with Gerta about the cause of the poor and oppressed and if this isn't them, I do not know who is. This fellow Lenin who Rubin idolizes: he could make a name for himself saving these forgotten wretches.

---

Perhaps I was over zealous declining the lawyer Shiner's kindnesses. If I stop at his quarters for one night only, I'm confident he will respect my privacy. After all, it was his idea that I stay with him. It might be best if I return to Leather Lane in the morning in hope of finding Shiner pattering on his soapbox about religion. Or better yet, I could ask Matron for directions to Furnival's Inn. I remind myself that I am no longer the lady of the manor and that beggars can't be choosers, as Maman used to say, at least twice a day.

***

At dawn, Matron enters the hall carrying a straw broom, which she flicks from side to side, sweeping the whores from their cots. Matron instructs me to get my belongings together and depart immediately if I refuse to listen to a Holy Roller sermonizing about redemption. To get a morsel of food for breakfast, the rule is you must listen first and then take your bread and tea.

I would rather go hungry. I reach under my cot to secure my things. Matron is shouting at me to get moving—now—as I fumble with my portmanteau.

"My paintings are missing!" I scream. "One of you pinched my Turners."

Matron locks the door so none of the dollymops remaining in the dormitory may leave; but it is too late. Whoever nicked the art is already out the door and probably down the street.

"Could you give me directions to Furnival's Inn?" I ask Matron plaintively.

"What business have you at Furnival's Inn?" she asks. "A worse collection of heathens can't be found in London. Stop for your morning tea with us and I'll call the peelers to help you recover your belongings."

The police are the last people I wish to bump into. Frederick might be dead by now, and Inspector Anniss on my tail, if Jack's told him I was bound for London. There's no telling what the lad will do. Or Albert, for that matter, once he has read Frederick's letter. Everyone has turned against me.

Out on the street, I reach into my reticule for a three-penny bit for tea, bread and a hard-boiled egg, but my purse is empty of coins. I break into a cold sweat. Inside the dormitory a clever whore must have stolen my money and inserted a stone weighing the same as my sterling. I am penniless and entirely alone. I don't even know where to go to trade my few jewels for money.

In the country, I would sit down and try to plot my course, but here with the soot and noise and the commotion of the gaggling crowds, I feel as if my brain is on fire. On one corner across from the Rescue Hall, a Gypsy acrobatic group has strung up a tight rope. Young women with raven hair tumbling down their backs are prancing across the rope. Their pink slippers are soiled. In another corner, a costermonger is hawking tickets to his *Punch and Judy* show. A dancing monkey, dressed in slave's attire, frolics beside the puppet stage. Kiddy corner from me, some blokes have fenced in a dozen rats, which are chewing each other to bits. The gamblers are throwing coins into various baskets balanced on an old woman's ample lap. Everyone is talking and smoking.

When I realize I do not even know the direction to Furnival's Inn, Otto Shiner appears, out of nowhere. He jumps down from a hackney cab. This morning he is wearing a stylishly cut frock coat, a fresh white shirt with shiny black buttons and a black cravat. On his head, he wears a top hat. His pinstriped trousers are neatly pressed and his black boots shine like water under a full moon. He looks every inch the successful city lawyer.

I, on the other hand, look a wreck. My hands and face, which I haven't washed since leaving the Devil's Stone Inn, are smudged in black soot and my red shirt is drenched in sweat. The hem of my checked blue skirt is covered in dried muck.

"Ah Miss Tilley, what have we here?" Shiner says, tipping his hat and bowing to me as if I was a lady.

"How'd you know I'd be here?"

Otto Shiner smiles. "There are only so many places a woman on her own might end up on her first night in Soho. My first stop was here, at the Rescue Hall on Beak Street. Did you sleep well?"

I have a half a mind to turn on my heel and walk away, but I am lost and friendless. What other option do I have but to indulge Shiner?

He looks down at my farm boots and my straw hat and says nothing.

---

"I am Jewish, you know. Same as you."

"You mentioned that Israel Zangwill is an acquaintance, so I expect you to be. Repeat to me how you know Mr. Zangwill?"

"I invited him to a dinner party at my house in Devon." I realize as soon as the words escape my mouth how ridiculous they must sound to Shiner.

"A dinner party that you gave or that you prepared?"

I could say I was the lady of the manor, but Shiner would never believe me and if truth be told, I can't see what good it would do me. If am to disappear into the mayhem of London, it must be as a servant and not as a lady.

"Yes, I was the cook for a fine family in Devon."

"And you left them . . .?"

I'm stunned for a moment, speechless.

"Trouble with the master? Well, I understand."

He looks into my eyes. "Splendid. It is difficult to secure an experienced cook in London these days. I assume you are searching for a position in a Jewish home?"

"Yes, preferably," I respond.

Shiner is inspecting me closely. As he does, an old man leading his donkey walks by us. His pushcart is overflowing with toffee and sour gums. The old man speaks to Shiner in Yiddish, but the lawyer answers in English and throws the ragged fellow a florin. The old man bows, pulling at his beard. Shiner inquires if I would like a toffee.

I am starving and thirsty; the toffee goes straight to my head. I am dizzy and fear that I will faint, but Shiner holds me by the shoulders and rushes me into his waiting hack.

Inside the vehicle, Shiner pulls a silver flask from his coat and offers me a dram of gin. It revives me.

"Shall we stop at the cook shop in Fetter Lane and get some food into you, Miss Tilley?" he asks.

What other choice do I have, but to acquiesce?

"Tonight shall we have potatoes, beans, marrows, beetroots and a little flounder for supper? Are you able to prepare that for me?'

Shiner is, no doubt, offering me a position as his cook. I imagine his home to be grand, he being a fancy London lawyer. "Yes, I can manage," I assure him.

"There's a bit of cleaning that goes along with the position of cook in my domain. Would you mind doing that as well?"

I am feeling groggy. I wish he would stop asking me questions and buy me breakfast. "A bit of cleaning is acceptable," I say.

Inside the cookhouse, I can barely make out the faces of the characters sitting down for their morning meal. The room is filled with smoke, caked with grime and smelling of bacon grease. Shiner orders three eggs and a half a rasher of bacon for me. I watch as the cook cracks the eggs into a pan of bacon fat. Next the brown bread goes into the pan as well, floating in the grease.

Shiner orders nothing. Before we sit on a bench in the corner, he pulls a handkerchief from his pocket with his expensively gloved hand and places it on the bench. He does not offer me the same courtesy. I am to sit directly on the filthy bench next to a toothless woman who is drinking her ale for breakfast. A congealing bowl of cold porridge and milk stands in front of her.

"We shan't be eating bacon in my quarters," Shiner announces.

Without his leather gloves, Shiner's hands are pale and spongy, same as dough before kneading. He places his hand on my knee and squeezes, but before I can remove it, he whisks it away. Perhaps it was an accident, it all happened so quickly.

"You shall earn eighty-two pounds a year." Evidently Shiner believes this salary to be a generous wage.

"You shall sleep in the kitchen on a cot beside the stove."

"Yes, sir." It is as much as I can expect since I am unable to provide him with a character reference.

"One more thing, Miss Tilley. Few women servants actually reside at Furnival's Inn so it is necessary that you remain absolutely quiet at night."

"Can I talk?"

"Certainly. To me, in a low voice. I've noticed that you speak rather loudly."

"I'll try to keep my voice down."

## – 3 –

Otto's chambers at Furnival's Inn, small as they are, lack nothing in terms of comfort. The outside of the Inn is dilapidated, but inside his furnishings are rich. His style of décor, however, is feminine, with cabbage rose slipcovers, white-lace curtains and pots of violets everywhere. The lawyer keeps his rooms overheated with the coal glowing crimson and a fragrant wood burning in the hearth. The wallpaper is striped with little green and purple flowers. To me, it appears that a woman lived here once.

My day begins at six o'clock when I dress, light the kitchen fire and fix breakfast. Afterwards I am to shake the carpets, doormats and rugs, sweep the wooden floors, wash the white-lace curtains, Otto's shirts and private linen as well as the table clothes and napkins. During the afternoon, I am to go by foot to market in Whitechapel to purchase kosher meat, poultry, cheese and butter.

By late afternoon, I am to scrub the front steps leading to the lawyer Shiner's door. All this must be done before he returns from the High Court of the Chancery, where he pleads his cases. Shiner habitually takes a whiskey and soda before dinner, but by seven-thirty, he is eager to see his plate set before him.

When he is finished, I am to do the washing up and prepare the fires and stove for the following morning. If I'm lucky, I might end my day by ten p.m.

After my first week, Shiner arrives home carrying a parcel of clothing wrapped in brown paper and tied with a string.

"Come here to me, Cordelia," he orders. "I would like you to wear a proper maid's attire when you serve me breakfast and dinner."

The maid's attire turns out to be the costume for a French maid: a white starched muslin cap, white cuffs at sleeve's end and a curly, white ruffle around my neck. The bodice, however, is low. I am to wear black stockings and fancy lace garters and black patent shoes with pointy tips.

"I can't wear these!" I object. "I'll be filthy by the time I'm to serve you your breakfast."

"But you must. It is *de rigueur* for a servant in my employ to look the part."

"I understood I was to be your cook and do a spot of housekeeping. You didn't tell me I was to become your personal maid."

"Or perhaps something more." Shiner gives me a peculiar look. "Prove to me that you can be trusted and we shall see if we ought to advance your station."

I understand that he is propositioning me. Although I am in no position to turn down any offer, I cannot fathom what my life would become as Shiner's paramour. Unlike my station at the manor house, I would have absolutely no status. Not even a housekeeper to anger me, or Jack to try my patience. I would become a caged animal in Shiner's menagerie. During the last week, I've watched his clients come and go. They are strange people, beasts, I'd describe them as, each with one foot in the underworld and another in business.

***

What I'd like to know is whether Frederick is dead or alive, but there's no way to find out. I certainly can't contact Jack. My servant boy has adroitly put the pieces together that explain my power of infection: his mother, the teacher Miss Staples; and finally Frederick and Olympia.

If I'm able to return to the County Devon to visit my boy William at his resting place, I might see a newly dug grave beside William's and it would be Frederick's. I miss my son so, being far away from him in London town and unable to console him during our daily conversations. The weather is turning frosty and I worry if he is warm enough during the windy Devon nights, alone in the churchyard of St. Peter and St. Paul's with only Frederick and Olympia for company.

## – 4 –

During my fifth week with Otto Shiner, after I'd served him his supper, attired in the French maid's costume, he offers to take me to Merchant's House in Whitechapel. We stroll along Petticoat Lane where the shops are jammed with rows of frocks in every colour, design and fabric. It is more of an Oriental bazaar than an English market. In the windows are huge sides of salted beef. Beef tongues and chicken livers are swimming in porcelain pans. Platters of fried potato latkes and steaming knishes abound.

At one dress shop, Shiner approaches a woman with purple-painted lips and hair dyed red.

"Ah, Mrs. Grabinsky. Delighted to see you. You look well."

Mrs. Grabinsky gives Shiner a comical curtsy and pushes me inside the shop. From inside I can hear her ask Otto if I am his new girlfriend, but I cannot make out what he whispers in response. He does not wish for me to hear him.

Inside the shop, I find a navy-wool dress with a demure linen bib. I imagine it would make me look like a proper lady. When Otto sees it, he orders me to return it in to the rack. "That won't do!"

"This is more like it,' Mrs. Grabinsky says, showing me a flouncy extravagance of yellow froth. This dress is not at all like the one I chose. It looks like cooked cream boiling over. Whalebone stays are protected by leather strips implanted in the revealing bodice.

"This bodice pulls them in tight and lifts them high," she says, grabbing my chest and pushing my breasts together. The sheer sleeves are shaped like three grapefruits held together by a string.

"That's more what I had in mind!" Otto says. "If you throw in a camisole, one of sheerest yellow, my dear Mrs. Grabinsky, we have a deal." Otto takes a handful of coins from his purse. "Wear it now, Cordelia," he orders. "Tonight we are going dancing."

Mrs. Grabinsky puts my old clothes in a sack and pats me on the shoulder. "I shouldn't worry, dear," she says. "He's not so bad once you get used to him. Lots of girls would give their eye teeth to be with the lawyer Shiner."

As she tries to calm me, I see a figure in a stained-tan raincoat circling the shop. It is Inspector Anniss. But he keeps his distance. He's watching me, but not approaching. I wish to run, to escape him, but Otto pushes me behind Mrs. Grabinsky and steps out into the street hurriedly to meet him. I watch as Otto places a large amount of sterling in the Inspector's palm. Anniss looks my way, tips his cap to me and suddenly disappears like a rat into the first alley off Petticoat Lane.

---

Otto Shiner has paid off the Inspector to keep me from the hangman's noose. I begin to speak, but Otto is already distracted. As we walk from the shop, Otto is approached by a powerfully built man, albeit one in ragged dress. He is carrying books in a satchel tied to his back. His hair is long, golden blonde and falls straight down to the middle of his back. His blue eyes, clearer than spring water, are alert. His lips are lush, but the angle of his jaw is square. Determined. As he pulls a slim volume from the satchel, I notice that his fingers are elegant, not calloused from work.

"What have we here? It's Simon, selling his poetry in the alleyways of Whitechapel," Otto says with slight trepidation in his voice.

Surprisingly, Otto and this man are acquainted. I recognize him from my first night in London. He was the man reciting poetry while Otto was pattering about Zion. The one who shouted a warning to me.

Perhaps this street-seller is also a client of Otto's from the underworld. His English is heavily accented.

Although Otto does not bother to introduce us, the poet says, as if reading my thoughts, "I'm Russian. From the land of Pushkin. My name is Simon."

"I'm Cordelia."

"Ah," he says, kissing my hand. "From Shakespeare. An English princess."

"Hardly," Otto interjects. "Cordelia is my maid-of-all-work. She does everything."

For a few moments the two men speak heatedly in Yiddish.

Otto's face is flushed. "Get out of my way," he shouts to Simon in English. He searches about for a peeler. "Go away, Simon!"

But Simon won't leave us. In disgust, Otto pushes me forward, toward the street-seller.

"Do you know who this man is?" Simon asks me. "How he lives?"

I am standing between the two men who are glaring at each other.

"Do you know who she is Simon? She is a murderess. She is free only because I have just now bought her freedom."

Simon is much taller and stronger than Otto. He makes a fist and turns to use it on Otto. The lawyer ducks cringing under the threat. "Take her," he shouts at Simon in English, "She is too much trouble. I have already paid too much for her! Good luck to you! Best not sleep too soundly beside her!" Shiner is still screeching as he scurries away from us. Simon grabs my hand, I squeeze it. His wrist is pale, covered in blonde hair. I like the look of him. He is rescuing me, I can sense as much.

Together we cut down an alley. Simon puts his mouth close to my ear and whispers, "If it does me no good knowing you it will do you no good, knowing me. I am destitute. I live on the streets selling my poems and at night, I rest with the fried-fish sellers, the lowest of the low in all of London town, but I can help you to escape from Shiner. The lawyer preys on women, beautiful ones, green to London. Let us trust each other."

No one has called me beautiful for a very long time. After tonight, I will never need to look in a mirror again.

"Shiner promised to help me and he did."

"No doubt, men like Shiner promise the world. You are so lovely and a Jewess."

"Not a very good one," I reply and Simon smiles. It is an enchanting smile, wide and open and as inviting as ever I have seen.

"My poems are written in Yiddish. You could translate them into English for me."

"I couldn't possibly. I hardly understand," I reply.

"Vey iz mir!"

"I could try. My mother taught me a little Yiddish."

The colours of the night are turning me inside out. I follow Simon through the pathways of Whitechapel. He holds my hand firmly in his broad, stronger one. We are both grinning. When he stops at a stall to buy a few shillings of chocolate, he places each piece carefully in my mouth. I am his bird, brightly plumed and contentedly round. He is feeding me. Then he is kissing me, gently, expertly. I fear his is the sweetest kiss on earth.

"Neither am I, a very good Jew, but I try hard to be a good man. What else can any of us do? Otto Shiner wishes to send us, the greenhorns, to the Levant. He believes we sully the atmosphere for the established English Jews."

"What does it take to be a good Jew?" I ask.

Simon believes my question to be rhetorical, but of course, it is not.

In the night shadows, we continue walking, slowly, his arm about my waist. Otto does not give chase. I am not worth it to him. The payment to Anniss, I tell myself, was inconsequential or why ever would he let me disappear with the poet? Unless he could sense immediately that I would never leave Simon's side once he drew me to him. Simon talks a great deal, rapidly, about poetry, about making me his muse. Neither of us bothers mentioning Otto again or the other grimy, little details of our existence. There is no need. We slip easily inside the mayhem that is London.

– 5 –

By morning, I discover for myself that Simon resides in a hovel underneath Leather Lane with his comrades, the fried-fish sellers. The smelly creatures who dare to roam the darkest streets of London town. To enter their den, I must descend from a rope ladder to below ground. Afterwards Simon clamps shut the piss-stained plywood door and bolts it securely. I am attempting to convince myself not to ruin this, to stay with this one good man.

The first time Simon makes love to me, I don't notice our bed, if you could call it that, or the dingy room, nor the cupboard in which he keeps his pallet and measly belongings. The second time he takes me, I cannot block the smell of the frying fish from my senses. Fish permeates everything in the warrens under the streets of London, which the fried-fish sellers call home. Why would Simon choose to abide with these people? They are Jewish as are we, but of the lowest order. The third time, I cannot go through with our lovemaking, no matter how deep my feelings for Simon.

Perhaps I am overwhelmed and frightened by London. Perhaps I am weary after so many years of fighting Frederick; of plotting, planning, scheming; wearied by being surrounded by enemies. Perhaps I simply have given up. But I so desperately wish to be attached to Simon, that I believe there to be a blossoming of fulsome love running between us.

This man must never discover what I have done. I would throw myself at Anniss's feet before I would allow him to find out about the poisonings. And then, there is Jack, who must never catch wind of Simon ... or all will be lost. God, forgive me! The first time we made love, I was certain that I felt it, love, overwhelming, my stomach turning upside down, my fingers tingling, my heart in my mouth.

But the smell of fish gets in. I loathe it. It's curdling my insides. It's as if I'm catching a fever. I can't keep much down. A drop of bread and tea is all I can manage. Everything was clean and precise at Otto's and, of course, at the manor, Mrs. Bullbrook's housekeeping was beyond reproach. I never worried about the dirt or becoming ill.

In the rookery, we exist like rats below ground. Rodents in a maze. Not that I can say a bad word about the inhabitants of our den. Hardworking. Open-hearted. Barely scraping by, they are all skin and bones. No one asks me why I am here. Secrets are respected. Some of the fried-fish sellers are pious, putting on *tfilin* to pray. During their long days and nights of work, they stand patiently outside the doors of the worst pubs in London, with their stinking baskets of greasy fillets slung over their shoulders. Like Simon, they are good people. They are not like me, the rotten apple, polluting the barrel with her effluence.

***

I want to love Simon more than I've wanted anything in my life. He's holding me in his arms, nibbling at my neck, caressing me, but my head is swimming. I feel as though I have a fever. Simon believes it's from the drains, the slew of sewage encircling our den. Typhoid, cholera, scarlet fever all sprout through the seeping drains like an infected wound.

Today Simon has written a poem and inscribed it to me. "Cordelia, the great love of my life." Simon explains that his inspiration comes from the street, the plain decent folk of the rookery. "Kind souls who do no harm," he says.

If I perish here under the ground, I wish for Maman to forgive me, to understand. Oh, please, Maman. Don't whisper in my ear. He's not good enough for you. It's the other way around. Maman, you've never understood the power of the loving heart.

Simon is a good man, so much better than I could dream to be. But the smell, the bloody smell of frying fish is tearing me apart.

Although I've lost track of the days, Frederick must be long dead by now. There is a light spattering of white snow on the ground outside the hovel where we exist. It turns black within minutes. Throughout my illness, Simon never leaves my side. He spoons droplets of water down my parched throat. My lips are cracked and bleeding. I must look a sight. How can Simon keep his gaze focused on me? He tells me that I am as red as a ruby and it must be scarlet fever. Or am I just burning for my sins?

If I were to survive and return to the manor, surely Inspector Anniss lies in wait for me. He'll have me. With Jack egging him on, he'll throw the noose around my neck. Jack's trap. Guilty as charged.

By the time I come to my senses, Simon is discouraged. I've been ill for weeks. He'd hoped I would be tough enough, committed enough to his poetry, to share his underground world. But I am not. I'll never be able to translate his poems from Yiddish to English. To earn our keep, I'll never be able to sell fish with the others. Shyly he tells me he left a wife and three babies in Poland. Her name is Freya, she shaves her head and wears a wig of horsehair. Simon postulates that it is best to leave Freya and the children at the edge of civilization, he, not able to imagine how they could adjust to his life in London.

Simon offers to take me to Israel Zangwill who I have spoken of in and out of my delirium. Of course Simon knows his name and reputation. Simon assures me that I will not be thrown into the street.

Simon bundles me into my clothes. The whore's threadbare party frock smelling of fish entrails. It is night when we arrive at Zangwill's Kensington home. The electric lights are burning brightly. The ornamental French doors are open wide to allow a cool breeze to circulate in the stylish, crowded room, overflowing with guests. I peer inside at the modern parlour, black and white sofas, black-enamel tables and chairs with white-geometric tiles decorating the fireplace. From the corner of my eye, I see Beatrice Webb holding court. Theodore Herzl, I recognize from photographs. Vladimir Ilych Lenin, too! Christians and Jews are mingling, laughing, enjoying drinks and *bon mots*. I overhear Lenin saying that the twentieth century will surely bring justice and equality to all the world. My heart is beating so quickly I cannot catch my breath.

---

Zangwill's servant does not turn us away. We are invited to stand in the foyer. When Zangwill approaches, in full evening dress, he extends his hand to Simon. He notices me, next. We smell of fried fish.

'Mrs. Wendice!" he exclaims. "Let me get you a chair."

I can barely stand. He and Simon confer. Zangwill looks perplexed, but shakes his head in agreement, patting Simon on the shoulder.

"Your husband, I know he is dead, Mrs. Wendice," Zangwill says to me directly.

"He perished. From typhoid fever."

"May I ask what brings you to London? Simon insists that he found you on the street, near Petticoat Lane. He tells me that you were in the employ of the lawyer Otto Shiner."

I notice that Simon is slipping out the door. Without a word. I'll never set eyes on him again. I begin to cry. Zangwill offers his handkerchief to me, but I will not oblige him. I dry my tears with the back of my hand.

"I needed to find work," I reply. I am crying and laughing at the same time. "I couldn't bear to stay on at the manor after Frederick perished. Shiner offered me a position as maid in his rooms at Furnival's Inn."

Zangwill uses both index fingers to raise his spectacles higher on the bridge of his nose. "Yes, well, Otto is a rather peculiar fellow. I have my doubts about him." Zangwill lowers his eyes. "He collects strangers."

He knows.

"I shall help you. Let's get some broth into you and tuck you into a clean bed for a good night's rest." He is looking at me reservedly. "A good night's sleep will do wonders."

When I catch my reflection in the hall mirror, I'm ashamed. My hair has fallen out in clumps and my skin is like *Papier Mâché* drying in the sun. I have become the witch that everyone has always expected me to be. "I am a sight."

"Jack will be delighted to accompany you to Holsworthy, where you belong."

I rise from my seat unsteadily. "Jack?" The room is spinning.

"Oh yes, Mrs. Wendice. Please, please! Do sit down. You'd be surprised how loyal he is, that lad. What great luck to keep a servant such as he. He's been searching for you for weeks. He was the one to inform me that Mr. Wendice passed away and that you were overcome with grief. He'd had an inkling that you would journey to London and eventually end up on my doorstop." He stops, embarrassed. "Well I didn't quite mean it that way."

"I am beyond all that now, Mr. Zangwill. Please, continue."

"He wishes to find you, to offer you a helping hand. To guide you back to your home where you will be safe. London is a harsh place for a woman on her own. You deserve better. Why, in Holsworthy there are servants to care for you."

Frederick is dead. I put my hand to cover my mouth, to stop myself from crying out.

"I'll send a missive to Jack now. He'll receive it by the first morning post. I've arranged for Jack to reside in a workhouse while he searches for you. Do you have any money, Mrs. Wendice?" Zangwill asks kindly.

"None at all."

"No matter, my dear. If you will allow me I'll secure two seats for you and Jack on the train to Holsworthy. Of course, yours will be in first-class and Jack in third. Did you know that Gerta and Rubin Stollman speak well of you? They've lost their business, the poor dears."

"No, I didn't know, not for certain."

If I recall correctly, they knew your mother, may she rest in peace."

"Yes my mother and my father."

***

The next morning, when Jack comes for me, I am prepared. I fully expect him to have Inspector Anniss lying in wait for me at Paddington, but I am mistaken.

"You've changed," Jack remarks.

"So have you," I reply.

"Inspector Anniss has disappeared."

I suspect that Otto Shiner must have paid him a great deal to make him go away. Even Jack cannot figure why the Inspector has not charged me now that the evidence must be crystal clear.

"One way or the other, we survive, you and I," he says without irony.

Although he doesn't know exactly why I haven't been charged, Jack does comprehend that I appear to have slipped out of the reach of

Inspector Anniss and, with that, he no longer has the power to undo me. A quick study, is Jack Livesay. This time I pray he is correct.

During the hack ride to the station, Jack is subdued. His movements are not as deliberate as before. His back is slightly stooped as if he has been combing the streets of London for weeks without rest. Life without me is harder than he imagined. At the manor, Mrs. Bullbrook refused to pay him his wages while forcing him to sleep in the stable with the animals. Without me, as his protector, it's back to the pits for Jack, unless I rescue him, that is.

Before we board the train, me to the first-class coach and he to third, he covers me with the tartan rug Zangwill has arranged to warm me. Jack places a hamper from Zangwill's kitchen next to me. It is a lunch of soup and other delicacies from the party of last evening. Thank goodness it does not include fish.

I shall never eat fish again. I am sitting alone in the first-class compartment. The space around me is glorious. The bright winter sun, reflected through the glass window, warms my face and hands. It is as if London were some kind of dream—or nightmare. How could I really have found myself brought so low? Did I imagine feelings for Simon, or did I simply see him as my only chance for survival in a place so hostile and foreign that my cleverness, my guile Wiseman called it, could not overcome its power. Yet I have survived and triumphed even, over the Wendice clan. After years of being accused of filthy crimes, of inadequate breeding, of stupidity and malice, it is Cordelia who carries on. That Cordelia was lost somehow in the vile streets of London. Have I claimed her back?

Once we leave London, the ground is covered in white snow. It will be Christmas in a less than a week and I imagine that Mrs. Bullbrook is preparing the goose and Christmas pudding. I could run away, disappear at St. David's Exeter where no one would recognize me. My real father could be alive still, but how would I be able to face him, rise to his expectations, me being a murderess?

At the rail station, Jack leaves me in the hands of the stationmaster whilst he runs to the manor to fetch the dray to carry me home. He helps me up into my seat. Since I have no bags, I am a light load. The greys rush through the streets to home. From the dray, I notice that the Stollman's tearoom has been replaced with a pub called the Elephant's Ear.

"I expected to be in irons by now. When are you intending to shop me to the Inspector?" I ask Jack, testing that my assumptions about Inspector Anniss are accurate.

"Who says I will?" He does not look at me, but he is gentle with me, putting his hand on my arm.

I am holding my breath. Waiting for the axe to fall.

Could Anniss be awaiting us at the manor? But, no.

"We might manage, the two of us. Respect it is, that will make things right." He wishes to make amends, but he's sending me his message. We know what each other is capable of. We know who we are. Each of us is vulnerable to the other. His future rests in my hands, mine in his.

"We might."

"Someone needs to watch over the miners at the quarries, ma'am, now that Master Frederick is gone," Jack says hoarsely.

"Someone does."

"You'll inherit everything, the mines, the manor, the Abbey at Hartland Point."

"So it comes to that. I am the last Wendice standing. By choice though not by birth." Now that I am certain that Frederick is dead, everything is coming into focus.

Jack pulls on the reins before we enter the driveway leading to the manor. Inspector Anniss is nowhere to be seen. I'll never know how greatly it cost Otto Shiner to set me free.

As for Jack, he is not acting out of loyalty since he has none; it is ambition catching him by the tail and shaking him hard. I understand perfectly. The London workhouse has both hardened him and sustained his resolve to rise above his natural station. He's eager to settle this deal before we go in. Jack doesn't fancy himself as a cringing servant or a slavish quarryman for the remainder of his days.

"What about Inspector Anniss?" I inquire.

"The Inspector lines his pockets from both sides. No one can figure out exactly how Frederick Wendice caught the typhoid. Scores of others have passed, too. Who's to say where it comes from? We have not the science for it in England. It's all speculation, isn't it? Even with spit and blood, no one knows for certain."

---

As usual, Jack knows everything. "Yes, it's all speculation and superstition," I say cautiously. "In Plymouth, Anniss was, indeed, lining his pockets with loot from the Royal Navy and cornering the girls into paying him for protection. He is an evil man."

Jack gives me a curious look, but I don't bite. I shall never forget the press of Anniss's body against me or the pool of my blood on the shed floor.

"You could tell Mrs. Webb about what goes on in Plymouth. She'd take up the cause. Or write a book about it."

"I suspect she would." Jack smiles. He has always been such a clever lad.

"You've suffered a great deal, ma'am ... Cordelia," Jack says. "There is the ghostly shadow of overweening ambition in his face. It has aged him rapidly. I can surmise that he realizes that it is all for naught without me. His plan is for us to live on equal terms. As brother and sister. No, not quite. Immediately, I shall hire a seasoned overseer to keep the mines operating. Over time, I shall ensure that clever Jack learns how to be second-in-command of the quarries on the coast of Devon, the copper works at Morwellham Quay, while I shall retain my high station as the lady of the manor. He's always been a quick study. And it's best to keep him close, though not give him entirely what he desires. He shall never be the boss at the quarries or rule the roost at the manor. He will always be a close second. That is his enduring punishment.

I imagine relaxing comfortably in my Catherine de Medici room, writing letters to Polly, the Reverend Kinsman and Israel Zangwill or anyone else who might catch my fancy.

"And Mrs. Bullbrook?" The fly in the ointment.

"Who would believe the old hag? Jack says at first haltingly and then with more determination. "She's a servant, hardly able to see straight and half in her cups day and night. These days she doesn't stray from the fire. Sleeps throughout the night in her old rocker, mumbling to herself about Master Frederick and how he didn't deserve to die."

"And you are in agreement with her?" I inquire. "In your heart?"

"What's done is done," he replies, firmly.

Jack is right. A clear thinker. A rational young man. No one would believe the housekeeper if she accused me, the lady of the manor, of poisoning my husband and my mother-in-law. What remnants of poison could be discovered? Ridiculous. Germs, if they exist at all, are said to be too small to be seen. They are of the imagination. The dreams of mad scientists and foreigners.

Before retreating to the manor, Jack and I pause at the graveyard. William's grave is covered in snow. I crouch beside his little tombstone to wipe the white blanket of flakes away with my bare hand. The snow is coming down hard. Frederick and Olympia's plots are next to William's. The earth covering their graves is still raw and uneven. I leave the snow to settle upon them. To quiet their voices, their unearthly protests.

"I've returned, William," I say soothingly. "... never to leave you again. I shall give the orders now and I shall see to it that you are safe and warm, as you should be. No one can harm you now."

***

Mrs. Bullbrook does not appear entirely surprised to see me, although she does not rise to greet me when I enter her kitchen.

"You've changed," she says.

"Scarlet fever," I inform her. "I am no longer beautiful. My skin is red and ruined as you can see. My hair will never grow back." Housekeeper is pleased. Another man will not want me in this state. "Stand up when I enter the room, Mrs. Bullbrook," I order.

Her face is close to mine.

"You needn't bother, threatening me, alerting the Inspector," I warn her immediately. "If one single word of recrimination leaves your mouth, I will tell the entire story of the Wendice family. The children maimed from birth. Frederick's eccentricities. It will ruin the Wendices' reputation in the County forever."

Her mouth snaps shuts like a turtle's after swallowing a fly. The loyal servant to the end. Her only concern being the impeccable name of the family.

After my long journey, I must rest. "My heart is weak," I explain. Climbing the stairs to my bedroom is a chore. My breath comes in thunderous bursts. Finally, I undress and it feels as if a thousand feathers are caressing me when I crawl under the eiderdown. If I could, I would never emerge again.

I instruct Jack to let Housekeeper know she may stay on. If I've learned anything, it is to keep my enemies close. However, I rule that

Mrs. Bullbrook be barred from the kitchen. No more overcooked, fatty mutton and brown sprouts. Jack informs me that the Stollmans reside in town and that they are in-service for Mr. Ealing.

I must make amends, so I steal away the couple to run my kitchen. They are delighted, complaining that the only meal the doctor wishes to consume is comprised of mutton, Brussels sprouts, and brown ale. Our daily fare is a cross between Viennese and Parisian cuisine. Gerta and Rubin never disappoint. The Sachertorte is creamier than ever.

At the manor, I don't stand on ceremony. Jack and I and the Stollmans take our meals together every day. What a shame, none but we dare taste the delicious fare!

Mrs. Bullbrook is ordered to eat alone below stairs. I have abandoned my love of the culinary arts.

The Stollmans live in, occupying fine rooms high above ground, transforming Frederick's study into their private parlour. To this day, I overhear them arguing over the merits of Socialism versus Zionism. Although Gerta suspects that I infected the villagers with my own White Ladies pudding, she has forgiven me. I believe she understands why I did what I did. She often reminds me that Olympia Wendice waged war to scapegoat the couple for the typhoid murders. As luck would have it, there wasn't a shred of evidence against the Stollmans. The kitchen at the Café Demel was the cleanest in all of County Devon. But for lack of trade, it closed down all the same. No one dared enter the shop after the fever blanketed Devonshire.

Once, on my daily outing to visit William, Inspector Anniss purposefully bumps into me. He had been waiting around the back of the church where he assumed I wouldn't see him lurking.

"You're a murderess and a Jewish whore," he hisses. His balding hair is greasy, running in stringy locks down to his shoulders. I notice he has the biggest feet I have ever seen. Mud encrusts his boots and there is dirt under his unclipped fingernails.

"You should have thought of that before taking the bribe from the lawyer Shiner. Otto had the evidence destroyed, I'd bet my soul on that—or were you and Jack just having me on?"

"You're the only one with motive and opportunity, Mrs. Wendice."

If he touches me I will dissolve, disappear into that dark place that has always threatened to destroy me, but I smile demurely. He is surprised by the look of my skin and hair. Even he notices that I am no longer beautiful. Before turning away from him I say coldly, "I could ruin you. You must recall Mrs. Beatrice Webb who sat at my table. She knows the Prime Minister and the Home Secretary." I threaten to tell Beatrice how he played the working girls off against the Royal Navy men in Plymouth. "She would write a book about it," I say.

I've never seen Anniss since.

***

After Griselda died, Albert bravely departed the Devil's Stone Inn to take the twins to Plymouth. He and Polly run the Purple Peony together and although we've never met again, we exchange cards at Christmas. Privately, Albert writes that it's me that Polly loves and that he is only a stand-in, like the cutout dolls one finds in fashion magazines. But I know differently. Polly is an honest woman.

Every spring without fail, I visit Maman's modest headstone in the far corner of the graveyard beside the Devil's Stone Inn. When we converse, she can't or won't disguise her disappointment in me. Each time I attempt to assuage her anger, I fail. It never dissipates. In death as in life, she remains unfulfilled.

Pa, too, is long gone. He passed away about the same time as Griselda died. If I recall, it was shortly after I snuck away from Shebbear for London. But then my memory is beginning to fail.

Tilleys no longer own the Devil's Stone. Instead it's a middle-aged couple, going by the name of Sharkey. When the proprietress smiles, blackened teeth stare out from her wide, bloodless lips.

The Sharkeys have knocked down Pa's old stone shed to erect more rooms for tourists. Maman would find it hilarious to learn that the Devil's Stone Inn is considered to be the most ghost-ridden pub in all of England. When Jack drives me to Shebbear, if the weather is fair, we find time to stroll along the River Torrington, each lost in our own thoughts, remembering the night so long ago, when he expressed his love for me. Or what he thought was love. He has never married or even bedded a woman as far as I know.

---

On winter nights, Jack and I enjoy lounging before the fire; me stretched out on the divan, Jack reclining in Frederick's old armchair. We are both great readers, me with my novels and Jack with his engineering journals. Jack has not aged well. His beard is already sprinkled with white and his spine has twisted his shoulders to a permanent stoop.

Trade at the mines is dying. The Americans have discovered their own slate reserves, and no one wishes to purchase the arsenic refined from the copper at Morwellham Quay. Too many accidental deaths. And women are particularly fond of using arsenic as their poison.

When word reaches the Stollmans that the red-haired pedlar has died, we attend his funeral in Exeter.

I wear a thick black veil, as I always do when I venture out from the manor. Not a soul suspects that I am his daughter. It is much, much too late for all of that. I imagine him as he once was, with his hand to his heart, waiting for Maman to blow him a kiss. I dwell inside their love.

From time to time, I send Jack on a wild goose chase to Bristol to search for a slim volume of poetry by Simon. He always returns empty handed. I reckon that Simon never encountered a woman, still beautiful, who could properly translate his poems from Yiddish to English. Perhaps he has never met anyone quite like me again. Whatever it was I felt for him, my love, or something other, it does not diminish. Was Simon that one great thing I longed for? The love, Maman so disdained. If so, I gave it, and him, up so easily. If it was love, I am not built for it.

My only reminder of the poisonings comes from the scullery girl, whose hands tremble whenever she cleans the grate in my fireplace, or more so, when she clears the table of the soiled dinner china.

"Why do you shake so when you are in my presence?" I ask her on the anniversary of my last dinner party, the one in August so many years ago, when Herr Wiseman accused me of guile.

"Ma'am," she says, "I couldn't say."

I stand before her. "Yes, you can. Tell me."

"In the village, ma'am, the elderly, who remember the great typhoid epidemic of 1895, they claim it was you who spread it round." The scullion is weeping now. "Please, ma'am, don't poison me."

I instruct her to stand tall. "I would never hurt you or anyone else." The next day I instruct Jack to let her go, but to ensure that he writes a brilliant character reference for her to take on her way. Away from here, from this house, from me.

Oddly, Frederick would be proud that I am so strict with the servants and that I have managed, over the years, to keep the manor running smoothly on the money he left me in his will. One day I will tell him, when he quiets down, what an exemplary Wendice I have become.

Always a big talker, Frederick shouts at me endlessly from his grave. He disturbs my sleep. On moonless nights, I swear I can hear him lecturing me from the church's graveyard. Mostly, he scolds me about poisoning Mater. Olympia, herself, has lost her voice for good and, therefore, can pester me no more.

Recently, as trade falls off to a trickle, Frederick's in a huff about the Tintagel mines. He advises me that it's Jack's fault, believing a quarryman's offspring is not the natural choice to captain the Wendice enterprises, even as a number two. He argues that I should have chosen a proper gentleman to help guide the business.

In 1915, by the time Mary Mallon is forcibly, inhumanly incarcerated on an island infirmary, for the remainder of her days, the world war has overwhelmed Europe. It took the New York authorities such a long while to catch up with Mary, to quarantine Mary, as they would a raging beast, no, a monster in a cage. Sadly, I sympathize with Mary, as I suspect she would with me, when she pleads, "This contention that I am a perpetual menace in the spread of typhoid germs is not true." Yet I could not claim the same for myself when she cries, "I have committed no crime and I am treated like an outcast—a criminal. It is unjust, outrageous, uncivilized. It seems incredible that in a Christian community a defenceless woman can be treated in this manner." For a lowly cook, she sounds strikingly eloquent to me, but my treatment at the hands of the community has been relatively slight and certainly just. I am, however, quarantined in a different way. In my own way.

Here, in England, with the shock of so many bright young men perishing in battle, no one much cares about an aged widow, scarred and hairless, living for years with her manservant in a dusty manor in the remote heartland of the County Devon. What matters that the lady of the manor was once rumoured to spread typhoid fever? Who would ever stop to put two and two together, particularly when the accusations always emanate from the servants?

# Afterword

While wandering through a church graveyard in Devon, England I came upon a weathered tombstone. The inscription reads:

*To the memory of*
*Cordelia*
*The Beloved Wife of*
*Frederick H. Martin*
*Of this town,*
*Who Departed this life on the*
*23rd day of October 1885.*
*Aged 33 years.*
*Watch for ye know not what hour your*
*Lord doth come.*

*Also to the memory of*
*William Frederick Ackland*
*Only son of Frederick H and Cordelia Martin*
*Who Died on the 12th day of April – 1885.*
*Aged 1 Year and 8 months.*

Reading this inscription on the gravestone in Holsworthy's St. Peter and St. Paul's churchyard, inspired me to a write a novel about an imaginary Cordelia and what might have happened to her before the death of her son and after her actual demise.

In the case of the historical characters appearing in the novel, Polly Turney, Inspector Anniss, Israel Zangwill, and Beatrice Webb, I have taken the liberty to transform their roles to match the plot of this story rather than the other way around. For this imaginative license, I beg the reader's understanding.

# Acknowledgments

Although *The Cook's Temptation* is a work of fiction, I did rely on books and articles about Victorian England for my research. Among the most prominent were Henry Mayhew's ground-breaking nineteenth century study *London Labour and the London Poor*; Jill Matus' *Unstable Bodies: Victorian Representations of Sexuality and Maternity; Parallel Lives* by Phyllis Rose; *Trials of the Diaspora: a History of Anti-Semitism in England* by Anthony Julius; *A Jew in the Public Arena: The Career of Israel Zangwill* by Meri-Jane Rochelson, and "'We Are Not Beasts Of The Field': Prostitution And The Poor In Plymouth and Southampton Under The Contagious Diseases Act" by Judith and Daniel Walkowitz. They were all catalysts for the creation of Cordelia's story. The description of the sickroom at Wendice Manor is from Judith Flanders' *The Victorian House*. The conversation about women and marriage between Frederick Wendice and Harald Salt is from *The Odd Women* by George Gissing. I am indebted to Gissing for his insight into Victorian romance.

*Typhoid Mary: An Urban Historical* by Anthony Bourdain was an invaluable source as was Daniel Rogov's cookbook *Rogues, Writers & Whores: Dining with the Rich and Infamous* from which the recipes for *Bombe Monselet, Peches Melba and Oeufs Careme* originated. The Chester pudding is from Favourite British Pudding Recipes.

I am grateful to Sheridan College for generously awarding me a sabbatical and Diaspora Dialogues for selecting me as one of the recipients of its mentorship program.

Without the support of my fellow writers and friends, this book would not have been completed. David Wayne and Sandy von Kaldenberg were constant sources of encouragement. My heartfelt thanks to Sheridan colleagues Michael Collins and Janet Fear for their initial encouragement and to Howard Aster and Mosaic Press for believing in this book. Donna Kirk, Rex King, Barbara Ledger and Susan Walker stood by me as I worked my way through numerous drafts. My editor and friend Michael Walsh is responsible for all that is worthy in this novel. And to Robin, who made it all possible.

Most of all, I thank my daughter, Hannah, who put up with me while I was writing this novel.

*Joyce Wayne*
*Toronto, Canada*
*2013*